# COLD
# GLORY

# COLD GLORY

## B. KENT ANDERSON

WITHDRAWN

A TOM DOHERTY ASSOCIATES BOOK
NEW YORK

COLD GLORY

A Forge Book
Published by Tom Doherty Associates, LLC
175 Fifth Avenue
New York, NY 10010

www.tor-forge.com

Forge® is a registered trademark of Tom Doherty Associates, LLC.

ISBN 978-0-7653-2861-8

First Edition: October 2011

Printed in the United States of America

0  9  8  7  6  5  4  3  2  1

*For Terri, my love*

*and*

*In memory of the real Dave Stanton (1936–2008):*
*broadcaster, reader, writer, musician, artist, colleague, friend*

# ACKNOWLEDGMENTS

Books come about in mysterious ways, and many people contributed large and small, directly and indirectly, to make this one happen.

At the top of the list is my agent, George Bick, who brought an infectious enthusiasm and a wealth of publishing experience to this project. He not only gave me input that made this a stronger story, but saw the project through with style and good humor as well. He's also quite adept at responding to e-mails from nervous authors. It's a joy to work with him.

For his early encouragement of this book, I would also like to extend my gratitude to John Talbot.

My amazing and insightful editor at Forge, Kristin Sevick, understood this story better than I did at times, and she helped me to look at it in different ways—quite a significant accomplishment. She has been a tireless advocate, a wellspring of ideas, and a creator of handy time lines. Plus she is a fellow baseball fan and connoisseur of random historical facts. My name appears on the front of this book, but it is very much hers as well.

Copy editor Eliani Torres did a masterful job of keeping me accurate and consistent.

8 ACKNOWLEDGMENTS

To Ray and Jean Miller, thanks for spending a Sunday afternoon working on the photo shoot, and for the terrific pictures.

For research assistance, I am grateful to the following:

Rodger Harris of the Oklahoma Historical Society; Richard Green, Chickasaw Nation tribal historian; Larry Marcy, superintendent of the Fort Washita Historic Site; Norman Rozeff of the Cameron County, Texas, Historical Commission; and Jeanne Burke, county historian for Clark County, Indiana, as well as several staff members of Falls of the Ohio State Park who patiently answered my questions. Additionally I would like to thank Bette and Ken Cullen for their hospitality and kindness while I was in the Louisville area.

I must acknowledge the late Chloe Sartin, the finest teacher of American history and government ever to enter a classroom. Not only did she instill in me a great passion for these subjects, but she also taught me how to take notes and organize data. Thirty years later, I still use a variation of the outlining technique she so lovingly pounded into all our heads at Madill High School.

Personal thanks to:

Connie Edmondson, Jim Lowery, and the people on the second floor, for their professionalism and compassion.

My colleagues and friends, past and present, at KCSC, the Oklahoma City Philharmonic, and Southwestern Publishing, for more reasons than I can count. Within these organizations, I am especially grateful to Brad Ferguson, Michelle Winters, and Elizabeth Meares for the many professional and learning opportunities I have been given.

My spiritual family at NWCC, who embody and exemplify the idea of unconditional love and understanding.

Friends from across the country, who have been so good to me through the years, with extraspecial thanks to those I always know I can call on at any time: Jeanette Atwood, Tom Clare, Brooke Harry, Darren Hellwege, Barb Hendrickson, Zena McAdams, Nancy Moore, Charles Newcomb, and Lane Whitesell. Rob Boss cheerfully answers all my e-mail questions about wine and firearms. JoLynda Ingram has been a steadfast friend through all the changes in my life. She also apparently harbors no hard feelings for the time I tried to teach her to drive a stick shift nearly twenty years ago, and she brought me a burger from Johnnie's when I most needed it.

My parents, Bill and Audrey Anderson, and my sister, Teresa Anderson, have helped me in various ways over the years, even at times when I did not realize I needed them. Perhaps that is the truest test of family.

My sons, Ben, Will, and Sam, are the joys of my life, and are three of the most unique and fascinating people on the planet. I have learned more from them than I could ever have imagined, and all four of us are still learning. Walk this way, boys . . . or at least this direction.

I have heard it said that those who believe in us create an actual physical environment in which it becomes possible to succeed. I never fully comprehended this statement until I met Terri Cullen. She believed in my writing almost from the moment we met, and this book would not exist without her love and support. She helped me see light, beauty, and hope after a long period of darkness and despair, and I am humbled by her faith in me. Terri offered encouragement at every turn, patiently listened to me ramble on about plot scenarios, and even offered excellent suggestions for settings. Plus she served as my technology and academia consultant and she makes terrific chicken curry. I am truly blessed.

Both sides forget that we are all Americans. I foresee that our country will pass through a terrible ordeal, a necessary expiation, perhaps, for our national sins.

—Robert E. Lee

The Constitution was not framed with a view to any such rebellion as that of 1861–5. While it did not authorize rebellion it made no provision against it. Yet the right to resist or suppress rebellion is as inherent as the right of self-defense, and as natural as the right of an individual to preserve his life when in jeopardy. The Constitution was therefore in abeyance for the time being, so far as it in any way affected the progress and termination of the war. . . . It would be a hard case when one-third of a nation, united in rebellion against the national authority, is entirely untrammeled, that the other two-thirds, in their efforts to maintain the Union intact, should be restrained by a Constitution prepared by our ancestors for the express purpose of insuring the permanency of the confederation of the States.

—Ulysses S. Grant, *Personal Memoirs*

# PROLOGUE

### *April 9, 1865*

### Appomattox Court House, Virginia

His name wasn't Edward Hiram, but it amused him to call himself that. Edward was Robert E. Lee's middle name, and Hiram was the real first name of Ulysses Grant.

He appreciated the humor and the irony. There was a shortage of humor in these last days of the war. No one cracked jokes anymore. The Union boys didn't act victorious, only tired. The Confederates still acted defiant, not defeated. As for the irony, that was his alone. He carried it with him like another saddlebag, just as he had been traveling at night, skirting picket lines and carrying messages for months.

It was Palm Sunday, and the dispatches had been moving between Grant and Lee since Friday. Richmond had fallen, Lee's troops were hungry, and no supplies would be forthcoming. The Army of Northern Virginia would surrender this day, within the hour.

For half a year, Hiram had traveled between the two armies. No one knew who he was. No one trusted him, for he wore neither blue nor gray. In fact, no record of him existed. There were no pay warrants, no records of assignment to a company or regiment or battalion. He was a civilian in this war, yet he moved in and out of the armies' picket lines as easily as if he were at a church social. No one trusted him, no one knew his name, but they all let him pass.

Hiram fingered the gold pin just inside his lapel. He'd first put it on less than a week ago, when it became clear that the end was coming quickly. It was solid gold and engraved with the ornate letters G.W.

Glory Warriors.

Only a handful of the pins existed. But others were already being made, and many more would come soon, when the war was officially over.

Hiram rode on toward the village of Appomattox Court House. The meeting was to take place at the home of Wilmer McLean, and there the bloody conflict would end. It was a safe location and easily accessible to both generals and their staffs. A rambling two-story house, dark with white trim, it had a magnificent Southern-style front porch that ran the length of the place. Officers and horses milled about the front dooryard. Someone was singing one of Stephen Foster's popular songs in a fine Southern tenor voice. Hiram stopped to listen for a moment: *"'Tis the song, the sigh of the weary, hard times, hard times, come again no more. . . ."*

*They believe the hard times will end with the war,* Hiram thought. *In reality, they may be just beginning.*

He rode around to the back of the house, unnoticed. *My greatest talent,* he thought. No staff waited there. Lee had told them all to wait in front of the house until he called them in to witness the surrender. The McLeans had left the home, aware of the momentous business that was about to transpire. Lee's famed horse, Traveler, was tethered to a fence post.

Hiram entered through the kitchen and, silent as dewfall, moved to the sitting room at the front of the home. The dark velvet curtains were drawn. Lee sat at a little oval table near the front window, one elbow resting on it. Even with the expression of drawn exhaustion on his face, Lee sat erect in his spotless gray uniform. His sword, jewels encrusted in the hilt, lay at his side. In an army where many of the men had no shoes at all, Lee's boots were new, stitched with red silk. His silver hair and beard were perfectly groomed. He looked like a man about to take high tea, not one about to surrender a cause for which many of his countrymen had bled and died over the last four years.

Hiram cleared his throat. "General," he said.

Lee did not look at him. "Is it ready?"

"It is," Hiram said.

Then Lee did look up, his face clouded.

"Sir," Hiram added. He rarely bothered with formalities. He was no longer a military man, after all, and even when he had been years ago, his work had been rather less formal than that of the Army regulars. Still, Robert E. Lee commanded a respect not due to many others, in or out of uniform.

"May I see it?" Lee asked, his voice ever soft, ever studied.

Hiram opened his saddlebag and withdrew the papers. There were three pages, the last one blank. Lee read them quickly, running his hand over the raised seal at the top of the first page.

Both turned as the front door opened and Ulysses S. Grant stomped in. Sixteen years younger than Lee, four inches shorter, slightly stoop-shouldered, he wore a uniform and boots spattered by mud. Aside from a pair of shoulder straps, he wore no indication of his rank, and his shirt and coat were those of a private soldier. He nodded to Lee, then to Hiram. "We haven't much time. The staff will need to be admitted in a few minutes."

Hiram pointed at the table. Lee held the papers out to him. Grant crossed to him and took the pages, rattling them in his hands. He looked up at Hiram. "You understand that it could not be in my handwriting, or General Lee's. The body of the statement itself, I mean."

"I don't concern myself with such things, General," Hiram said. He looked at both generals. "I have simply done my small part."

"Not yet, you haven't," Grant said.

He took a pen from his waistcoat and shuffled the papers, the blank page coming to the top. He scrawled his signature across it and handed it to Lee. The older man hesitated.

"General Lee?" Grant said.

"Yes," Lee said. "Yes. General, I would like to pray."

Impatient, Grant took off his hat. Hiram knew Grant had never been religious, and Lee was famously pious. There was a breath-filled silence while Lee bowed his head, eyes closed. After a moment, he looked up and signed the page, his signature just below Grant's. His hand shook a little. Hiram was startled. It was the closest thing to weakness he had ever seen from Robert E. Lee.

"General," Grant said, "the coming years will be difficult. You and I know this better than any others."

Lee waited a moment, then nodded. "The peace may well be more violent than the war." He looked at Hiram, then at Grant. "We must protect the people. *All* the people, North and South. As soldiers, it is our sworn duty."

"A precaution," Hiram said. "The nation—if indeed we are to again become one nation—will be volatile."

Both generals stared at him as if he'd spoken out of turn. Hiram felt a rising tide of annoyance at this silent rebuke from two men who'd been afraid to have the device in their own handwriting, and yet they had just affixed their signatures. Perhaps they were, after all, no better than politicians themselves.

Hiram took the pen from Lee, added the date and the time below the two signatures, and beneath that wrote, *Appomattox Court House, VA.*

"Go," Lee said. "Ride hard. The Glory Warriors await news of what we do here."

"The guardians are in place?" Hiram said, looking at both generals.

Grant rubbed his beard, looking at Lee, then glanced back to Hiram. "Yes, and a guide will be waiting for you to take you the last few miles."

"A guide?"

"The roads are not reliable in the area, especially when the rivers flood. One of the local Indians will show you the best route. I understand the man is quite respected in the Territory."

No one spoke for a long moment. "We are growing by the day," Hiram finally said.

Grant waved a hand at him, then sat down. "You heard General Lee. Go." He turned to Lee. "And on to the public business we have here."

Hiram folded the papers back into his saddlebag and left without another word. He ran his hand over the G.W. pin again.

*The Glory Warriors.*

They didn't trust him. Even after all of this, they didn't trust him. But he would be protected.

*I don't trust them, either,* Hiram thought as he mounted. *They have done what they must, and so will I.*

Within a few minutes, Grant was writing out the terms of Lee's surrender, while blue and gray stood close to each other, witnessing the end of four years of hell that had been unleashed upon the land. Hiram spurred his horse away from the house. He had a long journey ahead of him.

### Three Weeks Later

### NEAR FORT WASHITA, INDIAN TERRITORY

The Indian was waiting on the muddy road a few miles north of the Red River, where it divided the Territory from Texas, when Hiram met him. The old Chickasaw sat astride a magnificent horse, solid black with a white star on its forehead. The Indian was older than Hiram had expected. He had to be at least sixty, perhaps seventy. It was hard to tell with the Indians.

Hiram had traveled hard, but he hadn't come directly from Virginia to the Territory. He'd made a long detour, but one that would protect him. One that would protect the Glory Warriors from impulsiveness and stupidity, qualities Hiram found in abundance wherever he stopped.

He hadn't even made it to his first stop when the news reached him about Abraham Lincoln's assassination. *And so it begins,* he thought, *much sooner than any of us expected.*

He'd waited three days for more news—it would dictate what he did next. But there were no other killings in Washington. Not yet. He moved on. He saw Yankees and Rebs taking meals together as if the past four years were a grand illusion. He saw freed slaves working fields alongside poor whites. But he also saw revenge killings— North on South, South on North. He saw two starving farm women in Arkansas fighting each other over a single bushel of corn.

*The peace may well be more violent than the war,* Lee had said.

\* \* \*

He nodded to the old Indian, then turned the collar of his jacket out, showing the G.W. pin.

Without moving, the Indian said, "I am Jeremiah Colbert. I was told to wait here at noon each day. You have money? Northern money, no Confederate bills."

"Colbert? What kind of Indian name is Jeremiah Colbert? You don't trust me for the money? You think I speak with a forked tongue?"

"Don't mock me, white man," Colbert said. "I speak better English than you do. Most of my people have English names. But if it matters, I am also called Onnaroketay. And remember, our government didn't go to war with itself. My nation is more civilized than yours."

Hiram reached into his bag—not the one with the Virginia papers—and took out a wad of bills. Without any movement from Colbert that Hiram could perceive, the Chickasaw's horse moved forward. He took the bills from Hiram.

"How far?" Hiram asked.

"Ten miles," Colbert said. He turned his horse around in the road and trotted away. After a moment, Hiram followed him.


Fort Washita had been built more than twenty years earlier, and at the time of its construction was the U.S. Army's most remote outpost in the West. Built to protect the"civilized tribes" of the area—the Chickasaw and Choctaw, specifically—from marauding Plains bands like the Kiowa and Comanche, it was abandoned when the war began, then occupied and held by the Confederates through most of the war. It wasn't large—guardhouse, a few barracks, officers' quarters, hospital, and parade ground. The word *ramshackle* came to Hiram's mind as he and Colbert rode up to the guardhouse.

Hiram turned and looked at Colbert. "You can go," he said. "You've earned your money."

Colbert shrugged, turned the black horse, and trotted down the road. Hiram rode through the front gate into an overpowering silence. Just inside the gate, he stopped and dismounted, tying his horse to a tree.

The two men came from the far side of the guardhouse. One wore blue, one a threadbare gray uniform, but otherwise their similarity was striking—corn silk hair, blue eyes, drooping mustaches. The one in blue wore an infantry cap; the gray one was hatless, his hair matted and dirty. Both carried pistols on their belts.

Hiram showed them the G.W. pin without speaking. They each turned back their own jackets to show identical pins. One of the men Hiram had recruited to the Glory Warriors was a Union captain who in civilian life was a New York jeweler. He'd begun casting and engraving the pins and was awaiting Hiram's word even now to know how many more to produce.

"What's your name?" said the one in gray.

"I have no name," Hiram said.

The blue one shrugged. "Micah Garrity."

"Jonah Garrity," said the gray.

"What state?" Hiram asked.

"Missouri," Micah Garrity said.

Hiram nodded. There was a certain poignancy to it: Brothers from border states often wound up on opposite sides of this war. "It's all over," Hiram said. "Lee surrendered. The rest will follow, even here in the West."

Jonah Garrity nodded. "We've heard tell."

Micah Garrity scratched his stubbled face. A long mass of scar tissue ran from his left ear down the jawline to his chin. "Don't have to ask what's next, else you wouldn't be here."

"You have everything in place?" Hiram said.

Both men nodded.

Hiram opened his saddlebag. He withdrew a single sheet of paper, folded and tucked it into an envelope. With great deliberation, he sealed it.

"We don't get to look at it?" Jonah Garrity said, his voice low.

"Can you read?" Hiram said a little too quickly.

Both men glared at him, blue eyes hardening.

"Then don't waste my time," Hiram said. "What's inside there is for others to read. You have your part, I have mine, and they will have theirs, when the situation warrants." He handed the envelope to Micah Garrity. "You know what to do with it?"

"Dammit, we ain't fools," Micah Garrity snapped.

Hiram said nothing.

"You seen 'em?" Micah said. "Both Lee and Grant?"

"Of course," Hiram said. "Who do you think sent me?"

"Of course," Micah said.

Hiram looked at the man to rebuke him for his tone, and he missed the movement. Jonah Garrity's pistol was in his hand, and before Hiram could even turn to get his own, the big gun had sounded twice.

Hiram stumbled back against his horse. One hand went to his chest. He felt the warmth of his blood and thought, *Damn them. Damn them all.*

"It's not over," he whispered, clawing at his saddlebag.

Micah Garrity kicked Hiram's legs out from under him and stood watching as the man bled out. "It is for you," he said. He bent down and pulled the G.W. pin from Hiram's coat, tearing off a bit of the fabric with it.

"We don't want him to die in here," Jonah Garrity said. "Take him outside." He and his brother each took one of Hiram's arms and pulled. They dragged him along the path, through the gate, and into the mud in front of the fort.

"He had a nice horse, at least," Micah said. "That'll help."

A mist had begun, and the late-afternoon light was fading. Jonah and Micah Garrity walked away from Hiram, leaving him in the middle of the road to die.


Hiram didn't know how long he lay there. He floated weightless above himself in the rain, then felt as if he were being dragged back down into the mud. Nothing flashed before his eyes, as he'd heard happened with dying men. He just felt the floating sensation, then the dragging, over and over again. He rolled onto his back. The entire front of his white shirt was red. He saw the old Indian and for a moment thought, *Are you God? Are you to pass judgment on me?*

But Jeremiah Colbert—Onnaroketay—dismounted and looked at him without speaking. He lifted Hiram as if he weighed nothing at all and draped him across the saddle of the beautiful black horse.

Colbert still said nothing, but Hiram felt the horse moving. He was no longer floating, but his head felt incredibly light.

*It's not over,* Hiram thought. Then he closed his eyes, floating again, and this time he wasn't dragged back down.

# CHAPTER

# 1

*Present Day*

T hey first found out about the discovery at the same time and in the same manner as the rest of the world—via television. The Judge was watching one of his own networks, Heritage News Channel, in the middle of the afternoon, when the cable network inserted one of its fluff "feature stories." It was something the Judge might have missed, as he usually ignored such nonsense. Then again, even if he had missed it the first time, he was certain he would have been informed in fairly short order. One of the others would have picked up the significance and relayed it to him.

The graphic at the bottom of the screen read HISTORICAL FIND IN OKLAHOMA. The video was of an earthmover breaking ground in an open field. The reporter, male and young, spoke in voice-over. "I'm Dan Manning at the Fort Washita Historical Site, between Madill and Durant in far southern Oklahoma. A huge cache of Civil War–era weapons was found buried here, as ground was being broken for a new museum dedicated to the 1840s-era frontier fort."

The Judge leaned across his huge walnut desk, eyes riveted to the plasma screen TV. The video shifted to a long table, on which were piled rusting long rifles, their wooden stocks weathered, barrels encrusted with nearly a century and a half of grit. "This is only a portion of the weapons found. The Oklahoma Historical Society, which owns Fort Washita and the property adjacent to it, has turned the artifacts over to historian Nick Journey at nearby South Central College of Oklahoma. He estimates more than five thousand rifles"—the reporter came down hard on the word *thousand*—"were buried here. And that doesn't take into account dozens of disassembled artillery weapons. Some still bear the insignia of Civil War regiments. Interestingly enough, the heavier weapons seem to have come from both Northern and Southern units, yet they were buried here together."

The Judge grabbed a pen and pad and began to write, his heart pounding. The video cut to a middle-aged white man whose dark reddish brown hair was shot through with gray. He was of average height, slightly thick around the middle, lined face and calm brown eyes, thoughtful demeanor. He was wearing a blue denim shirt. The graphic identified him as NICK JOURNEY, PH.D., CIVIL WAR HISTORIAN.

"We're just starting the process of analyzing the artifacts," Journey said into the microphone. "It'll take a while to sort it all out."

"Any theories?" the reporter asked.

The Judge held his breath. "No," Journey said. The historian dropped his eyes away from the camera. "No theories. Not yet."

The video ran to an exterior shot of the Fort Washita guardhouse as it overlooked a narrow two-lane highway, then back to another table, on which rested a rusting metal strongbox, the kind that had once been made to transport gold and other valuables. The camera zoomed in for a tight shot of a gold pin that rested beside the box. The reporter, blond and fair-skinned with the well-scrubbed but unremarkable looks that permeated TV news, stepped into the shot and picked up the pin. "Adding further to the intrigue, this metal box was found buried at one end of the pit that held the weapons. Professor Journey tells us some documents were also in the box, but they haven't been released to the public as of yet."

The shot returned to Nick Journey. "The Oklahoma Historical Society has granted me custody of all these materials, and I'll be working to determine just how they came to be here at Fort Washita."

"What can you tell us about the papers that were found in the box?"

"Nothing at this time. But the documents will be secure."

"What is the condition of the papers?"

"Very good, from what we can tell. The box is made of tin and coated with copper. Someone was very serious about preserving the contents of this box. Our document conservators at the college are working on the papers now, to make sure we are physically able to handle them. After that, I'll start analyzing them for content to see if we can figure out where they came from and who buried them here. Believe me these items aren't going to be very far away from me for the foreseeable future. We have very specific chain of custody procedures for historic artifacts."

"Do you think you'll get to the bottom of this?"

"That's my job, Dan."

The camera cut back to the reporter, who walked to the table and picked up the gold pin. "This little bit of jewelry has been cleaned up, and it appears to be made of solid gold." He turned it toward the camera and ran his fingers over the letters. "Who was G.W.? Perhaps when we know that, we'll know more about this very curious discovery at this off-the-beaten-path historical site. Historian Nick Journey will be trying to find out just what all of this means. For now, though, it's a bona fide historical mystery. I'm Dan Manning for HNC, in Bryan County, Oklahoma."

The piece ended and the anchors in Washington were back on screen. The Judge muted the TV's sound and sat back in his leather chair. He folded his hands together as if praying, then unfolded them several times. He swiveled in his chair, facing the picture window that looked across the green West Virginia hills. The Judge had come here years ago, settling in this state that had been born out of the Civil War. It was a symbol of his commitment to the cause. He had spent most of his life searching, looking for what a random construction project had just turned up in Oklahoma, of all places. Not the old weapons, of course. But the "documents" buried with them—he needed the documents.

He and the others had waited. The names and faces came and went. The old ones died off and young ones were carefully recruited. Thousands of them waited now, in secret bases across the country—they came from the military, the intelligence services, law enforcement, even from the business, technology, and academia sectors. All waited for their opportunity to move into action. For many of them, their trails were obscured, their lives reshaped, just as he had reshaped his own life. The media, even his own employees, liked to call him "reclusive." And he was, since he had turned the day-to-day operation of his companies over to subordinates, MBA types who knew nothing of his real purpose. To them, he was just a rich old man who had once been well known and was now content to sit back at his home in the hills and make his money. Newspapers, magazines, radio and TV stations, cable networks, Internet portals . . . he owned them all, but they were only the means for achieving his true life's work—work that was closer to reality today than it had ever been. The Judge turned back to his desk. He had scrawled *Nick Journey, South Central College of Oklahoma* on the legal pad. He picked up his phone, waited a moment, then said, "Have you heard?"

"Just now," said the man on the other end of the line. "Did you see it?"

"Yes," the Judge said. "What this man has found will fill in all the holes. It's the actual document. Did you see the pin?"

"Of course."

"Yes. We must have the document in our hands. Start working on the man, this college professor, Journey."

His mind shifting, racing, turning like an undammed river, the plans that had consumed him for so long—just as they had ruled the lives of his father and grandfather before him—began to come into focus. After hanging up the phone, the Judge unlocked his desk drawer and withdrew the ancient pages. He read the ornate writing, ran his hands across the words. Then he pulled out another page and felt the raised seal: two swords, crossed at their points, with USA and CSA on their respective hilts, a single silver star occupying the space between the two points, and below that, between the hilts of the swords, a bloodred American eagle. This was all they knew for so many years. Now the other pieces would fit together. Now they would be complete.

The Judge turned the lapel of his jacket inside out and touched the gold pin there, a round piece of jewelry with the letters G.W. engraved on it.

# CHAPTER

# 2

On any given day, *tired* was the only word Nick Journey could think of to describe his life. One of his colleagues in South Central College of Oklahoma's Department of History was on sabbatical, so he'd had an extra undergraduate course added to his teaching load. His manuscript for a journal article had lain untouched since the spring semester ended, and his coauthor was constantly on his case about it. Then there was Andrew, whose needs were changing, seemingly by the day, and caring for a twelve-year-old with a profound disability was by definition a case study in exhaustion.

Then there was "the gun thing," as his students were calling it, and dealing with the aftermath of the Fort Washita discovery simply added another layer. Journey had little interest in the guns themselves, and having secured a couple of them for the tiny SCCO history museum, gave the rest of them back to the Oklahoma Historical Society. They'd sent three trucks from Oklahoma City to pick up the old ordnance. But Journey held on to the little strongbox and its contents.

So he put in his time as SCCO's resident celebrity. The college sat along the edge of Lake Texoma, the huge man-made lake that was fed by the Red River and divided Oklahoma from Texas. The town of Carpenter Center, with a year-round population of ten thousand, was equal parts lakeside resort and small college town, infused with the quintessential Oklahoma elements of Old West cattle culture, the oil industry, and Native American influence.

His office in Cullen Hall was cramped. With a decade on the faculty, he was a tenured associate professor, but office space at SCCO was notoriously tiny. The office was disorganized, the books and journals and student works piled around his laptop. The only adornment on the wall was his doctorate from the University of Virginia. A few pictures of Andrew fanned out on the desk. Physically, the boy was a carbon copy of his mother, with the pecan-colored hair and the gray-green eyes and high cheekbones. Andrew smiled in only one of the pictures, the one from when he was three years old, before his autism had become clear. In the others, his look ranged from frightened to completely vacant.

With his morning class over and no office hours scheduled today, Journey opened his window—the best thing about the office was that it looked out onto the tree-lined common—and unlocked his desk drawer.

He'd received the papers back from the document conservators, who had applied a humidification process to make the paper less brittle. Still, they'd encased the pages in a plastic sleeve for handling. Journey took out the sleeve and centered it on his laptop—it was the only place on the desk he could put it. He tapped a fingernail on the desk three times. It was a gesture that never failed to irritate students, colleagues, and his ex-wife—always the left index finger, always three times.

He looked at the thick, somewhat yellowed parchment, feeling the embossed seal of swords, star, and eagle through the plastic. The handwriting beneath the seal was flowing yet masculine. An educated man had written the words.

> *Whereas the late War Between the States has been ended, on this date and in this place; And whereas the conditions of the American continent in the conflict's aftermath bring to bear great uncertainty; And whereas Americans, both North and South, possess an interest in the general order and well-being of the continent; This clause is added to the terms ending the aforementioned conflict. As*

*such, it possesses the power of treaty and the import of law, to super-
sede all others, in accordance with General Order No. 100, "Instructions for the Government of Armies of the United States in the
Field," Section I, Article 3.*

   *This clause shall be enacted into law if three provisions of the
American Federal Government are present. If the leaders of the
three branches of Government are removed in short order from
their offices—to wit, the Speaker of the Legislative Branch, the
chief justice of the Judicial Branch, and the president of the Executive Branch—and if said removal is accomplished by conspiratorial means to destabilize the American Federal Government,
this clause shall be activated, and will supersede all other areas of
law and treaty until such time as the Government may once again
become stabilized. This clause shall not be enacted unless all por-
tions of this document may be authenticated, inclusive of our signatures following.*

A long black line of ink stretched across the page, and at the
bottom, in a slightly more hurried hand, was written: *The Poet's Penn
makes the waters fall and causes the strong to bend.*

   Journey had read the page at least fifty times by now, putting
himself into the time when it was written. The Civil War era, Reconstruction, and the Gilded Age that followed were rife with conspiracies, most of which turned out to be nothing more than a fanatic or
two planning here or there to do something to promote their cause.

   Never, to Journey's knowledge, had there ever been a plot to remove the highest officials of all three branches of the government.
That would have meant widespread panic, a descent into chaos, anar-
chy. In the 1860s, perhaps even a resumption of hostilities between
North and South. But such a thing could never have been accomplished. The planning would have to be too precise. A thousand
things would go wrong. They always did.

   Journey tapped his finger again. But *someone* was thinking about
such a conspiracy in the war years. Clearly referring to Lee's surrender at Appomattox, the writer of this page had envisioned just such
a conspiracy, and a "clause" to deal with its aftermath. The writing
didn't belong to either Lee or Grant—both men had left enough

writings behind to be preserved in many different archives. It had taken Journey all of fifteen minutes online to see that neither man wrote the words on this page.

He went back to his computer and typed *General Order No. 100* in the search engine. When the results settled onto the screen, he nodded to himself. He'd run across it in his research before, but usually under its more common name, the Lieber Code, after the law professor who drafted most of it. General Order No. 100 was an executive order issued by President Lincoln in 1863 to direct the conduct of the armies during the war. It was often cited as one of the precursors to the Hague Conventions that still governed modern warfare.

Journey scrolled down to Article 3 of the first section and read:

> *Martial law in a hostile country consists in the suspension by the occupying military authority of the criminal and civil law, and of the domestic administration and government in the occupied place or territory, and in the substitution of military rule and force for the same, as well as in the dictation of general laws, as far as military necessity requires this suspension, substitution, or dictation.*

A chill went down Journey's spine.
*Hostile country.*
*Martial law.*
What did the Lieber Code have to do with Fort Washita? What "conspiratorial means" was the author of this page talking about?

Journey returned to the old paper. There was no second page, no signatures as referenced in the writing. And the cryptic note at the end made no sense. The document was so precise in its language, so deliberate—the misspelling of *penn* leapt off the page.

*The Poet's Penn makes the waters fall and causes the strong to bend.*

"What *is* this?" Journey said, not realizing he'd said it aloud.

"Nick?"

Journey jumped and knocked papers off the desk.

"Sorry, didn't mean to startle you." The voice belonged to Sandra Kelly, one of the new young assistant professors, in her third year and not yet tenured. Her specialty was the history of third-party political movements and extremism in American politics. She was fully six feet tall with a mane of brilliant red hair and blazing Irish green eyes. She was fond of wearing loose-fitting tie-dye dresses. A small, simple silver cross hung around her neck. "Working on the gun thing?"

Journey made a face at her. "Stop calling it that. It's bad enough that TV reporters and bloggers with nothing better to do call it that. It's not about the guns."

She grinned. "Want to grab some lunch?"

"I suppose so." Journey was vaguely uncomfortable with Sandra Kelly, often sensing she was looking for something other than a professional relationship. She was a good dozen years younger than he, and had never said or done anything overt, but his gut told him otherwise. Even so, he and Amelia had been divorced for only three years. He suspected Sandra—or almost any other woman, for that matter—would be scared off by Andrew's disability. So he told himself with great regularity.

"Don't sound so enthusiastic."

"Sorry. I guess I'm distracted. You want to get Uncle Charley's? Today is the cheeseburger basket special."

"Very funny." Sandra was a strict vegetarian.

"Right. I'll eat your burger, and you can have a salad."

Journey dropped the gold pin into a plastic Ziploc bag and tucked the bag into the pocket of his tan chinos. Taking care not to fold or crinkle the sleeve, he picked up the paper and slipped it into the battered green backpack he used as a briefcase. Journey was notorious among the faculty for taking documents with him wherever he went, whether they were major discoveries or not. He worked on them at home, in coffee shops, sitting in traffic, anywhere he could snatch a minute to consider and analyze a new historical find. The pin was another question without an answer. Who was G.W.? On some vague level, Journey felt that he should know the answer already, and that if he found G.W., he found the rest of this strange little enigma.

Nick Journey and Sandra Kelly walked down the stairs and out of Cullen Hall into the bright September sunshine. As they did, a tall young man with a blond buzzcut, sitting in an armchair in the lounge area on the first floor pulled out a cell phone. He spoke quietly to his counterpart, who was leaning against an elm thirty feet from the front steps. The man outside watched the two professors as they passed, then snapped his own phone closed.

Journey and Kelly cleared the common, with its towering oaks and elms and its "memory garden" of wildflowers. Uncle Charley's, a campus institution that had been serving burgers and beer for half a century, sat diagonally across Whitesell Boulevard from the main gates of the college. One minute later, they were ordering lunch. Across the street, at a metered parking space, a man in the driver's seat of a navy blue Chevy Suburban spoke into a cell phone. "He's now off campus. Move in."

The young man in the lobby of Cullen Hall closed his phone, stood up, and headed to the stairs. Half a minute later, the one from outside joined him. Less than ninety seconds after the man in the Suburban had spoken, the other two were inside Nick Journey's office.

In three minutes, they called the man in the Suburban. "It's not here," said the one who'd been stationed outside. "He must have it with him."

"Acknowledged. Were you seen?"

"Negative. The hallway's empty."

"Good. Get out of there. They went to the diner across the street. I'll establish surveillance there."

The man in the car was a little older than the other two, wearing jeans, a polo shirt, and sneakers. He left the Suburban, turned the corner, and walked into Uncle Charley's. He spotted Journey and the red-haired woman three booths back from the counter. A waitress had just brought their food—an enormous cheeseburger with a side order of grilled jalapeño peppers for Journey, an equally substantial salad for the woman. The man glanced at their table once as he passed. The plastic sleeve rested on the table, Journey's right hand on top of it, as if he expected it to try to escape.

He went to the counter and ordered a cheeseburger to go. When it arrived, he took the white foam container and walked past the two professors again. They were eating, Journey's elbow resting on the page. Journey looked up as the man passed and for an instant their eyes met. The man from the Suburban shifted his eyes away to the sleeve. He saw the faded seal—the swords, the star, the eagle embossed in deep red.

Journey moved around a little, covering the page with his arm. The man from the Suburban walked outside and returned to his vehicle. His two associates were waiting for him.

"He's keeping it with him," the man said. "Let's go back over his schedule." He looked at the other two. "We're going to go operational. We have to take it from him."

"He's not going to want to give it to us," said one of the others.

"Our orders are clear. We do whatever it takes."

Journey lingered over his burger, Sandra picked at her salad, and the two of them talked about their colleague who was on sabbatical in England, about students who annoyed them, students they liked. Sandra didn't press him about the document, for which he was grateful. It was a welcome respite from all the hype surrounding it, and he sensed she knew it. It was almost two o'clock when they left Uncle Charley's.

Journey didn't have another class until evening, so he picked Andrew up from school and headed to his home, a brick 1930s Tudor six blocks from campus. Andrew wasn't especially vocal today, which was good—he'd been screaming a lot lately. He was also likely to break into hysterical laughter at any moment, and it was far different from his genuine, happy laughter. Today's sound, though, was whistling, the same three notes in the same pattern over and over again. Repetitive behaviors were one of the hallmarks of Andrew's autism. Journey thought of his finger taps—always the left index finger, always three times. Maybe he shared more with his child than he thought he did. The idea gave him a little comfort. Many times a day, he felt he never reached Andrew at all, that nothing he did made the least difference, so he took his common ground wherever he could find it.

He changed Andrew's diaper. Changing diapers on a boy who was five feet six presented its own set of challenges, but it had become so routine to Journey that he occasionally let himself forget that parents of other twelve-year-olds didn't have to do this several times a day. He rolled a ball back and forth with the boy for a few minutes; then Andrew grew tired of that and wandered off in search of a straw and a pencil, which he would beat together in rhythm for hours on end, if left to do so.

Journey checked e-mail, thought about working on his journal article, and didn't have the heart for it. He looked at the Fort Washita document again. What did it mean? Some 1865-vintage lunatic fringe stockpiling weapons to assassinate the president, the Speaker of the House, and the chief justice of the Supreme Court?

The line at the bottom, scrawled more hastily but in the same handwriting, was nonsense. *The Poet's Penn.* Penn with the double *n*. A reference to Pennsylvania? William Penn? Journey could think of nothing that coincided with the Civil War references.

Before he knew it, two hours had slipped away and he needed to get ready for class. The sitter, a special education major from the college, was on time and Journey said good-bye to Andrew. As usual, he had to say the boy's name several times to get a fleeting second's eye contact, and then Andrew pushed his flat hand forward in a sharp, jerky movement, his version of a good-bye wave.

He was almost late for class, which wasn't unusual. The class ran from five thirty until nine o'clock, an upper-division course called Congress in the Civil War. He had only eight students, and the discussions were lively and challenging. He hated the scheduling of it, but intellectually it was the high point of his week.

At a few minutes after nine, he walked upstairs to his office, intending to check e-mail and phone messages before leaving campus for the night. He pulled up short, three steps from his door.

It was slightly ajar.

Journey looked up and down the hall. He was alone. No other office doors were open. His was the only class that met in the building this evening.

He stepped into the office. His laptop was on the floor, the screen shattered. His desk was clear—all the papers had been swept onto the floor. The single drawer of his desk was pulled open. His file folders had all been opened. Student assignments covered his chair. Books had been ripped from the tiny shelf. His pictures of Andrew were all askew. The one of a smiling three-year-old Andrew, in a gold oval frame, was cracked. The fissure in the glass slashed directly across the boy's face.

He heard a footstep somewhere down the hall.

Journey turned halfway around, as abruptly as if someone had pulled him by the shoulder.

Another step. Cullen Hall was an old building with tile flooring in all the offices and hallways. Footsteps were always magnified, and there was a standing departmental joke that one person walking down the hall sounding like the entire student body stampeding.

Journey reached for his phone and punched *2-3-4-5*, campus security. "This is Nick Journey, history department. My office . . . someone broke into my office."

The young male voice said, "What room, Dr. Journey?"

"Cullen Hall. Two-oh-three."

"We'll be right there."

Journey stepped into the hallway. It seemed darker, the walls closer, the air stifling. "Hello?" he said to the walls.

There was the noise again, from the direction of the stairs. Three offices were between here and there, plus restrooms at the top of the stairway. He took a few more steps, a fast walk, then almost a jog.

He turned back toward the hall. It was empty, dark. He'd never realized what an isolated cave of a place Cullen Hall was at night after classes were over.

Journey tightened his grip on his backpack strap, flexed his hands, and put a foot on the top stair.


The three field operatives had moved from their base in Dallas into Carpenter Center, armed with a thorough dossier on Nick Allen Journey, Ph.D. The young man who had watched from the common as the target and Sandra Kelly walked to lunch eight hours ago was in an alcove just off the stairs at the opposite end of the building from Journey. His code name was Silver, and his backpack lay at his feet. He withdrew a Heckler & Koch MK 23 Mod 0, the pistol adopted by the United States Army Special Operations Command for Special Forces use in the 1990s. It came with a suppressor, which was already in place. Silver's field counterpart, code name Gold, was positioned outside, armed with an identical weapon.

The Judge's orders were very specific. The document was of paramount importance. Nick Journey was not deemed automatically expendable, but if the situation warranted, extreme measures were authorized, if it meant acquiring the document.

Silver peeked from his alcove. Journey had started tentatively down the opposite stairs. He held his gun in front of him, arms extended, elbows tucked in, ready to fire, and started down the stairs.


*Where the hell are the cops?*

SCCO was a small college in a small town, and real crime was rare, especially on campus. Journey wasn't certain they would even have procedures in place for dealing with breaking and entering.

He paused halfway down the stairs, listening. Now the acoustics of this old building were playing tricks on him. The noise seemed to come from somewhere else. His hands closed on the plastic bag. He jogged down the rest of the steps and half turned toward the opposite end of the building.

A man not much older than some of his students, in nondescript jeans and polo shirt, had just stepped onto the floor at the other side. His hands moved strangely, and Journey followed the motion. He saw the gun. He spun toward the front of the building and ran.


Silver adjusted the ultraslim headset that curled around his right ear and down to his mouth, then spoke into the little microphone. "Moving as expected. He's heading toward the front door. Stay in position."

He started to run in long, loping strides. Ahead, he saw the overweight middle-aged professor disappear around the corner of the wall that ran toward the front of Cullen Hall.

Silver smiled.

*Think!* Journey screamed inwardly.

There was a man with a gun in the building, coming for him. Coming for the document he carried in his backpack—this was no random campus break-in. He still didn't understand the significance of what he carried, but it was the only explanation that made sense.

*But it doesn't make sense at all.* Cryptic words about the Civil War and "clauses" and heads of government being removed by "conspiratorial means" and nonsense words about water falling and the strong bending. It was incomplete—there had to be more to it. . . .

*They may think I have more than I do. Whoever* they *are.*

The man with the gun moved closer, and Journey was already out of breath. Fifteen years removed from his days as a minor league baseball player—and not a very good one at that—and his idea of exercise now was chasing Andrew to make sure the boy didn't run into traffic.

*Andrew.*

Journey blinked. Part of having a child with special needs, especially a child who was nonverbal, was anticipating what he was about to do, to figure out if he was about to hurt himself or someone else. It was like chess, always thinking one and two and three moves ahead as to what Andrew was going to do.

The man with the gun was herding him outside. The campus would be almost deserted by now. If he had come for the Fort Washita documents, he wouldn't be alone. He would have another man stationed somewhere else.

*Right outside the front door.*

As he laid his hand on the glass front door of Cullen Hall, Journey turned away from it just as quickly. Three feet from him was a dark opening that led down a long wheelchair ramp and out a side entrance. Several students had complained about the poor lighting.

Journey was thankful that maintenance hadn't yet gotten around to replacing the lights.

He dodged into the hallway.


Gold waited at the foot of the rock steps that led outward from Cullen Hall. He also held a backpack, one hand wrapped around its strap, the other hand buried inside, grasping his own H&K pistol.

He was on full alert following Silver's transmission. He caught movement ahead of him, inside the building, but just a flash, a small glint in the lobby lights, and then nothing. Seconds later, Silver swung open the glass door at the top of the steps and shouted, "Where is he?"

Gold dropped the backpack, the pistol coming up in his hand. "He didn't come out!"

"Shit," Silver muttered. "He must have turned at the last second and I didn't see him. He has to be . . ."

Both men turned, their highly trained senses hearing the sound at the same time. Gold pointed with his gun, around the side of the building. They broke into an instant run.


Journey skidded at the foot of the ramp, just long enough to slap the blue and white wheelchair symbol with the palm of his hand. It took three excruciating seconds for the door to begin swinging outward, the mechanism grinding slowly.

*Now I know why the students in wheelchairs get upset,* he thought. The door opened a few inches. He got his fingers around the edge and put his shoulder against the glass. It opened a little more, inch by maddening inch. Journey put his entire body into it and slammed against the door.

The opening widened, but then as if in rebellion against unwanted attention, swung back a few inches. Journey kicked at the bottom and twisted his body through the opening into the warm night air.

A wide sidewalk bisected two lines of grass on this side of the building. On the far side of the second strip of green was Howell Hall, the science building, with an identical door and wheelchair ramp. Journey looked right. The sidewalk ran between Cullen and Howell and emptied into a parking lot. Diagonally across the lot was the field house.

*Yes*, Journey thought. Phys ed students, not to mention some of the varsity athletes, often worked out late into the evenings. Staff was in the building until midnight, and security was nearby.

He ran toward the lights of the parking lot.

# CHAPTER

# 4

The Judge sat in his study, with the smell of wood and leather and good whiskey, and watched his computer screen as the events in Oklahoma unfolded before him in real time.

*Amazing,* he thought. *The Internet has created possibilities that are endless. The information, the communication, the data . . .*

Still, he found it rather ironic that all the information technology in the world had not been able to find the document the Glory Warriors sought for all these years. That had come down to something as mundane as digging a hole in the earth. Perhaps the equipment was different, but the act itself was as old as humanity.

He sat straight in his leather chair, watching the monitor. All the field operatives had wireless cameras mounted on their headsets, the images uploaded to a secure server and broadcast to the Judge's computer. All the teams were coded as Gold, Silver, and Bronze, with further designations for their base and ranking. This was the top team from Dallas Base, known as Dallas One.

The men's motions were jerky as they ran, and of course, the lighting was poor, but the Judge could see the outline of Nick Journey as Dallas One Gold turned the corner between the two buildings. The men were equipped with all the information available on

Journey, and now he must let them do their jobs. They had been well trained, and a paunchy professor with high blood pressure was no match for the Glory Warriors.

He had been patient long enough. They had all waited too long. The Judge could taste success, as clearly as he had tasted the fine Thomas H. Handy rye whiskey in a glass at his elbow. He had put Dallas One into motion, and other teams were moving into position to orchestrate the remaining components of the mission.

The Judge watched as Nick Journey's outline disappeared into the parking lot.


With his gun hand, Dallas One Gold waved Silver around the other side of Howell Hall. He had seen where Journey was going, making for the parking lot. They would come at him from both sides of the science building. Gold would be in the parking lot in fifteen seconds. Journey would be in the open, and the lighting would be better.


Journey's lungs were on fire, his legs wobbling as he stepped out from between Cullen and Howell. He heard only one set of steps behind him. No doubt the other man was circling in from another direction, trying to trap him.

He bounded into an oval of light in the first row of parking spaces, steadying himself against a light pole as a campus police car, lights flashing, pulled into the far corner of the lot. He waved his arms. The police car angled toward him.

The car skidded to a stop, sideways across three parking spaces. The officer was barely older than some of Journey's students.

The kid's name tag read P. PARSONS. "Dr. Journey?" he said. The drawl was pure Oklahoma. "Why didn't you stay—?"

"Guns," Journey whispered. "Two men." He sank down alongside the concrete support of the light pole.

"What?" said Officer Parsons, his glance moving from Journey to the space between the two buildings. He stepped into the space where Journey had been standing a second ago.

Gold closed to within a hundred feet of him. Sighting the H&K's laser aiming module, and well within the pistol's range, he gave a gentle squeeze to the trigger, and the shot caught Officer Parsons just above his name tag.

The young officer made a sound like he'd been punched in the stomach and toppled toward Journey. Too stunned to speak, Journey raised his hands as if he were hitting a volleyball and pushed Parsons away from him.

From far across the parking lot, he heard a scream.

"Dr. Journey!" Gold shouted. "The document, now! Put it on the ground by the car!"

Journey said nothing, the backpack slipping halfway off his shoulder as he ducked into the open door of the police car.

The radio was squawking. "Parsons? Pete, what the hell happened? Pete, are you on?"

Journey slid into the still-warm car seat and dropped the gearshift down three notches. He didn't—*couldn't*—think. He turned the steering wheel hard left and stepped on the accelerator.

Silver was halfway across the parking lot, running steadily, as he saw what was about to happen.

He shouted into the night. He was still too far away, out of range with no good shot.

He raised the pistol anyway and fired.


Journey heard the shot from the other direction, but didn't look. He locked his hands to the wheel and plowed straight ahead.

The man in front of him raised the gun again and got off one more shot. But now Journey was a moving target, and the gunman was a second too late. He looked like he was about to lunge to the right, but the grille of the police car caught him at the waist. He bent like a question mark, whirled halfway around, and bounced onto the car's hood.

Journey screamed into the windshield. Beside him, the radio kept up a constant chatter.

The police car jumped the curb. Journey twisted the wheel and found the brake. The back end fishtailed around; then the front clipped into the side of Cullen Hall. The gunman's limp body slid across the hood and slammed into the brick building.

Journey saw blood. He felt nothing. He heard a siren.

The Judge stood up, knocking his glass to the floor. He'd been watching the split screen feed from both Gold's and Silver's cameras, Silver closing across the parking lot, then slowing and stopping as Gold's feed became a blur of images: the car, the wall, the ground.

The Judge picked up his phone. "Where's Bronze? Extract, extract! Get them out of there!"

"He's moving into position," said the voice, and then the phone went dead.

Silver turned and ran, circling back around Howell Hall, away from the carnage. He had been trained to leave no man behind, but he had also been trained to think of the mission above any individual loyalty, and the mission—at least this aspect of it—was blown. In two minutes, he had crossed the common and was sitting with Dallas One Bronze in the blue Suburban. In five more minutes, they had left Carpenter Center and were headed south.

Journey stumbled out of the car, holding on to the hood to steady himself. He pulled the gunman away from the brick wall, feeling for a pulse, finding none.

As he pulled his hand away from the gunman's neck, he brushed something hard. Journey fumbled around the man's shirt collar. Underneath it, concealed from view, was a round pin with the letters G.W.

The world tilted. Journey's mind went fuzzy for a moment, then came into sharp focus: the pin that was found in the ground, a few miles from here; this man, shooting at him, wearing a pin very much like the one from Fort Washita. Connections. History was about making connections.

*But maybe this is about more than just history,* he thought.

He felt along the back of the pin, unhooked it from the man's collar, and dropped it in his pocket—the same pocket with the Baggie. Then Journey slumped down alongside the car and waited.

# CHAPTER

# 5

M eg Tolman lived in two worlds. In one of them, the U.S. Government's Research and Investigations Office (RIO), a jointly administered agency of the Justice Department, Treasury Department, and Homeland Security, she was simply known as Meg. In the other world, she always used her full name, Margaret Isabell Tolman. She couldn't think of a single successful concert pianist with a name like Meg. So she begrudgingly went for pretense over familiarity. Even with as small a venue as the Falls Church Chamber Music Society, she felt obliged to use her "concert" name.

But, small venue though it was, the Falls Church women had a Steinway in their hall, and they paid better than the average group of old ladies. She stood alone just off the little stage and rolled kinks out of her back. One of the ladies was on the stage introducing her, talking about how Tolman had studied at the Curtis Institute in Philadelphia, followed by a year in Vienna, and had studied in master classes with Garrick Ohlsson and Emanuel Ax and Mitsuko Uchida. . . . Tolman tuned it out. She'd heard it too many times. She just wanted the keyboard.

The woman stopped blathering, there was polite applause, and she walked across the stage. The old ladies—and a few husbands who'd been dragged out on a weeknight for this—were slightly aghast that she wasn't wearing a dress. Old ladies typically didn't like her very short blond shag haircut, either, but she would not bow to convention on either count. Dresses were too damn uncomfortable, and she didn't have time to deal with hair, and if these ladies didn't think a woman could play Rachmaninov with short hair, in pants and a sleeveless blouse, then to hell with them.

She gave a nod to the audience and sat down at the keyboard, no score in front of her. That was Franz Liszt's fault—he'd screwed it up for every pianist who came after him, showing off by playing everything from memory. She refused to play Liszt to this day. One of her teachers at Curtis had told her she was being passive-aggressive. She didn't care.

But Rachmaninov was another matter. And Chopin and Schubert and Brahms and Beethoven and Debussy, and more obscure composers like John Field and Charles Tomlinson Griffes. But she started every recital with Rachmaninov, one of the preludes, a different one every time, each a gem in miniature.

Then there was nothing in the room except Tolman and her piano—while she sat at the keyboard, it was *her* Steinway—and the incredible and indelible emotions of the music. She played, lots of little pieces and one big one, the Beethoven "Pastoral" Sonata, without taking a break. She played for nearly an hour and a half, pausing only long enough for a bit of applause—which she scarcely heard—after each piece. She played an encore of Mozart's "Rondo alla Turca," then threw in a little jazz with the Paul Desmond–Dave Brubeck classic "Take Five." After a full evening of romantic and impressionistic music, it never failed to bring down the house.

Then she was offstage, steeling herself for the reception of terrible punch and worse baked goods. She collected her check, and one of the husbands insisted on driving her to the Metro station. It was not quite seven o'clock, warm in the District, the sun starting to hang low but still very much in evidence. *Might as well go to the office*, Tolman thought. There was nothing at home but a deaf cat and dirty laundry.

She got off at Farragut Park, with its famous statue of Admiral David "Damn the Torpedoes" Farragut and walked half a block up Connecticut Avenue to one of the twin office buildings that faced each other across the street. It wasn't a federal office complex. RIO was a small agency, and when it had been created five years ago, none of the three Cabinet-level departments that coadministered it had wanted to house it. Congress created the office, held a news conference about "data coordination" and "interagency discipline" and "research and investigative support," and then essentially forgot about RIO. The government leased the office space in this private building.

Tolman took the elevator to the fourth floor, made one turn down a narrow hallway that dead-ended at a wooden door with a small nameplate containing the suite number—427—and the words UNITED STATES GOVERNMENT. In smaller letters just below: RESEARCH AND INVESTIGATIONS OFFICE.

The outer office was dark. Most of the dozen RIO staffers worked on a strict eight-to-five clock. Four of them, including Tolman, were classified as "Research and Investigative Specialists." Two were former Deputy U.S. Marshals, one was ex-FBI. Tolman was the only one who'd come straight to RIO from the Academy, where she'd gone after her year in Vienna and another disastrous year spent trying to make a living playing music full-time. She made it through the Federal Law Enforcement Academy in Glencoe, Georgia, and stunned a lot of people, herself and her Secret Service agent father included, by her aptitude for it. Her eye for marksmanship and her endurance in physical training surprised her Academy instructors. Then she'd blown them all away with her investigative use of technology. That was the paradox: a petite woman with eyes the color of blue topaz, who could curse with the big boys, shoot like a SWAT team member, outrun most of her male counterparts, manage databases like a seasoned IT professional, and play piano professionally.

The rest of the RIO staff were "civilian" support people, as was Deputy Director Russell "Rusty" Hudson, who ran the office. Tolman found it curious that a Deputy Director was in charge, because in five years no one at RIO had met or reported to anyone with the title of Director.

Hudson would still be here, Tolman knew, for at least another couple of hours. He had no life. He was in his early fifties, an accountant and a lawyer, a career government employee, who by choice had no family. Tolman passed by his office door, which was open, and kept going. The suite was a narrow maze with offices that branched off it. Hers was at the end, which her coworkers found appropriate. Underneath her nameplate, someone had taped a piece of paper that read WHERE CASES GO TO DIE.

She tossed her purse and keys onto a spare chair, sat at the desk—institutional, fake wood, a half-moon shape that accommodated her computer—and let her mind work its way back from Rachmaninov and Beethoven to the world of RIO.

Within half a minute, she heard Rusty Hudson's heavy step in the hallway. The man was a study in contradictions: he was huge, at six feet seven and over three hundred pounds. But he had very fair skin, small, delicate features, always wore a suit, always spoke in soft and very precise tones. Yet he professed a love of Washington Nationals baseball and reality TV.

He towered over her. Hudson towered over most people, but Tolman, at five-one, felt especially dwarfed. In the annual departmental photo, they always stood next to each other. One of the wits in the office pointed to them as "diversity."

"How was the performance?" Hudson asked.

"Not bad," Tolman said.

"And the Beethoven piece? Wasn't this your debut with it?"

"Better than I expected. A little rough in the second movement, but I don't think the old ladies noticed."

"You've been working on it for several months. I know you were anxious about it."

Tolman looked up at him. Hudson wasn't really a classical music listener, but he never failed to talk with her about her music. "Rusty, you're the only person I know who gets it."

"Gets it?'"

"Me. The music. RIO. All of it. My father is supportive, but he still doesn't really understand it. My musician friends don't get RIO, and the rest of the people here don't get the music."

Hudson looked embarrassed. "I have enormous respect for the fact that you are able to function so well in two completely different spheres."

"Different spheres," Tolman said, and smiled. "I like that. So what are you working on tonight?"

Hudson dropped a thin file folder on her desk. Tolman arched her eyebrows.

"Do you remember hearing a few days ago about that discovery of Civil War–era rifles in Oklahoma?"

"No," Tolman said.

"You don't watch television?"

"Not if I can help it."

"More than five thousand rifles from the Civil War were found buried in the ground near an obscure fort in rural Oklahoma. There was also some sort of document and a strange old piece of jewelry buried with them. The artifacts were turned over to a history professor at South Central College of Oklahoma. The contents of the document were not released to the public."

"So?"

"The professor returned from an evening class to find his office ransacked. He says two men with guns chased him. A campus police officer entered the fray, was shot and killed. The professor ran down one of the gunmen. The local police in the town investigated. The dead gunman had no identification of any kind. Local police contacted the Oklahoma State Bureau of Investigation. No leads. The gun was an H & K MK23."

Tolman looked up. "Special Forces."

Hudson nodded. "Untraceable. Gun and gunman alike do not exist. OSBI called FBI, though on the surface it appears no federal laws are involved. Remanded to us for review."

"So what's in the papers? These documents the professor has."

"No one knows. Build a book on the professor. See if it leads anywhere. Write the report, send to the FBI, and they can then remand it back to state and local jurisdictions."

"Our kind of case," Tolman muttered.

"It would seem so," Hudson said. "Unsolved and unsolvable. Our reason for existence."

"Was that sarcasm, Rusty? From you? Surely not."

"Far from it." Hudson pointed down at the file. "Work him. Write the report. Create the paper trail."

Hudson turned and headed back to his office. Tolman opened the file. "Well, Professor Nick Allen Journey, it certainly looks like you've attracted someone's attention, haven't you?"

# CHAPTER

# 6

W here Cases Go to Die" was not entirely in jest, when applied to RIO. Cases filtered down to the office from one of the three coadministering departments, cases that made little sense but weren't necessarily worth solving, either. Of course, neither the departments nor RIO ever actually said or wrote anywhere that a case wasn't worthwhile, as cases were often referred from local or state jurisdictions before the lower-level agencies asked the federal government for help.

In suite 427 of this unassuming office building, away from the seats of Justice, Treasury, and Homeland Security and their notorious turf battles, the databases of the three departments talked to each other with great regularity, while Meg Tolman and her colleagues essentially gathered information that would explain to someone, somewhere, exactly why federal resources would not be committed to a given case.

It was nearly ten o'clock when Tolman felt she'd constructed a solid basic picture of Nick Allen Journey, Ph.D., of Carpenter Center, Oklahoma. Starting with just his Social Security number and driver's license, she'd made her "book," thirty-seven pages about the man. This case was different from some because Journey wasn't easy to classify. He'd been a victim of burglary and assault, but in defending himself, had killed another man. He wasn't being held, since the Oklahoma authorities had a credible witness from the parking lot who corroborated Journey's account that the two men had been chasing him and shot at him first.

Still, he held Tolman's interest. She printed out her book, added it to the file, and walked to Hudson's office. He was watching a Nationals baseball game with the sound off. Tolman glanced at the little TV.

"Winning?" she said. She had no interest in baseball, but enjoyed hearing Hudson's laments about "his" team.

"They're being destroyed by the Phillies," Hudson said. "It has been another long season, but such is life."

"Shouldn't you be at home by now? This is late even for you."

"And you?" Hudson said. They shared a wry smile. Neither of them particularly cared for their respective homes. At least Tolman had her deaf cat—Hudson didn't even have an animal.

Tolman settled into the chair across the desk from the big man. "Nick Allen Journey. Not Nicholas, just Nick."

"Anything interesting?"

"Lots that's interesting."

"I'll rephrase: What will our report say?"

"Hard to tell yet. I've worked him up, but I'm not sure. Might be worth a phone call or a couple of e-mails."

Hudson looked at her. "Really? Now that *is* interesting. You follow up only eight out of every one hundred cases with contact."

"You tracking my contact rate?"

"You know I am. I am a bureaucrat, Meg. I do what I must."

Tolman smiled again. "Our man Journey is forty-two, born in San Diego. Father was a civilian laborer at the navy base, mother a homemaker. Two older brothers. On New Year's Day the year our man was seven, his family was driving in a 1968 Chevy station wagon along the San Diego Freeway. They were northbound toward L.A., approaching mile marker 67, which is the location for the San Clemente Border Patrol Station."

"I've driven that highway," Hudson said. "All northbound traffic is stopped for inspection in the center of the road, and some are directed into the station itself for a secondary inspection."

"According to the report from the California Highway Patrol, the Journeys had just gone through the on-highway inspection and were accelerating when a truck merged in from the secondary inspection lane. The truck cut off the station wagon, Journey's father lost control, then two other cars hit them. They spun off the highway, flipping end over end. Nick was riding in the back of the wagon. Remember, this was in the days when they still made real station wagons. Based on that model of wagon, the rear gate apparently flew open and it probably saved Nick's life. He was thrown twenty feet out of the car when it first rolled. The rest of the family never made it out of the car. They were all dead at the scene, massive trauma and internal injuries. Nick received only cuts and contusions and a broken clavicle. I viewed the accident report, some insurance forms, the death certificates, even a couple of newspaper stories about it."

Hudson shook his head. "If you dig deeply enough, you always come up with a fistful of tragedy. That's a depressing aspect to our job."

"Kid stayed with various relatives in California, Missouri, North Carolina, and Florida. Graduated high school in Fort Myers. Four-point-oh GPA, but he got a baseball scholarship to Florida State."

"Really?"

"Thought you would appreciate that. I guess he was pretty good. Says he was a left-handed pitcher with a curveball. . . . I assume that's good."

"Teams always need left-handers with a curve."

"Right-O. He majored in history. Four-point-oh GPA as an undergrad. He went into the baseball draft, chosen in the thirty-eighth round by the Detroit Tigers." She looked up from the book. "Thirty-eighth round? Is that good? That doesn't sound very impressive."

"No. At that point in the draft players are usually filler for a team's minor league rosters."

"Journey played in the Detroit organization for five years before giving it up. Decided on graduate school. Master's and doctorate in history from the University of Virginia. While at UVA in grad school, he met and married Amelia Boettcher, who was studying for an MBA. Three years later, while he was working on his dissertation, their son, Andrew Bryan Journey, was born. The dissertation was on high-ranking officers from both sides of the Civil War, on their lives before the war, and tracking what they did after the war was over."

"That sounds like something you'd appreciate," Hudson said.

Tolman grinned. "Journey gets a job at South Central College of Oklahoma in Carpenter Center, Oklahoma, a small town right on the Texas line. It's a little liberal arts college, enrollment of about four thousand. Less than a year after getting there, his son is diagnosed with developmental delays. Undergoes tests for a couple of years and final diagnosis is severe autism. The boy can't talk, isn't toilet trained, the whole business. He's twelve now. When the boy is nine, Amelia files for divorce. Irreconcilable differences."

"More than eighty percent of couples who have children with special needs get divorced."

Tolman looked up. "You just pull that one out of thin air?"

"Television is not all evil, Meg. It is possible to learn from it."

"Uh-huh. The wife moves to Oklahoma City, lets Journey have full custody. She's landed as a bank executive and is doing quite well financially. Journey keeps the kid, who stays with him year-round except for two weeks with the mother every summer. Let's see here. . . . Journey owns a house in Carpenter Center, ninety-thousand-dollar mortgage. Pays his taxes. He does occasional consulting work for the Oklahoma Historical Society and a few other groups like that. Doesn't travel much, I would guess because of child-care issues. He drives a ten-year-old minivan that he bought right after moving to Oklahoma. It's paid off. What else? His credit rating isn't all that great, lots of little loans and credit card debt. Fallout from the divorce, I guess. Physically, six feet tall, two-ten, has high blood pressure and cholesterol issues."

"Outside interests?"

"Can't find a whole lot on that. Doesn't belong to any golf clubs or anything like that. He's in the PTA; does that count? His whole world seems to be the job and the kid."

"What about the guns and documents from last week? Please tell me you have something more than the television news."

"Not much, really. Thousands of guns, some papers, one piece of jewelry. I can't add much to the evidence on the scene with the burglary and assault. Shooter is a phantom, young guy, good condition, military haircut. . . ." Tolman lowered the pages.

"And a weapon known for being used by Special Forces."

"There is that. I uploaded crime scene photos, and I'll see if I can get DOD records. Maybe he's ex–active duty and there's a photo."

"The Pentagon doesn't like us wandering around in their database, since we don't belong to them."

"I know who we don't belong to." Hudson winced at the grammar, and Tolman grinned again. She frequently tried to annoy him with her speech. "You want to call them or you want to let me see what I can find?"

Hudson leaned back, cutting his eyes to the television. "Ten to four. What a team."

Tolman stood up. "Maybe they could use a left-hander with a curveball."

Hudson frowned, the wry humor gone. "Contact DOD if you must. For now, go home to your cat."

"Right." Tolman went to lock up her office, but she was still thinking of the puzzle: a middle-aged college professor, single father of a son with a disability, a horrific tragedy in his own past, a bunch of Civil War–era relics, and an attacker with no identity.

Tolman might as well have been a million miles from the Falls Church Chamber Music Society. By the time she reached her apartment, just across the river in Alexandria, she was still thinking about Nick Journey.

# CHAPTER

# 7

The Judge had called for a meeting of his inner circle, six other men who were highly placed, men whose counsel he sought both in the planning and execution of the mission. Two of the six were in charge of regional bases—Dallas and Chicago, respectively—and lived lives out of sight, assuming whatever identities were necessary for any given situation. The other four came from Washington, and their lives were infinitely more complex: they held jobs that placed them in the light, working in public, going about their everyday business and their not-so-everyday business—laying the groundwork for the Glory Warriors.

He had invited the others to his retreat at the summit of a mountain overlooking Matewan, West Virginia, the town along Tug Fork where one of the nation's most notorious battles between union organizers and coal operators had taken place in 1920. Ever mindful of history—a plaque on the Judge's desk read THERE IS NO PRESENT OR FUTURE, ONLY HISTORY THAT IS YET TO BE CREATED—he had chosen the spot well. It was isolated, but still close enough to Washington for strategic purposes.

The doors to his study opened and the other six men entered, fanning out onto deep leather chairs and a long sofa against the wall. Even though the Judge's house was swept for electronic surveillance several times daily, and even though the field men were under deep cover, names were never used when speaking between walls. Each base director was referred to only by the name of his city. The Washington men were simply known as Washington One, Two, Three, and Four.

The Judge rose to his full height and watched the other men. He was six-feet-three and age had not stooped him at all. He had lost weight as he grew older, passing seventy, and so gave the appearance of being somewhat frail. But his skin was tanned and healthy, his blue eyes sharp and focused as they had ever been. He met the eyes of all six men, then slowly settled his gaze on the man who led the Dallas regional base. "Report?" the Judge said.

Dallas, almost as old as the Judge but with a much more robust build, had a full head of silver hair that contrasted with his dark skin. He stood to address the group. "As you know, we lost Dallas One Gold. The operation was not a success, and we do not have the document."

"We all know that," said Chicago. "A meaningful report would be nice, something of substance. For example, why and how did this out-of-shape professor escape with the document and take out one of our men? Maybe Dallas Base isn't equipped to deal with—"

Dallas half turned in anger. "That's enough! Sometimes an amateur can be very dangerous. We can't plan for every contingency. My men were up to the task. There were simply variables we didn't foresee."

"Such as?"

"Such as, Journey did not leave the document in his office."

"Would *you* just leave it lying around in a college office?" This from Washington Four.

"Certainly not," Dallas said. "But we can't predict an amateur—"

"Journey has read it," Washington Two said. "He has to know what it means, even if he's not talking about it."

"Not necessarily," the Judge said, and all the men looked at him. "He's an academic. He'll want to be sure it's authentic. Chances are he doesn't know what he has, even if he has read it. But we must deal with Professor Journey. We must have the treaty. We will not be viewed as legitimate without it."

Washington Three was younger than the others, known as a rising star in his own circles. He was wearing an Armani suit and silk tie, and a mildly cynical expression. "Legitimate? Really now, let's be honest with each other. Nothing we are doing or planning to do is legitimate."

"Excuse me?" Dallas said.

"Let him speak," the Judge said.

"We shouldn't delude ourselves," Washington Three said. "Yes, we are right. Yes, we know what needs to be done and have plans to do it. But we aren't going to be viewed as legitimate—at least not at first. The 'document' . . . Come on, it's really just window dressing. I've never understood the obsession with finding it." He looked around the room at each of the men, finally meeting the Judge's eyes again. "The Glory Warriors have been around since long before any of us here were born, right? There have been hundreds of times that the group could have moved into action—*should* have moved into action, in fact—but didn't, because the all-important document hadn't been found. It's a crutch, and frankly, I'm tired of leaning on it."

There was a moment's silence. The Judge's antique clock, on a Louis XIV table behind his desk, chimed the quarter hour.

"You make your point as eloquently as ever," the Judge said.

"He's full of shit," Chicago said.

"And you have made your voice heard as well," the Judge said, looking at Chicago, then back to Washington Three. "We love our country. That is why we're here."

"No, it isn't," Washington Three said.

"I beg your pardon?"

"We're here because we want to be in power. We want to run things the way they should be run, and no one else is willing to do that."

"Because of love of country," Dallas said, "and what it stands for. Maybe you're too young to fully grasp—"

The Judge cut him off. "No. He has his contributions to make, his role to play, or the Glory Warriors would not have recruited him.

Perhaps his motivation isn't clear." He stared hard across the desk at Washington Three. "Be that as it may, don't ignore the historical significance of what we are. We must have the rule of law. That is why we must have the treaty, in its entirety, because it gives us the rule of law, the authority to do what has to be done."

"Does it?" Washington Three said. "I mean, really, does it?"

The Judge looked at the younger man, and for a moment saw himself more than five decades earlier, asking his father the same question. He could feel his father's rage at being questioned. The anger rolled off him in waves.

"The treaty is real," his father had said. "Never doubt that! And never doubt that it will transform America, and it's my responsibility to lead. Mine! You can't possibly understand the responsibility I have."

"Maybe not," he'd said, "but I do understand that you couldn't care less about Mother or me, or anyone or anything else. You never ask me how things are at school. You leave for months at a time, and when you do come back, it's all Glory Warriors and this Lee and Grant nonsense. Did you know that I won the state chess tournament? Would you care if you knew? That treaty is nothing. . . . I don't think it exists. I think you've built it up—"

And then his father had hit him. With lightning-fast reflex, he crashed a fist into the side of his son's face. The young man teetered but stayed on his feet, so shocked he couldn't react. His father hit him again in the same place, harder. His legs buckled and he fell.

"Never question me again," his father said, and walked away, leaving him on the ground.

And he never did.

The Judge looked at Washington Three again. All the others were staring at him. He cleared his throat. "The American people will accept it," he said, "if it's in black-and-white, and if they're told enough times. As you know, I'm in a position to influence public opinion. A document—something they can see, something tangible— will move them. Think about it. . . . This country wasn't real until there were documents: the Declaration of Independence, the Constitution. Deeply flawed documents, and by no means unanimously popular when they were created. But the people have a love affair with official papers. My father knew it; his father knew it. Grant and Lee knew it." He folded his hands together. "Oh, yes. It gives us all the authority we need. When the people see it—and I will make sure they see it—they will understand."

Washington Three held up his hands in mock surrender. "Look, I know I'm younger than everyone else here. Okay, fine. You guys have been living for the moment that damned treaty comes to light. So now it's come to light. I'm not going to argue the point. If it's what we need to have to make this country right again, fine. We go get the treaty from this professor, yes?"

"Yes, and no more slipups," Chicago said.

"But perhaps we should take a little time to reflect on the lessons of the operation in Oklahoma," the Judge said.

Dallas slowly turned to face the Judge.

"Let's say we don't have to forcibly take it from Professor Journey," the Judge said. "Let's pay attention to the good professor. He may give us an opportunity." He nodded at Dallas. "Stay with him. We'll get it, one way or another."

Washington One cleared his throat. He was a man of few words, and when he spoke, he commanded immediate respect from all who heard him, whether in this room or at the highest levels of "official" Washington. "Historically, we know what has to happen. It's been passed down to the Glory Warriors now from those who came before us. Before we have the treaty, before we go public, before we *must* have the treaty . . . can't we take the first steps?"

The Judge smiled, looking in Chicago's direction. Then he turned and walked back to the window that looked down from the West Virginia mountains. "We already are," he said.

# CHAPTER

# 8

On a typical warm September Saturday morning, Journey might take Andrew out for a drive in the countryside around Lake Texoma. Being in the car seemed to soothe Andrew—something about its rhythm slowed his sensory overload, and he would quietly watch out the window, attending to whatever slipped by, be it trees, the waters of the lake itself, other cars. Journey would keep up a commentary from time to time about nothing in particular—counting the number of blue jays and cardinals they saw, picking a color of car and pointing to every one of that color they passed, mentioning the names of people who lived along the road. And then at times it was silent, with just the rhythm of the road all that was spoken between them.

Journey missed the drive, but it was no ordinary Saturday. A few pebbles of glass had pricked his face when the assassin shot out the police car's windshield. None was especially serious, but one hunk scratched his neck and required a bandage—he was still wearing it.

There had been more reporters and more police. His department chair called and said his classes were covered for the rest of the week. He talked to Officer Parsons's mother on the phone—the kid had been on the job at SCCO for only five months, his first law enforcement job. His two older brothers were both deputies with the Marshall County Sheriff's Department, and young Pete's ultimate ambition had been to join them there. Journey wasn't sure what to tell the woman, other than her twenty-two-year-old son died doing his job.

Journey slept poorly, still seeing the gunman, hearing the shots, watching as young Pete Parsons toppled toward him, remembering nothing between the shot that killed Parsons and the police car skidding off the wall, the gunman's limp body sliding to the ground.

He remembered his hand touching the pin and the split-second decision, pulling the pin off the man who had tried to kill him.

G.W.

The two pins, one taken from the ground, one from the gunman, were identical in shape. The only difference was a barely perceptible variation in the shape of the letters. The pin that had come from Fort Washita was a bit more ornate in its engraving, the letters having an Old English look.

G.W.

Journey tapped each of the pins against the side of the desk in the corner of his living room. Andrew looked over at him, made eye contact for a fleeting second, then looked quickly back down to the puzzle he was working. Journey ran his hands over the pins.

He hadn't told the police about the pins, and he wasn't sure why.

*Because I don't understand them, that's why.*

Could giving the police the pins have helped them figure out who the two men were at Cullen Hall? So far, the man he'd run down hadn't been identified. There was no trace of the gun he'd used in any records. The local cops seemed unsure what to do next.

They'd asked him about the document. He told them it was safe. They asked him for it. He declined. Legally he wasn't compelled to turn it over. *Victims of attempted burglaries aren't required by law to turn over the property that they think the burglars were trying to take, are they?* he'd asked the Carpenter Center police chief.

*I don't think this is an ordinary burglary, Dr. Journey,* the chief had said.

Journey had just stared at him, and eventually the man went

away. The police had an officer cruise by his house several times a day. Perhaps it was their version of offering protection. Or maybe they were checking up on him.

The doorbell sounded.

Sandra stood on the porch in the bright morning sunshine, wearing running shorts and a UCLA T-shirt. "Hey," she said.

"Hey," Journey said.

They looked at each other for half a minute.

"Are you going to invite me in?"

"Oh," Journey said. "Sure, come on in."

Sandra moved with easy grace and came inside. "Hi, Andrew," she said. He didn't acknowledge her. Sandra sat on the couch and crossed her long legs. "First thing is this: I'm about to ask you a question. Being a question, it requires an answer."

"What?"

"How are you? That's a question, not just a greeting that someone says and then goes on without listening. So tell me how you are."

Journey looked at her. She was an unusual woman, undeniably brilliant, attractive in a wispy sort of way, more direct and forthright than any woman and most men he knew. "I'm fine."

"Wrong," Sandra said. "Try again."

Journey allowed himself a little smile. "You're quizzing me, Professor." He shrugged. "I feel strange, disconnected, out of sorts." Andrew screeched. Sandra jumped. "Andrew," Journey said.

The boy didn't look at him.

"Andrew," Journey said. "Look at me." The boy had picked up a straw and pencil and beat them together furiously. "Look at me, Andrew."

The boy glanced at him.

"Use a quieter voice, son."

The boy stood up, stamped his feet, and emitted a low, throaty noise. He walked past his father and Sandra, the straw and pencil tapping faster and faster. He disappeared around a corner. Journey heard the door to his bedroom close.

"Excuse me, Sandra," Journey said, and went to the bedroom to look in on Andrew. He was sitting on his bed, surrounded by white walls. Journey had tried livening the room up with some posters at one point, but the visuals seemed to bother Andrew, so the bare walls returned. "You okay?" he said to Andrew.

The boy hummed, not looking at him. He rocked back and forth.

"Okay," Journey said. "Sandra's just visiting for a little while. I'm going to go back to the living room and talk to her. You want your music?"

Andrew rocked and hummed.

Journey touched the little CD boom box on Andrew's dresser, and soft piano music filled the room. He went back to the living room and sat across from Sandra again. "Sorry."

"Don't be sorry. Must be hard."

Journey shrugged.

"Okay, that sounded patronizing," Sandra said. "I actually don't have a clue what it must be like."

Journey shrugged again.

"Do the police know anything?" Sandra asked after a moment.

"No. The guy who came after me had no identification, and no one got a close enough look at the other one. It's . . . I don't know what it is."

"You still have the artifacts?"

"I'm trying to figure out what they mean."

"You think this was treasure hunters? Except treasure hunters don't usually carry around assault pistols, I guess."

"I don't know. I—" Journey felt himself bending like a small tree, helpless in the face of the prairie wind.

Sandra's green eyes clouded. "Look, I can go. I just wanted to see how you were."

"No, I . . . Look, this document that was buried with the guns. It's strange. . . . I haven't talked to anyone about the contents. I wanted to do the proper research, to see what I had. But I—Sandra, I killed a man."

She put out her hand to touch him, then pulled it back slowly. "I know. He was shooting at you. It was—"

"Self-defense, I know. But *why* was he shooting at me?" Journey got out of the chair and crossed to his desk. He scooped up the paper and the two pins. "A cryptic reference to Appomattox and a special 'clause' and 'conspiratorial means' and a riddle at the bottom. That and a piece of jewelry."

Sandra was shaking her head. "Riddles and jewelry? Nick, you're not making sense." She looked at the pins in his hand. "I thought there was only one pin found at Fort Washita."

"There was. I took the other one off the man who was shooting at me—the man I killed."

They stared at each other. "Why are you keeping all this to yourself?" Sandra finally said.

"I don't know," Journey said. He rubbed his face. "It's not academic egotism, if that's what you're thinking, that I'm holding out to be the first to publish."

"I wasn't thinking that at all. You're not like that."

Journey looked at her in surprise for a moment, then lowered his eyes to the artifacts again. He palmed the two pins in one hand. "G.W.," he said. "Does that mean anything to you? I mean, in a historical context."

"No, not offhand. When those things were dug up at Fort Washita, I just thought G.W. was someone's initials."

"That's what I thought, too, until those guys came after me. You know what I've been thinking since then?"

"Tell me."

"In 1865, someone buried thousands of weapons in the ground in the middle of nowhere in Indian Territory. Along with them they buried this piece of paper, incomplete, cryptic, and pretty ominous. And they buried this pin." He tossed the older of the two pins to Sandra. "Now, nearly a century and a half later, these things come to light, there's a little news coverage, and suddenly my office is trashed and I'm tracked by a couple of guys with guns. One of the guys is wearing this." He held up the other pin.

Sandra thought for a moment. "So they're not initials. More of an insignia."

"Yes."

"Nick," Sandra said. She ran one hand over the smooth gold of the pin, tracing the lettering with her long fingers. "I've studied a lot of different kinds of movements, dating to the Revolutionary War. This is what I do."

"I know."

"And it sounds like it could be some kind of society."

Journey nodded. "Think about it. Yale, for God's sake, still has the Skull and Bones Club. As hysterical as people have been in popular culture the last few years about the Masons, one thing is true—they are a 'secret society.' The KKK wasn't the only one to come out of the Civil War."

"The Knights of the Golden Circle, the Order of American Knights . . . most of them lived only on paper, but some of them were real forces. The Klan is just the best-known example."

"And they all had some kind of signature. The Klan had the white hoods." He held up the gold pin again. "And G.W. had its members wear these pins."

"And apparently they still do," Sandra said.

Journey nodded. He heard Andrew humming again.

"You have to tell someone this," Sandra said. "You have to tell the police."

"You think the Carpenter Center Police Department is going to do something with this? No, what I have to do is find who G.W. is, and find the rest of this document."

"You mean there's more to it? Where?"

"It's incomplete. This page has lots of 'whereas' and 'what if' types of statements, but doesn't say what happens when 'what if' comes around. I think that whoever was behind this in 1865 was very smart, but didn't trust the others who were involved. I think he hedged his bets, and the rest of this document was hidden somewhere else. This little bit of nonsense at the bottom tells us what to do to find the rest of it. *That* is what I think the riddle is."

"You have to go to the police," Sandra said again.

"You think if I go in there with those two little pins and say, 'I was attacked by a secret society that has been around since the Civil War and is up to something, but I don't know what,' that the police are going to drop everything and launch a full-scale investigation? They would think I was nuts, and they'd be right. I need a full picture, not just a sketch."

Sandra stared at him. "You can't."

"I'm not calling the police. Not yet."

"Then I will." Sandra stood up. "You can't just—"

"Yes, I can *just*. Please, I have to work this out. That's the only way I can protect Andrew and myself."

"And what if G.W. comes after you again?"

"Then I'll be ready for them," Journey said.

# CHAPTER
# 9

Meg Tolman didn't own a piano, but she had an arrange-ment with the Alexandria campus of Northern Virginia Community College to give one lecture per semester, and in return, she enjoyed unlimited use of their prize Bosendorfer. She took no salary from the college, only traded her time for piano time. She had a key to the studio where the piano was kept, and was able to come and go as she pleased. The NVCC campus was half a mile from her apartment.

She played for two hours on Saturday morning. Her next paying gig was tomorrow afternoon, a wedding reception in Chevy Chase. She hated wedding receptions—they were worse than piano bars, and she spent hours playing love songs while no one listened. She tried to slip in a little Chopin when she could, but people didn't no-tice that, either. Still, she took whatever paying jobs came her way, like them or not. The money was secondary. Maintaining a status as a professional musician, albeit a part-time one, was vital.

After rehearsing, she took the Metro across the river to the office. Saturday was just another day as far as she was concerned—if she could get something done, she got it done, the calendar be damned.

Dr. Nick Journey had been much on her mind since she did the preliminary workup on him. From a purely objective standpoint, she didn't think federal resources could do much for the case. She could write the report and send it on to the FBI, and that would be the end of it. But something about the case made her stop, made her think, made her wonder. The cases in RIO that did that were few and far between.

As she expected, Rusty Hudson was in the office, clicking his mouse and talking on the phone. *What a sad pair we are,* Tolman thought, waving as she passed.

As she sat down at her computer, Tolman thought of Nick Journey again. Maybe she identified with the history professor because of her own history. Her own "fistful of tragedy," as Hudson had said. She thought of Nick Journey's family on the California highway when the boy was seven years old, and then of her mother turning to shout at her from the driver's seat—*"You watch your mouth and show me some goddamned respect, Margaret! I don't care if you can play the goddamned piano like Franz Fucking Liszt himself. If you can't get through geometry, then you are a failure and all the piano scales in the world won't change it!"*—and of herself screaming, "Mom, look out!" as the car swerved off the Rock Creek Parkway and down the embankment toward the Potomac.

Her mother's last words: *"You are a failure and all the piano scales in the world won't change it!"*

"Stop that shit," Tolman said aloud. Nick Journey had nothing to do with her, and the fact that she was mentally connecting the two probably meant she either wasn't getting enough sleep—*true*—or wasn't playing enough music—*also true*. She resolved that when she was finished here today, she would go back to NVCC and play for another hour or two.

She logged in to her e-mail, then opened another window and navigated to the file she'd created for the Journey incident. At the tail end of it, as was her custom, she'd placed contact information for the case's principals. She had Journey's address, phone numbers, and e-mail address.

She thought for a moment, then typed NJourney@sccok.edu in the address line. In the subject line, she put *Incident at South Central College*. That should at least get him to open the e-mail. She typed a quick, polite message informing Journey that the local and state authorities had requested federal assistance, and that she was the officer in charge of evaluating that request. She asked if he could provide any additional information about the materials he believed the gunmen were trying to steal, and encouraged him to contact her at any time. It was more or less a form letter, but it was still more contact than she made in 92 percent of her cases. She pressed SEND.

She sat back and closed her eyes for a moment, running through Rachmaninov's "Variations on a Theme by Chopin" in her mind. The final section had been giving her fits. She'd added the piece to her repertoire only in the last few months, and was going to play it in recital for the first time next month at James Madison University. That was a good paying gig, and her father had said he might even drive out with her. Dad was completely tone-deaf, and she knew he was still disappointed in her job at RIO, but he'd learned to hold his tongue about that as they both matured. He was trying. She had to give him credit for that.

She gave up on Chopin/Rachmaninov and went back to work, logging in to the Department of Defense's human resource database. Hudson was right—DOD didn't like to play well with the civilian departments, and she had to tread lightly. The wrong sorts of inquiries could set off a "bureaucratic crisis," a term Hudson had coined. She smiled a little at that.

She pulled up the head-shot photo of the first gunman, the one who was dead at the scene at South Central College. OSBI had e-mailed it to her. It was a crime-scene photo, and there was blood on the guy's face. Still, it was enough of a close-up for her purposes.

Then she opened the second photo, a still that had been taken from one of the parking lot's video surveillance cameras. It showed the second gunman, though at long distance and not good quality. *Cheap-ass video,* Tolman thought.

She zoomed in on the second gunman, resized the photo, sharpened up the definition, and tried to get in as tight on his face as she could, minimizing the parking lot surroundings. It still wasn't great, but might suffice. The second gunman looked a little younger than the dead man, with lighter hair and a more muscular build— the first one had been more slender, a runner's physique. Tolman couldn't tell eye color on the second one, but hopefully she had enough detail.

With Homeland Security as one of its "parent" departments, RIO had the latest facial-recognition software, the same program used by the Transportation Security Administration at airports to compare the faces of people moving through checkpoints to a database of known criminals and terror suspects.

Three-dimensional facial recognition was immeasurably more accurate than the older 2D programs, in that it measured the actual geometry of the face's features, which negated such variables as differences in lighting, facial expression, and the positioning of the head in the video or still image. The main challenge for several years had been to actually acquire three-dimensional images, but newer software solved that problem by projecting a grid onto the face and integrating the video into a 3D high-resolution computer model.

Tolman overlaid her grid onto the faces of the two gunmen and built the 3D model, admiring the graphics on her flat screen. When the models were ready, she began her search in the Pentagon database.

Over the next hour, she finished paperwork on a couple of minor cases and rearranged her desk while the computer flashed SEARCH-ING, PLEASE WAIT. When the search finished, 2 MATCHES FOUND scrolled across her screen.

"Now we're talking," Tolman said, then frowned when she clicked on the icon.

YOU ARE NOT AUTHORIZED TO ACCESS THIS FILE.

"Oh yes, I am," Tolman said, and confirmed the password she'd used to log in to the database.

YOU ARE NOT AUTHORIZED TO ACCESS THIS FILE.

"Now, that's fucking rude." She clicked and typed a little more with no luck. Fifteen more minutes got her into a large directory with the matching file numbers highlighted. But she still couldn't reach the files themselves. It was a bit like getting a ticket into a movie theater, but being able to go only as far as the lobby, and not into the theater itself. "You're pissing me off," she said to her monitor.

She copied down the file numbers, then exited the database and shut down the facial-recognition program. She'd already suspected that the two Oklahoma shooters might have been ex–Special Forces, due to their choice of weapon. But she'd fished in the human resource database before and found Special Forces files, both active and former personnel, and never had access issues on those occasions.

She went back through the process of getting into the DOD system and this time found herself completely locked out of the database. *This is horseshit*, she thought.

Tolman tried three more times to access the Pentagon database and found herself blocked at every turn. DOD may not have liked to play with the other children, but its resources were usually available, however grudgingly, to other government agencies with legitimate requests.

"Rusty!" she shouted down the hall. "I'm about to provoke a bureaucratic crisis."

Hudson stomped into the room, towering in the doorway. "You went fishing at the Pentagon."

"I got matches on the Oklahoma photos in DOD, but they wouldn't let me look at them, and then locked me out totally."

Hudson moved to one side of the door. "Is this worth pursuing?"

"It is now."

"Meg."

She looked up, recognizing the tone.

"Don't pursue it because you're irritated that DOD wouldn't let you play around in their systems. If the case has merit on its face, that is a different story."

"The very fact that I can't get into their system *is* merit. We have two shooters in West Nowhere, Oklahoma, one of them DOA, using Special Forces weapons of choice. If this is some weird DOD black op, at least we need to know that we have to stay out of it."

Hudson waited a moment. "I don't like being in the dark. I don't like being shut out of information. Go a bit further and we will talk again." He turned and moved off down the hallway.

Tolman pulled up her government agency phone directory on the computer and navigated through a Department of Defense labyrinth before finding a listing for the office that dealt with active-duty personnel files. She would start there.

She glanced at the clock—nearly noon on a Saturday. But Tolman knew that the Pentagon had people in its offices, even the mundane ones, seven days a week.

On the third ring, a female voice said, "Ann McAdams."

"Ann, this is Meg Tolman at RIO."

"RIO?"

Tolman sighed. "Research and Investigations Office. We're a joint office of Justice, Treasury, and DHS. I need to access a couple of files for an investigation we've been asked to review."

"Glad to help. Do you have a DOD authorization?"

"No, as I told you, I don't work for DOD."

"But you should still have an authorization to get access."

Tolman stared at the phone. "Can't I just tell you the file numbers and you look them up and e-mail them to me?"

"Hold on."

Tolman listened to badly synthesized music while on hold for sixty seconds, and then McAdams was back. "I wasn't entirely sure what RIO was."

"I get that a lot. You have the files?"

"Could you give me the numbers? Then your supervisor could write my supervisor a memo on Monday, and we'll backdate the authorization."

*This is more like it.* "Thanks, I'll do that." She read off the two file numbers.

"Just a moment."

This time she was on hold for nearly five minutes, and when the line clicked again, Ann McAdams's voice had been replaced by a deep male voice, older. "This is Colonel Meares. To whom am I speaking?"

*A colonel? In human resources on a Saturday? Now that is odd.* "Colonel, this is Meg Tolman with RIO. I was asking about two files—"

"You're not authorized to view those files."

"We're reviewing an investigation, and the two men whose files I'm requesting may be connected to it."

"Connected in what way?"

Tolman hesitated a moment. "As suspects in a burglary and assault. One of the men was killed in the incident."

"Impossible. You're mistaken."

"Why don't you just release the files, then, and I can eliminate your men as suspects?"

"They're already eliminated, Ms. Tolman."

"What do you mean?"

"The men whose file numbers you referenced are not suspects in your case, whatever it is, because those two men were Army Rangers who were both killed in action in Iraq in 2006."

# CHAPTER
# 10

Journey walked along the SCCO common with Sandra, Andrew in between them. Journey held Andrew's hand, and as always drew stares when Andrew vocalized. Journey was never sure if the stares were because of the vocalizations, or of people's puzzlement in seeing a child as large as Andrew holding tightly on to his father's hand.

Few students were on the common on a Saturday. A handful sat under trees with books and laptops. One couple simply lay on the grass next to each other. An impromptu jam session—acoustic guitar, harmonica, and violin—was in progress near Howell Hall.

It was the first time Journey had been back on campus since the night he was attacked, and the college felt strange, smaller. He avoided the space between Cullen and Howell. He'd already taken two blood pressure pills, and was feeling shaky.

"So," Sandra said, "two things."

"Two things," Journey said. "Find out what G.W. means. And find the rest of the document. That means the note at the bottom of the first page. 'The Poet's Penn makes the waters fall and causes the strong to bend.' *Penn* spelled with a double en."

"Misspelling or wordplay?"

"I think wordplay. The rest of the page is very precise. The writer was educated. If he knew how to spell *conspiratorial*, he should know how to spell *pen*."

"Good point."

Andrew whistled.

"I hear you, Andrew," Journey said.

"How do you do that?"

"Do what?"

"Talk to him, when he—" Sandra stopped, looking stricken. "I didn't mean—"

"It's okay," Journey said. "The truth is, we don't know all of what he can and can't understand."

"You're such a verbal person. It must be . . . tough." She shook her head. "I'm sorry, Nick. Everything I say sounds so trite. I don't mean it to."

"It's all right. If it makes you feel better, most people don't know what to say."

"You're so good with him," Sandra said, then stopped herself. "There I go, trite again. Talking about Civil War conspiracies was easier."

Journey shrugged. "At times it can be—" He squeezed his son's hand. "—overwhelming. I don't always know the right things to do. I see other parents of kids with special needs, and they're advocates and activists and they know exactly what to do in every situation. Most days, it's all I can do to get him fed and keep his clothes clean. I don't do nearly enough."

Sandra looked thoughtful. "You know what someone told me once? The people who think they aren't doing enough are usually the ones who are doing all they can. It wasn't about having a child with autism, but I think it applies."

"Maybe," Journey said. "I don't know. Most of the time, I'm too tired to even think straight, though."

They walked a few steps in awkward silence. "So . . . the Poet's Penn," Sandra finally said.

"The Poet's Penn," Journey said. "It makes the waters fall and causes the strong to bend. What waters? And how do the strong bend? Are the words part of an actual poem? The same person who wrote the rest of the page wrote the riddle. The writing is the same, but it's not as neat. It looks rushed, less precise."

"Like an afterthought," Sandra said.

"He didn't trust his partners, or they didn't trust him, so he decided to make it more difficult for someone to get the whole thing. In the top part, it says the clause will not go into effect unless the heads of the three branches of government are removed by 'conspiratorial means,' and that the document must be authenticated, including signatures."

"Whose signatures? Grant and Lee?"

"That's the implication. It refers to the time and place of Lee's surrender, and implies that this clause is a condition of the end of hostilities."

Sandra nodded. "Could they be talking about the Lincoln conspiracy? That was supposed to go much further than it did."

"It was," Journey said, "but no one ever seriously thought the Speaker of the House or the chief justice were in danger. On this page, G.W., or whoever it was, seemed to be planning for the likelihood that the highest-ranking officials in each branch of the government would be removed somehow, and their clause would be activated if that kind of crisis came about. They even referred to the Lieber Code article about martial law, which shows they'd done their homework. If Grant and Lee signed off on this . . ." He shook his head and let the thought hang between them.

They reached the edge of the common. Beyond it were two student dormitories, parking lots, then a beautifully landscaped area and the shores of Lake Texoma. Journey stopped at the edge of the parking area, still holding his son's hand. "G.W. was involved in this in 1865, and they exist today, and they want this document. Consider this: If they buried this document and the pin, they buried all those weapons."

"They were preparing for something."

"Armed conflict," Journey said.

"But why? They'd just come out of the bloodiest conflict in history. Lee and Grant sat there at Appomattox and agreed to end the hostilities. Why would they be preparing for another conflict?"

Journey shook his head, gazing toward the lake. Andrew wiggled his fingers inside his father's hand. "Okay, Andrew, we'll keep walking."

They rounded the edge of the parking lot. The day was hot, and Journey was starting to sweat.

Sandra glanced at him. He was looking at the ground, shuffling beside Andrew. "My brother teaches English at Stephens College in Missouri," she said. "He does a section on American poetry every fall. Maybe he's heard of the Poet's Penn."

Journey didn't look up. "You can't tell him why you're asking."

"I'm beginning to see that."

Journey nodded, still looking at the ground. He squeezed Andrew's hand, then slowly looked up at Sandra. Her eyes were wide and very, very green. They'd talked in faculty meetings and casual lunches and at various college functions, but he didn't think he'd really ever looked at her before. Her face seemed older than thirty. Not in an unflattering way, but her face and those eyes seemed to hold great depth and more self-awareness than most thirty-year-olds Journey knew. Sandra's red hair was pulled back from her face, and she wore a pair of dangling silver earrings in the shape of miniature dream catchers.

"Jewelry," he said.

"Excuse me?"

"The G.W. pins. They're gold, custom-made jewelry. Jewelers are artists. Artists sign their work. Somehow, some way, they sign their work."

Realization came over Sandra's face. "If you can find the origin of the pins themselves—"

"Then maybe we can find who or what G.W. is." Journey turned, pulling Andrew with him. The boy screamed, a keening wail. "Come on, son. You're okay."

"I think I'll go call my brother," Sandra said.

"And I think I should start learning about jewelry," Journey said, then turned toward home.

Jefferson Vandermeer felt every one of his seventy-three years, and the fact that Labor Day had passed meant winter wasn't far, and his arthritic bones would spend five months begging for mercy. Of course, most of that time would be spent farther south, where the winters didn't bite so hard, where six inches of snow would shut down the city. The thought made Vandermeer smile. In Sheboygan, Wisconsin, on the precipice of Lake Michigan, six inches of snow was scarcely enough to shovel.

He locked the front door of his house and stepped onto the porch of the stately Victorian. It was still modest for a man of his power, but it was where he had started fifty years ago, he and Beatrice, and he'd kept the home all these years. Beatrice had been dead six years now, and everything about the house reminded him of her—its modesty, its lack of pretense, its bookshelves, her handmade quilts everywhere. There were times, even now, that he swore he could smell her cherry pie baking early in the mornings.

Vandermeer stretched on the porch, his knees complaining, and walked slowly down the steps. For the moment, he was alone, and he needed the quiet time before heading south again. He needed to clear his mind, to think without people clamoring on all sides of him.

He could have had security guards here, even in Sheboygan—there were those who worried about his safety, and he simply laughed at them—but he had to have his solitude. These walks were sacred. His schedule was erratic when he was in Wisconsin, so sometimes the walks came early in the morning, sometimes the middle of the day, occasionally at sunset. But he made time to walk every day that he was here. Before the cancer took her, he had shared the walks with Bea. Now they were his alone.

Vandermeer's house was a block from North Point Park, with its overlook of the lake. *Better get going,* he thought. He didn't walk nearly so fast as he once had. He stretched once more, then started down the tree-lined sidewalk toward the park.

Chicago One Silver was a woman in her thirties with long blond hair that she had tied back in a ponytail. She wore runner's gear and a Brewers baseball cap with her ponytail pulled through the cap's rear opening. A small gym bag was slung over her shoulder. An earpiece curled into her ear from beneath her T-shirt.

She gave the appearance of total relaxation, a single young woman out for a run alongside the lake. But her entire being was on alert. She was keenly aware that she was one of the few female Glory Warriors in the field, and she had been given a mission that most of her male counterparts wanted. She had been chosen to set the plan in motion. Silver would not fail.

The cell phone in the pocket of her warm-up pants vibrated once, then stopped. After a few seconds, it vibrated twice more. Silver bent over to attend to her shoe, even though it wasn't untied. She glanced to her right. She could see the old man in his khakis and Windbreaker moving slowly along the sidewalk. If he held true to form, he would go to the overlook and spend a few minutes contemplating the lake before turning and beginning the slow walk back to his house.

Silver watched as Vandermeer moved toward her. She could begin to see some of the details of his famous craggy face and pure white hair. He was fifty feet away.

\* \* \*

Vandermeer had to catch a plane south tomorrow morning. This was his last day of peace until Thanksgiving. By then, the leaves would have fallen from all these trees. No doubt the first snows would have come. North Point Park would be a very different place in November, not nearly so hospitable as this pleasant September afternoon.

He saw the young woman ahead of him. She was his daughter's age, maybe a bit younger. It seemed that not many people came to city parks anymore—probably all inside on their computers, he mused—and he was happy to see a young, pleasant-looking woman outdoors enjoying the sunshine.

Silver had moved a few steps down the sidewalk, where she stopped to read a historical marker about the *Phoenix* Tragedy of 1847. The steamship *Phoenix*, carrying more than two hundred passengers, including many Dutch immigrants who intended to settle in the Sheboygan area, had caught fire five miles offshore. Less than fifty on board survived. So the story went, some of Jefferson Vandermeer's ancestors had been among the survivors.

Just beyond the marker was a set of playground equipment, monkey bars painted bright purple. A grassy area sloped down toward the great lake. A few steps farther on was a rocky outcropping into Lake Michigan. Vandermeer was twenty feet from Silver. She placed her gym bag on the sidewalk at the foot of the historical marker and reached inside it.

Silver pulled out the H&K MK 23, suppressor attached, and held it in her right hand, away from the sidewalk.

A bead of perspiration appeared on her upper lip.

*Focus,* she told herself. *Remember your training. Remember why we're here.*

Silver bent down to scratch her leg with her free hand. She angled her body to keep her gun hand hidden.

The young woman was certainly pretty, Vandermeer thought. He didn't particularly care for baseball caps on women, but he supposed that was the modern age at work. Vandermeer smiled his famous lopsided grin as he approached her. He wondered if she would recognize him. "It's a fine day to be out," he called.

"Sure is," the young woman said, and Vandermeer thought he heard a slight catch in her voice.

"I haven't seen you out here before," he said.

"I'm new in town, just moved up here from Arizona," the young woman said. "I like to look out over the lake. No lakes like this around Tucson."

"That's a fact," Vandermeer said, smiling as he came abreast of her. She certainly was pretty.

She turned to face him. She wasn't smiling, and her expression didn't match the words of a woman who'd just been talking about the lake. Her hand came up, and the last thought that United States Speaker of the House Jefferson Vandermeer had was that the last laugh was on him—maybe he should have had security in Wisconsin after all.

# CHAPTER
# 12

Distracted, his mind cartwheeling through everything that had happened, Journey finally realized it had been at least a couple of hours since he'd changed Andrew. He and Andrew walked the six tree-lined blocks from the campus to the house, and Andrew's pants were soaked by the time they walked up the driveway past Journey's old minivan, the one he and Amelia had bought when they thought they would have more children. "I'm sorry, son," Journey said to Andrew, then got him into the house, changed him, and put a dry pair of jeans on him.

He'd been terrified three years ago, when Amelia decided to file for divorce. Not so much of the end of the marriage itself—she'd been emotionally divorcing herself from Andrew and him for several years by then—but of becoming a single parent. It wasn't that Amelia didn't love Andrew. Journey knew she did—he still remembered her rolling around on the floor with him as a baby, and the way she'd always been able to get him to go to sleep when Journey couldn't. But as Andrew's condition grew more profound, she'd gradually begun to put up walls. It was her way of dealing with something she couldn't understand. For as long as Journey had known her, she prided herself on being a problem solver, and she couldn't solve Andrew. So Journey had been doing most of the parenting for a while before she moved out, but the idea of not having someone else to physically fall back on, someone to give him a break when things blew up, was the most frightening thing he'd ever faced.

He'd told Sandra the truth—he knew he didn't do enough with Andrew. He tried to keep up with the new therapies, to know all the educational processes and procedures, to network with the right people and organizations, but most of the time, he was a blind man in the dark. He didn't talk much about his life as a parent, and he wasn't sure why he'd said what he did to Sandra. He loved Andrew without question or reservation, and he tried to do the right things for him. When Andrew gave one of his genuine heart-stopping smiles, or held his father's elbow—one of Andrew's signs of affection—when they walked into a store, or seemed to truly understand something Journey was telling him, the stress and the frustration and the doubt fell away. But he also couldn't help the sadness that gripped him when he drove by a field of kids playing baseball, or heard one of his colleagues talk about their child who was in the school play or singing in the choir.

Journey's heart was racing, and he knew his blood pressure must be coming out the top of his head by now. He tried to calm himself, using the same trick he used with Andrew, the soft music on a CD. He put on an early Windham Hill sampler and listened to Alex DeGrassi's "Western" and George Winston's "Thanksgiving," but with no effect. He was all nervous agitation, his finger tapping its triplets repeatedly against the wall, his desk, his pants leg.

He felt the two G.W. pins in his pocket, read the strange document again and again. He felt a silent to urge to hurry, to *move*. Journey's mind clicked and whirred. *History is about passion. These people were passionate about something. They were committed. Fanatics, even. And they were preparing for . . . what?*

*Armed conflict*, he'd told Sandra a few minutes ago.

The missing piece was how G.W. got from 1865 to now, how a secret society protecting a secret treaty at the close of the bloodiest conflict in American history landed in the here and now, men with gold G.W. pins searching for this document and willing to use whatever means necessary to obtain it.

Knowledge was power, and what he'd told Sandra was true—he had to be ready for them. He had to know more than they did to keep himself and Andrew safe.

His mind still churning, and thinking of the way Sandra's earrings had glinted in the sunlight, he logged on to his computer and checked his e-mail. He deleted a few pieces of junk, skipped over two from students and one from his old advisor at Virginia, then stopped on the one with the subject *Incident at South Central College*.

The sender was *Tolman, Margaret I.*

Journey opened the e-mail and read it quickly. He'd never heard of RIO, but evidently the stakes were rising. The local authorities had bumped it up to Washington to look for answers, and Washington had circled back around to him.

He did an online search for the Research and Investigations Office. It appeared legit, a strange little arm of three different Cabinet-level departments. The Web sources he read included phrases like "evaluation and oversight" and "review of cases referred from state and local jurisdictions." One blog, from a man who had apparently worked for the office, referred to it as "the place cases go to die."

*The place where cases go to die is going to help me?* he wondered.

He thought for a moment, typed *I have nothing to say at this time*, then turned away from the computer. "Come on, Andrew," he called. A few seconds later, Andrew wandered into the room, a vague smile on his face, dragging an empty paper grocery sack. Journey let him keep the sack—he fixated on it less than he did the straw and pencil.

They climbed into the van and pulled out of the driveway. It was time to search for G.W.

Taylor Drive ran outward from the SCCO campus and wound to-ward the US 70 intersection. One more turn led to Texoma Plaza, an old-style town square with a small park instead of a courthouse at its center. A bronze plaque in the park honored Carpenter Center's war dead. The earliest were from World War I. The most recent bore last year's dates, from Iraq and Afghanistan.

At the corner of the square nearest the highway junction stood Colbert's Fine Jewelers. SINCE 1900, the storefront said, which placed it in Indian Territory days, seven years before Oklahoma Territory and Indian Territory united into the state of Oklahoma. Journey knew the name Colbert. The Colberts were one of the most prominent Chickasaw families in the area.

The jewelry store was a tiny place, with a bell over the door—an old-fashioned silver bell, not an electronic chime—and two wooden-framed display cases. One case contained watches, while the other held rings, earrings, and other jewelry.

He pointed Andrew to an old wooden chair by the door and the boy sat, rattling his paper sack. A young man in his late teens, with blue eyes but the high cheekbones and bone structure of a mixed-blood, looked up. "Help you, sir?"

Journey put the two pins on the glass top of the case. "What can you tell me about these?"

The boy looked at the pins, then at Journey, then at the pins again. He turned around and walked through a doorway into the dark background of the shop. "Uncle!" he yelled, then said something else Journey couldn't make out.

There was a shuffling step, and a minute later, an old man with much more Native blood than the boy stepped through the door. His long dark hair—so black, it looked almost blue—hung in a single braid to the middle of his back. It held only a handful of silver threads. "Jimmy said you had some pieces," he said, his voice carrying the soft lilt of the Chickasaw people.

"Are you Mr. Colbert?" Journey asked. "Can you tell anything about these?"

"I'm Mr. Colbert, but then, so's Jimmy. I'm Marvin." The old man took a pair of rimless glasses out of his shirt pocket and carefully put them on. "What do you want to know about them?"

"Anything. Where they came from, who made them."

"I think I saw you on TV. You were talking about all those guns out at Fort Washita."

"That's right."

"These come from out there, too?"

"One of them," Journey said.

"Uh-huh." Colbert poked at the pins. He picked up the older one and paid special attention to the clasp on its back. He ran a finger along it, looked up at Journey with a stony expression for a very long moment, then looked down again. "Old. Mid–nineteenth century. These kinds of clasps haven't been used in jewelry since the States War. Great-grandmother had a brooch with that kind of clasp, and it was from 1850."

Andrew hooted suddenly, kicking at his sack. Colbert looked long and hard at Andrew, and Journey was ready to give his "my son has autism and here is why he does some of the things he does" speech. But Colbert said nothing. He turned and opened a dusty file cabinet behind the display case. Much to Journey's surprise, he came up with a small round plastic yellow ball with soft protrusions that looked a bit like the quills on a porcupine. He ambled around the counter and handed the ball to Andrew, who immediately squeezed it. There was a little hole in the center, and when he squeezed it, air rushed out into his face. Andrew smiled.

"Porcupine ball," Journey said as Colbert came back around the case. "Thanks."

"I keep it around for the great-grandbaby," Colbert said. He waved his hand toward Andrew. "Needs to do things with his hands, doesn't he?"

Journey nodded and the two men looked at each other for a moment.

"What about the engraving on the pin?" Journey finally said.

"Nice work. Custom job, I'm sure."

Colbert hefted the newer pin. "Uh-huh. Newer, pretty recent, I'd say. You can tell because it's not as heavy. These kinds of pieces are lighter now, and the engraving's a little different. Letters are just a bit off-center, too. Tenth of an inch, maybe."

Journey looked at the two pins. He hadn't discerned the difference in placement, only the change in font. But with Colbert holding both pins, he could see it. "You can tell a tenth of an inch just by looking?"

Colbert smiled. He turned over the new pin. He tapped it, then flipped on a round jeweler's lamp and swung it down so Journey could see. "See this here?"

Journey looked. "What?"

Colbert angled the pin in a different direction, running his thumb along the edge of it. "This little notch on the back. See it now?"

Journey squinted. "I guess."

"That's AAJE work."

"AAJE?"

"American Academy of Jewelry Engravers. This means it's high-dollar work. AAJE has only about a hundred members in the whole country. They're like a big-city country club. Don't let the riffraff in."

"Are you a member?"

Colbert gave the little smile again, glanced at Andrew with the ball, then back to Journey. "I'm riffraff. Don't want to be in." He handed both pieces back to Journey. "But that little notch is the AAJE signature. Those'll be worth a lot."

"Thanks," Journey said.

He motioned to Andrew and the boy stood up, leaving the paper sack, still squeezing the ball, enjoying the little breath of wind on his face. "Here, son, let's give this back."

"He can keep it," Colbert said. "Got six more for the great-grandbaby. Your boy might get more good out of it. Don't you think so?"

"He might," Journey said.

As Journey got into the van and pulled away from the store, Marvin Colbert was still watching him, a strange look on his face.

When Journey pulled into his driveway, the Carpenter Center police officer assigned to watch him drove by and waved to him.

"Are you going to protect me?" Journey muttered as he unlocked the house.

He changed Andrew and popped in a CD for him. It was approaching five o'clock, and he needed to start thinking about dinner. It was strange, he thought, how in the midst of secret societies and weapons caches and thoughts about running down that gunman, life could still be rooted in the ordinary, in things every other parent did—finding something their child would eat.

Journey thawed ground beef and began to boil water to make something he called "poor man's Stroganoff." It resembled real beef Stroganoff about as much as he resembled a real chef, but Andrew would eat it, and it made abundant leftovers. While waiting for the water to boil, he flipped on the little portable TV he kept on a corner of the kitchen counter.

It settled onto CNN, the reporters and anchors talking in urgent tones, but Journey didn't catch any of it at first. He opened a package of egg noodles and started to dump them in the boiling pot when he heard the reporter say, ". . . the assassination this afternoon of the Speaker of the U.S. House, Representative Jefferson Vandermeer."

Journey dropped the package of pasta, noodles rolling at his feet. He turned toward the TV.

". . . no claims of responsibility thus far," the reporter said. Behind him was Lake Michigan and yards of yellow crime-scene tape. "The Speaker was scheduled to return to Washington tomorrow from the Labor Day recess, and was out for his daily walk in North Point Park. Since the death of his wife, Speaker Vandermeer lived alone, splitting time between his homes here in Sheboygan and in McLean, Virginia, just outside Washington."

Journey took a step.

"The nation is in a state of shock. Never before in the history of the United States has a Speaker of the House been assassinated. The House Sergeant-at-Arms, who is responsible for security for members of the House, said today that the Speaker had not requested a security detail and that no threats had been made against Vandermeer. Security details are not normally provided to members of Congress while they are in their home districts, unless they specifically request it."

The pot of water on the stove boiled over, hot water splashing. A little of it caught Journey's sleeve, and he pulled up his arm in pain at the scalding water. Without turning off the pot, he ran for the living room, crunching pasta under his feet.

Andrew was still squeezing the yellow ball. He hummed occasionally. He'd taken off one sock and shoe. Journey reached for the document on his desk and read it again.

*Conspiratorial means . . . to destabilize the American Federal Government . . .*

*The Speaker of the Legislative Branch.*

The removal of the Speaker of the House was first in the list of events that would trigger the activation of the unnamed "clause."

"No," Journey said.

Andrew looked up at him.

G.W. wasn't just trying to get this document—and the missing pieces of it, no doubt—as a historical curiosity in the here and now. They weren't just planning for a contingency of stepping into a power vacuum in Washington; they were *creating* the power vacuum.

Journey felt his heartbeat in his ears, his neck, his arms—it was everywhere, one gigantic beat, pounding faster and faster. He reached out and steadied himself against the desk.

He swiveled around to the computer, bumping against the mouse. His screen saver vanished, and the search results for RIO were still on the screen. He hadn't closed the window before heading to Colbert's.

He stabbed at the keyboard, logged back in to e-mail, and found the note from Margaret I. Tolman.

At the bottom of her e-mail was her electronic signature:

MEG TOLMAN
RESEARCH/INVESTIGATIONS SPECIALIST II
RESEARCH AND INVESTIGATIONS OFFICE
A JOINTLY ADMINISTERED AGENCY OF THE U.S. DEPARTMENTS OF
HOMELAND SECURITY, JUSTICE, AND TREASURY
202-207-2811—VOICE DIRECT
MTOLMAN@RIO.GOV

Now he had no choice. Sandra had been right, after all.

Journey picked his cell phone off the desk, but his hands were shaking so badly it slid off onto the hardwood floor. Andrew heard the clatter, looked over, stood up, and walked to him. He bent down next to his father and put a hand between their faces.

"I know, son," Journey said. "I know, I love you, too. I know." His stomach lurched.

He grabbed the phone and, his hands still shaking, punched in the number.

# CHAPTER
# 13

The Judge rose before six on Sunday, as he did every morning. He made a simple breakfast of toast, fruit, and juice, then took a walk along the winding road around his property. He appreciated the fact that he and Jefferson Vandermeer had apparently shared a fondness for quiet walks. The Judge enjoyed the rustling in the trees, the sounds of the birds, the smell of fresh honeysuckle.

After half an hour, he headed back to the house and wandered into his study. He read for two hours, part of a new Thomas Jefferson biography, then turned on the television to catch the Sunday-morning talk circuit.

Out of habit, he checked all four of his cable networks, including the flagship HNC, then settled in to watch what the competition was doing. On NBC, announcements had been running all week promoting *Meet the Press,* in which David Gregory would spend a full hour with the president. Gregory had already given his introduction, and the camera pulled back to a long shot of the two men sitting in the Oval Office.

President James Harwell *looked* presidential. He was tall and broad-shouldered in his mid-fifties, with pure silver hair and brown eyes that could be by turns empathetic and unwavering. A Connecticut native with roots dating back to before the American Revolution, he was a self-made millionaire, a skilled politician, and by all accounts, a terrible leader. Halfway through his second term, his administration had been a series of missteps almost from day one. But he *looked* the part, which crystallized for the Judge one of the most critical shortfalls of today's America: politicians with no substance and who refused to govern. Further proof of the need for the Glory Warriors

"Mr. President," Gregory said, "there are those who say America is in a time of national crisis. Our Middle East problems continue to be unstable, with no end in sight. The economy is still feeling the effects of the deepest recession in nearly thirty years. Health care costs continue to rise unchecked, despite the reforms that have been put into place. Terrorism is everywhere—a pipe bomb on a train in Atlanta, a carload of explosives at a mall in Minneapolis, snipers on the freeway in Los Angeles. And now the Speaker of the House has been shot and killed."

Harwell waited a moment, then saw that Gregory was finished. "Was there a question in there, David?"

"I could go on. Even the federal judiciary has been rocked with scandal in recent months, allegations of judges taking bribes from powerful corporate interests. Sir, the America we know is changing right before our eyes, and a great many Americans don't seem to like it. Our latest NBC News poll shows that seventy-six percent of the people disapprove of your job performance. There have been calls for you to resign, some from leaders in your own party. What do you say to them?"

Harwell crossed his legs. "Look, David, I say to them what I've been saying all along. We don't run this nation based on poll numbers. This administration is committed to doing what's right in sensible and bipartisan ways, to best serve the American people. Our economic-stimulus package is working through Congress now, and I'm confident the Congressional leadership will do what's right. But progress takes time, David. The American people know that. They elected me twice, and I'll take that vote of confidence over the poll of the day any time. We're attacking every problem on every possible front, and yes, it seems like we've taken a lot of hits in recent months. But the American people are strong, and their spirit shines through. I take comfort in the words of Euripides—'Somewhere human misery must have a stop. There is no wind that always blows a storm.'"

"Euripides notwithstanding, Speaker Vandermeer was assassinated when out for his daily walk yesterday. After the vice president, he was next in line for the presidency. What do you say to the American people when the Speaker of the House is assassinated?"

"My thoughts are with Jeff's family, his daughter Alice, his grandchildren. I knew Jeff Vandermeer for many years and worked with him on a lot of legislation. We didn't always agree on issues, but he served this country honorably for a long time. I'm holding his family and the people of Wisconsin in my prayers, and I know those who committed the crime will be caught. We will see justice done."

Gregory leaned forward. "But isn't the Speaker's killing just symptomatic of the larger problem in America today?"

Harwell mimicked the host's motion. "No, David, the Speaker's killing is symptomatic of some maniac who thought he could make his point through the barrel of a gun."

"So you believe the Speaker's assassination was a terrorist act."

"I believe all violence is a terrorist act. Look, the motivations may be different, but the results are the same. Someone believes they are above the rule of law, and they take matters into their own hands."

"What do you say to Senator Brenson, third-ranking Senator in your own party? On Wednesday, he said in a *New York Times* op-ed piece, 'The president has proven he is incapable of managing the affairs of state, and our country is spiraling out of control under this administration. The president cannot even control his own affairs, it seems. If he truly loves his country, he will step aside while he can still do so honorably.'"

Harwell sat back against the chair. He gave a loose smile. "Dane Brenson is a good man and a good Senator. But if he thinks I am going to walk away from the job the American people hired me to do, then he is sadly mistaken."

"What about the reference to your own affairs? The Justice Department is continuing its inquiry into fund-raising irregularities from your reelection campaign."

"The campaign legal team is dealing with it. I broke no state or federal laws, and I'm not going to let it be a distraction to the business of governing."

The Judge tuned out the rest. He'd heard what he needed to hear. Harwell was responding predictably, and all the good looks and personal charm and wealth in the world couldn't change the fact that his administration was crashing around him. His Secretary of the Interior had resigned six weeks ago when allegations came to light about his activities when he'd been national co-chair of the reelection campaign. Congress was in open revolt, refusing to deal with any of the president's programs. Harwell was stuck in political quicksand, and the entire country knew it.

The Judge turned off the television and sat back in silence. The stage was being set for the Glory Warriors. Grant and Lee's original vision, as articulated at Appomattox, would be realized. Even more important, his father's vision would become real. He was going to save the country he loved—that his father and grandfather had loved. Everything in the Judge's life—law, the military, the political system, business—had been about arriving at this point.

At seventy-one, and with his father dead for more than thirty years, the Judge still heard the old man's voice at times, as clearly as he'd heard the birdsong when he walked around his property earlier. The Judge wondered what his father would think of him now.

# CHAPTER

# 14

*D*r. Journey! The document, now!"

Journcy saw Pete Parsons's blood spurting, saw himself throwing up his hands as the young officer's body fell toward him. He heard the shots, felt himself diving into the police car, flooring the accelerator. He felt the sick crunch as the body of the gunman bent against the force of the oncoming car.

And then he was in another car on a highway in the bright winter California sunshine, and he was crawling around in the back of the station wagon, rolling a baseball back and forth. The family was going to visit Uncle Darren in Westminster, who lived very close to Anaheim Stadium, and who had been trying to teach his nephew to throw a curveball. Then there was a crash and the car was sliding sideways. Another impact, then another, the car shooting around in different directions. He felt himself being tossed from side to side. Glass was breaking, the world was tilting, his mother screaming, his father fighting the wheel. Danny and Mark were yelling, Mark reaching over the seat toward him, fingers outstretched . . . and then he was falling free.

Journcy woke up bathed in sweat, the sheets balled in his hands, his nails digging half-moon shapes into his palms. He was breathing hard, his heart thundering. He noticed that his legs were shaking.

He hadn't dreamed of his family in at least fifteen years. Journey closed his eyes again, but all the dreams—both of his family and of the parking lot at SCCO—were gone, wiped clean from his brain. Still, he'd killed a man. A man had lived and breathed and walked, and now he was dead because of Journey's actions.

*I killed a man.*

*A man who was shooting at me.*

*A man who wanted something I have.*

*Dr. Journey! The document, now!*

Journey made himself get out of bed, put on coffee, showered, and dressed. Within a few minutes, the door to Andrew's room opened and the boy walked out, his thick hair sticking up in all directions.

"Good morning," Journey said. "How you doing, big boy?"

Andrew hummed a little, then smiled, and Journey's heart nearly broke—he looked so much like Amelia that it still startled him at times, especially when he smiled.

"Come on, Andrew." He steered his son into the bathroom, holding his breath against the smell of Andrew's urine. He would put the pajamas and all Andrew's sheets and blankets in the washer in a few minutes, as he did every day. He got the wet pajamas off him and dressed him in sweatpants and a loose-fitting shirt for a day at home.

Andrew was growing fast. He'd probably be taller than his father within another couple of years. *Will I still be changing diapers then?* Journey thought, then chased that from his mind: *This is the way it is, at least for now.*

The two of them had breakfast; then Journey took Andrew for a walk and back home to do puzzles, his hand over his son's as they put the pieces in place. He knew he was distracted and that Andrew could tell, and after a while he patted his son's hand and said, "You do it for a while."

Journey wondered about the phone call he'd made yesterday. When would Meg Tolman from the Research and Investigations Office check her messages? Someone should be calling him, better yet coming to see him, and soon.

*Assuming they don't think I'm a nutcase.*

He took out the G.W. pins and found the little notch on the back of the newer one, the one he'd taken off the dead man Tuesday. He ran his hands over it, as if the metal could tell him something.

"Maybe it can," he said, and turned to his computer. In less than a minute, he'd found the Web site for the American Academy of Jewelry Engravers.

SERVING FINE JEWELERS SINCE 1922, read the banner headline.

Journey navigated around the site. It was the standard professional association site, with mission statements, services to members, how to apply for membership, a page of FAQs. He clicked that link and scanned the list. At the bottom was a link to a page listing the academy's 108 member companies.

He poured himself another cup of coffee, then returned to his computer and thought for a moment about how to narrow the parameters of the search. The AAJE had existed only since 1922, so there was no way to link to the G.W. of 1865. Still, he reasoned, if G.W. was a secret society formed in the Civil War era, and had existed in some form until now, perhaps the group started using a jeweler for its pins and continued with the same company for a long time. It was a starting point. Journey began clicking links to AAJE member sites—at least those who actually had a presence on the Web—and began looking for companies that had been in business for over a century.

He reached for the phone, then pulled his hand back. *Sunday,* he thought. Most of the jewelers wouldn't be open. He would start making phone calls first thing tomorrow morning.

*I'll find you,* he thought. *Whatever you are, G.W., I will find you.*

The wedding reception in Chevy Chase was as advertised, so-
cially and musically lacking. Tolman played some jazz standards, a couple of movie love themes, and lots of filler. She worked in
a few bars of the theme from the old *Perry Mason* TV series, but no
one seemed to notice.

No one except her father, that is. Ray Tolman had driven her to
the gig and stayed through the whole thing, sitting in a chair ten feet
away and listening to every note. He applauded at the end of every
piece, which made all the other wedding guests look at him, and then
a few of them applauded as well. *That* made his daughter smile.

Still, she was not at her best. Her worlds kept spilling into each
other, sitting at the keyboard while she chased thoughts of Nick
Journey and the anonymous assassins whom the Pentagon insisted
had been dead for several years. Her father drove her back toward
Washington from the suburbs, and she tried to enjoy just being in his
presence for a while. There weren't many words between them—there
rarely were—but it was an easy silence, not stiff or tense. They would
talk when they had something to talk about. They listened to the
radio, with news of Speaker Vandermeer's murder on every station.

"That's the damnedest thing," Ray Tolman said after a few miles.

"Vandermeer?"

"He was a crusty old fart, but to get blown away like that . . . it's a shame. First Speaker in history to be killed in office."

Meg closed her eyes. "You ask the average American on any given day who the Speaker of the House is, and I bet they couldn't tell you. But now they'll remember this one."

"When did you get so damn cynical?"

"I come by it naturally. You ever meet Vandermeer?"

"A couple of times when Clinton went up to the Hill." Ray Tolman shrugged. "He's no better or worse than any other Congressman."

When they crossed south into the District on Connecticut Avenue, Meg Tolman told her father, "Just drop me at the office, okay?"

Ray Tolman, a big man, muscular at fifty-eight, bald on top with close-cropped gray fringe, glanced sideways at her. "It's Sunday and you just played for two hours. Take it easy for a while. I can make you some dinner."

"Dad, if I want bad cooking, I can do that myself. I have some things to catch up on."

"It's Sunday, Meg."

"'There's no such thing as Sundays in my job.' Who do I remember saying that when I was a kid?"

"I was on personal protective detail. It's a little different."

"Not so different. Just because you protected three presidents and I sit at a computer, what's so different? The job is what it is. I heard that one a few times, too."

"Oh, bullshit," Ray Tolman said, but he was smiling. "Stop quoting my words back at me."

"See, I *was* listening when I was a teenager."

"Yeah, yeah, yeah. Well, I'm too old to protect anyone now. Deputy assistant directors only protect spreadsheets, and since I don't know a damn thing about spreadsheets, that is a bit of a problem."

His daughter punched him on the arm. "Now *that's* bullshit. You're in better shape than most of the guys on the detail now, I suspect. But be that as it may, don't give me that 'I'm too old' crap. Everyone in the Service drives a desk at some point, and you might still get promoted up to an assistant directorship."

"No, I won't, because I don't kiss anyone's ass, and I'm too old—don't look at me like that, Margaret—to start. And I really don't care."

Meg looked at him again. *I really don't care.*

*Yes, you do,* she thought. *You care more about a lot of things than you let on.* She found herself thinking of the only time she'd ever seen her father cry, in the hospital the day of the crash. She was relatively unscathed herself, aside from a bump on the head. Her mother had gone through the windshield and into the Potomac. Her father was with President Clinton at Camp David when he got the call. The president himself called later in the day to see how Ray Tolman was. By that time, her father had calmed himself, but she remembered sitting with him in the ER and watching him cry.

Everyone around him, even the president of the United States, kept telling him they were sorry for his loss—meaning her mother, of course. Only Meg understood that her father cried not because his wife was dead, although he certainly grieved. But he cried because of what his daughter had told him about those last few minutes. He cried not only for Janet Tolman, his manic-depressive wife who refused to take her medication, but he cried for his daughter as well, who would forever carry her mother's last minutes with her.

"I really don't," Ray Tolman said. "And it's not going to bug me to drive my desk into retirement. Four more years, and I'm going fishing."

"You don't even like fishing, and if the fish get one look at that bald head, they'll all swim away as fast as they can go."

"That's cruel, Meg."

She smiled. "It certainly is. Just drop me at the office."

Ray Tolman waited a moment. "Something's going on with you. I could tell even when you were playing."

"Yeah. Kind of an interesting case."

"Hmm, that's a change for RIO."

"Tell me about it. You ever have any trouble with DOD?"

"The Pentagon? Never had to deal with them much, thank God. What's up?"

She shook her head, thinking of her call to the Pentagon yesterday. "I'm not sure yet. Probably just a mistake."

"Yours or theirs?"

"Maybe both. Maybe neither."

"Ah. They've turned you into such a bureaucrat."

"But I'm a bureaucrat who can play Rachmaninov."

"Point taken."

They reached her office building, and her father pulled his Crown Victoria to the curb. "Thanks for coming today, and for the ride," Meg said.

Her father shrugged. "I haven't heard you play in a while. You should learn some Beatles songs."

She laughed. "Say hi to Granddad for me."

"Yeah, I'm headed out to see him now. Probably take him some dinner. He's not that wild about the food at the assisted-living place. Imagine that."

She watched as the long black car—he'd been driving government cars for so long, even his own personal vehicle looked like one—pulled away from the curb. A little uncomfortable at times, a little lost at being in the gray area between middle and old age, but he was trying. He always tried. She envisioned a stone marker in a cemetery not far from here: RAY TOLMAN. HE TRIED. There were worse epitaphs. She smiled a little at that.

The RIO office suite was empty. Tolman was slightly surprised that Rusty Hudson wasn't in, but even he went home sometimes. She drifted down the hallway, flipping on lights as she went. In her office, she tossed her bag on the spare chair and kicked off her shoes. She booted up her computer and let it cycle through the start-up routine. "Come on, come on," she said, restless to get started. "I don't have all fucking day."

Attempting to log in to the Pentagon database, she again found herself locked out. No surprise, given what had happened yesterday, but she still didn't like it. She folded her hands together, interlocking her fingers. Tolman sat still, replaying the brief conversation with Meares yesterday.

*"Those two men were Army Rangers who were both killed in action in Iraq in 2006."*

Tolman leaned forward and began working her mouse and keyboard. The U.S. Army Rangers were an elite unit, and in five minutes, she knew that there were only three posts where Rangers were based: Hunter Army Airfield in Georgia; Fort Lewis, Washington; and Fort Benning, Georgia.

Next, she accessed a Web site called Iraq Coalition Casualties, one of many that listed casualty reports, sorted not only by name, but also by date of death, unit, cause, and place of death. She started her search with Hunter Army Airfield. Ten soldiers stationed there had died in Iraq. None were listed as part of the Seventy-fifth Ranger Regiment. She went up the list to Fort Benning. Sixty-six from there were killed in action. Seven were Rangers. She scanned the dates: four of them were killed in 2003, two in 2005, one in 2007.

"Okay, then," she said. The office was feeling warm, and she opened the top button of her white blouse.

Fort Lewis had seen 179 of its soldiers killed in Iraq. Only six were Rangers. But four of them had died in 2006, two of them in March in Ramadi, the other two in August in Taji.

Tolman clicked on the name of the first March soldier and was instantly taken to Defense Link, the official DOD news-release site. A two-sentence statement reported the deaths of the two soldiers. Their names, ages, and hometowns were listed below, along with a contact phone number at the Pentagon for Army Public Affairs. A similarly worded statement was online for the August deaths.

"Dead end," Tolman said, staring at the screen. She tapped a bare foot on the floor, humming a few bars of the *Perry Mason* theme.

Tolman went back to the Iraq Coalition Casualties Web site, then copied and pasted the date the March soldiers died. She did a search for the date, cross-referenced with "Iraq deaths." Dozens of references came back, online news stories about that day's fighting in Ramadi. The Associated Press, HNC, NPR, the online editions of all the major newspapers . . . there were pages and pages. Tolman read a few of them and came away with a pretty good feel for the battle where the men had died.

She did the same search for the two August soldiers. Several pages of hits came back, but not so many as for the March date.

She clicked on the HNC link. The story discussed troop movements, new units being deployed in Baghdad, the IED explosion in Taji that killed members of the Sixty-sixth Armored Regiment, First Brigade, Fourth Infantry Division, based at Fort Lewis, Washington.

Tolman read it again, then blinked at the monitor. Back at the search screen, she clicked on the Associated Press story. Same story with a few variations. Soldiers killed from the Sixty-sixth Armored Regiment.

She read three more online news accounts of the day's fighting. No mention was made of the deaths of two soldiers attached to the Seventy-fifth Ranger Regiment at Fort Lewis.

*What the fuck?* Tolman thought; then she said it aloud, then said it again.

The Rangers were an elite unit, the army's pride. The deaths of two of its members were worth noting, worth reporting. Probably worth a sidebar story or two, feature-type stories that the media loved.

Slowly she went back to the names of the two Rangers who'd been reported killed on that date.

Sergeant Michael Standridge, 30, Moscow, Idaho
Sergeant Kevin A. Lane, 26, Pineville, Louisiana

Tolman searched for the newspapers from the hometowns. The *Moscow–Pullman Daily News* carried an obituary for Michael Standridge. The date was right. Tolman scanned it quickly. Standridge had been a high school basketball player and track star, was known as an outdoorsman and hunter. He'd joined the army straight out of high school. He was unmarried, but the story quoted his high school girlfriend about his sense of patriotism and duty. The photo posted with the story was from his high school graduation. She'd seen the face before, except it had been older, bloodied, and lifeless in the crime-scene photo from Oklahoma.

The newspaper in Pineville, Louisiana, was called *The Town Talk*, and its obituary of Kevin A. Lane called him a "bona fide hero" who felt called to serve his country from the age of six. He was third-generation army, excelled in science in high school, and was known locally as being able to repair anything, from cars to computers. He'd left behind a wife and a six-month-old daughter. His photo was from the army, in full dress uniform, wearing the Rangers' red beret.

Although the photo from the security camera at South Central College had been at long distance and poor quality, she recognized the shape of Kevin Lane's face, and a little scar beside his left eye.

"Shit," Tolman muttered.

Back to the media. There were no mentions of any U.S. Army Rangers from Fort Lewis dying on that date. But the DOD official news releases, and obituaries in hometown media days later, said these men had died in Taji.

DOD could control the hometown media, it could create an official paper or cybertrail and seal the records, but it couldn't stop the reports from the actual scene, not in this era of journalists "embedded" with military units.

Standridge and Lane hadn't died in Iraq in 2006, and they'd been in Carpenter Center, Oklahoma, a few days ago.

Tolman reached for the phone with one hand and her office directory with the other. Rusty Hudson answered on the first ring. She heard the sounds of wind and a crowd of people. "I think you should come to the office," she said.

# CHAPTER

# 16

Waiting for Hudson, Tolman sat back for a moment, then stood up, walked around the office, walked down the hall to the reception area, then back again. "Come on, Rusty," she muttered. "Get your ass in here."

She sat back down at her desk and clicked her mouse a few times. She checked her e-mail and saw the note from Nick Journey.

*I have nothing to say at this time.* The message had been sent shortly after her original e-mail went to Journey. She moved his reply into a folder she'd created for the case.

Two more clicks, and she checked phone messages. She had forwarded her voice mail directly to the computer, strictly a convenience factor so that she didn't have to hold the phone when checking messages.

The messaging program showed a single voice mail. It had come in yesterday, early evening. Tolman turned on her speakers and sat back in her chair.

Sixty seconds later, she was sitting up straight, holding her breath. She checked the time of the phone message and compared it to the time of Nick Journey's e-mail. He'd called her an hour and a half after he e-mailed her yesterday.

"Holy fucking shit," Tolman said.

She heard steps in the hallway, and a few seconds later, Hudson was at her door, wearing a golf shirt and khakis. It was the first time Tolman had ever seen him without a tie.

"What is it?" Hudson said.

Tolman shook her head.

"Meg?"

Tolman finally looked away from the computer. "I called you about the DOD and the shooters in Oklahoma. I found—Jesus Christ, Rusty, I just picked up this message, right after I called you." She clicked on the phone message.

"This is Nick Journey," said a man's voice, resonant but soft-spoken. Tolman detected no regional accent, remembering that Journey had grown up all over the country.

"You e-mailed me yesterday, about what happened to me a few days ago," Journey said. "I wrote you back a little while ago, but I . . . I just . . ."

There was a beat of white noise, a moment of hiss on the phone line. "I just heard about the Speaker of the House being killed. I think . . . I think the chief justice is going to be next."

Another pause. A high-pitched squeal sounded in the background of the recording. Hudson winced at the sound.

"Just a minute, Andrew," Journey's voice said, as if he'd turned away from the phone; then his voice was full volume again. "I think the chief justice of the Supreme Court is going to be assassinated, and very soon. I thought I . . ." His voice trailed off again. Another high-pitched wail. Journey made another sound, as if he were about to say something else; then the line went dead.

"Play it again," Hudson said, and Tolman did. "Make a copy of that message and bring it with you," he said after it played the second time.

Tolman pulled out her RIO-issued laptop and fished a USB drive from her drawer. "Where are we going?"

"There is a threat on the life of the chief justice. There will be a threat-assessment meeting. Bring your book on Journey."

Tolman plugged the USB into her desktop and started copying the file. "Who's in the meeting?"

"The Marshals Service, the Bureau, and us."

"But you'll handle the briefing on our side."

Hudson shook his head. "No," he said. "You built the case, you made the contact. You do the briefing."

The big man turned and strode down the hallway. Tolman finished copying the audio file, disconnected the USB, grabbed her Journey file and laptop. She stopped in the doorway, seeing her shoes under the desk. *Oh no*, she thought, then: *Fuck it. I'm not torturing my feet in those heels for the next God-knows-how-many-hours.* Barefoot, she jogged down the hall after Hudson.

"I'll drive," Hudson said. He knew how Tolman hated driving.

Like everything else about the man, Rusty Hudson's car was a paradox. When she first came to work at RIO, Tolman had pictured him as more of a Crown Victoria type, like her father, but he drove a bright blue Dodge Dakota pickup truck with a club cab. Tolman wondered how someone who obsessed over departmental budgets and time sheets could reconcile driving a vehicle that probably got all of thirteen miles to the gallon.

"Where were you today?" Tolman asked. "Ball game?"

Hudson shook his head. "Family reunion."

She stared at him.

"Believe it or not, I do have family, Meg. If you didn't call me about Journey's message, why did you call?"

"This whole Journey thing is tangled up in DOD. There's some kind of weird-shit deep cover operation going on."

"Facts, Meg. You need to give me facts."

As they turned south, Tolman outlined what she'd learned about Michael Standridge and Kevin Lane, and how she'd come by it. "I knew if you went into the DOD database, there would be trouble," Hudson said when she finished.

"Oh, don't be such a bureaucrat. This is not about protecting RIO's ass. Why would DOD go to all the trouble to make sure these guys were legally and officially dead, only to have them turn up going after Nick Journey? I mean, Lane and Standridge couldn't have faked their own deaths in Iraq, certainly not to the extent that the official army machine has covered it."

"No," Hudson said, "that isn't feasible."

"So someone with some real juice at the Pentagon had to be involved somewhere. Maybe this Colonel Meares I talked to. Maybe that's why I was transferred to him in the first place."

"No. To make two soldiers disappear would take something above a colonel."

Tolman paused a beat. "You don't have connections at DOD."

Hudson smiled. "As you're so fond of pointing out, I'm a bureaucrat. I have connections everywhere." The smile faded. "But I'm not convinced that this is some grand conspiracy on the part of the U.S. Army. It doesn't make sense for them to put these two men to death, officially speaking, and have them under deep cover. They were already Special Forces in the first place. On top of that, why would they attack Journey?"

"To get what Journey has: the document."

"Whatever that document is, it has been in the ground since 1865. What could possibly warrant the army expending that much time, effort, and money to obtain it? There has to be another explanation, a mistake in data entry somewhere."

"That's what I thought. I've been over it and over it—they were reported as dead by the DOD, but yet there were no casualties from their unit reported on that date."

Hudson was silent a moment. "What do you hope to find?"

Tolman lifted both hands, then let them drop into her lap. "I don't know. But this Journey thing . . . it started out as an obscure historical find, and now there are somehow two Special Forces guys—*dead* Special Forces guys—caught on camera going after Journey. I don't know if these guys faked their own deaths in Iraq and then somehow had the capability to hack in and create a trail that said they were dead . . . or if it's actually the army that wanted them to appear dead, and has them on special assignment. It impacts our case either way."

Hudson nodded. "Perhaps, but it doesn't seem quite right to me." He glanced at her. "And right now, we have a different priority."

They didn't speak the rest of the way to the meeting. Tolman closed her eyes and leaned back against the car seat. What did the

Speaker of the House and the chief justice of the Supreme Court have to do with a history professor and the non-deaths of a pair of Special Forces operatives?

*I don't know,* she thought, *but I'm sure as hell going to find out.*

# CHAPTER

# 17

The Judicial Security Division (JSD) of the United States Marshals Service is responsible for protecting members of the federal judiciary, including the justices of the Supreme Court. But the FBI has the responsibility for investigating threats made against the court and its members. While the Marshals and the FBI are both under the umbrella of the Department of Justice, the jurisdictional overlap produces gray areas, which can lead to the occasional bout of confusion.

*Certainly makes* me *feel right at home*, Meg Tolman thought.

Hudson had called the JSD Office of Protective Operations, and was told that the Senior Inspector in Charge was unavailable, until Hudson made clear that a threat against the life of the chief justice of the Supreme Court was involved, and that the threat was being reported by another government agency. The JSD duty officer promised to track down Senior Inspector Graves as soon as possible.

Hudson's next call went to the Special Agent in Charge of Threat Assessment at the Bureau, who was on the phone within three minutes. For once not asserting precedence in turf wars, the SAC, whose name was Gabriel Díaz, agreed to have the meeting at the Marshals Service complex in the Crystal City area of Arlington.

Then Tolman, Hudson, Díaz, two other FBI agents, and three people from JSD sat down to wait for the Senior Inspector. He was located in Norwalk, Connecticut, where he had attended the funeral of his mother-in-law the day before. A chopper was scrambled out of New York to pick him up and return him to D.C.: half an hour to get the helicopter to his location, just over two hours in the air from Connecticut to the Crystal City complex.

It was after eleven, and Tolman was napping when one of the other Marshals Service people knocked on the lounge door down the hall from the JSD conference room and said, "Graves is here."

She smoothed her blouse, rebuttoned the top button, and pulled at her hair, to no avail. Still in bare feet, she followed Hudson down the hall to the conference room. Tolman took a chair, opened her laptop, and plugged in the USB drive.

Senior Inspector Brent Graves was in his fifties, tall and lean, with the kind of graying hair people liked to call "distinguished" and WASP-ish features that made Tolman think of New England prep schools and old money. He didn't look as if it were late at night and he'd just spent two hours on a helicopter. He was dressed in a white shirt open at the throat and navy blue suit pants. His eyes looked a bit weary, but otherwise he seemed perfectly in control.

"Let's hear it," he said. "Who's presenting?"

Graves looked at Hudson, and the look lingered, as if he was registering Hudson's size for the first time. Hudson gestured to Tolman, and Graves's eyes followed.

"That would be me," Tolman said. "Meg Tolman from RIO."

"Why is RIO bringing this to us?" said Díaz, a slim Latino in FBI-standard black suit, white shirt, and red tie

"This stems from a case that was referred to us earlier in the week for review," Hudson said.

"By the Bureau, I might add," Tolman said.

Díaz glared, and Hudson shot Tolman a *Now, Meg* look.

"Here's the background," Tolman said, and spent ten minutes summarizing Nick Journey. She thought she'd lost a couple of people at the table, but Graves remained sharp and intent on the briefing.

"This call came in to my personal line at six-oh-eight P.M. on Saturday," Tolman said.

Tolman played the file. "This is Nick Journey," said the voice.

They listened, several of the group taking notes on legal pads or laptops.

"Play it again," Díaz said when it finished, just as Tolman expected.

After the second time, a beat of silence passed in the room.

"May I?" Tolman said. Hudson looked at her.

Graves looked down the table, his expression softening. "I'm not sure how to address you. I confess to not being familiar enough with RIO's operation to know the titles. Agent or Inspector or . . ." He raised his eyebrows.

"Actually, my title is Research and Investigative Specialist Two. But it would feel very strange for you to call me 'Specialist,' so let's go with just Meg."

Hudson shook his head.

"But Rusty here is a Deputy Director, if that helps," Tolman said.

"And did you lose your shoes . . . Meg?" Graves said.

"No, sir. I just didn't feel like wearing heels, in case we were here all night."

"Meg," Hudson said.

Tolman thought she detected a vague smile from Graves and a scowl from Díaz.

"All right," Graves said. "Your analysis, Meg?"

"It's not so much an analysis as a question. I understand that because of the content of the message, we have to be here, and I admit that when I first heard it, it really shook me up. But listen to the sound of the man's voice. When I think in terms of sound, I consider dynamics and the rise and fall of the voice and the pauses. I think something is going on with this man, something that relates to the document he has, but does that sound like a man who is planning to assassinate the chief justice?"

Graves looked thoughtful. "No, it doesn't."

One of the other JSD people, a woman about Tolman's age, said, "But we can't base our assessment on the dynamics of his voice. He clearly says the chief justice is going to be next."

"But he doesn't say he's going to do it," Graves said.

"And he doesn't mention any kind of reason or motivation," Díaz said. "He sounds disjointed, like his thoughts aren't all together. Speaker Vandermeer and Chief Justice Darlington have no connection whatsoever, and he makes a connection there. And trust me, all hell has been breaking loose at the Hoover Building since the Speaker was shot. But the two are apples and oranges."

"Yes and no," Tolman said. "As far as their responsibilities, they don't connect. But remember high school civics? Each of them is the highest official in a branch of the federal government."

Graves rubbed the bottom half of his face. "True. Tell me about Professor Journey and this mysterious document. He was attacked last week because of it?"

"That's the consensus of the local and state people."

"Does he still have it?"

"As of now, we believe he does."

"What's in it?" Díaz asked.

"We have no idea at this point," Hudson said.

"I have to tell you," Díaz said, "that this whole business of mysterious documents and old guns seems pretty far out. We have a hell of a lot to worry about right now, in the twenty-first century, and it just smells like bullshit to me. He's trying to get attention for whatever this thing is. Maybe he's trying to get tenure or something and he thinks this will help him get published."

Tolman rolled her eyes. "He already has tenure. I don't think—"

Díaz waved his hand. "Give me some real and credible evidence. Is RIO familiar with the concept of evidence?"

*Asshole,* Tolman thought.

Graves looked down the table at both Tolman and Díaz, then rubbed his face again. "Do you see anything in Journey's background that would lead to a threat against the Supreme Court?"

"Nothing at all," Tolman said. "The man's a small-town history professor. There's been no hint of extremism in any of the workup I did on him. He's had a . . . well, let's call it a bumpy life . . . but there's certainly no indicator of violence or any kind of political agenda. But I certainly think it would be worth talking to him, to see what he knows."

Graves stood up. "While the Supreme Court doesn't get near

the threats that the president does, we get our share. They'll pick up even more when the new term begins, and it'll be people with the usual issues: abortion, guns, school prayer. Both sides of the issues. Some are worth checking out; most aren't."

Díaz looked right at Graves. "Brent, sometimes you're too diplomatic for your own good. Why would the chief justice be in danger today because of some paper from as far back as the Civil War? Doesn't add up."

"I agree that this doesn't seem like a real and credible threat against Chief Justice Darlington, but I'm not ready to dismiss it without a bit of follow-up, either," Graves said, then glanced at one of his subordinates. "We have extra people at the chief justice's house?"

"Yes, sir. The detail was doubled as soon as we got the call from RIO."

"Don't alarm the chief justice. There's less than a month until the start of the new term, and she's always stressed this time of year. Plus, her husband has been ill. Make sure the house is secure. I'll order her a different car. Bring the other one back and comb through it, inside and out."

"What about Journey?" Tolman said.

"Meg, I'm going to follow your recommendation for follow-up. I'll send someone from our division here, and they can meet up with a Bureau person from the Oklahoma City field office, and go interview Journey. How far is this little town from Oklahoma City?"

"It's right on the Texas line," Tolman said. "A good two-and-a-half-hour drive."

"I hope they enjoy the scenery," Graves said, and the meeting was over.


As Tolman and Hudson left the Crystal City complex, Hudson said, "I'll drop you off at home."

"But my shoes are at the office."

"Surely you have more than one pair of shoes." He drove for a while and said, "You shouldn't antagonize our colleagues."

"They're not our colleagues. The Bureau, the Marshals,

everyone . . . they all think RIO was just a PR stunt by Congress, if they think of us at all."

Hudson sighed as he merged onto I-395. "Then why would they send us the number of cases they do?"

"You know very well why they send us cases. These are the cases they don't want to bother with. It's sure as hell not because they respect our investigative or research capabilities."

"You sell them too short. I've been watching you for five years, and you do this job so well. You're the best specialist in the office. You put together your cases brilliantly. But you are occasionally dismissive of our overall mission."

"Is there a point to this?"

"Meg, you've built up five years' experience. Your evaluations are perfect every quarter. You could get on with any number of other agencies."

"You trying to get rid of me?"

"Certainly not. I just do not understand why you stay with RIO with the way you feel about the office in general. I say this not only as your supervisor, but as your friend, too."

Tolman smiled. "It's about balance. Music is all emotion and expression and gut-wrenching feeling—at least it is when I'm doing it right. RIO is connections and information and assembling things, whether on paper or on a computer screen. Music is open-ended— it's always there, even when I'm not playing. With a RIO case, I immerse myself in it totally for days or weeks, and then it's closed and I move on. Balance. I've had precious little of that in my life."

"Your mother," Hudson said.

Tolman had told very few people about her mother's illness and the car crash. She'd told Hudson one Saturday at the office two years ago. She assumed he already knew, as it would have shown up in her preemployment background check. But he'd never brought it up, which earned him Tolman's respect. When she trusted him enough, she'd broached the subject herself.

"Yeah," Tolman said. "But not just her, not just her illness and the accident. My dad being in the Service, posted all over the coun try, moving every year or two. Then I was all about music, did the

Vienna year, flopped at it. Then the Academy, getting into that world. RIO helps me get a balance that I've never had. That, plus an understanding boss who doesn't give me shit about going off to perform."

"As long as you fill out your paperwork on time." Hudson smiled.

Tolman patted his arm. "Don't worry about me. You and RIO and I are all pretty well suited to each other, don't you think?"

"Speaking of performing, you have something at noon tomorrow, yes?"

Tolman closed her eyes. "The Vienna Kiwanis or Rotary or Lions Club luncheon or something like that. I can call and cancel in the morning."

"No, go ahead and play your performance. I can hold things down at the office for a few hours. I don't know if Graves and Díaz will need us again, but I'll deal with them."

Tolman looked at him in the dark truck. "Okay. I'll keep it, then. Thanks. It's not Vienna, Austria, but it'll have to do."

Five minutes later, the Dakota rolled down the Seminary Road exit, turned a sharp corner, and stopped in front of Seminary Hill Apartments. As Tolman put her hand on the car door, Hudson touched her shoulder and said, "Give me your best instinct. Is Nick Journey involved in a plot to assassinate Chief Justice Darlington?"

"No," Tolman said.

"Then tell me this: Does a plot exist to assassinate the chief justice and Journey is somehow connected to it? Or is he living a complete fantasy?"

Tolman hesitated a long moment. "I don't know."

Hudson nodded. "I thought you might say that."

"I may have more of a feel for it after I play the piano."

"You are a complicated and often frustrating woman, Meg. But I understand."

Tolman smiled. "I know you do," she said, and got out of the truck.

Journey dropped Andrew at Carpenter Center Middle School in the morning and stopped to talk for a moment with the special education teacher. The school was small, and Andrew was the only child with autism in the town, so there was no dedicated autism class, just a generalized special education classroom. Journey had fought for and won a personal assistant for Andrew, however, who had specialized training for children with autism. She was good with him, and he trusted her. After his experience with Amelia, that was rare for him, when it came to other people and his son.

He drove to the office and made it just in time for his eight thirty class, the jam-packed undergraduate section of U.S. History to 1877. He sleepwalked through the lecture and talked with a couple of students afterwards. Back upstairs, he went into his office and closed the door, wondering when Margaret Tolman—or someone like her—was going to get in touch with him.

He started to work on the jewelers. Of AAJE's 108 member companies, seventy-two had Web sites. Of those, Journey eliminated forty as not being in business long enough. Then he started making phone calls.

He called all thirty-two that remained. He reached two voice mail messages, three disconnect notices, and spoke to twenty-seven. None said the elliptical pin with G.W. engraved on it sounded familiar.

Journey went back to the AAJE Web site and started on the list of thirty-six companies that did not have Web sites. He would have to call every one of them, finding out how long they'd been in business. He started down the list.

The twenty-first jeweler was Detheridge and Company, with an address on West Forty-seventh Street in New York. A woman answered the phone, and Journey gave the now well-rehearsed speech.

"My name is Nick Journey. I'm a professor of history at South Central College of Oklahoma. May I ask how long your company has been in business?"

"Our longevity is our guarantee, Mr. Journey," the woman said. "We are one of the oldest family-run jewelers in the country. Detheridge and Company first opened in 1850."

"That's quite impressive in this day and age."

"Indeed it is. How may I help you?"

"I'm trying to trace a piece of jewelry to its manufacturer. Two pieces, actually. There's an older one that dates from around the time of the Civil War, and a newer one, very recent."

"Can you describe them?"

"They're both gold pins, with the kind of clasp that could go on a shirt collar. They're round, and have the letters G.W. engraved on them."

"Can you hold a moment, please?"

In less than a minute, the woman was back. "I thought it sounded familiar, but had to check with Don on the exact letters. Yes, we've been making those pieces for quite a long time."

Journey's hand tightened around the phone. "For how long?"

"I'm afraid I don't have details on the account, but Don is our senior engraver. He started with the company in 1953, and he remembers doing them every year."

"Do you . . . Do you know what the G.W. stands for?"

"Here, sir—I'll let you talk to Don."

In a moment, a whispery old man's voice said, "Don Ferguson."

"Mr. Ferguson, I'm asking about the G.W. pins that you've worked on over the years."

"What about them?"

"Do you know what the G.W. stands for?"

"Who are you?"

"My name's Nick Journey. I'm a historian from Oklahoma, and I'm—"

"Why do I want to talk to a historian from Oklahoma about some jewelry pieces? Let's say I don't want to. Let's say I have other work to do. You could be anyone."

"True," Journey said. "Does anyone else ever ask about those pieces?"

"No, never," the old man said a little too quickly.

Journey waited a moment, listening to Ferguson's wheezy breath. "You've been working on them for a long time."

"Hell of a long time. Have you seen any of them?"

"Yes, sir." Journey thought of the man in the parking lot, shooting at him, and how he'd taken the pin from his shirt. "One of them made its way to me not long ago. You do quality work."

"Damn right I do. New one, or an older one?"

"Fairly new."

"You have one?"

"It's in my hand right now."

"Turn it over. Tell me what you see on the back."

"You mean the little AAJE notch?"

"I'll be damned," Ferguson said. "Guess you do really have one of them. I never know what happens to those once they leave here. I never see any of the usual paperwork. Whatever member of the family is currently in charge comes down to me once a year and tells me how many to make. When I finish with them, I give them right back and that's it. No invoices, no work orders."

"The family? What family?"

"The Detheridge family, of course. We're still a family business. Little Gene Detheridge is in charge now. Every year, along about April, he comes down and tells me to make more of those pins, and tells me how many. Been that way as long as I can remember."

"Do you know what the letters mean?"

"See, that account's been active for as long as I've been around, and I've been here since Truman was president. Now *that* was a president, not like this dumb-ass Harwell in the White House now. Well, I took over that job from Ralph Detheridge himself. Members of the family used to do the actual work around here back then. Little Gene, he's not a jeweler. He just signs checks, doesn't do any real work. But he brings that G.W. order down to me every spring."

Journey felt like screaming.

"So," Ferguson went on, "Ralph used to do those pins, and he'd done them every year for thirty years or more. And you know, I asked him about those letters and he told me it was none of my god-damn business. His exact words. But I used to go out and drink with Ralph on occasion, and it didn't take much to get him talking. He told me that his father, Alden Detheridge Jr., and his grandfather, Alden Sr., made those pins, too."

"And?"

"One night when Ralph was loaded up on single-malt Scotch, I asked him about those pins, he said everything was going to be different when the Glory Warriors took over."

"Glory Warriors."

"G.W.—Glory Warriors. That's what he said. Of course, he was in his cups, and he never went drinking with me again after that. I think it was some kind of veterans' group. I'm a veteran myself. U.S. Marines, Korea, 1951. *Semper fi.* I belong to all of them, the VFW, the American Legion, and I never heard of these guys. Maybe it was just for officers or something. I don't know . . . the family keeps bringing me orders and I keep making the pins, though I'm going to have to turn the job over to someone younger one of these days."

"Glory Warriors," Journey said again.

"Don't know how Little Gene Detheridge is mixed up with them. He was never in the service, that's for sure. Hell of name for a bunch of old officers, don't you think? Like they never figured out the war was over. But then, look at this country now. I guess in one way or another, a war's never over, is it?"

Journey thanked the man and hung up. His heart was pounding again, and he felt a fringe of perspiration along his hairline. He realized he'd forgotten to take his blood pressure medication this morning. He fumbled around in his backpack and found his pills, then dry-swallowed two of them. He sat back down and tried to center his thoughts.

*Glory Warriors.*

*G.W.*

*"Dr. Journey! The document, now!"*

He'd been on the phone for over three hours, and hadn't checked for messages. He flipped open his phone again to see if he'd missed any calls. There were none.

He checked his e-mail again and copied down Meg Tolman's number, then called it. He heard the voice mail lead-in again: "This is Meg Tolman in the Research and Investigations Office. I'm away from my desk . . ."

Journey hung up. He thought again of the group whose name he now knew, and of the man from whose shirt he had torn the pin.

*The Glory Warriors.*

He felt very much alone.

# CHAPTER
# 19

Tolman's apartment was all neutral earth tones, neither cramped nor spacious. Much of the furniture had come from her grandmother's house, and the rest she had scavenged from yard sales. Friends had told her it looked like the home of a perpetual graduate student.

She woke early, called and checked in with Hudson—he was in the office by 7 A.M., even after the late night—then fed Rocky, her solid white, blue-eyed cat. She showered and dressed in black slacks and a simple white silk blouse. By ten thirty she was on the Metro, headed to Vienna in Fairfax County, the western terminus of the Metro's Orange Line. From the station, she walked two blocks to the small hotel where the monthly luncheon of the Fairfax County Kiwanis was held. Sixty or so members, mostly men, mostly middle-aged, ate the obligatory chicken and listened to three of their members talk about service projects and scholarships and the upcoming fall picnic. Tolman tuned them out—she'd played enough of these sorts of things to hear every possible variation on it many, many times.

Still distracted, she thought of Nick Journey.

*"I think the chief justice is going to be next."*

The words were softly spoken, hesitant. Tolman remembered the sound of the high-pitched wail in the background: the man's son, shrieking without words.

Tolman tried to drive the thoughts away. She heard "Margaret Isabell Tolman" off to her left, then a little polite applause. She rose, nodded to the group, and moved to the piano. She closed her eyes for a moment, letting the deep cleansing feeling of music begin to take hold. She raised her hands to begin a Rachmaninov prelude.

"Excuse me, Margaret."

Hands two inches above the keyboard, Tolman froze. She looked toward the voice. The man at the podium was looking at her.

"I know you have a program you've planned for us," the man said.

Tolman stared at him. The room was silent.

"But since our great tragedy this weekend with the death of the Speaker of the House, I wonder if you would take a moment and play our national anthem before you get to the rest of your program."

Tolman stared.

Feet shuffled, chairs scraped. People were getting to their feet and turning at a slight angle to face an American flag that rested on a stand in the corner of the room.

Tolman nodded. She knew the piece, of course. Any musician who played events like this had to keep it in their repertoire. *You'll have to wait a minute, Sergei,* she thought.

She lowered her hands, then stopped.

The national anthem.

*The rockets' red glare.*

*Bombs bursting in air.*

Michael Standridge and Kevin Lane. U.S. Army Special Forces, killed by improvised explosive devices in Iraq.

*Gave proof through the night, that our flag was still there.*

"Margaret?" said the man at the podium.

People began putting their hands over their hearts.

*The land of the free, the home of the brave.*

The brave. Elite troops. Standridge and Lane. Dead in Iraq in 2006, alive in Oklahoma last week.

*Our flag was still there.*

Still there.

*I know how to find them,* Tolman thought. *I know how to trace exactly where they are.*

She folded her hands back into her lap.

All eyes in the room were on her.

Tolman stood up. "I'm sorry," she said. "I have to go."

Before any of them could say a word, she was out the door of the meeting room, and then out of the hotel itself. She had to get to the office. She had to talk to Hudson. This wasn't something she could do alone. She would need the man's bureaucratic muscle.

Within fifteen minutes, she was on the Metro, headed back toward Washington.

"Rusty, I need a court order," Tolman announced as she walked into the office forty minutes after boarding the train in Vienna.

Hudson looked up from his computer. "Would you say that again, please?"

"I had a thought about how to track my anonymous shooters from Oklahoma."

"Meg, I thought you were playing the piano right now."

"I was, but I came back. They'll get over it." Tolman flopped into the chair across from Hudson. "I was sitting there in this hotel meeting room, with all these balding, graying men, and they asked me to play the national anthem, sort of as a tribute to Vandermeer."

"What does this have to do with a court order?"

"I was about to play it, and I thought of the words to the song, how our flag was still there and all that."

"Meg, I'm tired and not in a good mood."

"It made me think, that if these guys were killed in Iraq, there would be payments to their survivors. Land of the free, home of the brave. Brave guys who get killed defending their flag get benefits. If I get access to their bank records, and those of their families, I could see if benefits have been paid and when. If there were no survivors' benefits paid, then I can prove they aren't dead, even if the army says they are."

"You arrived at all this by thinking of the words to 'The Star-Spangled Banner.'"

"The power of music."

"Meg, these sorts of things aren't as simple as you seem to think they are. Digging around in our own databases is one thing, but accessing the bank records of private citizens is quite another."

"Jesus, Rusty, we're part of Homeland Security. File the request under the Patriot Act or something."

"Can you demonstrate a verifiable terrorist threat? You don't even know for certain that the men in the Journey incident are these same men who allegedly died in Iraq. I even called the Pentagon for you this morning. I got nowhere. I think that, for whatever reason, you're finding ways to look at this case that really have no bearing on the case itself."

Tolman leaned forward, folding her hands over the edge of Hudson's desk. "The facial-recognition program—"

"Perhaps you're putting too much faith in the program."

"Rusty, you got us the goddamn thing! Don't be such a fucking bureaucrat! What if someone—let's say whoever is behind the attack on Journey—really is after the chief justice?"

Hudson met her eyes. "Meg, I give you a great deal of latitude in how you speak to me and the way you go about your job. I do this because you are very, very good at your job and because I count you as a friend. But in most organizations, if a subordinate spoke to their supervisor the way you just spoke to me, they would be gone. You understand that, don't you?"

Tolman spread her hands apart. "Okay, I'm sorry. I have my father's mouth. But I can—"

"I think that because Nick Journey called you personally, and the threat assessment came about from that phone call, that you're internalizing a lot of this case. Díaz is far from my favorite person in the Bureau, but he's right—we have no evidence that shows anything about your shooters. Getting a federal court order to go about accessing private bank records is not done without having overwhelming evidence that the records will produce an indication either of criminal activity or the intent of future criminal activity."

"Rusty—"

Hudson stabbed a finger on his desktop. "I don't like dealing with the Pentagon. They are out of our realm of responsibility. I've told you this before. I called them, as a courtesy to you, but there is nothing there."

"Rusty—"

"That's enough. I'm sorry the case is frustrating for you." Hudson turned back to his computer. "By the way, you did very well in presenting at the threat assessment."

Tolman left Hudson's office without replying and fumed down the hall, kicking her own door closed behind her. *Where cases go to die.*

"Such a fucking bureaucrat," she said out loud. Tolman tapped her foot, thinking of "Weeping Willow," a Scott Joplin ragtime piece she'd been working on lately. Usually the thought of new music calmed her, but this time Joplin's syncopations didn't help. She rocked in her chair, moving papers around her desk.

"Shit," she finally said.

*"You are very, very good at your job,"* Hudson had told her.

Patronizing bullshit, or honest evaluation? She tended toward the latter. Hudson was a bureaucrat, but he was also honest with her.

*If he thinks I'm so good at my job, then I'm going to do my job.*

*With or without him.*

# CHAPTER

# 20

Journey somehow stumbled through a department meeting, though afterwards he couldn't remember any of what was said. He tried for an hour to work on his overdue journal article, typing a grand total of seven words. His mind was churning, and he couldn't seem to quiet it.

*The Glory Warriors.*

*"Some kind of veterans' group,"* the engraver from New York had said.

*This is no veterans' group,* Journey thought.

He left his office at two thirty. Three doors down, he leaned through the open door of Sandra's office, but she wasn't there. He felt vaguely embarrassed for having dragged her into this, for letting her peek into his life. When he saw her again, he would thank her and apologize for letting their professional relationship become muddled.

He paused for a moment at her door. A book sat on her desk next to her computer. Journey read the title: *Profound Autism in the Pre-Adolescent.* He'd read it a year ago himself. He looked at the book for a long moment, his feelings on unsure footing. Sandra had been very kind, and though she clearly didn't understand Andrew—most people didn't—neither did she seem put off by him.

Journey looked down at the book again. Sandra Kelly was smart, a good researcher, and by all accounts, very dynamic as a classroom lecturer. She was attractive and interesting, and Journey could not imagine that she was really interested in an out-of-shape, middle-aged man who had significant emotional baggage and a child with a severe developmental disability. That should set off all kinds of warnings for a younger, single woman, shouldn't it?

*Shouldn't it?* he thought, and for a few moments his mind wasn't on the Glory Warriors and Pete Parsons and the man he had killed. He finally turned from Sandra's doorway and walked away down the hall.

The Brekke Ranch was a small spread between Carpenter Center and Madill, which offered equestrian therapy for special needs children from across the region. Andrew rode two afternoons a week, and from the time Journey turned the minivan off Highway 70 onto the narrow, dusty gravel road that twisted a mile down to the ranch, the boy smiled. The twice-weekly rides were among very few things that Journey could say truly gave his son enjoyment.

In the larger of two arenas, horses made their way slowly around, each led by an adult and accompanied by a "side walker" on either side of the horse. On one horse sat a girl with muscular dystrophy. A boy from Ardmore, who also had autism, though not so profoundly as Andrew, sat on the other. The adults engaged the children during the ride, taking them through directions for the horse, playing games with large plastic rings and soft balls.

At Andrew's turn, he mounted the horse from a wooden platform to the side of the riding ring, and ever so subtly rubbed the horse's neck, the signal for the horse to move. Journey sighed. They were safe here. Andrew could actually engage in an activity he enjoyed under the September sun, with a hint of breeze from the south.

After the forty-five-minute ride, Andrew hooted and whistled happily as Journey buckled him into his seat. He drove up the winding path toward the highway, and as the blacktop came into view, he spotted a dark SUV parked on the far shoulder.

He'd seen it before. When he left Highway 70 and headed down the road to the ranch an hour earlier, it had turned off behind him, a few car lengths back, but had then stopped, executed a tricky turn-around, and headed back to the highway. He assumed the driver had simply taken a wrong turn.

The windows were tinted, but Journey could make out two forms in the front seats of the SUV. It had Texas plates. Journey stopped at the top of the ranch road, waiting a little too long to make his left turn onto 70. An eighteen-wheeler blew by, and then the highway was empty.

Journey sat still in his old minivan, gripping the steering wheel. Andrew whistled his three-note melody from the backseat.

Behind him, another car came from the direction of the ranch, a white four-door hatchback driven by a man of about his age with a salt-and-pepper beard and glasses. The man had three sons who came to the ranch with him each week, though only one of them actually rode.

Journey tapped the steering wheel three times.

He checked his rearview. The bearded man, whose name Journey could never remember, was peering through the windshield at him. One of the boys, a teenager with thick light brown hair and glasses like his father's, was leaning out the window. They were both staring at the back of the van.

The SUV hadn't moved.

The man in the white car tapped his horn once.

Journey slowly glanced into his mirror again. Andrew went on whistling.

*The Glory Warriors.*

So they weren't hiding from him. They weren't even trying to conceal themselves. They wanted him to know they were there.

He thought of the document, the startling yet ultimately inconclusive words of the page he'd been given at Fort Washita and that now rested in his backpack on the seat next to him.

*"Dr. Journey! The document, now!"*

The man in the hatchback leaned on his horn again, longer this time. One of the boys in the backseat—the youngest one, Journey thought—had lowered his window and yelled something.

He looked up at the SUV and its two shapeless forms in the

front seat. He nudged his foot off the brake and onto the accelerator. He turned in a wide arc onto Highway 70, then pulled slowly to the far shoulder.

The man with the three boys in the white car also turned left. They all stared at Journey's minivan as they drove past him.

Journey inched the old van forward, facing the wrong way on the shoulder, until he was nose-to-nose with the black SUV, their front grilles three feet apart. He put the van into park, lowered the window, and waited.

Andrew squirmed. He'd stopped whistling and was looking out the window, across the rolling green fields of Marshall County. In a moment, Journey heard a tapping—Andrew had found a straw and a pencil.

Journey thought he knew what the original Glory Warriors had done, stockpiling weapons for an armed rebellion in case the post–Civil War federal government was destabilized. But the details were presumably in the pages that had not yet been found. And why were the modern-day Glory Warriors trying to bring about the very de-stabilization their forebears feared?

He could just give them the document and be done with it. He and Andrew would be safe.

*And maybe they'd just kill me anyway, once they had it in their hands.*

Journey gripped the steering wheel, a muscle working in his jaw. Andrew hummed.

Dallas Three Gold sat behind the wheel of the SUV and stared as the professor's old minivan pulled up facing him. "What the hell's he think he's doing?"

"He's out of his fucking mind," said Silver in the seat beside him.

Gold waited. "Maybe. But maybe not."

He flipped open his cell phone and called Bronze, who was back in Carpenter Center. He explained the situation. "Call base and re-quest orders," he said. "Do we approach?"

"Roger that on the request," Bronze said. The Bronze member of every team was the transportation and communications liaison, while Gold and Silver were field operatives. "Keep this line open."

Gold looked out the tinted windshield. He could very clearly see Nick Journey, sitting there tapping his finger on the steering wheel. His son was in the seat behind him, his head moving in strange, jerky motions.

Bronze was back on the phone. "Do not approach. Stay alert, do not approach. He's only trying to tell us that he knows we're here. Remember that he is an amateur. That's direct from Dallas Base."

"Roger that," Gold said, then closed the phone. "But amateurs are unpredictable."


Journey sat still for two full minutes, staring through the windshield. A droplet of sweat formed and ran into his eye, making him blink.

Behind him, he heard Andrew fidgeting.

"Hang on, son," he said.

Several cars came and went on Highway 70. A couple slowed as if to help—this was rural Oklahoma, after all, and that was what people did—but Journey waved them away.

Another minute passed.

Journey flexed and unflexed his hands. He blinked again. He'd detected vague movement from inside the big SUV, but nothing else.

*Each of us knows the other is here. But they don't know what to make of me right now. I'm just a college professor with high blood pressure, and they can't tell whether I'm brave or just stupid.*

*Neither can I,* he thought after another moment, but the grain of anger, hot and hard, hadn't gone away.

Another minute. The interior of the van seemed stifling, as if he'd gone to a higher elevation with thinner air.

"Wait right here, Andrew," he said; then Journey slowly opened the door of the van.


"What the fuck does he think he's doing?" Silver said.

Gold shook his head without speaking and undid the clasp on the holster that held his H&K assault pistol.

*       *       *

Gravel crunched under Journey's feet as he shuffled out of the van. He passed between the two vehicles, feeling the heat from his engine. He crossed to the driver's side of the SUV, two steps away from the highway. A truck roared past, and Journey felt the blast of wind tugging at his clothes.

He stood at the driver's door, motionless. Another drop of perspiration ran into his eye, but this time he didn't blink.

There was a small electronic hum, and the window came down.

"May I help you?" the driver asked, as if he were a clerk in a store and Journey was a customer.

Journey said nothing, kicking at a stray piece of gravel. He settled his gaze on the driver, thinking of his baseball days, how he had stared down the hitters. He was never physically imposing, so he was always left to the mental game to gain an advantage. He'd been told he had quite a stare.

The silence stretched for a minute.

A breeze came up. A little piece of cardboard blew from one side of the highway to the other. Journey heard his son humming, even from within the van. Then Andrew suddenly loosed a scream.

The SUV driver's head jerked as if he'd been poked in the face by a pencil.

"I know who you are," Journey said.

The driver, looking confused from Andrew's shriek, glanced back toward Journey, staring through the lenses of his mirrored sunglasses. His lips parted slightly, then closed again.

"Glory Warrior," Journey said.

The man in the passenger's seat said, "What do you think you—?"

The driver silenced him with a look, then turned back to face Journey.

"I guess you don't wear your little pins on a T-shirt like that. No place to hide them. Where are they? In your pocket, maybe? I bet you have your pins on you somewhere."

The driver said nothing. Andrew screamed again.

"I have to take care of my son," Journey said, "but let me tell you one thing, and you can pass it on up the line. The document you want? I have it, and I've read it. It's incomplete. There was only one page buried at Fort Washita."

The driver's head dipped an inch or two.

"That's right. It's not all there." Journey leaned in. He could smell the leather of the SUV's seats. "But I'm going to find it, and I'm the only person in the world right now who has a clue how to go about finding it. You see, the person who wrote the document left a little mystery to solve."

The driver took off his sunglasses. His eyes were blue and cold.

Journey nodded. "You leave my son and me alone. If something happens to me, you'll never see the rest of the pages."

Journey turned around and shuffled back to his van. He slammed the door. He felt surprisingly calm, his fingers curling over the steering wheel. Andrew screamed, then hummed.

"Yes, we're going soon," he said. "It won't be long."

Thirty seconds later, he heard the SUV's engine turn over. The big vehicle backed away from him and pulled onto Highway 70.

Journey sagged against the wheel. He wiped his sweaty forehead.

"All right," he said. "All right, then."

Halfway back to Carpenter Center, his cell phone rang. It was Sandra.

"Nick, I'm glad I caught you. Are you coming back to the office today?"

"No, I was headed home. But Sandra—" He remembered the book in her office, how this woman had been reading up on autism in an effort to . . . what? To find more of a connection with him? He shook his head—she was still the only person he'd talked to about all that had happened. "I found out who G.W. is. Can you meet me at my house in ten minutes?"

There was a moment's silence. "Of course," she said. "We have a lot to talk about, because I think I found the Poet's Penn."

# CHAPTER

# 21

Washington Two exited the Beltway and headed west through the rolling Virginia countryside. At the town of Herndon, in the westernmost reaches of Fairfax County, he maneuvered the suburban streets to Spring Street Park. Passing towering evergreens, he left his car in the lot and continued on foot to a walking trail, winding deeper into the park. At a wide spot where a bench sat alongside the trail, he veered off and hiked into the trees. Thirty feet from the walkway, he bent down behind a tree and retrieved a manila envelope.

Two cell phones were in the envelope, one marked with a strip of red electrician's tape on the back. Tucked in with the phones were two sheets of paper filled with computer printing. He read the instructions quickly, skimming the technical description of how the phone with the red strip had had its lithium-ion battery modified, and about the general instability of lithium-ion batteries and what could be expected from the resulting explosion.

Washington Two read the pages several times, then pulled out his own phone and called the Judge. "I have the phones and the briefing papers," he said, then went silent.

"You didn't call to tell me that," the Judge said. "Speak up. If you have something else to say, get on with it."

"I've been trying to think of a way to make it happen without losing a man."

"What do you mean? No other Glory Warriors should be anywhere nearby."

"No, I don't mean us. I mean . . . the chief justice's driver. She has a driver. They work in shifts. I know all of them personally."

"Casualties of war," the Judge said. "You've been working your way to this position for nearly twenty years, to help bring us to this moment. You're not telling me that you're having second thoughts now, after all this time, are you? Just because of a driver whose name you happen to know?"

"No. I had just hoped there would be a different way."

The Judge said nothing.

Washington Two cleared his throat. "I'll handle it."

"Good," the Judge said. "It has to move quickly."

"I know."

He put the two phones and the papers back into the envelope; then Senior Inspector Brent Graves of the United States Marshals Service turned and headed back down the slope toward the trail.


Half an hour later, Graves pulled into the massive parking lot of the General Services Administration's Fleet Management Center in Springfield. Graves showed his ID twice and was led to the garage where fleet cars scheduled for pickup waited. He spied two of his team members and was waved toward a black Town Car. Graves slipped the phone with the red strip into the pocket of his suit coat.

Senior Inspector Pickett, a tall black-haired woman who had taken part in the threat-assessment meeting, met Graves halfway across the garage. "We're good to go," she said. "Inspection is complete, and we just need to sign her out."

Graves nodded. His grip tightened around the phone in his pocket. "Okay, you two go and finish the paperwork. I want to do a quick once-over myself."

Pickett looked at him. "You really think this one's any more serious than the garden-variety nutcases?"

"No, not really. But it's just strange enough that I feel justified in sweeping the house, switching the car, and doing the extra detail."

"Mmm, overtime."

"Your tax dollars at work," Graves said.

Pickett walked away, smiling, to meet up with Thornton, a tall young soft-spoken officer. Graves watched them go. *I know them personally,* he'd told the Judge. Them, and twenty others like them, part of the permanent detail for Supreme Court security. He worked with them every day. He knew their spouses and children. By contrast, he'd met the Judge face-to-face only a handful of times over the past twenty-plus years.

Graves circled the Town Car. Pickett had left the driver's door open. He felt the underside of the seat, then ran his hand along and under the instrument panel. He repeated the action on the opposite side, then for the backseats. Graves popped the trunk and inspected the spare tire storage area.

He leaned farther into the trunk, his hand closing on the phone in his suit pocket. He made a show of pulling up the carpet in the trunk and running his hands all along the spare tire compartment. In one smooth motion, he pulled the phone out of his pocket, holding it flat against his palm. He wedged it alongside the Town Car's wheel well, directly behind the gas tank. He replaced the carpet and smoothed it out.

When he straightened, his heart was pounding. Graves brushed his upper lip. Pickett and Thornton were headed back toward him. He would have to check the duty roster—he wanted to know which of them, or of the remaining members of the detail, would be assigned to Chief Justice Darlington tomorrow morning.

*Casualties of war,* the Judge had said.

*A hell of a different kind of war,* Graves thought. The politicians talked a lot about wars on poverty or drugs or terror, and not much ever changed. Graves no longer had the same fire for the cause as he'd had twenty years ago. Until recently, the Glory Warriors had even become a bit of an abstraction to him. The "Washingtons" gathered from time to time and talked in sweeping tones about what they would do when the time finally came, and then they all went back to work and lived their everyday lives. The nation's problems were attacked from the right or the left, and still nothing was accomplished.

Graves had no illusions about Robert E. Lee and Ulysses S. Grant and their grand secret agreement the Judge had talked of for so long. Graves was just weary of stupidity and ineptitude. He wasn't even gripped by the "patriotic" fervor of so many of the other Glory Warriors, who professed to be disgusted by how the nation was viewed from both within and without and wanted to "take back their country," whatever that meant. Graves was a practical man, not an ideologue. He just wanted to make things work, and they hadn't worked for a long time.

But first, he had to get through tomorrow, the first time his two worlds—the one he lived in the shadows and the "real" one, though after this many years, it was hard to say which was which—would meet, with thunderous results.

Graves swallowed, trying not to think about Thornton and Pickett and Hagy and Crowson and Gill and all the other members of the Judicial Security Division, the people whose faces he saw every day.

*Casualties of war.*

"Looks good," he said. "You know me, though. I have to double-check for myself, control freak that I am."

Pickett and Thornton smiled. They knew their boss, after all.

"All right," Graves said. "Put it in service, and sign the current car back in. I'm headed to the office."

He walked back to his own car, and Washington Two made himself stop thinking about his Marshals Service subordinates. He couldn't afford to be distracted now.

When he turned onto his street, Journey immediately saw the two cars: one was a silver four-door, something generic like a Toyota or Honda, the other a green VW Beetle, one of the new ones. Both cars sat in front of his house.

As he approached the house, he saw the three figures in the yard. Two were men in dark suits, white shirts, nondescript ties. Sandra stood with them, talking and gesturing with both hands.

Journey pulled into the driveway, cut the ignition, and sat for a moment while the engine ticked. He reached over the seat, unbuckled Andrew's safety belt, and motioned at the boy to open his car door. By the time Journey was out of the car, Sandra was striding toward him.

"Nick, these men are from the government," she said. "They were here when I drove up."

"It's about time."

Both men were of indistinct middle age, well built but clearly not gym freaks, white. One wore round silver glasses. They both produced ID cases. The one with the glasses spoke first. "Mr. Journey, I'm Special Agent Winters, FBI, Oklahoma City field office."

The other man nodded. "Senior Inspector Hendrickson of the

Judicial Security Division, U.S. Marshals Service, Washington. We'd like to talk to you for a few minutes, sir."

"Judicial security." He met Hendrickson's eyes.

"Let's talk inside, if we may, sir."

"What about this Tolman woman?"

"Could we please go inside, Mr. Journey?"

Throughout the exchange, Sandra watched all three with a critical eye. She lagged behind as the three men started for the house. "Come on in, Sandra."

Special Agent Winters looked uncomfortable.

"Dr. Kelly is aware of everything that I know," Journey said. "She should hear whatever you have to say."

Hendrickson made a *lead the way* gesture with his hand. Andrew hummed. Inside, Journey tossed his keys onto his desk and said, "Just a moment, gentlemen." He quickly took Andrew to the bathroom and changed him, then took the boy to his bedroom and turned on his music. In another minute, Andrew was whistling.

When he returned to the living room, Sandra was sitting in the armchair. The two government men were still standing. "Sit down," Journey said, and motioned them to the couch. "You're here investigating a threat against the chief justice."

Hendrickson nodded. "A threat assessment was convened last night based on your phone call to Meg Tolman at the Research and Investigations Office. I'm here to determine whether the threat merits further investigation."

Journey nodded. He unzipped his backpack, withdrew the plastic sleeve, and handed it to Hendrickson. "Here's the original document. Under the circumstances, I think the Oklahoma Historical Society will understand if I surrender custody of it to you."

Hendrickson looked at the page for a couple of seconds, then at Journey. "Tell us what happened, please."

Journey told them all of it, starting with the Fort Washita discovery, the attack at the college, the dead man, the Glory Warriors, ending with the assassination of the Speaker of the House. Winters and Hendrickson listened without interrupting. Winters looked at the paper occasionally, taking off his glasses and tapping them against his knee. The motion reminded Journey of Andrew with his straw.

When he finished, they were all silent for a few moments. Sandra was in the chair, hands steepled in front of her face, fingertips to her lips. She met Journey's eyes with a *What more can you do?* look.

"You believe the shooting of Speaker Vandermeer is related to a threat against the chief justice," Winters said. It was a statement, not a question.

"Read the wording," Journey said. "Ultimately, they'll go after the president."

"What is their reasoning?"

"I've told you all I know. My guess is that they're preparing for some kind of power grab based on this." Journey pointed at the page in Winters's lap.

"A power grab," Hendrickson said.

"You're aware," Winters said, "that the prevailing theory at the moment is that Speaker Vandermeer's death was an act of random violence. There's no evidence of an organized group. Believe me, the Bureau is investigating every possibility, but ordinarily there would be some claim of responsibility, and there's been no credible claim so far."

"You say there's more to this document?" Hendrickson said.

"Yes. I mean, I think there has to be. This page alone doesn't make clear what their goals are. It just lays out the circumstances."

"And you believe this document was signed by Robert E. Lee and Ulysses S. Grant in 1865?"

"At Appomattox, yes."

"And it's your contention that the group you're calling the Glory Warriors is using this as a rationale to conduct assassinations today?"

Journey raised his hands and let them drop back to his lap.

"Surely you don't believe in coincidences," Sandra said.

Everyone looked at her.

"This document comes to light," she said, "with the first 'provision' on its list being the assassination of the Speaker of the House, and then Vandermeer is killed."

"Ms. Kelly . . . ," Winters said.

"It's *Dr.* Kelly, thank you."

"Dr. Kelly, this paper says nothing about assassination. It says 'removal is accomplished by conspiratorial means.'"

"What exactly do you think that is?" Sandra said, leaning forward. "It's not talking about elections and Senate confirmation hearings, is it?"

Winters was silent, then handed the page to Hendrickson.

Journey looked at both of them. "I sound like a conspiracy nut."

No one spoke.

"Don't patronize me," Journey said. "You think I'm crazy. Go ahead, run your background check on me, if you haven't already. You won't find any kind of extremism there. I'm an academic, a scholar, a father. I'm not an anti-government nut, and I'm not a radical. My politics are dead center."

Hendrickson rattled the paper, tracing a finger along it. "What's this business at the bottom? The Poet's Penn and waters falling. What do you make of that?"

"I think . . . ," Journey said, then stopped.

"Yes?"

"I think it's meant to lead to the rest of the pages."

"Like a clue," Winters said. With effort, a small smile worked its way onto his face.

"Something like that."

"Sort of like a puzzle," the FBI agent said. "Like *The Da Vinci Code*?"

Journey felt his temperature rising. He looked at the two men, then at Sandra. He remembered her words on the phone—*I think I've found the Poet's Penn.* Her green eyes found his again.

*They don't believe it,* the look said. *They're going through the motions. They won't believe anything you tell them.*

Journey dropped the gaze after looking into Sandra's eyes for a long moment. He turned back toward the couch. "You gentlemen are familiar with the Oklahoma City bombing, aren't you?"

Both men nodded.

"Do you remember the man in Arizona, the one who was a friend of McVeigh's? McVeigh told him what he was going to do. He didn't believe it, so he didn't tell anyone. The FBI found him later, and he was convicted of knowing about the plot but not telling anyone about it."

"What's your point?" Winters said. The smile was gone, the voice hard.

Journey pointed at the paper. "I've tried to do my duty, to let the proper authorities know about what I think is a real threat. What more can I do, if you choose not to believe me?"

"No one said we didn't believe you," Hendrickson said. "As a matter of fact, we've increased security on Chief Justice Darlington's detail. We take threats very seriously."

"Some more than others."

"Yes."

The two government men stood. "We'll see what the investigation turns up," Winters said.

Journey watched them leave, watched the silver four-door pull away from his house. Sandra stood beside him at the door. "They think I'm insane," Journey said. "Granted, it sounds that way."

"You gave them the page. It's out of your hands now."

Journey turned to face her. She was so close, he could feel her breath. "I made a copy," he said. "But if I were them, I wouldn't buy it, either." He shook his head and backed away from the door.


In the car, Special Agent Winters drove, passing back through Carpenter Center to Highway 70, where he turned toward Madill. "You came a long way for this," he said.

"Tell me about it," Hendrickson said. "And I'll get on a plane and be back in D.C. tonight."

Two and a half hours later, they were in the FBI's Oklahoma City field office, in a new modern complex along Memorial Road in the far north part of the city. Winters let Hendrickson use a spare computer, and the JSD man logged in to the Department of Justice database. He got no hits for "Glory Warriors" in the extensive files on terrorist cells or domestic extremist groups. In fact, there was no reference to the name in any of the DOJ databases at all.

After an hour on the computer, Hendrickson gave up and called D.C. "We met with Nick Journey," he said. "He spun a pretty good historical tale, but in the end, there's no evidence to support the existence of any kind of organized plot against the chief justice, and nothing tying her to Vandermeer. There's nothing anywhere in the database to indicate the existence of the group Journey talked about.

I think the guy is wrapped up in his history, and is attaching a lot more importance to this old document than he should."

"Did he give you the document?" said the voice from Washington.

"It's in my hand now."

"Bring it. Write your report and we'll add it to the file; then the file will be closed."

"Maybe this one should have stayed with RIO," Hendrickson said.

"They had to bring it to us, though. You know they did."

"Yeah. You going to keep the extra people on the chief?"

"Just through the night, I think, to be on the safe side. Come on home, and be sure to fill out your travel paperwork."

"Will do," Hendrickson said.

"We had to check it out," said Senior Inspector Brent Graves. "At least we can say we did our job."

# CHAPTER

# 23

Sandra watched the two agents drive away while Journey checked on Andrew. When he returned to the living room, Sandra said, "They didn't buy a single word of it. I have a lot of cops in my family. I have one cousin who used to be a deputy U.S. marshal, one in Customs, and lots of others who are city police. I know a lot of cops, and I'm telling you, these two didn't get it and they think this is just another stupid conspiracy theory, and they're not going to do a damn thing about it."

Journey looked up at her sudden vehemence. Something kicked at the back of his mind. "Sandra . . . why are you here?"

She turned her head halfway, as if the question had caught her off guard. She tucked a strand of red hair behind her ear. "What do you mean? You asked me to meet you here."

Journey made an all-encompassing gesture. "No, I don't just mean right now, this minute. I mean all this. You don't need to be part of it. Don't you have a class?"

"I had class this morning. I'm just trying to help."

"Why? I mean . . ." Journey went quiet for a moment—he couldn't quite grasp the thoughts tumbling through him. "You don't have to help me."

Sandra's eyes—those intense, burning green eyes—bore into his. "I can't just go home and forget about it now. Like I said—"

"I know, you're just trying to help. I saw the book on your desk."

"The book . . ." Sandra's voice trailed away.

"The one on autism."

"Oh. I don't know that much about it, so I thought I'd do a little research. Being around Andrew a little bit has made me . . . curious." She cleared her throat. "That sounds lame, doesn't it?"

"You don't have to do anything for me. I appreciate it, but you don't have to."

Sandra took a step forward. "I think you're not used to anyone offering to help you with anything. And I'm not just talking about this whole thing with the treaty and Vandermeer."

Journey said nothing.

"I never met your wife," Sandra said. "She was gone before I started here. But some of the other people in the department have told me she was—"

Journey looked up at her. "Say it."

"That she couldn't deal with Andrew. That she sort of signed out where he was concerned."

Journey was silent.

"You know, people respect you," Sandra said. "For doing what you do with him."

"Well, they shouldn't," Journey said. "He's my son. It's my job."

"I know that. *Everyone* knows that. Believe it or not, accepting a little help from someone doesn't make you a lesser man or a lesser father. Look, I really don't have any expectations, Nick. You trusted me with the document. I know that was a big deal for you. I can help you a little."

Journey looked up at her. In the other room, Andrew hooted. Finally he dropped his eyes from Sandra's. "These two cops . . . I wonder what happened to the other one, this woman who e-mailed me asking for information. The one I called. Why wasn't she part of this?"

"If it was perceived to be an actual threat against Justice Darlington, they'd have to hand it off. The FBI investigates threats, the Marshals Service provides security."

Journey looked at her.

"I told you. Cops galore in my family. I hear a lot of this kind of thing."

"Maybe I *am* losing it, and maybe there isn't any threat against the chief justice. But *something* is going on." He went on to tell her what he'd learned about the Glory Warriors, and about his encounter with the two men on the highway.

"And you faced them down, just like that?" Sandra said when he'd finished.

"Brave or stupid, do you think?"

"Maybe a little of both." They shared tight smiles. "What were you thinking?"

Journey hesitated. "They were just sitting there, pretty as you please, not even trying to conceal themselves. I called them on it. I'm not going to hide from them."

"Nick, these are the kind of people who shoot at you. *They shot at you.* You can't just walk up to people like that and have a reasonable conversation with them."

Journey shrugged. "What was I supposed to do?"

"I don't know, but marching up to them and getting in their faces a few days after what happened to you would not be high on my list."

"What they did to me, and to Pete Parsons, makes me angry. The other things they're doing make me angry. And the fact that no one is taking this seriously just makes matters worse. I'm trying to do what's right, and the only ones paying attention are the ones who were shooting at me."

"Well, I'm paying attention," Sandra said.

"You know what I meant."

"I guess I do." She sighed. "Let me tell you about the Poet's Penn."

"What is it?"

"I told you my brother is an English prof. Even he had to dig to find it. *The Poet's Penn* was a very small, very obscure literary journal that was published in Louisville, Kentucky, from 1858 to 1864."

"It ended the year before the war was over," Journey said.

"Right. And the double n *was* a wordplay. The editor—and as far as my brother could find, the only contributor—was named

David Stanton. He had originally come from Pittsburgh to settle in Louisville."

"So the double n was for Pennsylvania."

"Stanton's clever way of paying tribute to his home state."

Journey leaned forward. "Did your brother know about the reference to the waters running and the strong bending?"

"No such luck. Remember, this was a very small journal. Stanton evidently had a patron, a Louisville banker, who supported him because he liked Stanton's work. The journal was never circulated very widely; then it folded, presumably because the funding ran out. Stanton lived until 1908, but never published another word. He was apparently something of a traveling photographer for the rest of his life."

"Is there an archive of the journal? Even the most obscure publications show up *somewhere*."

"Randy couldn't find any evidence of a library archive, but there is one place where some issues of the journal are transcribed online."

"But I already did an online search for it."

"That's because in this archive, the person doing the posting refused to spell the title of the journal with the double n. She insisted on using the standard spelling of *pen* and then putting an asterisk beside it with a note about Stanton. Here's the Web address."

Sandra pulled out a piece of notepaper and handed it to Journey. "Belgium? You must be kidding. The archive of an obscure American literary journal is on a Web site originating in Belgium?"

Sandra shrugged. "Stranger things have happened. It's a grad student in literature, who is studying American poetry of the nineteenth century. This isn't the only journal she's put up. There are several others, equally obscure."

"Have you looked at it yet?"

Sandra shook her head. "I wanted to bring it to you first."

"Let's see what we have, then." Journey turned toward his computer and began typing in the URL, which was long and filled with numbers and symbols. When the page settled onto the screen, it was very simple, with few graphics and a generic light blue background. Three buttons filled the monitor: NEDERLANDS, FRANÇAIS, ENGLISH.

"Dutch, French, and English," Sandra said, reading over Journey's shoulder, her hand resting on the back of the chair.

He clicked on the English button and waited for the page to change, then read the new page.

Hello!

This is the Web page of Sherri Blake. I am a doctoral student in Comparative Literature at the University of Liege, Belgium. Originally from Sioux Falls, South Dakota, USA, I earned my undergraduate degree from the University of Sioux Falls. My master's degree is from the University of Lausanne, Switzerland. My research area is mid-nineteenth-century American literature, with special emphasis on the distinctive voices of regional literary and poetry journals and the work of "undiscovered" writers whose works were known regionally but never achieved wider recognition. This Web site is dedicated to archiving several such journals.

Journey scrolled down the page to a list of the journals Sherri Blake was in the process of archiving.

*Minnesota's Voice*—Minneapolis, Minnesota (1835–1838)
*Quarterly Literature Review*—Mobile, Alabama (1842–1861)
*The West*—Los Angeles, California (1852–1868)
*Once I Dream'd*—Chancellorsville, Virginia (1860–1861)
*Authors and Poets*—Somerville, Massachusetts (1830–1888)
*The Poet's Pen**—Louisville, Kentucky (1858–1864)

Journey read the appended note about the double-n reference, then clicked the title.

*The Poet's Pen**was published in Louisville, Kentucky, and appears to have been solely dedicated to the poetry of David Stanton, a native of Pittsburgh, Pennsylvania, who settled in Louisville in 1853. At its highest circulation, *The Poet's Pen* published 300 copies in the summer quarter of 1864. Stanton's work, though not widely known, was highly regarded in the area. His publication of a poem in a local newspaper caught the eye of prominent banker Samuel B. Williams, who financed the journal for six years. David Stanton's poems are generally reflective of the area and its people and paint an enlightening picture of a border area during the period leading up to and during the American Civil War.

Journey looked at his watch—it was past six o'clock. He glanced at Sandra. "Don't you need to do something, Sandra? This is going to be tedious work. I can—"

Andrew came into the room, tapping his straw and pencil. He passed both adults and lowered himself onto the floor in front of the couch.

"Hi, Andrew," Sandra said, and waggled her fingers at him.

He jabbed a flat hand in her direction.

"Hey, he acknowledged me," Sandra said, and grinned.

"We've been working on that," Journey said. "The waving is a big deal, getting him to acknowledge coming and going, or that people are talking to him." He looked at Andrew and smiled. "That's good waving, son."

"Do you want me to leave?" Sandra said.

Journey was silent a moment. "I think I need some time to process this."

Sandra nodded. "I'll take that as a yes, then."

"I'm not trying to be rude," Journey said.

"I know." Sandra stood up. "This is one of my nights to work out at the gym anyway, and I have a couple of other errands to run." As she passed the couch, she said, "See you later, Andrew."

Andrew looked at her and made the flat-hand motion again.

Journey smiled. "That's good. He's really acknowledging you well. It usually takes him a lot longer to get used to someone new— what they look like, what they sound like, maybe even what they smell like."

Sandra paused with her hand on the door. "Talk to you later."

"Yeah." She stepped through the doorway onto the porch. "Sandra?" he said, and she turned.

"Why don't you go to the gym, do what you need to do, then stop back by later? Maybe I'll know something in a few hours."

"Maybe so," she said, and walked to her car.

Journey watched her go, closed the door behind her, and stopped at the couch. He found the porcupine ball that Marvin Colbert had given Andrew, and tossed it back and forth a few times before the boy decided he was more interested in squeezing the ball and feeling the little puff of air against his face. Journey looked at his son for a long moment. Sandra's scent was still in the room. He wondered if Andrew could smell it as well.

Journey didn't feel like cooking, so he opted for the traditional fall-back of the single father: pizza delivery. Plain cheese pizza for Andrew, sausage and jalapeños and mushrooms for himself. They ate quickly, and Journey washed the pizza sauce from his son's face. He let Andrew watch Animal Planet on television for a while as he was drawn back to the computer, to *The Poet's Penn* and the verses of David Stanton.

By seven thirty, he'd read up through the 1862 editions of the journal. He gave Andrew his bath, as always trying to get his son to use the washcloth on himself. Andrew rubbed the cloth halfheartedly around his hands and neck, then became fixated on the bathtub faucet and flapped both hands in the water while vocalizing loudly. Same routine with drying—Andrew dried his face and feet repeatedly, ignoring the rest of his body while he dripped all over the floor. Journey helped him into his loose-fitting nighttime sweatpants and SCCO T-shirt. Their usual routine involved getting him to bed and reading to him, everything from Dr. Seuss to historical journals. Andrew never wanted to look at pictures in books, but he understood that it was bedtime when his father sat on his bed with a book. Sometimes the routine worked. Sometimes Andrew was agitated and would lie in bed, screaming and laughing at nothing, for an hour or more. Tonight he was calm, and Journey slipped quietly out of his room after reading to him.

Back at the computer, he touched the keyboard and the screen saver—an image of him holding Andrew as a newborn, with Amelia carefully cropped out of the picture—vanished, replaced by *The Poet's Penn*.

David Stanton had come from Pittsburgh, so Journey assumed his wartime sympathies lay with the Union, though the poet never took sides in his writing, which was highly unusual for the time.

He lived in Louisville, Kentucky, a border city in a border state. Kentucky had remained part of the Union, but with strong Southern tendencies. Louisville itself, thanks to its strategic position on the Ohio River, was an important supply depot for the Union throughout the war. Still, Stanton appeared neutral, chronicling in verse the horrors of war to both sides, to all sides.

At three minutes after nine, Journey read:

*In the gloaming of day, Twilight between blue and gray.*
*Where the strong river bends, Toward its bitter and bloody end.*
*There is no grace nor light, O'er the battle's hot black night.*
*So to leave the dead and forget the lame, All these men who sleep with*
  *no name.*
*'Tis a cold glory crowning warriors all, Lo! The waters rage and fall.*

Journey looked at the words again. He slowly pulled the photocopy of the Fort Washita document from the pile on his desk.

*The Poet's Penn causes the strong to bend and makes the waters fall.*

Journey reached out his hand and touched the computer monitor.

*Where the strong river bends . . .*
*Lo! The waters rage and fall.*

It was one section of a long and rambling poem Stanton had published in the summer of 1864. Journey scrolled back up the screen to the top of the page, where he read the poem's title: "Ruminations on the War, At the Falls of the Ohio."

# CHAPTER

# 24

Sandra was back at nine thirty, wearing workout gear and sipping from a bottle of water. "The Falls of the Ohio," Journey said before she was through the door.

She raised one eyebrow at him. He motioned her to the sofa and handed her a printout of David Stanton's poem.

Sandra read it, her brow furrowing. "The strong bends and the waters fall. Esoteric, but it fits."

Journey nodded. "It raises more questions, but it seems to answer one, at least, and that is that the next piece of this thing has to do with the Falls of the Ohio. I was in Louisville a few times when I played ball, but I don't know that area well."

Sandra drank water. "I grew up in southern Illinois, not all that far downriver from there. My parents took me to the Falls once when my brothers and I were little. It's really not a falls per se, not like Niagara, but more a series of rapids, and the river lowers in elevation over the course of a couple of miles. It's famous for the fossil beds that are uncovered when the river is low."

"I did a little online research a few minutes ago. There's a state park there now, on the Indiana side of the river. A lot has changed since the Civil War."

"They put in dams through there a long time ago. At one time, it was considered the only real navigational obstacle on the entire Ohio." Sandra put down her water bottle. "So this cryptic note points to the Falls of the Ohio. What is there? The rest of this document? More weapons, or something else altogether?"

"Good question," Journey said. "And here's another question: Who did this? David Stanton? How would he have been able to get close to both Lee and Grant? Besides, if you read some of his prose pieces in the journal, and then you read this first page of the Fort Washita document, it doesn't sound anything like him."

Sandra read the poem again. "Here he talks about 'the bitter and bloody end' and 'cold glory crowning warriors.' But the Grant and Lee paper is so . . . I don't know, more formal, businesslike."

"So if Stanton didn't write this—" Journey tapped the photocopied document three times. "—then who did?"

"And what's the connection between this and the Glory Warriors?"

"I think the answer is in the rest of the pages to this document. Whoever did this went to great pains to protect it. We think he was in Appomattox on April ninth, 1865, at Lee's surrender. At some point after that, he was around Fort Washita. He could easily have gone from Appomattox to Louisville, either on horseback or even part of the way by train. Some of the rail lines were still running. The war had cut off a lot of them, but not as much the farther west you went. Louisville was a major steamboat port then. He could get on a boat there and go to the Mississippi, then get another boat on the Arkansas River to Fort Smith, buy a horse, and ride the rest of the way here."

"But again, why?" Sandra said. "What's the purpose of all this?"

"I'm hoping I find that out at the Falls of the Ohio."

"You're not thinking of going there yourself? Aren't you going to give this information to the cops? Call those two who were here."

"You said yourself that they didn't take me seriously, that they're not going to do anything."

"You can't just take off like that. What about your classes?"

"My TA, Clark, will cover them. He's a good kid, and he'll do fine with the material until I get back."

"Nick, I don't think you should do this. Look, walking up to those guys on the highway was one thing. And even that was crazy of you to do. I get it that you need to deal with this, but I don't think you can just go halfway across the country—"

Journey tapped his finger three times, then shook his entire hand from side to side. "I think we'd better establish some boundaries here, Sandra."

Sandra sat back. "What are you talking about?"

"Look, I appreciate the fact that you got in touch with your brother and put out the effort to get this information for me. You didn't have to do that, and it means a lot to me. But you—" Journey swallowed. Sandra was looking straight at him, her eyes never wavering. "My life is complicated, and I don't think you want to get tangled up in this any further."

"Everyone's life is complicated. That's a cop-out."

"Excuse me?"

Sandra stood up. "If you don't want me around, say so. But please don't insult my intelligence with this line about your life being complicated. And I certainly don't need you or anyone else to tell me what I do and don't *want* to do."

"You're overreacting," Journey said, working to keep his voice level. "I don't want to see anything happen—"

"I'm a big girl. I can take care of myself." Sandra's voice had been rising steadily. "And what about your son? Have you thought about what you're going to do with him while you run off to Louisville?"

"Well, there's really no one here in town that I'm comfortable leaving him with overnight."

"You think I don't know that? *Everyone* knows that, Nick."

Journey tapped his index finger against his lip. "I was thinking I would drop him off with his mother in Oklahoma City."

"And just pull him out of school? Won't that disrupt his routine? What will his mother think about that? Hasn't she already done her token two weeks this year?"

"Don't you presume to tell me how to take care of my son!" Journey shouted with sudden anger. "You know nothing about my life!"

"And whose choice is that?" Sandra yelled back.

Journey absorbed the words like a slap across the face, and the two of them stared at each other across the living room. After a moment, Sandra picked up her water bottle and strode to the door. "I should go."

"Sandra . . . I have to go to the Falls of the Ohio. I have to see what's there. You don't understand."

"Yes, I do," she said. "That's what I've been trying to tell you." Then she turned and was gone.

# CHAPTER

# 25

The chief justice of the United States Supreme Court possessed the figure and demeanor of a jolly, round little grandmother from Alabama, one who still liked to can her own vegetables and made jams and jellies. She was also the sharpest legal mind of her generation, and when President Harwell nominated her to be the top jurist in the land two years ago, she'd been confirmed with only twenty-four "no" votes on the Senate floor. After years of a Supreme Court that had been directed by ideological chief justices, Nan Darlington was a pragmatist, a centrist in every sense of the word.

Now sixty-four, Darlington had come to Washington a decade earlier upon being named to the D.C. Court of Appeals, which was well known as the "training ground" for the Supreme Court. She'd been on the federal bench in Birmingham for the decade prior to that. The chief justice and her husband, Professor Edmond Norman, who taught criminal law at Georgetown, lived in a beautiful old row house on O Street in Georgetown, not far from the law school.

Darlington was a creature of habit. When in D.C., she rose promptly at six o'clock each morning, ate a breakfast of two scrambled eggs, bread, and juice, exercised on her StairMaster for exactly thirty minutes, and spent a few minutes in her study, silent and alone, praying and meditating on the day ahead. Then she would quickly dress in one of the forty or so black suits she owned, would talk to her husband about what his day held, then would kiss him at the front doorway. She would be on her stoop at seven fifteen, awaiting her car and driver. She never kept them waiting.

This morning, two officers were stationed outside her front door, and they had been on the property all night. Periodically, Brent Graves assigned extra officers to her for a day or two as part of what he called "training operations." But Darlington was not naïve. She suspected the extra security people at times coincided with threats against her or the Court. The extra officers at her door this morning were young and fairly new. She'd seen them both a handful of times—a woman with coal-black hair and a very tall young man who rarely spoke. "Good morning," Darlington said to them. "I take it all is well?"

"Good morning, Justice Darlington," the young woman said. "Everything is fine. How are you this morning?"

Darlington patted the woman's arm, being the Alabama grandmother. "I'm well, thank you. September is a fine month, the weather is good, my back isn't bothering me too much, and I have work on my desk. I don't think I could ask for much more."

At that moment, the black Town Car pulled to the front of the house. Darlington waved to the driver and started down the steps.

Graves had made his way through the ranks of the Judicial Security Division, first working security for federal courthouses in Kansas City, Denver, and Richmond before making it to D.C. He'd then been assigned to the D.C. Court of Appeals, and later the personal detail of Associate Supreme Court Justice Greene. When Darlington was appointed chief justice, he was named to head the Office of Protective Operations.

Six months after Darlington was sworn in as chief justice, Graves bought a house five doors down and across O Street from her. It was pushing the limits of his price range, but his wife loved it, and it put

Graves in the position of actually seeing Darlington from time to time in a nonofficial capacity. He had no doubt that the chief justice considered him a personal friend by now. She trusted him.

Graves had juggled the duty rosters around a bit, and neither Thornton nor Pickett would be driving this morning. The driver was a middle-aged officer named Hellendaal, who'd joined the detail only three months ago. Graves had done some checking—Hellendaal was divorced, with no kids. Both his parents were deceased. His only family was a sister in New York. It was the best Graves could do.

He finished his first cup of coffee and prowled the empty house, thankful that his wife was still in Connecticut, dealing with her family and setting her mother's affairs in order. He read the *Post*, drank more coffee, and pulled two cell phones out of his pocket, placing them on his mahogany dining room table. Just down the block, Darlington would be stepping onto her porch. She would banter with Thornton and Pickett, then make the short walk down the cobblestone walkway to where Hellendaal was waiting with the car.

Senior Inspector Hendrickson pulled into the Marshals Service's Crystal City complex at a few minutes after seven. Tired from yesterday's flights to and from Oklahoma City, plus a total of five hours in the car between the city and Carpenter Center, and frustrated by the wasted time he'd spent on Nick Journey, Hendrickson just wanted to fill out his travel vouchers and finish his report.

He went to his cubicle in the JSD section of the Marshals Service headquarters and completed his forms. He saved them to his computer, then printed copies. He took the old paper in the plastic sleeve that Journey had shown him yesterday and looked at it for a moment before tucking it into the file.

*Damnedest thing I ever saw,* Hendrickson thought. *"Whereas" and "to wit" and all that archaic language, not to mention that strange symbol with the swords and star and eagle. Journey was reading ancient history and letting his imagination run away with him.* He closed the file and walked it down the hall. Neither Graves nor his assistant was in yet, but he left the file on the assistant's desk with a Post-it note asking her to give it to the boss. She was an efficient woman, and Hendrickson was sure she would see that Graves got it.

Graves was tempted to walk outside, just to be sure that Darlington was where she was supposed to be. But that would have been a break in routine, one that could be possibly witnessed by neighbors. Graves never went outside in the morning until he was ready to leave. Georgetown had no Metro stop, and he drove himself to Crystal City every day.

Graves had timed it over and over. He knew the chief justice's habits as well as he knew his own. Darlington would stand and chat on the porch for thirty to forty-five seconds. Then it was forty seconds down the walkway, ten to actually get in the car. The driver would shut the door. It would take him fifteen to twenty seconds to move around to the front and get in the driver's seat.

Graves checked his watch. Darlington should be climbing into the backseat right about now. He flipped open one of the cell phones, the one he'd picked up in the envelope at the park in Herndon. With his other hand, he absently jingled the contents of his pants pocket. Along with the keys and coins there, he felt the gold pin, the one with *G.W.* engraved on it. Its solidity calmed him, steeled him for the task.

His thumb hovered over the phone's keypad.

Darlington took the driver's arm and held it as she lowered herself into the Town Car.

"How is your back, Madam Chief Justice?" Hellendaal asked her.

She squeezed his arm. "Please don't call me 'Madam.' 'Justice Darlington' is fine. My back is fair today, thank the Lord."

"Glad to hear it, ma'am," Hellendaal said.

"This is a different car," Darlington said.

"Yes, ma'am. Time to switch them out."

"Really, I don't need the largest car in the fleet, you know. I bet this thing gets terrible gas mileage, and with the price of gasoline, the taxpayers really shouldn't have to pay all that much for me to ride in this big old boat of a car."

Hellendaal smiled. "Gas certainly isn't getting any cheaper, ma'am."

He closed the door, waved to Pickett and Thornton on the porch, and started toward the front of the Town Car.


Graves looked at his watch again, remembering the instructions: the number of the other phone, the one with the red strip, was programmed into this one as speed-dial number two.

He flexed his fingers like a pianist sitting down to perform, then pressed the number two on the phone's keypad and the green button that would connect the call.


Darlington didn't carry a briefcase, only a small purse. Work stayed at the court, and she never brought it home. She had a cell phone, but saw no need to carry it on the short drive to and from the office. She occasionally used it when traveling, but found it to be more of a nuisance than a beneficial tool.

She smoothed the lapel of her jacket and watched as the driver walked around to the front of the car.

She heard the muffled trilling of the phone, and her first thought was that it had come from behind her. But that didn't make sense— her hearing must be playing tricks on her. First it was her back, now the hearing. Her eyesight would go next, no doubt.

"Is that your phone?" she called to Hellendaal, and the car exploded.


Hellendaal screamed as a part of the Town Car's wheel well smashed into his head. A jagged edge raked across his face, narrowly missing his right eye and slicing a deep cut all the way to his ear.

He twisted and stumbled but stayed on his feet, shambling around the edge of the burning car. The car's back half was enveloped in a halo of flame. Glass from the shattered windows crunched.

Smoke boiled into the clear September sky. Hellendaal couldn't see Darlington through the smoke and the flames.

Pickett and Thornton ran down the walkway. Pickett already had her phone out, talking quietly, urgently. People in the stately row houses of O Street began to drift outside. At least two senators, an ambassador, and the Secretary of Commerce lived on this block.

Within ninety seconds, sirens cut the air. Washington Metro PD and Fire and Rescue units arrived on the scene. Hellendaal was treated by the trauma team and loaded into an ambulance to Georgetown University Hospital. Professor Edmond Norman, the chief justice's husband, came to his doorway. He first looked down at the pieces of burning metal in his yard; then his eyes trailed toward the car. He took another step. Thornton ran back up the sidewalk and held him back.

"Not yet, sir," Thornton said. "We have to secure the scene first. I'm sorry, sir."

Thornton looked toward the car, as if he weren't sure of what he'd seen. Norman did the same; then the older man sagged into Thornton's arms.


Just over one minute from the time the car exploded, a tall silver-haired figure emerged from five doors down, on the opposite side of the street. He stood still for a moment; then his feet began to move. Within three steps, he was moving at a dead run. He passed Commerce Secretary Newcomb and his wife, a bathrobe-clad Senator Brenson, and a growing crowd of spectators. He felt the intense heat from the car, and he almost gagged on smoke and the unmistakable and sickening smell of charring flesh.

A few seconds later, Brent Graves was in command of the scene, and before Chief Justice Darlington's body was even extricated from the car, the investigation had begun.

# CHAPTER
# 26

Tolman needed Kerry Voss.

Voss was one of the non–law enforcement people at RIO, strictly on the research end of the spectrum. She'd joined the agency eighteen months ago, and all kinds of rumors about her past floated around: that she'd been a stripper, or a kindergarten teacher, or a substance abuse counselor, that she had a doctorate in sociology, that she'd had something to do with finances at DOD. There were even more tantalizing tidbits about her family background: one said that her original family name had been Vostrikov, and that her grandfather was a Stalin-era KGB agent who defected to the West.

Voss remained carefully coy about her background, and Tolman resisted the urge to investigate her coworker. Besides, she rather liked the paradox that Voss presented. She and Voss were about the same age and height, which bonded them instantly in an office full of taller people. Voss had tattoos, one of a yin/yang symbol and one of Big Bird from *Sesame Street*. Still, her office was filled with pictures of her three kids. Most important to Tolman, she could follow money. Tolman had no equal in finding people, in reconstructing scenarios and lives, but she was weakest on financial tracking. That, on the other hand, was all Voss did for RIO: follow money trails.

After a restless night—she'd walked to the NVCC campus but had been too distracted even to practice piano—Tolman was in the office before dawn. She turned on lights, started coffee in the break room, read meaningless e-mails as the staff started to trickle in. Voss had taken a personal day on Monday, something to do with one of her kids, and Tolman knew she'd be in early today.

As RIO's activity level built after seven thirty, Tolman walked out of her office and passed Hudson's. Hudson was already at his desk, but Tolman passed by without slowing. She went past the front reception desk and turned right into Voss's office. Voss was settling in at her computer, one hand on the mouse, another holding a pen that she tapped against a legal pad. Today she had longish brown-blond hair—Tolman was never sure of her natural color—and it was in a braid. Occasionally she showed up to work with it in cornrows. Voss's quirky nature made Tolman like her even more.

Tolman closed the door and sat down across from Voss.

"You closed the door," Voss said. "It's trouble when you close the door."

"Morning, Kerry," Tolman said.

Voss pointed with her pen. "Door. Closed. What do you want?"

"How are you, Kerry? I haven't gotten to talk to you in a couple of weeks."

"You have no gift for bullshit small talk, Meg. I can read you like a book with a broken spine. You want something. But I'll play. Let's see, my daughter has developed a serious case of preteen attitude—she's only nine, by the way—and my two boys fight constantly. My ex-husband just got remarried, my ex-mother-in-law wants to be my best friend, my car needs a new battery, and my garage-door opener doesn't work."

Tolman laughed out loud. "You and I should go out and drink sometime, when things settle down. Sounds like you need it. What about the guys?"

"Things never settle down. You remember I had met these two guys named Ramirez?"

"No relation, and you met them about a week apart, right?"

"Yep. Ramirez number one moved back to Texas. Ramirez number two stood me up for dinner at a fondue place."

"You're not making this up, are you?"

"No one could make this up. But I do have a good prospect, my youngest son's soccer coach. Code-named Hot Soccer Guy. Ready to tell me why you're in here with the door closed?"

Tolman raised both hands. "I surrender. Just don't tell me anything else about your life. I need access to some bank records."

"So? We do bank records all the time."

"Yeah, but I'm a little weak on the financial stuff."

Voss let that pass. "Do you have paperwork from Hudson?"

"No."

"Now I know why the door is closed. What's this about?"

"You did some time with DOD, right?"

"Let's say I did, hypothetically."

"Hypothetically, if a couple of soldiers died in action in Iraq, their survivors would get benefits, right?"

Voss nodded. "There's an immediate death benefit of a hundred thousand dollars, and that's usually paid within thirty-six hours after the death is confirmed."

"Then isn't there some sort of ongoing payment, like a pension?"

"Right. If your hypothetical soldier were married at the time of death, the spouse would get a monthly payment. There's also a monthly payment for each minor child."

"Okay, I need to know if a couple of soldiers' families got these benefits."

"Well, Meg, if they're dead, they definitely got the benefits. That's the way the system works."

Tolman crossed her legs at the knee.

"What?" Voss said.

"I'm not exactly sure they're dead."

Voss put down her pen.

"They may be or they may not be," Tolman said. "That's really what I want to find out."

"There are easier ways to do that," Voss pointed out. "You can get death certificates, all the usual stuff. That's much more up your alley than mine."

"Some things about this case may or may not contradict each other, so I'm trying to verify independently."

"And independently of Hudson, too?"

"Something like that."

"Why?"

"Because he's a bureaucrat and wants to cover his ass."

"Well, I'm a bureaucrat, too. So are you, for that matter. Just because you can carry a gun and get to call yourself 'investigative specialist' doesn't change that fact."

"No," Tolman said. "I know what I am."

"Besides, you get along great with Hudson."

"I certainly do. But he won't give me what I need on this case."

"You want this done without authorization. I can see it now— one of those 'federal agencies run amok' sorts of projects. The reasons certain people believe the government has too much power. Privacy, civil liberties, all that jazz. Am I right?"

"You are right."

Voss sighed. "I thought I left this kind of crap behind when I left—"

"Yes?"

"Never mind. It doesn't matter. This is big or you wouldn't ask. I know you well enough to get that." She sighed again. "It may take a little while. I have three other cases—"

"Just get me what you can, when you can. Please. I'm hoping the money trail tells me something I don't already know."

"Oh, it probably will," Voss said. "Money is kind of like a bloated corpse. It's ugly, and after a while it starts to smell bad, but if you poke at it long enough, it will tell you something. Give me what you have."

"Thanks. I will definitely buy you a drink sometime."

"Promises, promises."

Tolman didn't want to muddy the waters any more than necessary, so she gave Voss only the names of Michael Standridge and Kevin Lane, their army assignments, the dates the army had said they'd died, and their hometowns. She said nothing about Nick Journey or Fort Washita or Speaker Vandermeer or Chief Justice Darlington.

Tolman left Voss's office and headed back toward her own. As she passed the break room, she saw a cluster of half a dozen people around the small TV set. She caught snippets of the audio: ". . . driver was injured in the blast as well . . . the chief justice's husband reportedly watched from the porch . . . no claim of responsibility . . . on the heels of Speaker Vandermeer's . . ."

Tolman elbowed her way into the crowd. "What the hell's going on?"

Hudson turned and looked at her. His face was gray. He said nothing, his eyes boring into hers. Somewhere out in the office, a phone rang, then another, then another. Hudson said nothing, turned, and left the break room.

"What?" Tolman said.

The crowd parted and Tolman saw the TV. The HNC graphic on the bottom of the screen read, CHIEF JUSTICE DARLINGTON ASSASSINATED.

Without saying a word, Tolman ran back down the hall and threw open the door to Voss's office.

Voss, startled, looked up at her.

"That project I asked you to do just got a lot more important," Tolman said.

As she ran back toward her own office, she noticed that Hudson's door was now closed.

# CHAPTER
## 27

Journey called the school, telling Andrew's teacher there was a family emergency. He packed a bag for Andrew and a small one for himself. He called the student who served as Andrew's occasional caregiver and dropped off his spare house key with her, removing it from its hiding place under the back doormat. It would be safe with her. Then he called Amelia. On reaching her voice mail, he said, "I'm coming to the city. I can meet you at the usual place in two and a half hours. Something's come up, and I need you to take Andrew for a day or two."

He clicked off the phone and drove west on Highway 70, then north on Interstate 35 through the Arbuckle Mountains—small hills, really, but mountains by Oklahoma standards—and the red clay cattle and horse country beyond. It was a day trip he made once a month on average, to do his consulting projects with the Oklahoma Historical Society, to do some networking with other academics in the state, and to just spend some time in a city. Oklahoma City was sprawling but comfortable, of a perfect size to offer the right balance of urban culture and amenities and small-town charm and friendliness.

He'd been surprised that Amelia chose to settle in "the City" after the divorce. He expected her to move back to Virginia, where all her family lived. But the bank where she'd worked in Carpenter Center was headquartered in Oklahoma City, and they created a position for her there. Now she was a vice president of corporate development, easily making five times what Journey earned as a professor. She bought and renovated a Victorian house in an historic neighborhood, she skied in Aspen and went scuba diving off Key West, and had very little to do with Journey outside of the two weeks in June when Andrew stayed with her.

Amelia Boettcher—she hadn't taken the name Journey when they married—never allowed Journey to drop Andrew at the house. Journey assumed it was because a man was living there with her, and had been for nearly two years now. He'd answered the phone twice when Journey had called to talk about various Andrew-related issues. If Amelia had bothered to ask, he would have told her he didn't care in the slightest that she had a live-in. But she never asked, and consequently they always met at a little coffeehouse on Classen Boulevard.

The Red Cup might have stepped living and breathing from 1968, with its largely vegetarian menu, asymmetrical room configurations, and flyers for everything from yoga to Irish dance to hypnosis classes. A framed plaque proclaimed it a FAIR TRADE CAFÉ.

Journey ordered a latte for himself and a fruit smoothie for Andrew, then found a spot in a "quiet room" in the corner. There was no table per se, but a low wooden shelf, painted bright yellow, with chairs in front of it. Reading lamps lined the shelf.

Amelia was late, and showed up with her phone pressed to her ear. Journey watched her as she stood at the counter: the tall, full figure, the nut-colored hair, the gray-green eyes, high cheekbones, the graceful way she moved. None of those things had changed since they met in graduate school. What *had* changed was that she'd become hard-edged, blunt, and impatient in middle age. He waved her over to the little corner area.

"Hi," she said.

"Hi."

She looked down at Andrew, who was fidgeting with his straw and his pencil. The boy looked perplexed, then broke into a heart-stopping smile. "Hi, honey," Amelia said. She kissed his cheek. He turned his head and she kissed the other cheek. The smile stayed on for a few more seconds; then he lowered his head and tapped his straw and pencil together.

She slid into the seat next to Journey and lowered her voice. "What's this all about?"

"I can't really explain," Journey said. "I have to go out of town for a day or two, and I need you to take him."

"You pulled him out of school?"

"What other options do I have?"

"Haven't you found anyone in Carpenter Center who can look after him if something comes up?"

"No, I haven't. But I—"

"Can't you take him with you?"

"No, not on this trip."

"And why is that?"

"It's really too complicated for me to go into."

Amelia stared at him for a moment. "Is this related to that thing at Fort Washita? I saw you on TV, you know."

Journey tapped his finger three times, then remembered how much Amelia hated it when he did that. After a few seconds, he did it again. "Yes, it's part of that. Can't you just take him for a little while in an emergency? God knows I don't ask you for much."

"What is that supposed to mean?"

Journey held out his hands. "Nothing. Look, I can't do this. I'm on edge enough as it is. I've packed three days of clothes for him and a full package of Pull-Ups, his yellow ball, and a couple of his puzzles."

Amelia's phone chirped, and for once she ignored it. "Nick, don't make me out to be a bitch of a mother just because I won't drop everything for you to go off chasing your fifteen minutes of glory."

"Even though you don't have custody, you're still a parent. That's the way it is."

Andrew, mesmerized by the circle of light on the yellow counter from one of the reading lamps, suddenly laughed out loud, followed by a series of whistles, followed by more, increasingly loud laughter.

"Andrew, shhh," Amelia said. The boy didn't look at her. Amelia looked at Journey. "He's doing a lot more of the laughing thing."

Journey nodded. "It may be puberty. We'll see a lot more changes in his behavior before too much longer."

They both waited.

Amelia softened her tone. "You want to know something? When he's with me, during our two weeks in June, I think I spend most of my time crying."

Journey looked up at her.

She smiled. "Don't look so surprised. I know you think I never cry. Bank executives with MBAs don't cry, right?"

"No," Journey said. "I remember you crying sometimes when we were younger."

"It's just . . ." Amelia looked away for a moment. "I think of all the things he can't do and won't ever do, and it's just overwhelming. And it's hard for me to admit that he's better off with you." She raised her head. "But I shouldn't have to feel ashamed for doing what was best for all three of us."

Journey said nothing. Andrew whistled.

"Now you don't have a life, and won't get a life," Amelia said, "because you believe I failed both of you and now you think you have to do everything. Don't bother denying it. I just understood what was happening to us before you did. Maybe you still don't."

"That's not—"

Amelia held up one of her hands. "I don't want to fight with you, Nick. God knows we did enough of that." She glanced at Andrew. "He's such a beautiful kid, he's still so beautiful . . . and it hurts like hell."

She met his eyes, and for a moment he saw the woman he'd met fifteen years ago in graduate school—smart, tough, but still vulnerable, tender. Then her eyes changed and he saw her retreating behind her walls. "I need to tell you something else," she said. "Paul doesn't know about Andrew."

"The man you're living with doesn't know you have a son?"

Amelia looked at him. "You figured out that he's moved in? Don't answer that. I should have known you'd figure it out."

"You didn't tell him—"

"No, no, he knows I have a son," Amelia said. "He just doesn't *know* about him. You get my meaning?"

Journey blinked at her. "So what does he do in June?"

"I just tell him that it's my two special weeks with Andrew, and he goes and stays at his brother's house. He's been very understanding."

"And you've been with this guy how long?"

"Dating right at two years. He moved in a little over a year ago."

"My god, Amelia."

"I have to tell him," Amelia said. "I know. You don't need to say it. I've just been so busy. . . ."

Journey shook his head, but he held his tongue.

Amelia surprised him by smiling a little. "Yeah, you *do* think I'm a bitch. You're just using that typical forced restraint of yours to not say so. Having a life of my own doesn't make me a rotten mother, Nick. It just makes me different from you. You could make some different choices and still be a good dad."

Andrew screeched. Amelia winced. One of the workers behind the counter of the Red Cup looked over at them, then went back to work.

"We could do this differently, you know," Amelia said. "You don't have to take everything on yourself. I don't think I would be very good at full custody, but there are options. You're always saying you wish I was more involved in his life, and I could be. Maybe not the way you think of it, but we have some choices."

"What are you saying?"

"I'm doing pretty well financially, and we could look at working out something for him that would be good for all three of us. I could feel like I was doing something more for Andrew, and you wouldn't be quite so locked into things the way you are now."

"I can't have this conversation today, Amelia," Journey said. "I need you to take our son, and I will be back to get him as soon as I possibly can. I know it's the last minute, and I know last-minute things generally don't work in your life, but I need you to do this. Where I'm going—"

"Yes?"

"It might not be safe."

"What does that mean?"

"I'm not sure. But I'd feel more comfortable knowing Andrew was with his mother."

Amelia folded her arms. "You're a history teacher. You don't do things that aren't safe."

Journey spread his hands in a *What can I say?* gesture.

"All right, he can come hang out with me for a day or two. Stranger things have happened, I suppose. The world is full of strangeness these days, isn't it?"

"What do you mean?"

"Didn't you hear the news this morning?"

"The news? No, I had music on in the car for Andrew. What are you talking about?"

"Someone blew up the chief justice of the Supreme Court in her car."

Journey stared at her. Suddenly the room felt intensely quiet, even with Andrew hooting and giggling beside him, dishes clanking, other people talking. Journey laid both his hands flat on the yellow counter.

"Nick?"

Journey reached under the counter and slid Andrew's bag across to his ex-wife. "I'll call you when I can, Amelia."

"Nick, dammit!"

Journey pushed back his chair. Andrew stopped giggling and looked at him. Journey put his arms around the boy and squeezed once, then stepped back. "Stay with Mom for a little while," he said. "I'll be back as soon as I can."

"Nick, will you please tell me what's going on?"

Journey looked down at her, his eyes boring into hers, those intriguing greenish gray eyes that had so attracted him fifteen years ago. They were Andrew's eyes now. "I have to go. I'll call—"

"But I—"

"He's your son, Amelia. Keep him safe."

"Nick, have you lost your mind?"

Then Journey was up on his feet and moving out of the Red Cup.

\*   \*   \*

Dallas Four had followed Journey all the way from Carpenter Center. For this surveillance, they traveled in a light blue Honda Civic that blended in with almost every other four-door on the road. They had trailed the professor along I-35 and through the warren of streets leading to Classen Boulevard. They sat parked at a 7- Eleven across the street from the coffeehouse and watched Journey emerge.

Within Dallas base, the Four team was often referred to as the poster group for diversity. Their commander called them the "face of the Glory Warriors for the modern age." Gold was a trim, compact, first-generation Vietnamese-American man; Silver a tall, lithe African American woman in her mid-thirties; Bronze a middle-aged, heavyset, balding Anglo male. Silver was at the wheel of the Honda. She spoke with a clipped, precise tone. "The boy isn't with him."

Nick Journey's van was parked along the street, and they watched him hurry to it. In a moment, he had a phone to his ear. Thirty seconds later, the tall, well-dressed woman came out of the Red Cup, with Andrew Journey hanging on to her arm.

"Who's this?" said Gold, in the passenger seat. "Is this the ex-wife? It has to be the ex-wife. Why the hell did he meet her here?"

"Get plates and I'll run her," Bronze said from the backseat.

They watched the woman strap the boy into the backseat of a red Lexus; then the car roared out of the parking lot and turned toward Classen. It passed within twenty feet of them.

"Oklahoma plate seven-five-eight *X-L-K*," Gold read as the Lexus passed.

Bronze opened his laptop. "The Lexus is registered to Amelia Kay Boettcher, address on Northwest Fourteenth Street, Oklahoma City."

"That's the ex-wife, all right," Silver said.

"I'll call Dallas Base," Gold said.

In less than a minute, he was off the phone. "We stay with Journey," he said. "Team Three is going to come up and monitor the ex-wife and the boy."

"Why?" Silver asked, glancing at Gold.

Gold looked at her hard. "Covering the bases. All of them."

"How far do we go with Journey?" Bronze said.

"As far as we have to," Gold said.

*    *    *

His hands shaking, Journey sat in the van and unzipped the back-pack. He'd printed out the first e-mail, the one from Meg Tolman. He wasn't going to contact Winters or Hendrickson—they'd prob-ably be after him soon enough as it was. Yesterday, they'd treated him like a paranoid nut job. Today, or sometime soon, they would want to talk to him.

But Tolman had been the first one to contact him. Before Van-dermeer. Before Darlington. The tone of her first contact wasn't pa-tronizing or irritated. It was curious and businesslike.

He turned on the radio and found the local NPR affiliate. The coverage was wall-to-wall assassination. Chief Justice Darlington's car had exploded in front of her house at just before 7:30 A.M. East-ern Time. Her Marshals Service guard/driver had been badly injured in the blast. Pundits were speculating about an IED in the chief justice's car, a simple bomb on a timer or something of the sort. There was even speculation about it being a cell phone bomb, set off re-motely, just as in the Madrid train bombings in 2004.

*The Speaker of the Legislative Branch.*

*The chief justice of the Judicial Branch.*

Next they would be after the president.

He punched Tolman's number into his phone. A moment later, a voice said, "Meg Tolman."

"This is Nick Journey," he said.

There was a moment's silence.

"Dr. Journey," Tolman said.

"Do you believe me now?"

Another pause, then Tolman said, "Yes."

Journey exhaled. "Two men, one FBI and one from the Mar-shals Service, came to see me yesterday. Have you seen any kind of report from them?"

"Not yet."

"Don't you government people talk to each other?"

"Where are you right now?"

"It doesn't matter where I am now. But where I'm going . . . that's what you really want to know."

"All right, then. Where are you going?"

"The Ohio River, on the Indiana side just across from Louisville, Kentucky. The Falls of the Ohio. Are you familiar with it?"

"No," Tolman said, "but give me fifteen minutes, and I'll know everything there is to know about it."

Journey liked Tolman's attitude. He explained the first page of the Fort Washita document, and the cryptic notation that led to the Falls of the Ohio. He told Tolman what he'd learned about the Glory Warriors. "The next phase of this, whatever it is, has something to do with the Falls of the Ohio. I'm getting on a plane to Louisville."

Journey listened to Tolman breathing on the phone. He could hear her moving around.

"I'll meet you there," Tolman said after a moment. "Is this number your cell phone?"

"Yes. I'll have it with me."

"Here's mine." She gave him the number. "I'll call you when I get to Louisville, and we'll coordinate then."

"All right," Journey said.

Journey disconnected the call. He pulled onto the street and began working his way south toward Will Rogers World Airport. Even though keeping Andrew didn't fit into Amelia's life, at least she'd taken him. At least, Journey thought, his son was safe.


When Tolman put down the phone, she looked up and saw Hudson filling her doorway. From down the hall, she heard the sounds of the television, with its nonstop coverage of Chief Justice Darlington's death. There was a buzz of voices from the outer office, and several phones were ringing.

"Journey?" Hudson said.

Tolman nodded. "I'll need some backup."

Hudson arched his eyebrows.

"I'm going to Louisville," Tolman said, taking care to give the city its proper native pronunciation—*LOO-uh-vuhl*—as she'd been taught by a college roommate who grew up in Kentucky.

"What?"

"Journey is headed to Louisville. There's something along the Ohio River. . . . I'm going to meet him there and bring him in. Can you get me some backup?"

"Díaz from the Bureau is going to want to talk to you."

Tolman unlocked her lower desk drawer. "I think Journey trusts me. Everyone else thinks he's a nut. I can get him in, but I'll need backup. Whoever is behind Vandermeer and Darlington is after Journey."

"Meg—"

"No, don't 'Meg' me. The Bureau will have a field office in Louisville. Have them call my cell, and I'll tell them where the meeting is once I have it set with Journey."

"Díaz has jurisdiction. I'm not sure I have the authority to do this."

"Then, dammit, convince Díaz!" Tolman shouted. "You're bigger than he is. Journey knew what was going to happen and tried to tell us, and we didn't take him seriously. Well, we have to take him seriously now. And if Díaz can't see that, then he's too fucking stupid to be in the Bureau anyway."

Hudson waited a very long moment. "I believe you overestimate my influence at times."

Tolman smiled. "I knew you'd come through."

"Louisville, Kentucky," Hudson said.

"That's what the man said. Something about the Falls of the Ohio. I'll read up on it at the airport."

Hudson nodded and turned away. Tolman reached into her desk drawer and slowly withdrew her holstered sidearm. She qualified at the FBI range at Quantico every year, and went to a private range with her father once a month to stay sharp. But Tolman had never drawn her weapon on the job. RIO didn't lend itself to armed confrontation.

Still, she kept the SIG Sauer 9 millimeter maintained, and she kept her skills up to date. The various federal law enforcement agencies all had different standard-issue sidearms, but any officer was free to use their own money to purchase a different weapon. Some agencies had contracts with Glock, some with SIG, some even still used Berettas. She'd been issued a Glock five years ago, but had instantly felt that it was too big for her hand, and balanced all wrong. She'd bought the SIG out of her own pocket.

Tolman started for the door. Several of her colleagues took notice of the weapon. She hoped she wouldn't need it.

# CHAPTER
# 28

It was after ten o'clock when Journey landed in Louisville. He'd suffered through a layover in St. Louis, where the fatigue began to catch up to his body. He rented a car at the airport, then checked in to a motel along Interstate 65, not far from the airport. He'd just dropped his backpack and small travel bag on the motel bed when his cell rang.

"Where are you?" Tolman asked without preamble.

"Just checked in to a motel in Louisville. We'll need daylight to look around Falls of the Ohio. Are you here yet?"

"I'm stuck at O'Hare. I'm having trouble getting a connecting flight. I'll meet you in the morning."

"Do you know where to go?"

"I told you, Dr. Journey, all I need is my computer and fifteen minutes. Just across the river in Indiana, Exit 0 from I-65 and follow the signs. Sounds like a fascinating place."

"That it does," Journey said.

"Dr. Journey?"

"Yes?"

"I'm not jerking you around, I don't think you're crazy, and I'm taking you seriously."

"I think they're going to go after the president next. And if they do . . . I think we'll know more when we find the rest of the document."

"I'll meet you at eight o'clock in the morning."

Journey hung up, waited a moment, then called Amelia. "How's Andrew?" he asked her.

"He's still in his bed, laughing," Amelia said. She sounded frazzled. He remembered what she'd said about crying when Andrew was with her.

"Sing to him. He's always liked your voice better than mine."

"I will."

"What did you tell Paul?"

Amelia was silent for a long time, then said, "He's spending the night with his brother; then he's going to meet Andrew tomorrow."

"Okay," Journey said, then could think of nothing else to say. "Good night."

After he broke the connection, Journey showered, undressed, and lay down on the bed. It was well after midnight before he fell asleep.

More than four hundred miles separated Washington, D.C. from Matewan, West Virginia, but Baltimore Two Gold made the drive with only one stop for gasoline. With a task force convened to handle the investigation of Chief Justice Darlington's death, Brent Graves could not leave Washington, but he was able to slip away for fifteen minutes and meet his fellow Glory Warrior in downtown D.C. He gave him the document that Inspector Hendrickson had brought back from his interview with Nick Journey—the document Hendrickson unknowingly delivered into the hands of the Glory Warriors.

Baltimore Two Gold then made the drive to the Judge. The Judge let him into the door of the mountain retreat, then went to his study without speaking.

"Let me see it," he said when the oak doors had closed.

Gold handed him the paper.

The Judge took it as if it were Holy Scripture. In a way, he thought, it was, but with more far-reaching power. The Glory Warriors had always been a work in progress, an incomplete picture, and his father knew that. But he told his son what he did know, how the original Glory Warriors had waited patiently for their time, and their time had never come. Still, the name and the objective were passed down, and those of like mind were chosen, carefully researched, and entrusted with the mission. At first only men, then women as well. At first only whites, then those of all races. Gender made no difference. Race made no difference. The *mind-set* was the difference—the understanding of power in governance, and how that power should properly be applied. The American government had long since stopped governing. The Judge felt that true government had actually ceased the moment shots were fired at Fort Sumter and the Civil War began. Everything since was shallow and inept and corrupt, and unworthy of men like Ulysses S. Grant and Robert E. Lee.

*"You will be leader of the Glory Warriors one day,"* his father said to him, years before the day his father's fist had crashed into the side of his head when he dared to question the mission. He was only a boy, eleven or twelve at the most, thinking a boy's thoughts: chess tournaments and football games, school and vacations. *"Educate yourself,"* the old man said. *"Learn the law, the military, learn politics, learn how things work. When the time comes, be ready. When Lee and Grant's words are found, when we can document their true intentions and present them to the American people, you will be ready. The people will want us. By the time that happens, they will have no choice."*

*"Father, I don't understand. What are you talking about?"*

*"Power, son. I'm talking about power, and about doing what's right for America, no matter what it takes, no matter how long it takes."*

Son.

His father never called him "son." Never. He heard other fathers call their boys "son"—for that matter, other fathers called *him* "son" a few times—but never his own father. The only time in the Judge's memory was that day, nearly sixty years ago, when he first mentioned the Glory Warriors, first said the names of Grant and Lee.

He had done as his father instructed. His family name opened many doors, but he took every opportunity to learn. He went to Vietnam, then worked in the highest levels of the Judge Advocate General Corps at the Pentagon, and was then elected to the House of Representatives from California, serving three terms during the era of the first Gulf War. He was a deputy Cabinet secretary; then he ventured into the media, consolidating his power base until he was able to come here to this symbolic place, this state that had been born of the Civil War.

It had been a sometimes painful journey—occasionally the Judge found himself rubbing his cheek as if his father had just struck him—and his own relationship to the Glory Warriors had grown more complex over the years. The quest had consumed his life, as it had his father's and grandfather's. Now it was about to come to fruition. Was he a better man than they? Would he be a better head of government than they would have been? Was he worthy of Grant and Lee's vision?

On his deathbed in 1980, his father had said, "It's in your hands now. Don't fail."

*Don't fail.*

The Judge's hands trembled a little as he slipped the page out of the plastic. He touched the embossed symbol of the Glory Warriors, a twin of the one in his desk drawer. He read the opening words:

*Whereas the late War Between the States has ended . . .*

The Judge read it five times, mindful that he was the first Glory Warrior to read it since 1865.

*We are on the right path*, he thought.

Vandermeer and Darlington were dead. The Judge had considered it before, how the original Glory Warriors foresaw the government's instability, but never intended to have a hand in creating that instability.

That was his creation. Anyone who was paying attention could tell that the government was unstable, and had been for decades. Perhaps the three heads had not been lopped off, but those were just three people, and the government was bigger than the three. Speakers and chief justices and presidents came and went, and still the government failed to govern. Ideologies mattered little—whether they claimed to be right, left, or center, they accomplished very little, doing only enough to ensure their own political survival while mouthing platitudes about "the American people" and "rolling up our sleeves and getting to work" and "moving beyond partisanship." Year after year, decade after decade, the governmental machine limped along, sustaining itself while the country as a whole disintegrated around them.

So what if the Judge had helped bring about the circumstances that would hasten the Glory Warriors' ascension? He had only helped to create the right climate, implementing the vision, going deeper than his father had ever imagined, taking bolder steps.

*Don't fail.*

After a moment, the Judge gradually became aware that Gold was still in the room and was speaking to him.

"What?" he finally said, staring across his desk at the man.

"There are other pages, isn't that right, sir?" Gold said. "Won't we have—?"

"We'll have the rest of them soon," the Judge said.

"The professor?"

"Yes. One of the Dallas teams has stayed with him."

Gold looked at him questioningly.

"Dr. Journey said he would find the rest of the pages," the Judge said. "We're going to let him. Then we're going to take them from him."

# CHAPTER
# 29

Tolman finally rented a car in Chicago and drove the five hours to Louisville. She arrived after 3 A.M., slept for a few hours, and was up again at dawn, running on pure adrenaline and espresso. After leaving a phone message for her father to go to her apartment and feed Rocky, she grabbed her laptop, tucked her SIG into her shoulder bag, and pulled the Ford Focus back onto I-65.

She passed the University of Louisville campus, with its ten giant concrete columns facing the highway, spelling out the university's name. Past the sprawling Jewish Hospital complex, she crossed the Ohio River into Indiana and immediately exited the highway.

A couple of traffic lights, stop signs, a double back under the interstate, and she was on a small street that curved toward Falls of the Ohio State Park. The river was on her left. Seeing it at eye level, as opposed to when she crossed it on the I-65 bridge, made her realize that the water was very high. It had been an extraordinarily wet summer in this part of the country, and she remembered hearing about floods throughout Kentucky, Indiana, and Illinois in the last few weeks.

A few high clouds floated above, but otherwise it looked like there would be no rain today along the Ohio. With the rising sun behind her, she bore left past a bronze sculpture of Lewis and Clark shaking hands, at the ostensible beginning of their westward trek. Beyond the statue, a curving stone sign announced FALLS OF THE OHIO INTERPRETIVE CENTER.

Tolman slowed the car to a crawl. No one was around the place this early. She knew from her online research that the interpretive center didn't open until nine o'clock. She was left thinking of what Nick Journey had told her on the phone.

Glory Warriors.

Tolman opened her laptop, logged in to Homeland Security's custom search engine RACER—Retrieval, Assessment, Correlation, Expression, Review—and typed in the words "Glory Warriors."

Fifteen minutes later, the search was complete and one hit popped onto the screen. Tolman scrolled to it and clicked with the thumb bar.

A white four-door rolled slowly past her. She looked up in time to see the man behind the wheel peer at her as the car proceeded toward the parking lot at the rear of the interpretive center.

Her first impression was, *He looks older and grayer in person than I expected.*

Tolman let out a breath she hadn't realized she'd been holding. She angled her laptop screen away from the glare of the sun and looked at the file she'd just opened.

In a few seconds, she said, "That can't be right."

She looked at the screen again, then raised her head. The white car had stopped. Nick Journey—she knew it was him, since she'd pulled his driver's license photo when she first worked him up—was getting out, a backpack slung over one shoulder. He cast a glance toward her, then walked away from his car. In a moment, he was out of her view, behind the stone building.

Tolman looked at the computer. *Can't be right,* she thought again.

She closed the laptop, slid it under the passenger seat, dropped the car into gear, and headed toward the parking lot.

It was still not quite seven thirty, and Journey walked slowly around the back of the interpretive center and onto a curving wooden deck that extended from the building and overlooked the river. He saw that the main tourist attraction of Falls of the Ohio—the Devonian era fossil beds—was a moot point now. This was typically the dry season in the area, and when the river was low, the fossil beds lay exposed and people could literally walk almost halfway across the river. Now, with high water from the recent flooding, the beds were covered and a large amount of driftwood and garbage abutted the shoreline.

Journey walked halfway across the deck, then stopped and leaned over the fence. Gazing in the direction of the road, he could see an iron railroad trestle spanning the great river.

The Ohio had always been of critical and strategic importance. Journey had stood at both ends of it, on the spot at Point State Park in Pittsburgh where the Monongahela and Allegheny came together to form it; and on the little spit of land south of Cairo, Illinois, where it emptied into the Mississippi.

But here had been the only obstacle to the river's navigation. It bent, the water rushed, and its level dropped twenty-six feet in two miles. Many an early navigator saw their boat splintered to pieces here.

*The Poet's Penn makes the waters fall and causes the strong to bend.*

He thought of the steamboat trade, of how vital Louisville had been to the river's life. He thought of Kentucky staying in the Union in the Civil War, but its strong Southern culture making it the ultimate border ground, a place of confused loyalties and shifting ideologies.

*I'm missing something here,* he thought.

He heard the footsteps before the voice, and his entire body tensed. He straightened and took a step back from the fence.

"Dr. Journey, I'm Meg Tolman."

Journey turned and looked at the small woman with the short blond hair. Her Nordic-blue eyes were constantly moving, scanning the area, finally settling back on him.

"Let me see some identification," Journey said.

Still a good twenty feet from him, Tolman produced a leather case and flipped it open. "Put it on the deck and take ten steps back," Journey said.

She did. Journey picked up the case and read it, then folded it closed and extended his arm. "Anyone could have something like this made."

"That's true," Tolman said. "But if I wanted to hurt you, I could have shot you in the back while you stood there, couldn't I?"

"That's reassuring."

"I thought so." She came forward and took the case from him. "What do you think?"

Journey turned back toward the river. "I don't know. It's not . . . it's not right. Something about it isn't right."

"You understand that you are a material witness in the investigations into the deaths of Vandermeer and Darlington," Tolman said.

"I hadn't quite thought of it in those terms."

"You'll need to come back to D.C. with me. You've made arrangements for your son?"

Journey gave her a sharp look. "He's with his mother in Oklahoma City, but he can't stay there long."

"Why not?"

"Because he can't."

"I know about your son," Tolman said. "When your case first came to me, I did a full profile on you."

Journey said nothing.

"I know about Andrew's condition," Tolman said, "and I get the impression you're not one to let others take care of him."

"He's my son. It's my responsibility."

Tolman shuffled her feet on the wood planks. "I don't have any kids, just a deaf cat, so I'm not going to debate it with you. That's just my impression."

Journey shrugged. "These people that are after the document—they'll be here somewhere. They may already be here."

"I must say, you haven't tried very hard to keep away from them."

"I don't hide from things."

"Don't you?"

Journey looked at her again. "Meaning?"

"I've just met you. Maybe I'm way off base. But we all hide from something."

Journey shook his head. "I tried to tell you people about Darlington."

"Yes."

"You didn't believe me."

"Well, *I* believed you. Just because the FBI and the Marshals Service didn't believe you . . . that's not the same thing. Unfortunately, they're the ones with the jurisdiction."

"Does that matter?" Journey said. "The chief justice is dead, and the Glory Warriors killed her."

They both heard footsteps. A young couple with a very blond toddler had come onto the deck. The father lifted the little girl onto one of the benches. "Lots of water!" she exclaimed.

Journey turned away and started toward the parking lot, Tolman following. A winding sidewalk with steel railings on either side sloped down from the deck toward the river. Journey took it all the way down to the spot where it dead-ended in a pile of driftwood.

With his back still to Tolman, he said, "What about the president? Is the Secret Service aware of the threat to him?"

Tolman hesitated a moment. "We need to get you in, to make sure you are safe, to figure out exactly what is going on."

"You didn't answer my question."

"I can't answer your question just yet."

"They're going up the list. They've killed the Speaker, they've killed the chief justice." He raised both hands and let them drop to his sides. "And you're the only one here, from the obscure Research and Investigations Office."

"RIO has its place in the overall picture. But, Dr. Journey, I sat in the threat assessment and listened to the FBI say they thought it was all bullshit, that this was some kind of stunt on your part. You tried to tell us, I tried to tell them, and the chief justice was killed anyway. You're not insane, you're not making this up, and the document is real. I believe that."

Journey clenched a fist, then unfolded it slowly. "Why? Why do you believe me when no one does?"

Tolman looked surprised. "Because of your son."

"What do you mean?"

"You take care of a child that a lot of people probably would be uncomfortable around even for five minutes. You have no motivation to do anything that would take you out of being in a position to raise your son. You have no reason to lie." Tolman exhaled. "Then again, people are more complicated than that. No one really does something just for one reason, whether they know it or not. I don't know you well enough to know the other reasons that I believe you."

Journey shifted around again. "You're very interesting, Meg Tolman. You're not what I would expect from someone who works in a place called the Research and Investigations Office."

"If that's a compliment, thank you," Tolman said.

Journey shrugged and began picking his way through some of the flotsam. He could see a set of concrete steps that led up to the deck. After a moment, Tolman followed him. "What are you doing?" she called.

"Thinking," Journey said. "Something's not right about all this, about being here." He looked at his watch. "The interpretive center opens at nine. Maybe they can answer some questions."

The team members of Dallas Four had stayed with the professor all the way from Carpenter Center, through the airports in Oklahoma City and St. Louis and Louisville. They had taken shifts in the motel, stayed with him as he entered Falls of the Ohio State Park. Thus far, they were undetected. Nick Journey was, after all, an amateur.

They had split up into two rental cars this morning. Silver was dressed in walking shorts and a dark tank top and new Nikes. She was a tourist. Journey would not be expecting her.

She walked onto the deck, guidebook in hand, camera around her neck, taking in the entire area. Journey was below, picking his way through the driftwood, scant steps away from the river. Then her eyes narrowed as she saw the short woman with the shoulder bag three steps behind Journey who appeared to be talking to him.

Silver turned away from the river and walked to the far end of the deck. She raised her wrist and spoke into the microphone there. "We may have a problem," she said.

# CHAPTER

# 30

At nine o'clock, the doors to the Interpretive Center opened and a handful of people trickled in. The receptionist, a gray-haired man with a kindly face, gave them a short speech about the center's theater and exhibits.

Journey continued to look around. The family with the blond toddler was just ahead of them. Several elderly people had come in. A young black woman wearing shorts lagged a little behind.

Journey looked hard at the young woman. Had he seen her before?

He looked at her again. She was studying her guidebook, forehead furrowed. He turned away.

"What?" Tolman asked.

"Nothing. It's nothing. I'm more jumpy than I realized."

They went down a short flight of steps to the auditorium, which held eight rows of seats. The walls were stark and plain. After a few minutes, soft synthesized music filled the room and a video projection appeared on one wall.

Journey squirmed. The film was on the natural history of the area, how in the past this area had been near the Earth's equator and part of a vast sea. The voice-over launched into a narration about the Devonian era.

There was *something* here. *The Poet's Penn* had led here, to this spot on the Ohio River, a river that was at one time a major commercial highway. But the thought wouldn't take shape, flitting away from him instead.

"You want to say something," Tolman said.

They exited the auditorium and walked through the building, looking at the well-developed dioramas and graphics about the area's history. They wound to the back of the building, and Journey stopped dead in his tracks, causing Tolman to bump into him. He stared at a graphic depicting how the river had been dammed beginning in 1866.

"Nothing's the same," he said.

"What?" Tolman said.

Journey didn't answer her, jogging around the corner. They'd come full circle to the reception desk and a gift shop that sold books on the area's history, right alongside pens and pencils and plastic boxes full of colorful rocks.

Journey leaned on the counter. The man with the kind face said, "How do you like the exhibits? Sorry the fossil beds aren't exposed. It's been the wettest summer we've had in thirty years here. Where are you folks from?"

Journey ignored the man's question. "I'm a historian, and I'm doing some research on the area, particularly with regard to the Civil War era."

"Oh, the Falls had quite an interesting history at that time. You know, there were Union Army posts here on the Indiana side in Clarksville, and in Jeffersonville, too. There was a real panic during the war when word came back that the Confederates were going to invade Louisville, so civilians were evacuated across the pontoon bridge to Jeffersonville. And you know what the Union Army did?" The man laughed. "They erected logs into the riverbank to look like cannon, which might fool the Confederates into thinking Jeffersonville was fortified. Maybe it worked—Louisville wasn't ever invaded."

Journey shook his hand from side to side. "All right . . . the first dam was built at the falls in 1866, right?"

"Yes, sir. Now the McAlpine Lock and Dam system—"

"But is anything here today the same as it would have been in 1865?"

"Excuse me?"

Journey gestured around the room. "This whole area. With everything that's been done to the river, none of this is as it was then."

The man picked at a fingernail. "I can't say—"

Journey's mind was racing. "What about the railroad trestle? When was it built?"

"That was 1895. I guess when you put it that way, there wouldn't be anything just the same. Can't expect things to be the exact way they were that long ago."

Journey pulled at Tolman's arm. "Come on."

They stepped back outside. A few more clouds had rolled in, and the day had become overcast.

"What?" Tolman said. "What is it?"

Journey leaned against the railing, his back to the Ohio. "Think about this. Tell me . . . think in terms of 1865. How would this area around Louisville have been different from the area around Fort Washita in Indian Territory?"

"I don't . . . I wasn't a history major."

"Think! Where was the country at that time? What was going on here? What was going on in Oklahoma?"

"I don't . . . I don't know anything about Oklahoma. Indians, I guess. The Indians were in Oklahoma. This isn't a classroom lecture, Dr. Journey."

"But you're right. Fort Washita was where the first page of the Appomattox document was found. At the time Washita was built in 1842, it was the most remote outpost the U.S. Army had. It was truly the frontier. The Native people who had been brought there on the Trail of Tears from the Southeast were in the area, but there weren't many white settlers."

"All right, I get that."

"But here. How would Louisville compare?"

Tolman thought for a moment. "It was more settled. You said it was a major supply point for the Union in the Civil War."

"Exactly! It was settled. It was a city, and it was growing. It was

a steamboat hub. Things were happening here, things were changing all the time."

"But I don't—"

"The man who wrote that document knew that Fort Washita
was in the wilderness, and he knew that *this* was settled. He couldn't
have known what kind of growth the West would undergo after the
war. Oklahoma Territory and Indian Territory didn't merge into a
state until 1907."

Tolman looked surprised. "That's really recent. I didn't realize
that."

Journey nodded. "We're a young state. But at the time of Appomattox, no one could tell what was going to happen in the West. So
he felt that he could safely bury something in the ground there—he
wasn't expecting it to stay there for nearly a hundred fifty years, after
all."

Tolman began to see it. "So he wouldn't have done the same
thing here. This was a major city. But that still doesn't tell us anything about your missing pages."

Journey was quiet for a moment, then started toward the steep
concrete steps he'd climbed earlier. There were six sets of nine steps
each. At the bottom, he turned back to Tolman and said, "I've been
thinking about this all wrong. *The Poet's Penn* wasn't to tell where
another clue was. It *is* the clue."

Tolman sat down on a step. "Explain."

"He meant to lead whoever found the first page back here, back
to Louisville."

"What do you mean, *back* here?"

"Because he was from here. He didn't bury anything or hide
anything at the Falls of the Ohio. But this was his home base. He
figured that whoever found the Fort Washita page would understand that the whole business about the poem and the river bending
and the waters falling would make us understand who he was, and
bring us to his hometown."

Tolman noted his use of the word *us*, and smiled. "All right, I can
see that. But Louisville's a big city—how do we find someone from
1865 who would have gotten close to Grant and Lee?"

"No, the answer's right in front of us: *The Poet's Penn*."

"The poet?"

Journey sat down beside Tolman. "No. Not him. The writing style doesn't match. His writing was very vivid, lots of imagery and description." He folded his hands together. Far off to their left, a whistle sounded as a freight train started across the trestle.

"I keep thinking of something Sandra told me," Journey said.

"Wait a minute . . . Sandra. Who's Sandra?"

Journey hesitated a moment. Tolman noticed the hesitation. "Sandra Kelly. A coworker of mine," Journey said. "A friend."

Tolman nodded and said nothing, watching the subtle shift in his dark eyes.

"When she read the first page of the Washita document, she said it sounded . . . what was the word she used?" He gazed off across the river at Kentucky, then looked at Tolman again, as if he were in a trance. "Businesslike. She said it sounded businesslike."

He took his backpack off his shoulder, unzipped it, and pulled out the legal pad where he'd made notes to himself. His slanting cursive filled margins. He slapped the pad against his knee. "*This* is who we should be looking for."

"Who?"

"David Stanton published *The Poet's Penn* for six years. His money ran out in 1864. But for that entire six years, the journal was funded by a Louisville banker."

"Holy shit," Tolman whispered, then in a louder tone, said, "A banker. He would have had money."

Journey nodded. "It makes a lot more sense for him to get close to Grant and Lee than an itinerant poet." He thumped the pad again. "This is who we need to find. His name was Samuel B. Williams."

# CHAPTER
# 31

D o you trust me?" Tolman asked him.

Journey looked down into her clear blue eyes. A droplet of sweat ran from his hairline, past his cheek, and under his shirt collar. His gaze shifted down, and he pointed at her hands.

"Tell me something. Are you a musician?"

She unfolded her hands, revealing the long, slender fingers and short nails. Tolman nodded. "Pianist. You're observant."

"My son has great hands. Are you any good?"

"Pretty good. I get a few paying gigs."

"How does that work with the government job?"

"I have an understanding boss."

"You play jazz or classical or what?"

"Classical, mostly. But a little of this and a little of that."

"They're good hands," Journey said. "They remind me of Andrew's."

Tolman nodded.

"I guess I don't have any choice," Journey said.

"Nope," Tolman said. "Come on. My laptop's in the car."

They took Tolman's rental to a McDonald's near I-65 in Clarksville, not far from the park. Both ordered coffee and they sat in a corner booth. When she opened her laptop, it was still on the result of the database search she'd done earlier. *Can't be right*, she thought again. She made a mental note to look into it later. Right now she had more concrete, immediate concerns. She saved the search, and she and Journey sat next to each other, Tolman's hands working the keyboard, Journey scribbling more notes on his pad.

In half an hour, Tolman sat back and said, "So the Williams family founded First Commercial Bank of Kentucky in 1840. Henry Benjamin Williams was the founder. He died in 1858, and his oldest son, Samuel Benjamin Williams, took over. There's mention of another son, John Jefferson Williams, who was killed in the war."

"Eighteen fifty-eight is the same year *The Poet's Penn* started."

"A cousin on Samuel's mother's side, Estes Atwood, took over the bank in 1864. It stayed with the family until 1901. It's been through nine mergers and acquisitions since then, but the current River National Bank of Kentucky is its corporate descendant."

"So Samuel Williams took over running the bank the same year he started funding Stanton and *The Poet's Penn*." He counted on his fingers. "Eighteen sixty-four. The Civil War is winding down. *The Poet's Penn* ceases publication. A cousin takes over the bank. Which tells us . . ."

"That something happened to Samuel Williams," Tolman said.

"I would say so."

"I'm beginning to like him for this," Tolman said. "But how do we find what he may have left behind?"

"I'd say we start with the bank."


Journey climbed into her car and Tolman said, "I need to make a phone call." She called Hudson's direct line and heard, "You have reached Russell Hudson, deputy director of the Research and Investigations Office. . . ."

She wasn't surprised. He was probably somewhere with Díaz from the FBI and God only knew who else. After the tone, she said, "Rusty, I haven't heard from the local Bureau here in Louisville. I think Journey's on to something, and we're tracking it down. But I'm a little nervous, and I'd like that backup as soon as I can get it."

She broke the connection, then called the office's main number. The receptionist sounded harried when she answered.

"Tina, it's Meg. Is Rusty in there?"

"He's been gone all morning. Things are not very nice around here. I think the Bureau's blaming us for what happened to the chief justice."

Tolman sighed. "Have him call me ASAP, okay?"

"Okay, but I think he'll be at the Hoover Building for a long time. He said he'd be back here late, if at all. You just can't believe how crazy this is, Meg."

"Yes, I can. Thanks, Tina."

She closed her phone and got behind the wheel of the car. Journey was looking at her. "Trying to get us covered," she said, and pointed the car toward the highway.


On the Kentucky side of the river, they drove downtown to the corporate headquarters of River National Bank, in its own office tower at the corner of Fourth Street and Liberty.

Fourth Street, between Liberty and Muhammad Ali Boulevard, had been turned into a pedestrian mall and renamed "Fourth Street Live." An arch-shaped roof covered most of the block and a raised walkway spanned the street. Retail shops, chain restaurants, nightclubs, and a huge bowling alley called X-Bowl fronted the street. Foot traffic flowed easily.

"Looks like downtown Louisville is doing pretty well," Tolman said.

In the main lobby of the blue-tinted River Tower, Tolman asked a bored twenty-something man wearing a headset for the bank's community relations office. He punched a few buttons on a telephone console and directed them to the ninth floor.

On the ninth floor, a blond woman, who in four-inch heels was as tall as Journey and a full foot taller than Tolman, greeted them. "I'm Janine Pierce," she said. "Assistant vice president of community relations. How can I help you?" Her voice was soft and pleasant, not deep Southern, but neither was it Midwestern. Tolman suspected it was a common accent in Louisville.

Tolman showed her government ID. "Thanks for seeing us, Ms. Pierce. We're in the midst of an investigation that is connected to the Williams family, who founded First Commercial Bank."

Pierce was walking in long strides toward a small office. "First Commercial? Hmm, I think you may have the wrong . . . Oh no, wait a minute. First Commercial was the original bank. Oh my, it hasn't been First Commercial in a long, long time."

"I understand that," Journey said, "but we're looking for any kind of historical information we can get on the Williams family, who started First Commercial. We thought the bank might have some records."

"Oh, I don't think our records would go back that far. We've been River National Bank of Kentucky since 1997, and before that we were part of Cornerstone Bank for a long time. Have you looked online?"

"That's what led us to you."

"You can find almost anything on the Web," Pierce said. "It's amazing, isn't it? My two girls are seven and nine, and they just can't imagine a world without computers. And I'm not even *that* old."

They waited.

"Let me just check on something," Pierce said, uncomfortable with the silence. She left the room and returned in a few minutes with a note written in large round printing on a River National Bank notepad. "I asked Donna. She's been here forever. She said a few years ago there was a man here in town who wanted to write a book, and the bank donated a lot of its historical records to him to help with his research. He passed away a while back, but Donna thinks his son has all those papers. He has an office downtown, not far from here. Maybe he can help you."

Tolman and Journey were back on the street in five minutes, mingling with the increasing crowds along Fourth Street Live. The clouds had broken somewhat, and small rays of light pierced the pedestrian mall's roof, casting little squares onto the walkway. A bluegrass band was playing on a stage in the middle of the street, doing a blistering acoustic cover of the Beatles' "Ticket to Ride." Under normal circumstances, Tolman might have stopped to listen. She liked the vocal harmonies and the interplay of the mandolin and banjo in bluegrass music.

She watched the crowd as they passed the stage. "It'd be hard to pick up a tail in this kind of place."

"They're here," Journey said. "They want the pages. The first page says that all the pages, including the signatures, have to be intact for the document to have the force of law."

Tolman stepped around a pair of tables that sat in front of a Borders bookstore. "Forgive me for saying so, but these people don't seem overly concerned with the force of law, if they've really assassinated Vandermeer and Darlington."

"No, it makes a kind of strange sense. These Glory Warriors came into existence with the writing of this document, something that Grant and Lee supposedly agreed to at the same time as the Appomattox surrender. Several of the eyewitness accounts at Appomattox said that the two generals were alone in the house, just the two of them, for several minutes before the staffs were allowed in to witness the actual surrender. Until those rifles and the G.W. pin and the first page of that document were dug up, no one ever thought anything of it. But the Glory Warriors want to justify themselves. It's like the KKK trying to use the Bible to justify white supremacy. The documentation is important to these groups. Never mind what they're willing to do on the way to whatever their goal is. Once they get there, they all crave legitimacy in the eyes of the people."

"So this thing has become something of a holy grail for them."

Journey nodded. "Someone's behind them—someone who has money and resources to do all this, to keep looking for the holy grail year after year."

They walked in silence for a few steps, passing the bowling alley and out from under the roof. "I'm sorry about what happened to you," Tolman said. "The attack, the campus police officer, the man you killed. It's a lot to process."

"What do I say to that? Yes, it's a lot. They put me into that position. And because of it, Pete Parsons is dead, and the man who shot him and was trying to shoot me is dead. They're waiting around for me to find that page and take it from me, and then probably kill me." He put his hands in the pockets of his khakis. "Can't let them do that."

"No, we can't," Tolman said, but she wondered why she hadn't heard anything about her backup.


They turned the corner from Fourth Street and walked a block. To their right, just before Fifth Street, was a quiet garden courtyard. A brick building sported a blue awning that read CENTER FOR INTER-FAITH RELATIONS. Several people sat in the garden, reading. They crossed the street to a dusty glass storefront. Journey checked the address on the notepaper Janine Pierce had given them.

"This is the place," he said.

There was no sign on the door, only a business card taped to it. The card read

### ASSOCIATION OF MINOR LEAGUE ENTHUSIASTS
#### Evan Lovell, Executive Director

An address, phone number, and Web address followed.

Journey and Tolman looked at each other. Tolman pulled on the glass door and they went in. The small corner office was furnished with a single desk. It seemed to be wood, but only small patches of it showed. The rest of the space was piled with papers, books, and magazines. Baseball posters were tacked to the walls. Baseball cards spilled out of envelopes and boxes and cartons.

A man in his mid-thirties sat at the desk. He had a round body and string-straight brown-blond hair that hung in a ponytail to the middle of his back. His bushy mustache was a little darker than the hair, and he wore round glasses. He was wearing a Louisville Red-birds T-shirt and a Sacramento River Cats cap.

He looked up at them, as if he weren't used to visitors. "Hi. Do you need directions or something? Fourth Street is that way." He pointed back the way they'd come.

"Are you Mr. Lovell?" Journey asked.

"That's me," the man said. "Do I know you?"

"I don't think we've met. My name is Nick Journey, and I'm from—"

"Oh my god!" Lovell stood up, and a few papers fluttered around him. "Nick Journey, left-handed pitcher, Tigers organization, 1989 to 1994. Incredible progress through the ranks to AAA Toledo. Record of fourteen and five in 1993, ERA of two-point-eight-one. Opposing hitters hit two-thirty-six that year. The next year you had elbow injuries and were two and ten, ERA of six-point-zero-two. You retired after that. Nick Journey." He stopped for a moment. "You're the same Nick Journey, right?"

Tolman was looking at Journey. He thought she was almost smiling.

"Yeah," Journey said. "You . . . you follow the minors."

"That's what we do here. We track the players who never make it to the big leagues. We have supporters all over the world. Our Web site gets over half a million hits every day. Can I interview you?"

Tolman stepped between the two men. "I'm sorry, Mr. Lovell. I'm Meg Tolman." She showed her ID. "We'd like to ask *you* a few questions."

"Shit. Oh, shit . . . IRS. You're IRS." He looked at Journey. "You retired from baseball to join the IRS?"

"No, actually I'm a history professor, and she's not IRS," Journey said. "We understand your father was writing a book that had to do with the history of First Commercial Bank."

Lovell looked at both of them. "That's why you're here?"

"Yes," Journey and Tolman said together.

"Nick Journey, right here in my office, and he wants to talk about the book my dad was always going to write." Lovell waved at two dusty folding chairs. "Just toss that crap off those chairs. He never wrote it. He spent forty years gathering material, but he never would write it. He got all kinds of people to give him all kinds of stuff, and he went over it and over it, but he never wrote a word of it down. Finally it got to the point that all he did was look at that stuff. Wouldn't do anything else. My mother found him keeled over dead in the middle of all those papers, eleven years ago."

"So the book was a history of the bank itself? We're really more interested in the family that founded the bank."

Lovell barked out a laugh. "Of course you are. You want to know what happened to Sam Williams."

Journey leaned forward.

"Dad never solved it," Lovell said. "He spent forty years re-searching it, and he never realized that no one even cared anymore. You're the first people who've come around asking."

"What do you mean, your dad never solved it?" Tolman said.

"You mean you don't know? I don't get it. Then why are you here?"

"You tell us," Journey said.

Lovell put on a sly look. "Will you autograph some cards for me?"

"As many as you want."

Lovell smiled like a kid on Christmas morning. "I just need to find the key to that locker where I put all those papers. You can have them all, if you want. It was a big deal at the time, but you know how things are. People forget after a while. It gets to be a hundred years or more and people *really* forget. No one cares about what happened to a banker in Louisville way back then."

"I do," Journey said.

"Wow. Yeah, it's really something else. Sam Williams was this rich guy, his family started the biggest bank in Louisville, and they owned a lot of land. Lots of old money there. When his old man died, Sam took over the bank. He had been in the war that came before the Civil War—the Mexican War, I think—and some people said he'd been a spy for the army before he came back here. So he in-herited all that money and the bank and everything. Then . . . poof!" Lovell clapped his hands together suddenly. A little plume of dust rose from the desk. "He disappeared in the fall of 1864, while the Civil War was still going on. Gone without a trace . . . No one saw or heard from Sam Williams ever again."

# CHAPTER
# 32

The noon Mass at Cathedral of the Assumption, across Fifth Street, had just let out, and Dallas Four Gold stopped to take a few photographs of the gorgeous 1852 church with its tall white spire. He nodded to a few of the parishioners as they exited the cathedral, and he took a few more pictures with his small digital camera.

Then he turned and walked back to the corner, facing the dirt- and grease-streaked window of the Association of Minor League Enthusiasts. He had watched Journey and the woman go in, had seen them talking to the heavyset man with the mustache and ponytail. He was growing impatient and tired.

Hands on his camera, pretending to look at the image of a photo he'd just taken, Gold glanced again at the building across the way. The man behind the desk had just brought out several cardboard boxes and placed them in front of Journey and the woman. His pulse quickened, and he reported to Bronze, who talked with Chicago base, who had jurisdiction over the Louisville area.

Gold fiddled with his camera a little more and walked back toward the cathedral. He had to stay alert now.

\* \* \*

"Oh, he was obsessed with it," Lovell said as he pulled the lid off a cardboard box labeled WILLIAMS 1958–1963. "And to be fair to the old man, it *was* sort of a famous unsolved mystery around here way back when. My dad was really into Louisville history, and he thought he was going to solve it and write a bestseller and make a lot of money and go on the *Today Show*. You know, that kind of crap. He got lots of stuff the first few years, mainly old newspaper clippings, but there were even some police reports from the early twentieth century when it was still technically an open case. It kind of fell off after that, but he'd get two or three new things a year. Then finally, not too long before he died, the bank released a bunch of papers. Turns out they'd been in the vault for a long time and no one ever did anything with them. The bank's new CEO wanted all that crap out of there. Can't say that I blame him. So it all came back here."

"What do you mean, *back* here?" Tolman said.

"This place," Lovell said. "It was the old man's real estate office. He left it to me. I live upstairs. Don't ever have to leave if I don't want to."

Journey laid his hand over a bulging envelope. "Do you mind?"

"Go ahead. I've got stuff to do. But you promised to sign cards before you leave."

"I will."

He unfolded a yellowed newspaper clipping dated October 1, 1914. HALF CENTURY MYSTERY, the headline read, with the subhead, SCION OF LOUISVILLE FAMILY WAS MISSING DURING CIVIL WAR.

It was a short piece marking fifty years since prominent banker Samuel Benjamin Williams disappeared from his Louisville home, never to be heard from again. There were tantalizing tidbits: Williams was reputed to have been a member of Major McCulloch's renowned company of army "scouts"—a euphemism for spies, Journey knew—in the Mexican War of 1846–1848 before returning to Louisville high society. Further intrigue: a longtime employee of the bank swore he'd seen Williams walking out of the bank late one night "about six months after he went away." The man, in his eighties in 1914, was not believed to be credible, and was rumored to have "imbibed generously in spirits." Journey smiled at the language of the period journalism.

Paper-clipped three pages down was a smudged photocopy. Journey stopped cold when he saw the handwriting.

*I wear no uniform, but I am no less a warrior, a warrior to reclaim the glory of this American land. I leave all to my younger brother, John, who has crossed the river to join the Federals.*

"This is his writing," Journey said.

Both Tolman and Lovell looked up, Tolman from her own box, Lovell from his computer monitor and a small assortment of Nick Journey baseball cards he'd scavenged from a filing cabinet.

Journey dug in his backpack and withdrew his copy of the page from Fort Washita. He placed it on one knee, the page he'd just found on the other knee. Tolman looked at both, smoothing the pages on Journey's knees. Lovell looked at them with mild interest, then went back to clicking his mouse.

"Look at the shapes of the letters," Journey said.

"Are you really that much of a handwriting expert?" Tolman said.

"No, no, but when you read a lot of original documents from a period, you get used to analyzing them. It's the same."

Tolman ran her finger along the top of the page that had just come out of the box. In the same script was written the date, *1 Oct 1864*.

"You know what it reminds me of?" she said. "A suicide note. Like he was telling the world he was leaving."

"But a suicide without a body. Aside from one admittedly dubious sighting, no one ever saw him again after this. According to the 1914 newspaper story, he simply didn't go to the bank that day. His house was neat and orderly, all his clothes were in the closets, even his watch was on his dresser. His housekeeper said everything looked exactly as it should look, except for the note—*this* note—on the dresser. He was just . . . gone." Journey shook his head.

"Where was he between October first and the end of the war?" Tolman asked.

"Maybe getting close to the generals. Maybe putting the Glory Warriors apparatus into place. Here's something to think about: This newspaper story says he was one of McCulloch's 'scouts' during the Mexican War. Lee and Grant were both in Mexico—most Regular Army officers were. It's not inconceivable that Williams could have met both Ulysses Grant and Robert E. Lee nearly twenty years earlier."

Tolman looked at the newspaper clipping. "And he was from an influential family."

Journey nodded. "Not just an influential family, but one from a strategic city in a border state. That, plus the fact that they would consider him a 'brother officer,' a Mexico veteran, might have made them willing to meet with him. If he'd been just some obscure civilian Kentucky banker, they probably wouldn't give him the time of day." He shook the note Williams had written. "He even mentions being a 'warrior to reclaim the glory.' And maybe the dubious sighting wasn't so dubious after all." He picked up the 1914 clipping again. "This bank employee, supposedly after locking the bank one night a few months after Williams disappeared, said he saw him coming out a side door. Maybe this really *was* Williams after all, on his way from Appomattox to Indian Territory. . . ."

"And he locked the page in the vault of his own bank."

They looked at each other.

Lovell stared over his computer at them. "So you guys think you really know what happened to Williams? I mean, my old man never solved it, in all those years. He let his real estate business fall off, he pissed off his whole family . . . and you really think you know?"

"I'm not sure," Journey said. "It's a lot of maybes. But the time frame is right. Just like I told Sandra, he could have ridden here from Virginia, placed the page in the bank—right under everyone's noses— then taken boats from here to Fort Smith, bought a horse there, and ridden to Washita."

"And where else would be more secure than a bank vault?"

"*His* bank vault, no less. And that was what he was trying to tell us with *The Poet's Penn*. He was telling us who he was, telling us that he came home to Louisville before heading to the frontier for the last phase of the plan."

They were silent a moment; then Tolman picked up the note. "What about his brother? John?"

"I can answer that one," Lovell said. "My old man mentioned

him a few times. He was a lot younger than Sam, and he joined one of the Indiana regiments. He was killed in the war. That's no mystery. He didn't work in the bank and didn't want anything to do with it. He was a blacksmith, but he got killed in the war."

"So he left the bank to his brother," Tolman said, "but his brother was killed in the war. That's when the cousin took over, and the strange disappearance of Samuel Williams just faded out of everyone's consciousness after a while."

Journey looked at Lovell. "Evan, did you say that the bank donated a lot of papers to your father just before he died?"

Lovell nodded. "Yeah. They cleaned out their old vault."

Journey and Tolman looked at each other again. Neither one spoke for half a minute.

"Then more than likely," Tolman finally said, "the pages we're looking for are somewhere right here."

Journey and Tolman sat on the floor and began sifting through the dusty cardboard boxes. Lovell watched them while continuing to work at his computer and answering an occasional phone call.

Hours passed. The piles grew. Thomas Lovell seemed to have collected every possible scrap of paper that had anything to do with the disappearance of Samuel Williams, though there did not appear to be much of a filing system. A letter from Estes Atwood, Williams's cousin who eventually took over the bank, rested alongside a copy of a newspaper photo of Williams. The picture showed a man of medium height and build, with dark hair parted in the middle, and a dark mustache. He wore the black frock coat of the times and a string tie. The photo was unremarkable, Journey thought. Samuel Williams looked average, a man no one would notice in a crowd.

Journey put the photo aside, atop the "leaving" letter. At the bottom of a box, Tolman pulled out a manila envelope, opened it, and withdrew a single, brittle sheet. "The seal," she said.

Journey looked up. "What?"

"You were telling me about the seal of the Glory Warriors? I think I found it . . . but this is no treaty."

"What is it?"

"Looks like a receipt of some sort."

Tolman handed him the paper. Under the Glory Warriors' seal, in flowing handwriting—not that of Samuel Williams—was written, *Enclosed fifty (50) G.W. jewelry pieces, per specifications.* The page was dated January 2, 1865, and signed *Layton P. Detheridge.*

"The jeweler," Journey said. "He was one of them, one of the original Glory Warriors. It makes perfect sense."

"What do you mean?"

"When Williams was recruiting people to his cause, he made sure he found someone who could make the pieces of jewelry. The company's still in business, and the Detheridge family is still making G.W. pins. You know what else this proves? It proves Samuel Williams was still around after October of 1864, if this wound up in his papers."

"So this was one of the things he put in the bank vault."

Journey pointed at the box. "We're on the right track. Keep looking." He added the jewelry receipt to his growing pile of items to keep.

"Um, do you want something to eat?" Lovell said from behind his desk. "I can go get something, if you want."

"That's not necessary, Evan," Journey said. "You've really done enough for us."

"I can get you some great barbecue," Lovell went on as if he hadn't heard. "There's a place a few blocks away. You like ribs? They have wonderful ribs."

Lovell eased out of the office without waiting for a reply. When the door closed behind him, Tolman said, "So you're a sports celebrity."

"Hardly. Not too many people would remember my playing career. Then again, there are those hard-core minor league fans. It was a long time ago."

"You miss it?"

"No. It's not who I am anymore."

"I see. So tell me about this Sandra," Tolman said.

"Is this professional interest?"

"Maybe."

Journey put down the clipping in his hand. "She teaches in the same department I do. She's younger, a fairly new faculty member. She's . . . she's been a sort of friend."

"You've mentioned her twice."

"She's the only other person who knows about this. Other than the Glory Warriors and the U.S. government, that is. I'm sorry, I shouldn't have told her. It was wrong of me to get her involved."

Tolman shrugged. "Better than you carrying it around all by yourself."

"No, it's not like that. She actually found what *The Poet's Penn* was. I would never have found it. . . ."

"But you told her about it, trusted her with it."

Journey thought of what he'd shouted at Sandra: *"You know nothing about my life!"*

*"And whose choice is that?"* she'd shouted back.

"I don't want to talk about this with you," Journey said.

Tolman looked at him. "You're an interesting man, Dr. Journey. When you're talking about history-related things, your whole body language changes. Your eyes even open wider. But when it comes to anything personal, you close yourself up like one of those little antique fans."

Journey said nothing.

"And you force yourself to rein in what you say," Tolman said. "You hold yourself back a lot."

"I think of Sandra Kelly as a colleague and, recently, as a friend," Journey said. "That should answer your question."

"Does she know about your son?"

Journey settled his gaze on Tolman's blue eyes. "Of course. I keep a lot of things to myself, but I don't hide. I don't walk around with 'Poor me, I have a child with autism' tattooed on my forehead, but I don't hide him, either."

"But I bet his mother does, doesn't she?"

Journey was silent.

"I've made a book on you, and it's over a hundred pages by now," Tolman said. "Not to pry, not to get some vicarious thrill, but to try to understand you as I was researching your case, trying to figure out what happened to you when those guys attacked you on the college campus."

"His mother—," Journey said, then stopped and looked out the dusty window. "His mother thinks we should put him in a residential care program. She's never come out and said it in so many words, but that's what she wants. She as much as offered to pay for it."

"How do you feel about that?"

"I don't—I can't. He's my son. It's my job to raise him. It's not that there aren't excellent residential programs around. With the autism explosion the last ten years or so, there are a lot more treatments out there. And I know Amelia wants what's best for him, even if she can't handle doing it herself, hands-on. But what would it mean if I put him away somewhere at twelve years old?"

"I don't know. It might mean that was your best option at the time. People do what they have to do."

"Yes, and I have to raise Andrew. I may not be great at it, but I try to do the right things for him."

Tolman was quiet a moment. "I know about the car accident that killed your family."

"So? I suppose that's public record."

"I understand a little bit about you. I think it even partially explains why you're so committed to your son."

"You knowing what happened when I was seven doesn't mean anything." Journey's voice was even.

Tolman hesitated for a long time. "Dr. Journey, when I was fifteen, my mother drove her car off the Rock Creek Parkway and into the Potomac. I was in the backseat. She didn't survive. She was screaming at me, and that's why she lost control of the car."

Journey's tone changed. "Why are you telling me this?"

Tolman thought of Hudson's words: *If you dig deeply enough, you always come up with a fistful of tragedy.* "I'm not sure. I don't tell many people. But I think I understand some things about you, and maybe it's partly because of my own experience."

"I don't think about them anymore," Journey said. "They're gone. It's almost like . . ." He let the sentence fade, shuffling papers.

"Like they never existed," Tolman said.

Journey looked up at her but said nothing.

"I can do the math," Tolman said. "It happened when you were seven. You're forty-two now. You were with them for seven years; they've been gone for thirty-five. I get it."

"Yes," Journey said. He looked as if he were about to say more, but stopped himself and gave a slight half nod.

"I still think about my mother a lot," Tolman said. "I ask myself a lot of 'what if' questions. You can't tell me you haven't done the same. Maybe not in a long time, but I'll bet you have."

Journey locked eyes with her, then looked away, back to the pages in his lap. "We need to get through these papers."

Tolman went back to her own pile. A few minutes later, Lovell was back with armloads of plastic containers. They ate ribs and cole-slaw and potato salad and drank Pepsi.

After eating, Lovell joined them. "I want to help. I can stop working for a while. I want to find what you're looking for. Maybe I owe it to my old man." He took the lid off a box and went to work.

At five twenty, Lovell thumbed a page and said, "What about this one?"

He'd said the same thing every ten minutes or so since he started, but Journey took the clear plastic bag containing a sheet of paper. Journey saw immediately that it was not a photocopy.

He began to read, then looked up. "You found it," he said in a whisper.

Journey looked around at the fourteen file boxes and the hundreds of scraps of paper they'd already seen; then he began to read. Tolman angled her body so she could see the page as well.

"I found it," Lovell said. "Cool."

*This clause concerns the group of dedicated men of integrity, men of both North and South, who shall henceforth be known as the Glory Warriors. These officers and soldiers, both within the armies and without, shall assume exclusive executive control of the American Federal Government, in the event of the circumstances preceding.*

*With firmness of governance and efficacy of operation the primary objectives, other branches of the American Federal Government shall suspend their operation until reorganized by the controlling executive. Said executive shall be the leader of the Glory Warriors, chosen from within its ranks. He shall possess executive*

*power and shall function as Commander-in-Chief, with the other*
*members of the Glory Warriors to be organized into a new*
*governing body to assure effective governance.*

*Members of the Glory Warriors are to assume control of posts*
*throughout the American continent, in areas both Union and*
*Confederate, with direction and governance under the authority of*
*a regional commander, to be chosen from within the ranks.*

*Pursuant to the presence of conditions (outlined preceding) that*
*warrant such transfer of governmental operation to ensure stability*
*and tranquillity for all, we enact these provisions into law by virtue*
*of affixing our signatures.*

Written in the same hand, but with a different pen and slightly
darker ink, was *At Appomattox Court House, VA.*

"Jesus," Tolman whispered.

"Is it what you thought?" Lovell asked.

Journey looked at him. He felt hot. He didn't speak.

"And this just sat in the bank vault for over a century," Tolman
said.

"Just like the other page was buried in the ground for all that
time," Journey said. "Waiting for them to find it." He looked at
Lovell. "Evan, I think your father had something very explosive in
his possession and he didn't even know what it was." He glanced
back to Tolman. "See, it doesn't make sense without the first page.
Without the first page laying out the conditions, it's just gibberish.
I mean, there were all kinds of so-called plots to overthrow the government during that time. John Wilkes Booth couldn't pull it off,
though he tried. Right at the end and immediately after the war,
there were radical groups everywhere, in practically every state, all
with their own ideas about how to run things."

"But this one actually laid out the conditions that had to be present, then stated what they were going to do if those conditions arose."
Tolman shook her head. "Jesus. This is—"

"But they never did it," Lovell said.

The other two looked at him.

"I mean, obviously they didn't. I guess you're saying Sam Williams was behind this thing and he hid this in his bank vault for all

those years and no one figured out what it meant, and then my dad had it . . . but no one overthrew the government. So it doesn't matter, right?"

"Evan," Tolman said, "we need to take this with us."

Lovell's sly look crept back onto his face. "But maybe it's worth some money now."

"Evan, I'm telling you that we are taking these papers. I am confiscating them for the U.S. government. Your contribution will be noted."

"But the signatures," Journey said. "Both pages specifically state that all the pages have to be present, including the signatures, for the clause to take effect. Grant and Lee had to sign it." He looked at Lovell again. "Did your father ever say anything about having a page with Grant and Lee's signatures?"

Lovell held up both hands. "Whoa. I don't know anything about history, but I know who *they* were. I think if the old man had something like that, he would have said something. You think Sam Williams got them to sign this thing and he hid it in the bank, too?"

"Maybe," Journey said. "I don't know. We need to keep looking."

"Hell," Lovell said, "if I had a page with those guys' signatures on it, I'd put it up on eBay. I bet you could get a lot of money for it."


They had combed through almost all the boxes already, and it took only another half hour to empty them.

"No signatures," Tolman said, rubbing her eyes from fatigue and dust.

"No signatures," Journey said.

"They have to be here," Tolman said. The fingers of her right hand were moving, as if touching unseen piano keys.

Journey watched her hand, and he thought of Andrew's hands, the beautiful long, tapering fingers that would never play piano. He thought of the rhythms Andrew made with his straw and his pencil. Perhaps, he thought, there was music—beautiful, expressive music— in Andrew's mind, all from a straw and pencil. In Journey's world— and Andrew's—things were not always what they seemed to be on the surface.

Journey gazed around at the piles of papers, at the forty years' work Thomas Lovell had put into the disappearance of Samuel Williams, never to find out what happened to the banker. All the time, the creation of the Glory Warriors was here, on a page that at first glance could have been construed as the mindless ramblings of a Civil War–era conspiracy nut.

*Things are not always what they seem.*

"We need to get the signatures," Tolman was saying. "Before *they* do. We have to take this in."

Journey looked at her.

The straw and the pencil. Rhythms.

*Things were not what they seemed.*

"The signatures were never here," he said.

"What?" Tolman said.

"No. Williams was too smart for that. We don't know if all of this was his idea, or if one of the generals came up with it and he became the go-between. But we do know he wrote this for the generals to sign. Then he split it up. Maybe they told him to; maybe he just didn't want it to be too easy for all this to fall into place. So he came home to Louisville, left this page in the vault, then went to Indian Territory. He left the first page there, and that's where the cache of weapons had been gathered. He wrote the note about *The Poet's Penn* on the front page so that whoever found it would eventually find page two."

"But if he'd split up the first two pages, then he'd keep the signature page as far away from both of them as he could."

Journey shook the pages. "The generals didn't trust him. Or he didn't trust them. Either way, the signatures have to be somewhere else."

"Where?" Lovell said. "And you still don't know what happened to him. I mean, to Sam Williams himself. Say he did all this stuff . . . but where did he go then?"

"I think when we find that," Journey said, "we'll find Grant and Lee's signatures."

Gold had sat in the peaceful garden of the Center for Interfaith Relations for hours, standing up to stretch at intervals. He kept a map of downtown Louisville at his side, and he had read most of a book on Norse mythology through the course of the afternoon.

He walked to the corner. Through the dusty window, he saw all three of them standing. The man with the mustache and ponytail was stuffing some papers into a manila envelope. He handed them to the woman. Gold watched their body language—they were tense, tight, excited. The woman handed the envelope to Journey.

The two of them emerged from the office at a fast walk and turned toward Gold.

"We have to get you in," Tolman said, pulling out her cell phone.

Journey didn't protest this time. "My car. My rental car is still at Falls of the Ohio."

"We'll go get it, turn it in, and then you're with me. They have to believe you now." She was punching buttons on the phone. "Don't look up. The guy over there in front of the courtyard, the Asian guy in the jeans and the gray shirt. He's been around here all afternoon. How long can one tourist hang around a courtyard?"

Journey made himself keep his eyes forward as they crossed the street. They fast-walked halfway down the block to Tolman's car. Tolman kept the phone pressed to her ear, and in a moment heard a familiar voice. "Hudson."

"Rusty, where's my fucking backup?"

"Meg?"

"Goddammit, yes, it's me! Where is my backup?"

"Listen to me," Hudson said, his voice even. "They will *not* authorize people without some kind of evidence. I couldn't—"

"Rusty, if they want evidence, all they need is what's left of Nan Darlington. He was right, Rusty. Journey was right. We have another page of the document."

"Things are very difficult here right now," Hudson said. "They think that there may have been someone inside the chief justice's protective detail. Brent Graves is calling in everyone in the division. The media are all around. They haven't descended on RIO yet, but they may."

"Shit. *Shit!* Someone inside . . . these people could do that. I think they have pretty long arms, and I have one on me right now." She unlocked the car doors and slid in, motioning to Journey to do the same.

"You have someone following you?"

"Pretty sure."

"Meg . . . I am on a secure phone line. You're on a cell."

Tolman nodded. "I know. Just believe me when I tell you that Journey called it. There's one more piece we have to get—"

"Stop right there, Meg."

Tolman slapped one hand against the steering wheel. "Rusty, listen to me. I think . . . I think you may need to talk to the Service."

Hudson was silent.

"Rusty? Do you understand what I'm saying?"

"Damn," Hudson said, and his voice was very soft. It was the first time Tolman had ever heard him curse. "Can you put it together?"

"Jesus, I hope so," Tolman said.

"I'll do what I can here. Don't come back until you have it all and can show it to Díaz and anyone else who needs to see it. Do you have somewhere you can go to ground?"

Tolman thought for a moment. "I think so. It's a stretch, but I think I can make it work."

"Talk to no one but me, Meg," Hudson said, "and only on secure lines. If what Graves says is true, this burrows very deep. If what you're saying is true, then it is significantly bigger than RIO. Don't trust anyone you don't know well. If there is someone inside . . ."

"There could be lots of people inside."

"Exactly. Call me when you can talk. I'm sorry I did not believe you before, Meg. Bring me evidence. And take care."

Tolman started to hang up, then said, "Hold on a minute, Rusty." Tolman turned to Journey. "Did you say you gave the original of the first page to the agents who came to your house?"

"Yes, of course. They weren't taking me seriously and I—"

"Who were they?"

"One of them was from the Oklahoma City FBI office. I think his name was Winters. He did most of the talking. The other was a federal marshal from the Judicial Protective Division. His name was Hendrickson."

Back into the phone: "Rusty, did you hear that? There's your evidence. Page one of the document. Find this guy Hendrickson. Find out where he went after he came back to D.C. That paper is somewhere in D.C. right now!"

"Meg, don't say any more. You're on a cell phone."

Tolman snapped her phone closed and said, "God*damn* bureaucrats."

"What?" Journey said.

"My boss."

"The understanding one? The one who lets you play piano?"

Tolman smiled without humor. "The same. A great guy, even a big-brother type to me, but he's also the consummate paper-shuffler, the perfect administrator. He's covering the office's ass, and I guess that's his job."

"And what does that mean to us?"

"It means we cross every *t* and dot every *i*. It means we have to have the rest of this in hand, and hope to God your friends the Glory Warriors can't get close to the president. It also means—" She looked sidelong at Journey. "It also means that we are on our own."


Gold watched as the Ford Focus pulled away from the parking meter, made a sharp right on Fifth Street, and headed north. He went to his own rental car, a black Suburban, and called Silver.

"Yes?" she said.

"They picked up some papers. I'm going to find out what. I heard them talking as they went back to their car. They're headed back to the park to pick up Journey's car."

"This may be our opportunity," Silver said. "Hold the line."

Sixty seconds later, she said, "Bronze just talked to Chicago Base. We are green light to do whatever is necessary."


Evan Lovell was still coming down from the rush of the afternoon, the intensity of emotions he'd never felt before. Nick Journey—former Tigers organization pitcher and now a history professor!—had been in his office all afternoon, going through his dad's things.

And he'd helped. He'd found what Journey needed. All that business about Grant and Lee and Glory Warriors and Sam Williams, right in the middle of it. His old man would have loved it, and for a few fleeting moments, Evan Lovell thought the old man might have been proud of him for being the one who found it.

Back at his computer, making updates to the association Web site, he looked up when a man came in. "Hi," he said. "Do you need directions? Fourth Street is that way."

"I don't need directions," the man said. A black fanny pack—Lovell had always wondered why they were called that—was strapped around his waist.

"Well, it's my big day, then," Lovell said.

"You spent a long time with the two people who were just here," the man said.

Lovell's eyes narrowed. "Yeah. How do you know?"

"You gave them some papers. What were they?"

Lovell drew himself up. "Hey, that's a little rude, mister. That was Nick Journey, former pitcher for—"

The man reached into his fanny pack and pulled out a gun, aiming it at Lovell's chest.

"Hey, whoa, whoa! I don't have any money!"

"I don't want money. What did you give Journey?"

"Papers. Some of my dad's old history papers."

"You read them. What were they?"

"Look, I don't want any trouble, mister." Lovell started to tremble. "That was just my dad's old stuff."

"I can kill you with one shot, and I assure you, I will," the man said, his voice calm. "Talk to me and I won't."

"I . . . I . . . I . . . look, it was all about Sam Williams. He was this banker in Louisville and he disappeared in the Civil War, and he left some stuff in the bank vault, and there was this page about a—what do you call it?—a coup, like people overthrowing the government. There was a group that Nick and the lady kept talking about . . . the glorious warriors or something. Don't shoot me!"

"And you gave them these papers?"

"Yeah, yeah, yeah! They acted like they were important, and I

found the important page, and they're going to make sure I get credit for it—"

Lovell didn't even hear the shot that killed him. He saw the muzzle flash, though he didn't think the man had moved. How could he do that and not move at all? Lovell felt one moment of incredible pain in his chest, and he saw red gushing out all over his desk. It splattered his computer monitor, and all his spreadsheets that he'd printed out. He'd been working on stats from the New Orleans Zephyrs teams from 1995 to 2000, and now his spreadsheets were ruined.

Then Lovell felt himself pitching forward. In an instant of bright clarity, while the world blazed around him, he thought that in all the excitement, he'd forgotten to get Nick Journey to autograph the baseball cards for him. Then Lovell felt nothing at all.

Tolman drove as fast as she could through the tail end of rush hour traffic on the I-65 bridge. She cast an eye for watchers with every move, every lane change, every acceleration. Journey used his cell to call Amelia, who sounded rushed. "How's Andrew?" he asked her.

"He's eating, Nick. What do you want?"

"Oh," Journey said.

There was a silence; then Amelia said, "What, are you surprised I actually feed him?"

"No, no, of course not. I was just hoping you could hold the phone up to him and he could hear my voice."

"Now's not a good time," Amelia said. Andrew screeched in the background. "See what I mean? When will you be back?"

"I don't know. This may take longer than I expected."

Amelia was silent.

Journey cleared his throat. "So did Paul meet him?"

Amelia said nothing. Andrew screamed again, then whistled in the same breath.

"Was there anything else?" Amelia said.

"You're safe, then."

"Oh, God, Nick, don't be melodramatic."

She hung up in his ear. Journey bowed his head and rubbed his forehead. His face felt hot again. He couldn't remember if he'd taken his blood pressure pill in the morning. This morning seemed like a long time ago.

Tolman came off the bridge, cut across three lanes, and took the first exit on the Indiana side. She came down into Jeffersonville, then two left turns and a right turn later, passed into Clarksville, "the home of the Falls of the Ohio." They passed through Ashland Park, wedged between Riverside Drive and the river itself. They passed the dam, then under the railroad trestle that spanned the Ohio immediately behind the dam.

Tolman bore the car left and passed the interpretive center, with its Lewis and Clark statue, pulling around to the parking lot in the rear. Journey stuffed the envelope with page two of the document deep into his backpack, along with his copy of the first page. Tolman leaned out the door and said, "I'll follow you back to the airport so you can turn your car in." Her eyes flickered to the rear-view mirror.

"All right," Journey said, climbed in his car, and drove toward the front of the park.


Silver and Bronze's car, another dark Suburban, was in a loosely graveled parking area on the other side of the railroad trestle. "This is him," Silver said into her wrist radio, watching as Journey's rental passed the stone sign announcing FALLS OF THE OHIO INTERPRE-TIVE CENTER and onto Riverside Drive.

Silver felt in the pocket of her shorts and ran her fingers across the G.W. pin. She was ready.


Tolman snapped her phone closed after scribbling directions on the back of one of her own business cards. She and Journey would have to make a long drive together, but it would be safe, and would give them a place to think. The man had been surprised to receive her call—he'd thought they would never see each other again.

*Put that away,* Tolman thought. *For now, it will be a safe house, and it's a place where the Glory Warriors won't be looking.*

Journey's car was almost to the railroad bridge when Tolman turned the Focus in that direction. The sun was well on its westward arc, but it was still over an hour from setting, and the light was cascading out across the Falls of the Ohio. Tolman could see it glinting across the river.

Journey had turned on the radio as soon as he got in the car, and every station was airing news. Federal officials vehemently denied a connection between the killings of Speaker Vandermeer and Chief Justice Darlington. The attorney general called it a "horrible, terrible coincidence of timing, and a tragedy for our nation," but stressed that the crimes were too different to be remotely connected.

*Idiots,* Journey thought. As he approached the railroad trestle, a black SUV suddenly backed out of the parking area to the right. Gravel sprayed the road.

Journey shouted into the windshield and whipped the steering wheel to the left. The SUV backed up farther. The vehicle was large enough that it blocked both lanes of the narrow roadway.

He slammed on the brakes and the car fishtailed. The grille crashed into the limestone structure at the base of the trestle, and Journey whipped forward, restrained by his seat belt as the car's air bag burst forth. His hands flailed.

A car door slammed somewhere outside.

Tolman lost sight of Journey as she drove around the edge of the interpretive center. Her mind was in overdrive—Hudson's steadfast refusal to take risks; the strange document that Nick Journey had unearthed; Journey himself, a multifaceted man who was still an enigma, her own assertions to him notwithstanding; the Glory Warriors . . .

The thoughts came faster and almost on top of each other, like practicing scales at the keyboard . . . first slow, then with increasing pace, almost into a frenzy. Ulysses S. Grant, Robert E. Lee, a military coup of the United States, a secret group of warriors waiting patiently for a century and a half . . .

She merged onto Riverside Drive from the park. Ahead, she saw the SUV back into the street from behind the bridge support on the right. Journey's car crashed into the wall.

Tolman flinched, as if she'd struck the wall herself.

Then, of all the things to notice, she saw a woman in shorts jogging along the trail beside the road.


Journey sat, breathing hard, the air bag warm against his forehead. He heard footsteps slapping the pavement, coming fast.

He fumbled with the door lock, undid the catch on his seat belt, and tumbled sideways out of the car. His shoes slipped on the gravel and he went down, palms breaking his fall, scraping against the gravel. Then he remembered. . . .

He reached into the car, grabbed his backpack, and started to claw his way up the steep railroad embankment.


They had him on two sides, Silver thought, and he was an amateur. Her H&K pistol was in her hand, and she gestured with it to Bronze, who was already out of the SUV and moving toward the professor.

She wished Gold were back, but he was still en route from downtown. Bronze was not a field operative. He was actually an electronics engineer, with specialized training in communications, but every Glory Warrior, even the Bronze members, went through some field training. Still, Four Bronze was not known as a marksman, and he was not in excellent physical condition, either. Better shape than Nick Journey, to be sure, but still not in the shape of a field operative.

Silver was thankful that this operation was not being uplinked live to the Judge. Dallas One had been ordered to do that on the first operation with Journey, and One Gold had wound up dead. The teams at Dallas Base had developed a bit of a superstition about live feeds.

Silver preferred to do her business with no one watching.

No one but the target.

# CHAPTER
# 35

Journey looked back once, in time to see the man from the SUV—who was short and balding, wearing suit pants and a white shirt—raising a gun. Journey twisted his body around, flattening against the embankment, as he heard the shot.

He was already breathing hard as he worked his way around the limestone and up toward the railroad tracks. He heard the man say, "Dammit."

Then a woman's voice: "Go around the other side! Move!"

Journey's foot slipped again, and he almost slid all the way down. But he dug his hands in and pulled himself forward. In thirty seconds, he was at the top. To his left, the railroad track ran into a wooded area. To the right, it opened onto the river bridge. A three-foot-wide metal catwalk extended between the track and the waist-high metal safety railing.

He heard steps across the track. Journey cocked his head, judging exactly where they were. He steadied himself against a metal sign atop a rusting pole. The sign was bowed inward on the sides, as if someone had taken a hammer to it, and read: KEEP OUT—PRIVATE PROPERTY.

He strained to hear the footsteps. Journey swung his backpack off his shoulder and stepped across the railroad track.

Tolman saw the gun in the woman's hand, saw her jogging faster. The man from the SUV had disappeared on the other side of the trestle.

Now her training came back to her—she had never been in a real situation like this. It just didn't happen in RIO. But this was no longer about databases and computer searches and historical abstractions. She braked the car and tumbled out the door. In three seconds, the SIG was in her hand and she was moving forward, but still a good sixty feet from the woman with the gun.

She moved, zigzagging, the gun held straight in front of her in firing stance, not pointed at the sky or ground, as movies so often liked to portray. In the real world, an officer was always ready to fire, and the gun felt like part of her hands. She was thankful she'd bought the SIG and hadn't stuck with the standard-issue Glock.

"Federal officer!" she yelled at the woman. She didn't bother with the melodramatic *stop* or *drop it*. She'd identified herself—that was all she had to do.

The woman in the shorts turned, and Tolman instantly thought that she had been trained well, too. The woman came out shooting, and Tolman dived back down alongside her car.

Journey listened, hearing the man scrabbling for purchase on the embankment just as he had.

Timing was everything. The Glory Warrior would expect him to run, to put as much distance as possible in between the two. Journey would have a couple of seconds at best when his assailant would be surprised. He would not have force or strength on his side. All he had was his sense of hearing, and the right timing.

Journey stopped at the spot where the railroad track began to cross the road as it headed toward the river. He wrapped his hands around both straps of the backpack and held it at waist level.

He listened. He had perhaps five seconds.

He adjusted his feet, spreading them apart, bending his knees.

Three seconds.

He could hear the man's breathing, and gravel sloughing away under him.

The man's head appeared, then the rest of his body in a crouch. At the instant he began to straighten, Journey swung the backpack straight around his own body.

The man was holding the gun in his right hand, close to his body, and the backpack caught him perfectly. His hand opened; the gun fell. The man's feet slid out from under him as though he were walking on ice. He swung his arms in a wide arc, then he reeled backwards down the embankment.


Tolman shot back, and the other woman dodged behind a tree. From somewhere, a man's voice, low but strained, shouted, "They've got guns!"

The woman in the shorts emerged from the tree, keeping low. She was in the open for five steps; then she was behind the black Suburban. Tolman couldn't see the man, and she couldn't see Journey, either.

"Dammit, dammit, *dammit*!" Tolman whispered.


As soon as the Glory Warrior fell out of sight, Journey ran back across the track and scrambled down the other side, feet skidding. He hit the ground six feet away from where the car was crumpled against the limestone, door still standing open. He pulled himself into the seat, then instinctively covered his head as a shot shattered the passenger side window.

He couldn't see where it had come from, but he didn't think the man he'd hit with his backpack could have recovered, found his gun again, and been in position to take a shot that quickly.

*So there are two of them.*

In both his encounters with them—in the SCCO parking lot, and on the highway near the ranch—they had worked in pairs. He crawled back out the way he'd come in and hugged the side of the car. At the rear fender, he popped his head above the trunk and scanned the road.

"Dr. Journey!"

A woman's voice. All the other Glory Warriors he'd faced had been male. Journey was still, listening to his own breathing.

"We only want the document," she called. "Surely you know that."

"Like hell," Journey whispered. He looked over his shoulder. Tolman was moving, coming from her car, which was stopped in the middle of the road, twenty yards or so in the direction of the park entrance.

Tolman was holding a gun.

"Well, I'll be damned," Journey said.

He caught her eye, the two stared at each other for a long second, then he turned back toward the car.

*Cover me,* he thought. *I'll draw them back out. Please cover me.*

He thought of his son, and he suddenly wished the boy hadn't been eating when he'd called, and that Andrew could have heard his voice on the phone.

Journey bolted from behind the car and ran across the road toward the river.


"Where the hell are you?" Silver said into her wrist radio.

"There was a goddamn accident on the goddamn bridge," Gold coughed back. "A truck just spilled a load of pallets, and six cars are piled up. I'm still on the highway, on the Kentucky side."

Silver shook her head, but saw the opportunity here. "I'm in control of the situation, but there are a few people around. We may have local police here soon."

"Then maybe this wreck actually works in our favor. Local jurisdictions from both sides are working it. They may be delayed in responding to your location. Exfiltrate as soon as you can."

"Acknowledged."

Silver would be the one to take down Nick Journey and to retrieve the document that generations of Glory Warriors had sought.

Silver sharpened her focus, watching the professor run. She turned slightly, angling her body to take her best shot.

Someone was still shouting from down the road—"Call nine-one-one! Someone's shooting! Someone's shooting by the bridge!"—as Tolman watched Journey run from his spot behind the car.

*Stupid, stupid,* she thought, and then hard on the heels of that: *He's trusting me. The man is trusting me with his life.*

She watched him run, the green backpack slung over his right shoulder. The female assassin stepped from behind the Suburban, took one step, and fired at Journey. The shot went low, kicking up concrete a few inches from Journey's feet. The professor dodged away from the road, toward the sidewalk the woman had been jogging down a few seconds ago.

The woman's head moved an inch or so in Tolman's direction. Tolman gripped the SIG and sighted it. She didn't want to kill the Glory Warrior, only disable her . . . and then bring her in. Hudson and Díaz and Graves and the attorney general and the president would have their evidence.

The woman's eyes didn't meet Tolman's, but settled somewhere over her left shoulder.

*Oh shit,* Tolman thought, and half turned as the short man in the white shirt swung the butt of his pistol and smashed it into the back of her head.

Journey saw Tolman go down. He'd had his back to the road, and hadn't seen the short man come sliding down the embankment, gun in his hand again. He winced as Tolman fell.

The young woman—the same one from the interpretive center this morning—ran toward him. He angled away from the sidewalk. A large red sign with white lettering warned: LEAVE FOSSIL BEDS WHEN YOU HEAR SIREN—WATER SUBJECT TO SUDDEN RISE AND VIOLENT TURBULENCE WHEN GATES ARE OPENED. A smaller sign, just below it, announced that fossil and rock collecting were prohibited.

The woman was behind him. She was young and fit, and she would overtake him in a few steps. She thought she had him. He was in a place where there was no way out. There was nowhere to go behind Journey.

Nowhere but the Ohio.

Journey had seen the steps this morning, when he first drove into Falls of the Ohio State Park. They angled away from the shore, down to the river. In good weather—meaning a typical August to October dry season, when the water level was down—they led to the uncovered fossil beds.

*Now they're steps to nowhere,* Journey thought.

He ran for the steps, which were made of the same wooden planking as the deck behind the interpretive center. A short flight led down to a small rectangular platform, and a second, steeper set of stairs descended farther.

"Journey!" the woman shouted. For a split second, she was out of his view.

He raced to the edge of the rectangle. His momentum carried him down onto the next step, his body turning almost ninety degrees. As he twisted, the strap of his backpack slipped off his arm and caught on the wooden stair railing.

Journey stumbled. One foot came down on the second step. The other slipped, his momentum still propelling him downward.

For one instant, everything seemed to stop. Journey looked up and saw the female Glory Warrior at the top of the stairs, aiming the pistol at him.

He lunged, trying to grab the backpack. But his balance was off and his feet wouldn't work. The backpack was out of his grasp.

"No!" he shouted.

He thought he saw the woman smile and nod in his direction. She pulled the trigger. He heard the shot.

Then Journey slipped backwards off the steps, rolling down into the swift muddy water of the Ohio River.

The pavement was hot against Tolman's cheek, and the thought was hard in her head: *Now who's the stupid one?* She'd let herself be decoyed, focusing only on the woman, forgetting the man who'd backed the SUV into the road, until he was right behind her.

Her father had always said, *Any agent who lets someone sneak up on them from behind deserves to get shot.*

Tolman's head throbbed, and she felt blood. It ran from the wound on the back of her head, through her hair, and down her cheek into her mouth. She could taste it.

She blinked several times. The man's shoes, black and expensive leather, were right beside her, unmoving.

Then she heard the shot, some scrabbling, and Journey's voice— "No!"

He'd trusted her, and she let herself get cold-cocked by the butt of a gun. Not only her father but also her instructors at the Academy would be disappointed.

A siren sounded. She couldn't tell from which direction it came. The pavement was still spinning.

The woman's voice: "Let's go!"

The man with the expensive shoes said, "What? Where's Journey?"

"He's in the river. But I have the backpack."

Tolman heard the sound of a zipper, papers shuffling, a deep breath being drawn.

"This is it," the woman said. "This is *it!*"

"What about her?" said the man.

"Leave her. We have to go. Locals are coming—no time to clean up. Another team can finish her later if the Judge orders it."

The expensive shoes stepped over her. She saw the man's face for a second as he bent over and picked up her SIG from the pavement. The steps moved away. Tolman moved her head an inch. She saw the woman, with Journey's backpack in hand, sliding into the passenger side of the Suburban. The short man drove.

A wave of nausea hit her, and Tolman put her head down. She wasn't sure if she felt sick because of the blow to the head, or because the Glory Warriors now had all the papers. The Fort Washita page, the one Williams had hidden in the vault, Williams's "suicide" note—all of it. They had it all.

# CHAPTER
# 36

The sun was already down in the West Virginia mountains when the Judge assembled the secure conference call of the Washingtons. One of the group was absent—Washington Two was in the midst of the firestorm surrounding Chief Justice Darlington's assassination. The Judge had even seen Brent Graves on television during the day. He and an FBI agent named Díaz, alongside the attorney general, were becoming the public faces of the investigation. Graves acquitted himself quite well.

Standing at his desk, the phone on speaker, the Judge clasped his hands behind his back. "I spoke to Chicago a short while ago," he said. "The Dallas Four team took the papers from Journey, and they're on their way here with them now."

Washington One, the man with the military bearing, spoke first. "And Journey? Did they eliminate him?"

"Apparently not," the Judge said.

"And exactly why is that?" demanded Washington Three, the youngest and brashest of the Washington men.

"There were witnesses in the vicinity," the Judge said. "The team did not have time or a window of opportunity to finish Journey."

"Or the government woman," Washington Four said.

"The woman," the Judge said. "The rather tenacious researcher."

"She has gone considerably beyond research now," Four said.

"So she has." The Judge shrugged. "She's the only one who believes Journey. And in turn, only one person believes her, so she and Journey are not the pressing need. They will show themselves and we will know about it, and we'll take care of them then. In the meantime, the pages will be in my hands in a few hours. The base commanders are all moving their infrastructure into place." A moment's silence passed. "Once we present the evidence of the document to the mass media, the people will be with us."

"There will still be pockets of resistance," Washington Four said.

"Of course there will," the Judge said. "The American people do not like change . . . at least on its face. But the people want us, whether they know it or not. Have you seen President Harwell the last few days?"

The others murmured assent, some more vocally than others.

"We're doing the people a favor by creating the circumstances that Lee and Grant feared. There may not be as much resistance as we think. We'll sweep into Washington within minutes after the president is dead. There will be no chance to swear in the vice president. We'll occupy the White House, the Capitol, the Supreme Court, and the Pentagon. The people and the equipment are already moving into place."

"In the last twenty-four hours, we've processed nearly a thousand of our people through Baltimore Base," Washington One said. "Another fifteen hundred will be here within the next twelve hours, then they'll move out into the safe staging areas in Rockville, Silver Spring, Arlington, and Alexandria. The choppers and the trucks are ready to move them into the District and the Pentagon. We'll also have patrol boats on the Potomac ready to secure the District once we're in command of the targets."

"What about the airspace restrictions in D.C.?" Washington Three asked.

A trace of impatience crept into Washington One's voice. "Leave that to me. You doubt that I have the resources to deal with it?"

Washington Three almost laughed. "No, no. I know you do. I know you guys have the invasion planned perfectly." He paused;

then his tone was darker. "Seems strange to talk about an invasion of Washington, D.C., doesn't it? Calling the White House a target."

"Your cynical nature is showing itself again," the Judge said. "Maybe you'd prefer the term *objective* instead of *target*. After all, we aren't going to destroy it, but liberate it."

"Okay, okay, no grand speeches, Your Honor," Three said. "I get it. I'll do my job and everyone else will do theirs. So what about the second wave?"

Washington One cleared his throat. "The heavy equipment is staging behind the Blue Ridge in Virginia now. The tanks, the Humvees, more choppers."

The Judge smiled. "Just as General Lee used the same mountains to shield his army's movements when he invaded Pennsylvania in 1863."

"Yes," One said. "Though to me, it's more logistical than symbolic. We own large tracts of land and buildings there that let us warehouse the equipment. But it's still close enough to D.C. for us to move quickly. After the first raiding teams occupy the objectives—" He put a subtle taunt into his voice. "—the next wave will overpower any resistance and start moving the members of the old government into holding facilities."

"Even though there will be bits of insurgency around the country, we'll be swift, we'll be strong, and we'll have control of the bureaucracy," the Judge said. "There won't be time for them to react. We will simply overwhelm them, my media will tell people what they should think, and I'm already working on my own address to the people."

More positive murmurings came down the line from Washington, and the Judge said, "Your patience is about to be rewarded. We will soon be in a position to reclaim our country's glory, to fulfill Lee and Grant's vision. America will command respect once again, thanks to all of us. No more bought-and-sold politicians ruling in thirty-second sound bites, no more partisan bickering, no more corrupt courts and ineffective executives. Our power *will* be respected, by our own people and by the world."

He ended the conference call and sat down slowly. Now he needed rest, his aging body growing weary. But he would wake when the Dallas Four team arrived. They were under strict orders to drive straight through, to bring him the pages. He would finally hold all of them in his hand.

The troops were moving. All the disparate pieces were coming together. It would all happen very, very soon.

Still, the Judge couldn't help but wonder at all he had done to bring the country—and himself—to this point. He believed in the Glory Warriors' mission; of that, there was no doubt. The United States of America needed the Glory Warriors—needed *him*. That much was painfully obvious.

But had he ever really had a choice? And what of achieving the objectives? If one strives for a single objective for an entire lifetime, what does one do upon achieving it?

*Never question me again,* his father's voice whispered.

The Judge slapped his hand against the side of his chair. These ruminations were poison. They clouded his thinking, obscured the mission. They were the thoughts of either a child or an old man, and neither would serve him well now. The Judge undressed and lay down on top of his sheets. The mountains were utterly silent and dark. It felt as if even the natural world were waiting, waiting for what was to come.

Despite his exhaustion, the Judge could not sleep.

# CHAPTER
# 37

In the water, Journey had no concept of time. He'd heard the gunshot just as he slipped from the wooden steps. He felt the rush of air, and he thought the bullet tugged at his shirtsleeve and touched the flesh of his upper arm. His last thought before he fell into the water was that if he hadn't been off balance, if he'd been standing right where he was a few seconds before, the shot would have hit him squarely in the chest.

As it was, he slipped backwards and rolled onto his side, his ribs coming down hard on the piles of driftwood at the water's edge. When he moved from his side to his back, it felt as if someone had kicked him from a raft made of logs into the river itself.

With the water level as high as it was, the Ohio was moving swiftly. Journey's head went under. Water flooded his nose. He waved his arms, trying to turn his body yet again. He slapped the surface of the river. He kicked out with a leg; then his foot caught on something—the tightly packed logs where he'd just been. His foot wedged between two pieces of wood.

He tried to twist his body so that he could get on top of the water. He couldn't free his foot from the logs, but then the logs themselves were turning, and with a mighty jerk—the rest of his body flopped like a rag doll, now pulled by one foot—the wood broke free of the shallows by the shore and drifted into the river proper.

Journey's head broke the surface of the water, and he let out a growl, water running out of his nose and mouth. The two logs had some kind of vine wrapped around one end of them, binding them together, and his foot was tangled in the vine. He tried to shake his leg, and the vine loosened only about half an inch.

Now the logs were headed straight out toward the river, where the current was stronger. His head went under again, and he twisted his body in violent motions. He raised his head, slamming his temple into the side of another floating log, and for a couple of seconds, everything was black. He blinked, coughed, raised his head again.

He could see an outcropping of rock where the river bent slightly. Far above the rock was the curving rail of the Falls of the Ohio Interpretive Center's observation deck. Journey glimpsed it for a couple of seconds before his head went under again.

His foot, dead weight with the log, dragged him relentlessly, but he wasn't into the swiftest current yet. He had a few seconds before he would be carried into the center of the Ohio.

He hung suspended for a long moment. His neck was sore from lifting his head against the current. The next time he came up, he gulped air, and as soon as he went back down, put every ounce of strength he had into changing his body's position. His hands worked like a swimmer, cupping the water and displacing it. His body contorted, and for a crazy moment, he was almost upside-down, his foot directly above his head.

He felt his foot slam into the rocks, and for several seconds, nothing happened. Then he felt the vine around his foot loosen and finally break. The logs bounced off the rocks and floated toward the center of the river.

Journey whipped his body around, even as his foot screamed in agony, and he clawed at the rocks. Several fingernails split and began to bleed. A few rocks sloughed away.

*This is it*, he thought. *I don't have the strength to hold it. . . .*

But he did, and then he wasn't moving anymore. From the waist down, he was still in the river, but his grip on the rocks held. He heard a child's voice from above: "Hey! Hey, Mom, there's a man down there!"

He heard footsteps thumping on the wooden deck, and a woman's voice: "Oh, Dylan, don't be silly. There can't be a . . . Oh my God!"

The woman was young and had brown hair tied back in a ponytail. The little boy, who looked about six, looked just like the woman.

"I told you," the boy said, then waved down at Journey. "What are you doing down there?"

Journey laid his head against the rocks and tried to smile in the boy's direction. "Just waiting for you," he said.

# CHAPTER

# 38

Kerry Voss was often oblivious of the law enforcement aspect of RIO's mission. Of course, she knew that people on the staff were former federal marshals and FBI agents and such, and they had authority to arrest people, though that seldom occurred. Arrests— and the credit for them—went to the "real" law enforcement agencies.

Voss liked what she did, as well as the fact that RIO was away from the noise and the stress of some other government agencies. She spent her days digging through financial records, she wrote reports, she turned them in. She'd made a couple of friends in the office, including Meg Tolman, and she went out to lunch nearly every day. At night, she was either with her kids or, if they were with her ex-husband, she had time to herself, time to read, to think, the occasional date.

Five o'clock came and went. The TV in the break room stayed on with more news about Chief Justice Darlington's death. Hudson was gone, Tolman was gone, other people in the office were coming and going. Her children were with their father this week, so Voss stayed. She didn't know how the strange request Meg Tolman had made tied in with Darlington, but she'd read the urgency in Meg's voice and face.

Voss wouldn't do an off-the-books inquiry for just anyone. She'd worked for the government long enough to know where such things could lead. The law enforcement people in the office made fun of the "career bureaucrats," but the truth was, the word *bureaucrat* didn't have to be an insult. It meant a sense of loyalty to the organization, an understanding that the government ran on procedures, and that without those procedures, the infrastructure could break down and nothing would ever get done.

But Voss liked Meg Tolman, as Tolman was a bit of an enigma. Voss smiled at that—she knew she presented her own set of paradoxes to RIO, as the newest member of the staff, and that suited her quite well. So Voss found AC/DC's "Back in Black" on her iTunes and went fishing in her databases to see what she could find out about the possibly deceased Sergeants Standridge and Lane.

She first used the Social Security database to find the numbers for both names, checking the dates of issue to make sure the ages were right. Once she had them, she went into the Department of Defense's section for active duty personnel. Voss had backdoor passwords into DOD that no one else in RIO had, though no one here—not even Deputy Director Hudson—knew it. Even more important, Voss still possessed the clearance to use those passwords.

Still, once she was inside the massive database, she couldn't access anything having to do with Lane and Standridge. Electronic walls blocked her at every turn.

"Well, that's not very nice," she said, in the same sort of tone she would have used with her nine-year-old.

She found all the same information Tolman had found, and it matched, the dates of death in Taji in 2006, the units to which the soldiers had been assigned, their hometowns.

Voss stretched, went to the lounge area, and bought a Diet Coke from the machine. Tina, the receptionist, was gone, but lights were still on in offices down the hall, and the TV was still on HNC.

Back in her office, she started digging, first for Michael Standridge of Moscow, Idaho. His parents had been paid the standard benefit of one hundred thousand dollars within two days of their son's death. There was another lump-sum payment of twenty thousand dollars that she tracked to an insurance company.

Kevin Lane of Pineville, Louisiana, was married at the time of his death, and he and his wife, Brianna Hailey Lane, had shared a joint checking account. They had a daughter, Skyler Marie Lane.

Voss confirmed that Brianna Lane had received the immediate death benefit payment from DOD. Sergeant Lane's wife was also entitled to Dependency and Indemnity Compensation (DIC), and her daughter received a monthly benefit as well. Brianna Lane had set up a savings account for her daughter in the fall of 2006, and the regular payments had been deposited like clockwork ever since.

Voss checked the numbers for both accounts, then stopped, her finger tracing a line on her computer monitor.

She scrolled down through the account transactions until she came to the previous month.

*There it is again.*

The number leapt out at her—$7,500.00 had been deposited in this account beginning in September 2006 and continuing monthly, right up through the last month.

*So what?* she asked herself. Maybe Brianna Lane was a lawyer or an investment banker or . . .

Not making that kind of money in a town the size of Pineville, Louisiana. It was way out of proportion for an army widow in her twenties in a very small town.

"Let's just see about this," Voss said.

She began tracing the deposits, following the digital footprints deeper and deeper. No money was completely clean—all transactions left a trail, no matter how hard certain parties might try to cover it. Voss had been down that road before as well, and with numbers much, much larger than this.

Voss kept following the trail. Lights clicked off in the offices around her. She called her ex-husband's house, said good night to each of the kids as she always did, and turned back to her monitor.

The funds were transferred to Brianna Lane's account in Pineville each month from a bank in Dallas, Texas. The account was registered to a company called Beasley Holdings. Its address was a post office box. The account was nothing more than a pass-through. The funds arrived in the Beasley account on the same day each month, and were automatically transferred out to Brianna Lane within one hour.

Voss took it back another step, which led to a New York bank and an account registered to Eastern Investments. Same thing as the Dallas account—funds arrived and left within one hour. It took Voss a little longer to find that the money came to New York through an offshore account in Aruba.

As she expected, the trail ended there, at least temporarily. Even RACER wasn't able to immediately access foreign accounts. The account information was encrypted, and without some more sophisticated hacking, she'd never be able to break through the labyrinth and find where the money came from before it went to Aruba.

In her past life, she'd known just the person for such a job. He had the tools, he was a professional hacker, and he owed her several favors. Not wanting to use the office computer, she sent him a text message from her phone and asked him to call her. When he did, she told him what she wanted. He didn't hesitate, just said, "Sweet!" and told her he'd get on it.

Voss's eyes were blurry. She was hungry, and her butt hurt from sitting in the chair for so long. She reached for the phone, then pulled her hand back. She didn't know where Meg Tolman was, just that she had left town quickly.

Voss didn't have all the information Tolman might need, either. This was more than just a favor for an office colleague. With any luck, in the morning, Voss would know where that money had come from. *Then* she would call Meg Tolman.

The Clarksville, Indiana, police unit came from behind Tolman, where Riverside Drive diverged from the state park and wound into residential suburbia. Tolman's car was still in the middle of the road. Journey's sat with its nose crumpled against the base of the railroad trestle.

Tolman turned as the police car approached. Her gun was gone, taken by the Glory Warrior with the black shoes, but she wanted the city cop to see that she had nothing in her hands. She spread them apart, palms out.

"Federal officer!" she called. "I'm unarmed!"

The back of her head throbbed with no mercy. She was sure she looked frightening, with blood in her hair and running down one side of her face. She heard running footsteps from the direction the black Suburban had gone, and saw an old African American man carrying a cell phone and a fishing pole.

"They were shooting!'" he shouted toward the police car. "I saw it. The ones that shot went the other way."

The police officer, who was younger than Tolman and smelled of cigarettes, got slowly out of his car, keeping one hand on the butt of his pistol.

"Ma'am, are you all right?" he said. His eyes moved over the entire area.

Tolman nodded, which made her head hurt more. "Yes, I'm all right. It's a bump on the head. But there's a man in the river. Do you have rescue units? The man who's with me went into the river."

"They shot him," said the man with the fishing pole. "They drove off that way. It was a black girl and an older white guy. They were in a big car, a big new Suburban or something like that. Kentucky plates. I saw them." He looked at Tolman. "You shot back at them."

The police officer looked at the witness, then at Tolman. "You identified yourself as a federal officer, ma'am."

"Did you hear me?" Tolman said, her voice rising. "There's a man in the fucking river! My ID is in the car." She turned away from the car, toward the river, fighting dizziness.

"Fire and rescue and ambulance are on the way, ma'am. Tell me what happened here."

The dizziness intensified. Tolman stumbled.

"Maybe she ought to sit down," the man with the fishing pole said.

"No," Tolman said. She stretched her arms out to steady herself. Her head throbbed. She ran toward the river.

"Hey!" the cop yelled. "Freeze!"

*God, spare me from suburban cops who watched too many episodes of* Law & Order, she thought.

"Nick!" she shouted. "Nick Journey! Can you hear me? Nick!"

Two more police units arrived, one stopping by Journey's car, the other nose-to-nose with Tolman's. The rescue unit was next. Tolman pointed to where Journey had disappeared onto the steps. Radio calls were made and more units arrived. Within four minutes, two boats were patrolling the river, spotlights shining on the Indiana shoreline in the fading light.

Tolman heard steps behind her and turned to see the same cop, holding her ID case. "I've never heard of the Research and Investigations Office," he said. He looked more closely. "Justice, Treasury, and Homeland Security? You can't be under all three."

Tolman kicked at a stray piece of gravel. "Officer, you see that card next to my official ID? You're going to call that number in

Washington, and you're going to talk to a man named Russell Hudson. I don't have time for you to write your report."

The officer folded his arms. "I don't have the authority to make that decision, and I sure won't walk away from this crime scene."

Tolman pointed at the card. "Then have your lieutenant or your captain—hell, your chief of police—call Deputy Director Hudson. That gets you off the hook. But I'm not going to stand here and dance around with you and get bogged down in a jurisdictional pissing match."

"Ma'am, I'm sorry, but I can't—"

"Call the fucking number, Officer!" Tolman shouted.

The young officer took aside a sergeant who had arrived in the second car and talked at length. One of the paramedics looked at Tolman's head. "It doesn't look serious, but we'll need to take you in and take a closer look at it. You should have X-rays."

"No," Tolman said.

"But you should—"

"My pupils are responsive, right? I'm on balance, I'm coherent. Clean it up and put a bandage on it. I'm not going to the hospital."

"But—"

The sergeant and his officer were looking at Tolman. Around them, rescue teams had fanned out all the way to the interpretive center. The sergeant took Tolman's card and went back to his car. In a moment, he was on the phone.

The spotlight from one of the patrol boats played across Journey's back, and it was followed by an amplified voice: "Don't move! We'll get you out of there!"

Within a few seconds, rescuers from above scrambled down the rocks. Four sets of hands moved Journey onto a gurney without wheels, strapped him in, and attached cables to it. They made the cables fast, and Journey felt himself being pulled.

In two minutes, he was on the deck. "Tell me where it hurts," a man's voice said. Journey thought about it. He wasn't really in pain, except for his chest from holding his breath. He shook his head.

A light—small, not like the huge light from the boat—shone in his eyes. He squinted. "Wiggle your fingers," the voice said.

Journey wiggled his fingers.

"And your toes."

Journey wiggled his toes, and his left foot screamed. He sucked in air.

"Which foot?"

"Left," Journey said.

"Okay."

Then there were hands on his foot, then more than one set of hands. After a few minutes, a second voice: "I don't think it's broken, but it's a bad sprain."

He felt another hand near his shoulder, feeling his soaked shirtsleeve, palpitating his upper arm. The first voice said, "What's this?"

Journey remembered the gunshot. He remembered how his backpack had snagged on the railing, how he hadn't been able to keep his balance. "They shot me," he said.

There was silence for a while; then the first voice said, "You're damn lucky, mister. That shot barely touched you, just creased the skin. A quarter of an inch the other way, and you would've been in a world of hurt."

Another silence, then more hands felt his arm. It stung a little, but not too much.

"*Very* damn lucky," the first voice said again. "What's your name?"

Another voice, above his head: "His name is Dr. Nick Journey."

Tolman.

Journey twisted his neck to look at her.

She knelt beside the stretcher. "Hey," she said. "How you doing?"

Journey shrugged. Tolman smiled.

"They got the pages," Journey said. "They got all of it."

Tolman nodded. "I know."

"We have to—"

"I *know*," Tolman repeated, and Journey knew by her tone not to say more with all these people around.

Journey looked around at his rescuers. The stretcher was in a corner of the interpretive center's observation deck. The mother and

son were hovering at the back of the crowd. Journey winked at the
little boy, and the boy grinned.

"I can sit up," Journey said.

The straps holding him were unsnapped, and he sat up slowly.
Water ran off him and onto the wooden planking of the deck. He
swung his legs off the side. The left one hurt, and he grimaced.

"We'll wrap that," the first paramedic said, "and get you to the
hospital for—"

Journey shook his head.

The paramedics looked at each other. "What is it with you
people?"

"Just wrap it and give me something for the swelling," Journey
said.

"But you might—"

"Do it," Tolman said.

Behind her, a police officer wearing a sergeant's stripes approached.
"Ms. Tolman," he said. His expression wasn't friendly. "Our chief of
police has spoken with a Mr. Hudson in Washington."

Tolman waited.

"And we did verify independently that your Research and Investigations Office exists. You seem to be one of those departments no
one knows about, but that has a lot of pull."

"We're all just doing our jobs, Sergeant," Tolman said.

The sergeant smiled and spit on the deck. "Don't patronize me,
Ms. Tolman." The smile, which wasn't very genuine in the first place,
faded. "I'm told we need to offer you whatever assistance you may
need."

Tolman nodded. "You can take care of Dr. Journey's car. He
rented it at the Louisville airport."

"And the people who shot at you? We have witnesses." The sergeant gestured back at the old man with the fishing pole, and a
crowd of a dozen or so people along the road.

"Dr. Journey and I have to go," Tolman said.

"And he's a part of this RIO, too?"

"No, he's a—" Tolman hesitated. "—he's a witness."

"A witness." The sergeant spit again. He and Tolman stared at
each other for a moment more; then he looked at the young officer

who'd been first on the scene. "Release the scene," the sergeant said. "Call a wrecker to get this other car out of here. These people are free to go."

"Do I need to get—?" the young cop said.

"You don't need to get shit," the sergeant said, and started back to his patrol car.

# CHAPTER

# 40

"Take stock," Tolman said to Journey as they got into her Focus.

Thanks to a neighborhood resident from just up the hill, who had come onto her porch to watch the rescue of the man from the river, Journey had dry clothes. They were a little large, but the "carpenter" jeans and a soft button-down shirt were clean and dry.

"Lost my wallet in the river," Journey said. "My driver's license, credit cards, insurance card, everything. All my cash. My keys." He leaned against the headrest. "I left my phone in the rental car, though."

Without a word, Tolman walked to Journey's car, retrieved his phone and his overnight bag, and brought them back. "Anything else in the rental?"

"No, that's it. I travel light."

Tolman started the car and drove out of the park. In five minutes, they were on Interstate 65 headed south back into Kentucky.

"I want to go back to Oklahoma," Journey said. "I need to get Andrew."

"Look, Nick—I'm calling you Nick because after what just happened here, I think it's a little silly for me to keep calling you Dr. Journey—I'm sorry."

Journey looked sideways at her as Louisville slipped past outside the window. "What do you mean?"

"Lots of things, actually. I let that guy sneak up on me from behind while I was focusing on the woman. I'm out of practice." Journey saw the determined set to her mouth. "But it won't happen again, I'll promise you that. Look, we can't get anywhere near Oklahoma. Not just yet."

"What?"

"They'll be looking for you to go back there. They'll be waiting for you."

"They're not going to kill me now," Journey said.

Tolman nodded. "When they figure out that the signature page isn't there, they'll be pissed off. Then they'll figure that either you're holding out on them . . . or, just like with page two, that you'll lead them to it."

Journey closed his eyes. "*Then* they'll try to kill me again. I need to see Andrew."

"He's with his mother, so he should be safe, right?"

Journey hesitated a moment too long. "He should be."

"You don't have a choice right now," Tolman said. "And if we don't get on top of this, I don't think anyone's going to be safe."

The lights of the city and its suburbs faded behind them. Journey didn't speak for a time. "I need to at least call."

"Not yet," Tolman said. "Everything's changed, Nick. My boss told me not to talk to him over an open cell line, and I think the same applies to you. We have to get somewhere secure."

"You have somewhere in mind?"

"Yes. Somewhere the Glory Warriors won't look. We need time to put it together. We're going to get rid of this car first. Planes, trains, buses—no good. We have to drive and stay anonymous. I hate driving, but there you have it."

"You can't rent another car without a credit card. If they're that good, they'll have both of our credit card numbers." He rubbed the bridge of his nose. "Mine's at the bottom of the Ohio, but they don't know that."

"We'll buy something cheap along the road somewhere. For a few hundred dollars cash, you can buy a used car at almost any time, in almost any town in America. It should buy us some time, and I made sure I had emergency cash before I left D.C."

"Where are we going?"

"The middle of nowhere," Tolman said, and didn't elaborate.

An hour later, passing signs for Fort Knox, they exited the highway in Elizabethtown, Kentucky. After driving around the town for ten minutes, they found a twelve-year-old Toyota Camry with a FOR SALE sign parked at the end of a small shopping center. Tolman called the number scrawled on the sign and offered the car's owner an extra two hundred dollars if he would come immediately to finish the transaction. A few minutes and seven hundred dollars later, she had the Camry's keys in hand. As soon as the owner, a white-bearded man in his sixties, had gone, they left the Focus at the other end of the shopping center parking lot.

"Can you drive?" Tolman asked.

"As long as it's not a manual transmission and I don't need my left foot to do any acrobatics, I can drive," Journey said. "And I'll drive the speed limit, since I don't have a driver's license. Are you sure it wouldn't be safe for me to call Amelia and check on Andrew?"

Tolman waited, then said, "I'm worried that they might have her under surveillance, which means they might have access to her phones. If I were doing the surveillance, the ex-wife would be a natural."

"If they're watching her, then they know Andrew's with her!"

"You said it yourself," Tolman said. "They're not going to do anything to you until they know for certain what they do and don't have. We have a little window of time where everyone is safe for a while. By the time that window closes, we have to make sure we have what we need, and by then, I should be able to get backup anywhere in the country, even people to protect your ex-wife and your son."

Journey tapped his finger three times on the leg of the too-large jeans, looking out at the lights of the parking lot. "I just need to know he's all right."

"You're a very stubborn man."

"You don't have kids, do you?"

Tolman exhaled. "You know what? It irritates the crap out of me when people who have kids say that to people who don't. You act as if we live on different planets because we don't have children, and that we can't possibly understand, and so on and so on. And frankly, Nick, it's a crock of shit. I'm a human being, and I care and I have morals and ethics and all that. Just because I haven't birthed a baby doesn't mean I don't. I understand where you are coming from, and I even understand your very unique situation with your son. Don't think that I don't."

Journey leaned forward a little. "I'm sorry. I probably deserved that. But I just—I can't explain it. I don't always know the right things to do as a parent, but I don't like to depend on other people very much when it comes to Andrew."

"We're talking about him staying with his own mother. She's that bad?"

Journey shook his head. "No, it's not that his mother's bad. Andrew bonds well with her. In fact, if Andrew sees the two of us in a room, he'll run to Amelia every time. Even the last couple of years we were married, when it was clear she didn't want to be there anymore, he would run to her. I'm the one who feeds him and changes him and dresses him and always goes to school when he has a meltdown. I'm the one who gets scratches up and down my arms when he gets aggressive. I do all that every day, fifty weeks out of the year. And you know what, Meg? Just once I'd like to have him run to me the way he runs to his mother." He leaned back against the headrest and closed his eyes again. "None of that has anything to do with what you asked, does it?"

"Actually, it does. It tells me quite a bit. It tells me that because your boy chooses his mother every time, she probably figures she's doing everything right, even if she sees him only two weeks a year. You do all the heavy lifting of being a parent and she gets the credit, so to speak. There's some sexism there, too—I bet a lot of people think that because you have a penis, you can't possibly be as good a parent as the mother."

"You always talk this way to people you've just met?"

"Pretty much. Am I right?"

Journey turned to look at her. "Yes."

Tolman nodded.

"Your father," Journey said. "What was he like after your mother . . . after the car wreck?"

"He tried," Tolman said. "He really, really tried. Most of the time, he didn't have a clue, but it wasn't for lack of trying."

"I feel that way a lot."

"Yeah, and I was just a normal mouthy, smart-ass teenager. Your kid has a severe disability that may or may not ever change. I think you have the tougher job." She glanced at him. "Maybe he'll run to you instead of her one of these days."

"Doesn't matter. I shouldn't have brought it up. I just want him to be safe."

"I know. For that matter, Nick, so do I." Tolman was quiet for a long time, then said, "Thank you."

"For what?"

"You let me see a little bit of yourself, something beyond what I can find out from databases and official documents."

Journey looked away. "I guess my guard is down."

"You think?" They each got out of the car and changed places. "You want something to eat? Getting shot at and knocked in the head has made me hungry, now that I've had a few minutes to breathe."

"I could eat," Journey said.

"Let's go back to the highway and find something. Then we need to talk some more. We have a long night ahead of us."


Journey drove to a Plaza 94 truck stop on I-65. Eighteen-wheelers idled in the huge parking lot, belching exhaust. Tolman paid cash in advance for gasoline, and Journey filled the tank. Then Tolman grabbed her laptop bag and they went into the restaurant. They ordered cheeseburgers with thick-cut french fries, and Journey said, "Hmm," when his arrived at the table.

"What?" Tolman asked.

"Oh," Journey said, "I was just remembering the last burger I had. It was at Uncle Charley's, a little campus place in Carpenter Center. It was lunch with Sandra, a few hours before those guys came after me on campus. Sandra's a vegetarian and I remember I'd made some crack about it being double cheeseburger special day. She had a salad."

"Sandra again," Tolman said.

"Don't."

"I'm not. All I do is listen to what you say."

"I wish you'd stop trying to get into my head, Meg."

"Why?"

"There's nothing—" Journey sat back and laughed, lightly at first, then a full-throated, deep laughter. Tolman smiled a little, the smile of someone who can't maintain a straight face while another person is laughing, even if they don't get the joke.

"I'm sorry," Journey said after a minute. "I just—I was about to say that there was nothing in my head, and it struck me as ridiculous."

Tolman smiled again. "Oh, no, there's definitely a lot in your head. No doubt about that."

Journey let the smile stay on his face a little longer. Then he rubbed both sides of his neck with his hands. "Sometimes, when you're faced with total insanity on all sides of you, all you can do is laugh."

"That's true. Except I usually play piano. But I'll deal with that when I can." Tolman ate a french fry. "We still have something we need to talk about, but I have an idea first. It sounds kind of strange and convoluted, but then, that goes right along with everything else, right?"

Journey raised his eyebrows at her.

"You could probably use a pay phone here," Tolman said.

Journey put down his burger. "I thought you said they might have access to Amelia's phone."

"They might. But I've been thinking about it, and it would be a stretch for them to be on Sandra's phone, too. She's just a colleague, a coworker . . . The Glory Warriors couldn't possibly tap the phone of every single one of your coworkers. You could call Sandra and ask her to get in touch with Amelia to check on Andrew. Have her call Amelia at work, but not her direct, personal line, in case they are on that one, too. Then have Sandra do something like leaving you a message on an online bulletin board."

Journey looked hard at her. Her face was open, her eyes very large. He remembered the gun in her hand back at the Ohio, the way the two had communicated without speaking. They'd fallen into a wary rapport, understanding how each other moved, how they reacted.

"I know you want to see if Andrew is okay," Tolman said. "Don't you think Sandra's wondering how you are, too?"

"I don't know," Journey said, but he stood up anyway. Tolman gave him three dollars in coins, and he went to the row of pay phones in the hallway that led to the restrooms. The hallway smelled of disinfectant and too many human bodies coming and going. He pulled Sandra's number off his cell's address book, then dropped coins in the slot and made the call.

"It's Nick," he said when she answered.

There was silence; then Sandra finally said, "Are you all right?"

"More or less."

"What does that mean?"

"It means it's a very long story, and I'll be glad to tell you at Uncle Charley's one of these days. I'll buy you an extra-large salad. Look, Sandra, I don't have much time—"

"Where are you?"

"I think it's better if you don't know. This thing we found is big. Much bigger than we thought. I'm with an investigator from Washington, and we're trying to put some things together."

"How—?"

"Listen, I'm sorry about what happened back at my house." Journey felt a coldness in his stomach. He opened his mouth to say something else, but wasn't sure what. He wanted to talk to her, but he didn't want to talk to her.

"I was upset," Sandra said. "You're right, there are boundaries. I crossed one."

Journey shook his head. "No, I—" He swallowed. "We'll talk again, all right? But may I ask you a favor? I'm sorry to—"

"What do you need?"

"Andrew is with his mother. I can't call her. I'm afraid they may be watching her house. But I want to check on Andrew. I just need to know that he's all right."

"God, Nick. What do you want me to do?"

"Call her. I know this is a strange request—"

"What's the number?"

Journey gave it to her. "That's the main number at her office. I just want to know that Andrew's doing all right."

Sandra hesitated. "I'll do this, Nick. But you'll tell me about it when you get back."

*When I get back.* Journey had trouble thinking that far ahead. "Yes, I will. After you talk to her, leave me a message on the Civil War Geeks online message board."

"Civil War Geeks?"

"What can I say? My screen name there is 'On A Journey.'"

"Okay, I'll get on it."

"I have to go, Sandra." He felt an awkward silence. "Thanks."

"Of course. Nick . . . take care."

"You, too."

Journey hung up and went back to the booth. "I won't ask you how it went," Tolman said.

"It went fine."

"Mmm-hmm. Finish your food. I have something to show you."

When they had both finished eating, Tolman opened her laptop and put it on the table between them. She found the link from the search she'd done in the morning. "When I was waiting for you to show up at Falls of the Ohio," Tolman said, "I did a search for the Glory Warriors. Then we got a bit sidetracked."

"There's nothing online," Journey said.

"Not in ordinary search engines."

"What?"

"Look, my job is mining data, finding people and things that in a lot of cases aren't meant to be found. The programs RIO uses can go a lot of places, can search places most people can't. I can get to millions of pages of scanned documents that might not be readily available."

"What are you saying?"

"I'm saying I got a hit on the Glory Warriors, and I'm saying it confused the hell out of me. I kept thinking, 'This can't be right.'"

"Are you talking historical data or contemporary?"

Tolman thumped her computer. "Historical. But I don't get it."

Journey leaned toward the screen. "What? Is it something connected to Grant or Lee? I've read most of what's out there, but—"

"No, not Grant or Lee."

"Then what? Samuel Williams?"

"No."

"Then who, for God's sake?"

"You're not going to believe this. *I* don't believe this, and it's right in front of me."

"Just tell me!"

"Mark Twain," Tolman said. "The Glory Warriors are mentioned in some of the private papers of Mark Twain."

# CHAPTER

# 41

Journey sat back against the booth, closed his eyes, and nodded.
Tolman looked at him in disbelief. "You don't seem surprised."

"You know that Ulysses S. Grant was elected president, right? He was elected in 1868, three years after the war ended. He was an international hero, practically worshipped by much of the country. Even the South respected him because the terms he offered Lee at Appomattox were so generous. Grant was a rock star. Then he became president."

"And this has what to do with Mark Twain?"

"Stay with me here, Meg," Journey said. "Grant was one of the most honest men in America, but he surrounded himself with corrupt, unscrupulous, and often stupid people. He was a terrible president. Corruption, bribery . . . you name it and it happened during his two terms in office. By the time he left office in 1877, he'd squandered all his fame and popularity."

"What did he do then?"

"He traveled, went into business, did a lot of different things. But remember, there was no presidential pension then, and he'd given up his military pension when he became president. Within a few years, he was completely destitute, and then he was diagnosed with throat cancer. After all the years of smoking, it was already in an advanced state, nothing that could be done for him."

"But I still don't get—"

"Sam Clemens, aka Mark Twain, had been an admirer of Grant's for years. When Twain saw that Grant was dying, he told Grant to write his memoirs and that he—Twain—would publish them. Grant saw that it was the only way he could provide for his family after he was gone. He and his wife, Julia, moved to Mount McGregor, New York, and he started writing."

"Did he finish? Did Twain actually publish the memoirs?"

"Oh, yes. *Personal Memoirs of U. S. Grant* was a great success. Grant finished writing the book in the summer of 1885, and he died a few days after sending the manuscript to Twain. Twain had just started a publishing company with Charles Webster, who was his nephew by marriage, and it was the first book they published. It sold hundreds of thousands of copies, which was huge. And it did provide an income for Julia Grant until the day she died." Journey stopped and leaned toward the computer. "And you found a connection between the Glory Warriors and Mark Twain?"

"Here," Tolman said, manipulating the thumb bar. "One hit. It's a document that's been scanned as part of an archiving project at the University of California at Berkeley."

"Berkeley," Journey said. "Seems like I remember seeing a while back that a lot of Twain's later letters and some scattered obscure papers had been donated to Berkeley. But you say this isn't online? Then how can you get to it?"

"I use a program called RACER, which can go anywhere and find pretty much anything in the digital world. Part of its function searches out computer networks. If there's a network, and if *somewhere* in it, the network is linked to the Internet, we can find it. This document isn't posted online, but it's scanned into a computer on a network that has an online connection. You see what I mean?"

"So you can read my e-mail. Or, say, the president's e-mail."

"It's a research tool."

"There's really no such thing as privacy anymore, is there?"

"Look, that's not for me to decide. Someone way above my pay grade makes those policies. For me, it's a technology that lets me do my job. Do you want to have an academic debate about the government's research methods or do you want to see what this document is?" She opened the file and angled the screen so both of them could see.

The scanned document seemed to be a letter from Mark Twain to someone named Leon, and was headed with the date *April 8, 1910,* and *Redding, CT.*

"I don't know exactly when he died," Journey said, "but I think this was very late in his life."

The document was in a thick, heavy handwriting, with the look of a letter that had been written slowly. Tolman and Journey read through two pages of Samuel Clemens's ramblings, talking about family, how he still terribly missed his two daughters who had died, even years after their deaths. He went on to describe the spring flowers in Connecticut, and the certainty that he would never see spring flowers again. Halley's Comet would soon be visible to Earth, he wrote, and he expected his own death as it passed, just as he had been born in 1835, the last time the famed comet passed close to Earth.

Tolman and Journey kept reading. Journey drew in a hard breath on the third page.

*And so, good man, one of the most rewarding—and I daresay the most confounding—experiences of this long and occasionally ill-lived life, was my association with General Grant.*

*The man saved our Union, and yet at life's end found himself penniless. Once I persuaded him that his life's story could be sold to the American people, that it was indeed a story worthy of recounting, thereby providing for his dear wife, Julia, and family, he threw himself fairly into the task. A fine writer he proved to be, one with more style and a sense of economy of words than yours truly!*

*Confession, at this late date, is advantageous to the soul, or so I am led to believe. I confess great perplexity on the whole business of the Glory Warriors, of which the General wrote, then entreated me to reconsider the publication of said pages. I was obliged to hastily correspond with Webster and have him remove the pages from the book. What Webster did with the pages, I do not know. The General passed from this life within days, and of course Webster himself met his own end not long thereafter.*

*A perplexing business, indeed, and quite unlike the General. At first I had thought the General to be spinning a yarn, amusing himself at the end of the manuscript, perhaps distracting himself away from the horrors of his disease. But General Grant never joked about matters of war, so I can only surmise this unexpected coda to the memoir is a matter that confounded the General himself. As the conditions he described never came to pass, the notion must have faded from consciousness. General Lee was deceased many years by then, and Grant elected not to include the business in his memoir. It all seems to have been left with the dead, and as my own passage is imminent, so it shall stay.*

A computer-printed note was appended to the bottom of the file, declaring that Samuel L. Clemens died on April 21, 1910, thirteen days after composing this letter. The letter was never sent, and the Leon to whom it was addressed remained unknown. The letter was found by the author's surviving daughter, Clara, among his other papers after his death, and finally came to the archive at Berkeley in 1962, on Clara's death.

Journey sat back, his heart pounding. Suddenly feeling closed in, he said, "I have to get out. I have to move around." Tolman tossed money onto the table, and they left the restaurant. Journey walked around the edge of the parking lot and onto a grassy area between the truck stop and the highway service road. He paced up and down the grass, in and out of the lights that ringed the parking lot, limping on his left foot.

"What are you thinking?" Tolman finally asked him.

A truck went by on the service road, and Journey waited for the sound of the diesel engine to pass. After another pace, he stopped, turned to Tolman, and slapped the knuckles of his left hand into the palm of his right. "Grant wrote about the Glory Warriors. *He* did. Up until now, all we've had are these documents in a third person's writing, presumably Samuel Williams. But Mark Twain, practically on his deathbed, says that Grant himself wrote about it."

Tolman walked beside him for a few steps. "But then Grant

changed his mind and told Twain he didn't want it published in his memoir."

"So Twain wrote to his nephew Charles Webster, who actually ran the publishing company, and had him remove those pages."

"And you say the Grant memoir is well known?" Tolman said.

Journey glared at her.

Tolman raised both hands. "I didn't study history, Nick. You have to remember that not everyone is as into this stuff as you are."

"Yes, yes, Grant's book is considered a classic military memoir."

"And you've read it?"

"Of course I've read it."

"Never saw anything in it that remotely sounded like the Glory Warriors? Nothing that would point to it?"

"No, nothing."

"What about Lee's writing?"

Journey shook his head. "Lee wasn't a writer. He never did a memoir, and really only left behind a few letters. After the war he was president of Washington College. But no, he never mentioned anything remotely resembling this, in the few writings that did survive and have been accessible to historians."

"Okay, so Grant's publisher—who just happens to be one of the most famous authors in the world—writes on his own deathbed, years and years after Grant's death, that Grant mentioned this, then pulled it from the book. Twain also says that the nephew . . . What was his name?"

"Charles Webster."

"Right, that Webster died not long after that, and Twain didn't know what Webster did with the pages."

"Right."

"Is the publishing company still in business? Even as a subsidiary? I'm thinking of Samuel Williams's bank, still doing business after all this time, even though under a different name."

Journey sighed. "No. I can tell you that much. The company published a few more books, including Twain's *Huckleberry Finn*, but none of them were as successful as Grant's. It folded a few years later."

Tolman stopped in a circle of light and leaned against a pole, transferring her laptop bag from one shoulder to the other. "Those pages have to exist somewhere. Come on, you can't seriously tell me that what amounts to outtakes from a bestseller didn't find their way into someone's hands. A collector, a treasure hunter . . . Hell, Nick—" Tolman waved an all-encompassing hand. "—they could be sitting in a museum somewhere for all this time, with no one knowing what they had."

"They're not in a museum," Journey said. "Someone in the history community would have uncovered something by now if they were. If the pages are that explosive and outlined the fact that the two most beloved generals in America had at one point put their names on something like this, well, that would have come to light by now, even if the other puzzle pieces, the ones we uncovered, weren't in place. No, they had to have stayed hidden."

"Okay, they're not in a museum," Tolman said. "I wish you didn't know so goddamn much about all this stuff. Half the time, I feel like I should be getting course credit when I'm talking to you."

"Occupational hazard. I'm always a teacher, even when I'm not teaching."

"My, that's profound. So the pages have stayed underground somewhere." They both turned back toward the parking lot, to the old Toyota. "God, I really need a piano. And I really need to get to a secure phone so I can call Rusty and tell him what's happening." She slapped her hand against the car door. "And we need those fucking pages and those fucking signatures."

Journey stood beside her, taking his weight off his bad foot.

Tolman glanced sideways at him. "They're going to try to kill the president," she said in a low, resigned voice.

Journey nodded. "Yes."

"What's their timetable? I mean, let's say they kill the president. Now there's this huge power vacuum that activates the Glory Warriors. They have to have weapons, wherever they are around the country. They think they have a right to do this, because of what Lee and Grant signed. But Jesus, Nick, these people think they have a legal right to suspend the Constitution and basically overthrow our government! I mean, our government's not very efficient, I realize.

Hell, I work for it and I know that. But we don't have coups in this country. Russia, Bulgaria, Pakistan, Chile, maybe, but not here."

Journey shook his head. "Why do governments anywhere get overthrown? There's instability, people are restless. Look at us now. Yes, we have the best government on the planet, and things are *still* a mess. When a fanatic or group of fanatics steps into a mess and promises to make things orderly, it will get the attention of some people."

"And that's when you get a Hitler or a Lenin or the Taliban."

"Or a Glory Warrior invoking the names of two American heroes." He thumped the car door. "But I still don't understand why Grant and Lee would agree to it in 1865. It doesn't seem in character for them."

Tolman scuffed a foot on the pavement. "Okay, I'm not the historian here, but as you've told me, it was a different time. Can anyone alive now really, truly understand what the Civil War was like? You couldn't tell if someone was a spy, because he might look just like your brother. He might *be* your brother. There's no way we can understand. As logical and practical and strategic as people like Robert E. Lee and U. S. Grant were as soldiers, they were also people, and they were just as susceptible to emotions as anyone else. They may have *felt*, as least for a time, that they had no choice but to join together at the end of the war to create this contingency plan. They weren't thinking about the fact that it would stand the entire Constitution on its head. Maybe they were thinking a lot of people had died, and by then, they were sick of people dying, and just wanted to find a way to deal with all the blood. And this thing, however it came about, gave them an out, gave them a way to prepare."

Journey was staring at her. The look was intense, the lines on his forehead deepening into slash marks. Then they slowly softened.

"Sorry," Tolman said. "Now I'm the one who's lecturing."

"But you're right," Journey said. "Especially in that time, men didn't write their deepest fears and feelings into memoirs. It just wasn't done. Grant's book is a great recounting of his life up through the end of the war, and of his thinking as a military man. But it's hard to tell how he—or anyone—*felt*."

"We need to see those pages that Grant asked Twain to take out of the book."

"Yes. But in the meantime, we know they're going to go after the president, and we still can't prove any of this. What if we get the evidence, but it's too late?"

"I'll be able to talk to my boss when we get where we're going," Tolman said.

"And that would be where?"

Tolman shook her head. "Later. We may have to go at this a different way, as far as the threat against the president."

"What do you mean?"

"I happen to have a contact in the Secret Service."

"Someone you trust?"

Tolman thought of her father, crying in the ER after the car crash fifteen years ago, and of him a few days ago, sitting at the wedding reception in Chevy Chase, applauding her performance while everyone else ignored her. "With my life," she said.

# CHAPTER

# 42

When the members of Dallas Four drove up the mountain to the Judge's retreat at just past midnight, they didn't know what to expect. None of them had ever met the Judge face-to-face. Few of the rank-and-file Glory Warriors had. But Dallas Base, and later Chicago Base, had confirmed their orders: Take the pages to the Judge. They'd received directions to his house as part of their briefing.

When Gold rang the Judge's bell, he felt surreal. It seemed an anticlimax, driving up this mountain in the dead of night and simply ringing a doorbell. It took several minutes, but lights came on and the Judge opened the door. Gold felt even more off-balance then: The Judge was old, but even in the middle of the night and wearing pajamas with red stripes under a faded terry cloth robe, he had a certain bearing. The dignity of a soldier, the charisma of a born leader, Gold thought. Even without saying a word, the man communicated strength and leadership and power. Gold had seen video of the Judge in his younger days, at a time when he was in the public eye, and he seemed to have lost very little of his presence.

"Dallas Four, sir," Gold said. Glory Warriors didn't salute, but the members of the team stood at attention.

"Come in, come in," the Judge said. "You must be tired. Would you like coffee?"

Again, there was the faintly ridiculous sensation. The Judge made coffee for all of them and positioned them in the large, open living room. It was rustic, with an abundance of pine and deep leather furniture under a wrought iron chandelier. "The pages," the Judge said at length as they drank coffee.

Silver handed him the backpack and gave him a precise verbal report on what had transpired in Louisville and at Falls of the Ohio. The Judge acknowledged her with a nod, opening the backpack and slipping the pages into his hands.

He read, a look of knowing and understanding on his face. He smiled; then he sifted through the papers.

"Where's the other page?" he asked.

"Sir?" Silver said.

"The signature page. It isn't here."

Silver looked at Gold. They both looked at Bronze. No one spoke.

"We must have the signature page," the Judge said. "It isn't here."

"Sir," Silver said, "these are what Journey had with him."

"No," the Judge said.

"She's correct, sir," Gold said. "We recovered all the pages he had."

The Judge slapped the pages onto the wooden coffee table. The sudden motion startled Dallas Four. "Then he's fooled you! He's put it somewhere else."

"Sir—"

"Do you understand?" the Judge said, shouting now. "All of this is useless without Lee and Grant's signatures. It says as much on the first page. All must be here for the treaty to have the full weight of the law." He leaned forward, a vein throbbing in his neck. "Do you have any idea how many have sacrificed their entire lives for this? Do you know what *I* have sacrificed for the Glory Warriors? It is within our reach . . . right now! We are two-thirds of the way to satisfying the conditions on page one. We've always known what to do, but we must have the signatures! The people will not accept us if we don't!"

The team members sat rigid, eyes fastened on the Judge.

The Judge stood and backed away from his chair. "The professor—where is he now?"

"I shot him," Silver said. "He fell into the river. There were witnesses, and there wasn't time to clean the scene. We had to—"

"Journey has that page!" the Judge screamed. "He's alive and he knows where it is. We have to be ready when all three of the conditions of page one are met. As soon as it happens, we must be ready, and that means the signatures. They need to be where people can see them. When I go on TV and radio and the Internet to explain to the American people, they need to know we are real. The cameras must do a close-up of Lee and Grant's signatures."

The team members looked at each other.

"Are you completely ignorant of history? America's history—*our* history? In 1865, Lee and Grant gave us our authority. With the Lieber Code as the point of legal reference, and with their agreement at Appomattox, the provisions are law. If the people don't see this and understand it, they won't accept us. They'll view us as glorified terrorists. They'll think we're some sort of silly militia group. No, the treaty is our legal authority, and the people must see it! Do you understand?"

They were all quiet for a time; then Bronze said, "Sir, we should call Dallas Base to check in."

"No!" the Judge yelled. His terry cloth robe fell open, and they all saw his chest heaving, as if he were laboring for breath.

"Sir, are you all right?" Gold said.

"Get out of my house!" the Judge bellowed. "You are relieved of duty! Go back to Dallas and do nothing! Do you hear me? You are relieved. Now, *get out*!"

They left, and the Judge stayed behind, breathing hard. After the taillights of their car had faded down the mountain, he made his way to his study, slammed the door, and picked up the phone.

It took ten minutes for the Dallas duty officer to locate the Dallas Base commander. When he came on the line, the Judge said, "Your team failed. They didn't get the signatures, and I've relieved them of duty. Nick Journey and the woman have the page, or they've put it somewhere."

"We'll find them," Dallas said.

The Judge ran his hand through his thin white hair. "See that you do. Team Four will not be involved. Put them on arsenal guard duty or something equally humiliating. They failed."

"All right, sir," Dallas said. "I'll put my Team One on them. We have a new Gold, and Silver is anxious to be a part of this."

The Judge nodded, feeling his heartbeat begin to slow. He thought he felt a flutter in his chest. "Call the other base commanders. Have each of them put their own Team One on alert. Have all your Bronzes do what they can to track every possible way to find Journey and Tolman. I'll call my Washington people."

The Judge hung up, then called Washington Three, who answered with a sleepy "Yeah?"

"You have a green light," the Judge said.

"What?"

"Wake up! I'm telling you to move forward. You are cleared to move into the operational part of your mission."

"Sir?"

"Yes." The Judge planted a closed fist on his desk. "Start looking for your opportunity to enact the third provision."

The Judge hung up, his heart still pounding, hands shaking. He should not have raised his voice to his subordinates. It accomplished nothing. Showing temper to underlings only displayed weakness.

Now was the time for strength, for control. Soon after President Harwell was dead and the Glory Warriors had secured Washington, he would be addressing not only his troops, but all the American people. Control was paramount. Calm was essential. There could be no more outbursts.

They would find the signatures. They would find Journey and the woman. There would be no more mistakes.

*Don't fail.*

The Judge sat back down behind his desk and closed his eyes. But an hour later, his heart was still thundering and his hands were still trembling.

# CHAPTER
# 43

Tolman fell asleep before they crossed into Tennessee. Journey's fingers hurt from where he'd clawed at the rocks, and his left foot was sore, but he held his leg as straight as he could with his right foot on the accelerator. He kept the old Camry pointed south through the night, then turned west on I-40 at Nashville, per Tolman's scrawled instructions. Just past two thirty in the morning, he coasted into a truck stop in Jackson, Tennessee.

Tolman woke, and they both washed up in the trucker-sized bathrooms, then walked into the restaurant to order coffee. The layout was typical American truck stop: booths along three walls, tables in the center, a counter with stools. Homemade pies sat under glass at the counter. Classic rock played over the speakers.

"How do you feel?" Journey asked as they settled into a booth.

"Head still hurts, but not too bad. You?"

"I'm ready for you to drive," Journey said. "My foot's very sore, and I'm tired."

"Thanks for driving."

Journey nodded. "Now will you tell me where we're going?"

"A little speck of a town in Arkansas called Gravelly. There's someone there I trust. It'll be safe, it'll be secure, and the Glory

Warriors would really have to be stretching to make the connection. The man who lives there is named Darrell Sharp. I knew him at the Academy. I got to know him because of the piano."

"The piano?"

Tolman smiled. "We all lived on campus at the Academy. That was a requirement. But Darrell also rented an apartment in town. One day in class, I think it was Advanced Database Investigations, someone made a crack about him renting an apartment just for a piano."

Journey looked at her.

"It was true."

"So he was also a pianist," Journey said.

"No. He can't play a note. But his father was a concert pianist who taught at the University of South Carolina. His father had died of cancer the year before and left Darrell this piano. But not just any piano—a Steinway concert grand. He didn't want to leave it in storage somewhere, and he didn't want to sell it or give it away, so he kept it and hired professional piano movers to take it wherever he went."

"Isn't that expensive?"

"Very. But his father had done well as a concert pianist and left Darrell a decent trust fund. So anyway, after class I went up to him and asked him about the apartment and the piano. He offered to show me, so the next time we were both free, I went over and saw it. He let me play it. I'd just come off a year of trying to make a living as a musician, then coming to the realization that I wasn't good enough to do that, so I went into the family business and applied to the Academy."

"And you and he started seeing each other."

"It's not what you think. We didn't really 'date' or anything like that. I just . . . went and played his piano. Sometimes he made dinner. A few times things went further." Tolman stopped, turning the memories over in her mind. "But there was never anything beyond that. Then he graduated and joined the U.S. Marshals Service. His first job was in Miami. I was still at the Academy."

Tolman had already downed a full cup of coffee, and she signaled the waitress for another. "Six months after Darrell got to Miami, he was sent on a prisoner escort. A major cocaine dealer who'd been a fugitive for more than five years had been recaptured in Key West. Darrell and one other deputy marshal were sent to bring him back. Some of the dealer's 'employees' somehow broke through security and tried to blast him out during the transfer. Between the holding cell and the car, they broke him out. Darrell's partner had his head practically blown off. They killed the DEA agent who'd found the dealer, and two local cops."

"My God," Journey said. He put down his coffee cup.

"Darrell ran around the opposite side of the truck, with them shooting at him the whole way. He got to one of the guys, knocked his gun away, but the guy turned around with a knife and slashed Darrell across his stomach. So there he was, bleeding from a belly wound. They scuffled, Darrell got to his shotgun and put a round through the guy's neck. The two other guys turned on him, he rolled into a ditch, got around the other side of them, and shot them both. The dealer got into the middle of it and Darrell shot him, too." Tolman looked down at the table.

"That's eight people dead," Journey said, counting on his fingers.

Tolman nodded but didn't look up. Her eyes were far away. "Darrell was the only one of either the druggies or cops left alive. Bystanders corroborated everything, he received citations for bravery, newspaper and TV stories were done on him. But he couldn't sleep, couldn't eat, couldn't even move some days. He'd go for a week or more at a time without talking. He was put on administrative leave and sent to a counselor."

"Posttraumatic stress disorder."

"PTSD and severe depression. He woke up crying one morning, and he couldn't stop. He simply couldn't stop crying. He had the presence of mind to drive himself to a hospital, and he spent three weeks in the mental health unit. He resigned from the Marshals Service the day he walked out of the hospital. Eventually he was awarded a disability pension. So there he was, retired on disability at age twenty-six. He found this remote place out in the woods in Arkansas, and just walked away from everything."

"And you talked to him while all this was going on?"

"He called me from the hospital. I'd finished the Academy and joined RIO in D.C. by then. I went to Florida over two weekends and saw him in the hospital."

"What does he do now?"

"He paints," Tolman said. "The guy actually paints landscapes on cups and bowls and plates, and he sells them online. I haven't talked to him in a couple of years now. He rarely leaves the house. He's worried that people are coming to get him. He's on meds, and he's better than he was, but he's not quite whole yet. He always feels that he's on the edge of either killing someone or being killed himself. But I know his communications are secure, and I know he has weapons. We'll be there in the morning."

Journey looked at her. "And he's going to just welcome us, with all our baggage, into his remote little life out there in the country?"

"He's ready for us," Tolman said. "Ready as he can be."

# CHAPTER
# 44

Voss came to the office at her regular time, though it had been well after 1 A.M. when she finally went to bed. She said a quick good morning to Tina, the receptionist, then headed for the lounge to get a Diet Coke. Hudson was there, pouring himself a cup of coffee.

"Morning," Voss said.

"Good morning, Kerry," Hudson said. His voice was tired.

"Any news?"

"No." Hudson poured sugar into his coffee and stirred it. "I don't think I'm going to have to be at the Hoover Building today, though. Special Agent Díaz is running the investigation, with the attorney general personally overseeing. I understand the president himself even called Díaz. For all of our sakes, I hope this is a quick investigation."

He stirred his coffee some more.

"Have you heard from Meg?" Voss asked.

Hudson looked down at her. "No," he said, and left the room.

*Strange,* Voss thought. Everyone in the office knew that Tolman and Hudson got along famously, though it was an odd pairing. One of the law enforcement guys swore they were sleeping together, which of course was nonsense. A woman could tell, and Voss knew that what Tolman and Hudson had was more a big brother–little sister relationship. Voss went to her office and settled in to work. She followed up on a few e-mails, killed some time online, and her hacker called her cell at just after ten o'clock.

"Hey, Kerry."

"Morning, Duke. What do you have?" Voss turned off her computer's media player in the middle of Guns N' Roses' "Mr. Brownstone" and pulled at a strand of her hair. She'd meant to do more with it, but wound up pulling it back into a ponytail. She'd been too tired to face her hair this morning.

"Oh, yeah," Duke said. "Yeah, yeah, yeah. I rule the world, Kerry."

"I know you do. Where does the money originate?"

Duke made a clucking sound with his tongue. "You want to go out sometime, Kerry?"

"No. I've told you this every time you've asked, Duke. We'll keep it on a professional level. And you seem to forget that I have three kids."

"Damn, that's right. I hate kids. All right, never mind. Got your money, though."

"Tell me."

"Of course, there's no name on the account in Aruba. Can't get names on offshore accounts. This was a good challenge. It took me a couple of hours to get into the bank, but once I was in . . ."

"Duke."

"Yeah, yeah, yeah. Okay, so from Aruba it comes back to the States. I got the computer that initiated the transfer of funds to Aruba, who transferred it to New York, who sent it to Dallas, who sent it to its final destination in Louisiana. And you know what? The original account is right here in the D.C. area."

Voss sat forward. "Really?"

"Ha, now you love me, don't you? Yeah, it's a branch of one of the big banks. The branch is in Silver Spring."

"And?"

"And . . ." Duke drew out the silence.

"I don't have much patience with drama this morning, in case you're wondering," Voss said.

"Yeah, I'm getting that from you. And there is one big shitload of money going out of that account. We're talking millions every week, and it's sent to other accounts all over the place. Jamaica, the Caymans, Luxembourg, South America."

Voss whistled. "And I bet all those are pass-throughs."

"I bet you're right. That money goes *everywhere*, but it all eventually winds up back in the States. There is a *lot* of it."

"Okay, so who owns the account in Silver Spring?"

"It's something called GW One. You want me to spell it? No, okay, I won't spell it. GW One."

Voss wrote *GW1* on her pad.

"And I got the IP address of the computer that initiated the funds transfer. It came from a wireless network that's part of the Hubopag server. You know them, right?"

"Local ISP for the D.C. area. Yeah, I know what Hubopag is."

"Right, right. One step further back, the Wi-Fi signal was from a place called Around the Ground. Its physical address is in downtown D.C. You know what that is? I don't go downtown. I don't want to deal with tourists all over the place. You know what Around the Ground is, Kerry?"

Voss looked out her window at Connecticut Avenue, squeezed her eyes closed, then opened them again.

"Kerry? Hello?"

"I'm here, Duke. Sorry, I zoned out for a minute there. I'm tired. Up past my bedtime last night."

"Hoo, you're a wimp. I haven't been to bed yet. I spent all night doing this for you, just because—"

"I appreciate it, Duke. The GW One account—did you get names? Are there real people's names on the account?"

"I pulled up the signature card itself. Two names on it."

Voss listened as Duke gave her the names. She didn't recognize the first one, but the second name she knew well.

So would Meg Tolman.

Voss hung up without saying another word to Duke. She sat for a minute, then another, in the quiet stillness of her office; then she opened a desk drawer and pulled out a thin booklet, a stapled-together directory assembled by the Government Printing Office. She flipped pages, then ran her index finger down a page. She read the name, then the phone number and address beside it. The address was in Silver Spring, Maryland.

Her cell phone still in her other hand, Voss stood and walked out of her office, turned at the reception desk without speaking to Tina, then took the elevator to the first floor and walked into the lobby of the office building. She passed through the revolving door and felt a gust of wind. She heard traffic sounds, a few voices. The morning was cloudy and it felt like rain.

Voss turned right and walked to the end of the block, to another office building almost identical to the one that held RIO's offices. She pushed through its revolving door, walked twenty or so steps, and rounded a bank of elevators. She smelled coffee.

To her left, at the rear of the building, was a little glassed-in coffee shop. A stylized painting of a cup of coffee was etched on the glass. The sign on the window, in bold blue letters, read AROUND THE GROUND.

# CHAPTER

# 45

Tolman drove through the night, crossing the Mississippi River at Memphis. They listened to various radio stations, catching snippets of an evangelist thundering on about the impending rapture, a few minutes of Beethoven's "Eroica" Symphony, Tim Mc-Graw singing about how choices and mistakes all knew his name, but mostly news. The newscasts were all from Washington: Speaker Vandermeer's memorial service had been held at the National Cathedral. President Harwell delivered one of the eulogies for his longtime colleague and frequent sparring partner.

More news: The Speaker's killing had been officially classified as a random act of violence, a possible robbery, though nothing was reportedly taken from the body. The Darlington investigation, on the other hand, was rife with intrigue and speculation about a terrorist cell that had an inside contact close to the chief justice. Journey and Tolman exchanged grim looks.

The sun rose behind them as they passed through Little Rock. Tolman looped onto I-430, crossed the Arkansas River, and exited on Cantrell Road. It wound west out of the city and became two-lane State Highway 10 heading west, then sharply north, then west again. In Ola, on the edge of the Ouachita National Forest, Tolman stopped in the parking lot of a Baptist church and said, "I *really* hate driving."

Journey had been awake since Little Rock. "Want me to take over?"

"No. We're almost there. I just need to check my directions. Don't want to get lost way out here in the middle of fucking nowhere."

"You were right about one thing," Journey said. "I don't think the Glory Warriors will be looking for us here."

At Ola's only crossroads, they bent back to the southwest on Arkansas 28, winding deeper into the trees between the Dutch Creek and Fourche Mountains. Forty-five minutes later, with the sun high over the brilliant green hills, the Camry rounded a bend into Gravelly: a handful of scattered frame houses, mobile homes, and a tired post office with a gravel parking lot. A dusty black Jeep Cherokee sat beside the post office. Tolman pulled the Toyota next to it and said, "Stay right here."

Journey watched as she got out and walked around the front of the car. The Cherokee's door opened and a man got out. He was tall and muscular, with a shaven head and a thick mustache. He and Tolman didn't embrace, didn't shake hands. Tolman said a few indistinct words; then the man said, "Follow me."

Tolman returned to the wheel. The Jeep pulled out of the parking lot and back onto the road. "How far—?" Journey said.

"He lives a little bit out of town," Tolman said.

They drove another mile. At a barely perceptible opening off the highway, the Jeep turned right and Tolman followed. The rutted trail wound another half mile into the backcountry before ending in a wide clearing before a small flat-roofed house. A miniature satellite dish sat at one end. There were few windows. Journey and Tolman each took their bags and followed the man inside.

"Put your stuff in the corner there," the man said; his voice was a Deep South drawl.

Tolman stood between the two men. "Nick Journey, Darrell Sharp," she said. Journey extended his hand. Sharp looked at it as if he didn't know what to do, then slowly shook Journey's hand. Neither man spoke.

Sharp was even taller than Journey had thought, at least six-five.

His body was muscular, though it looked more like manual-labor muscle than air-conditioned-gym muscle. His skin was tanned, his eyes dark and always in motion. Sharp's mustache was brown, and although he had to be at least ten years younger than Journey, it was speckled with gray.

The floor was concrete, the furniture all wooden and cheap, but very clean. A modest TV sat on a stand in one corner. A desk holding a computer, two telephones, and a fax machine sat in the other. Small shelves lined the walls, filled with china—cups, bowls, plates—all painted with bright, vibrant colors of gold, red, green, and blue. A short hallway led away from the front room, and to one side, Journey caught sight of a doorway to another room. It was filled with a black concert grand piano, a bench, and nothing else.

"You can rest up a little on the couch out here if you want," Sharp said, and it took Journey a moment to realize he was talking to him.

"Thanks," Journey said.

"Meg, I got a spot for you in the back," Sharp said. "You want something to eat?"

They hadn't eaten since Elizabethtown, nearly twelve hours ago. Sharp made scrambled eggs and thick sausage, and they ate at the butcher-block table while he watched them. He breathed loudly, moved in his chair, sniffed the air. He was the noisiest silent man Journey had ever met.

When they had eaten, he stood, still saying nothing, and walked out of the room. "We should rest a bit," Tolman said to Journey. "An hour, maybe two at the most. How's your foot?"

Journey seesawed his hand back and forth. "Sore. Not too bad, though. How's your head?"

"Sore. Stretch out, close your eyes for a while, then we'll get busy."

Journey nodded, then watched as Tolman followed in the direction Sharp had gone.

Journey fell asleep the instant his head touched Darrell Sharp's couch, but an hour later he woke up gasping as if he were drowning, clawing at the cloth edges of the old couch, just as he'd clawed the rocks at Falls of the Ohio. His fingers ached where the nails had split.

He'd awakened with a thought at the edge of his mind. Not quite a dream, but a little corner of realization, like a slightly smudged fingerprint in his memory. It was Samuel Williams and Robert E. Lee and Ulysses S. Grant and Mark Twain and Charles Webster. It was Andrew and Amelia and Sandra Kelly, and the woman shooting at him on the bank of the Ohio River. It was the man he'd killed in the parking lot at SCCO. It was gold pins with G.W. gleaming on them. And it was Meg Tolman with her probing insights. It was even his parents and his brothers, reaching out to him from the place where he'd mentally locked them away long ago.

*"We all hide from something,"* Tolman had said.

*"I don't hide,"* he told her.

*Yes, I do.*

*I hide behind Andrew, and I hide behind my students, and I hide behind the Civil War.*

But he still couldn't reach it. The waking thought stayed hidden. He sat up on the couch as a form appeared in the doorway.

"Meg?" he said.

Sharp stepped into the room. As his eyes adjusted, Journey saw the pistol in the man's hand.

"I wasn't sure that was you making that noise," Sharp said.

"You could hear me? I'm sorry." Journey swung his legs to the floor.

Sharp stood between Journey and the back of the house, unmoving, silent.

"Could I—?" Journey swallowed, looking down at the gun in the man's hand. "Could I just get a glass of water or something?"

"Yeah."

Uncomfortable with Sharp's brooding presence—not to mention the gun in his hand—Journey edged past him to the kitchen, fumbled for a light switch, and dug in cabinets until he found a glass. He ran some water over his hands, splashed his face, then drank some from the glass.

When he turned back toward the living room, he saw that Sharp was bare-chested and wearing only gray sweatpants. An inch-wide tangle of scar tissue ran horizontally across his stomach, just above the navel.

"I was in the hospital a while back," Sharp said. "Meg was the only person who came to see me when I was there."

Journey nodded, not sure if he should acknowledge how much of Sharp's story he knew.

"She tells me you killed a man," Sharp said.

"Yes," Journey said. "He was shooting at me."

"How did it feel?"

"I don't know. All I know is that he was shooting at me."

"Yeah," Sharp said. "I guess that's about all any of us really knows. You don't know how you feel until a lot later, and then sometimes you still don't."

Sharp turned around and walked down the hall, the gun still in his hand.


Journey showered in Sharp's small, square bathroom, then dressed again in the clothes the woman in Clarksville had given him. When he came out of the bathroom, he heard the piano.

It was a strange and incongruous sight, the elegant Steinway in a tiny room of a house deep in the Arkansas woods, a house owned by a gun-toting man who painted on china. It took a few moments for Journey to reconcile the picture he had of Meg Tolman as well, the woman who carried a gun and cursed a lot and mined databases, with this petite figure at the keyboard.

She stopped when he came in. "I had to play," she said.

Journey gestured at the instrument. "The same piano?"

"Same one. He gets a tuner from Little Rock to come out and make sure it's tuned every now and then."

"But he doesn't play."

"Not a bit."

"You play well."

Tolman tilted her head dismissively.

"I'm glad you got to play some," Journey said. "What was that piece you were playing?"

"A Rachmaninov prelude, number eleven, opus thirty-two." She smiled. "That probably doesn't mean a damn thing to you. Sorry. It's not Rachmaninov's most famous prelude, but I love it. B-major is an interesting key." She looked embarrassed. "You don't want a musicology lecture. We have work to do. But we should be safe here, to get some time to think."

"I liked the piece. It sounded . . . I don't know, hopeful, maybe?"

"Maybe. Maybe so."

In the living room, Tolman said, "Darrell, we need your phone and your computer."

"My phone's secure," Sharp said, then turned and disappeared into the back of the house. A moment later, a door slammed.

Journey stared after the man, and Tolman said, "This is who he is. Don't worry about him. Why don't you check your message board and see if there's anything from Sandra? Darrell said the computer is already on. You'll just have to open the Web browser."

Journey navigated to the Civil War Geeks Web site, logged in, and found a single message from the screen name "Radical Redhead." He smiled a little at that, but the smile faded quickly.

ON A JOURNEY: AJ IS OK. AB SAYS AN INTERESTING CAR IN THE NEIGHBORHOOD. AB CRANKY. YOU OK?

Journey read it again.

AB SAYS AN INTERESTING CAR IN THE NEIGHBORHOOD.

So they were watching Amelia's house. They knew where Andrew was, and just like before, they didn't care who knew it. Journey felt the anger begin to rise again. "They know where Andrew is," he said. He mashed his knuckles together, then interlaced his fingers, looking at the floor.

"Nick?" Tolman said.

He said nothing. The feelings tumbled through him like dice, as he thought of the way Andrew smiled at him in the mornings, pulling his blanket up to hide his face. A toddler in a twelve-year-old's body, playing peekaboo. Journey closed his eyes.

"They know exactly where my son is," Journey said, "and they could just go in there and take him at any moment. That's what scares me the most. He wouldn't understand what was happening to him. He wouldn't even know to be afraid. He doesn't know danger—it's a completely foreign concept to him. The only thing the kid's afraid of is dogs."

Tolman looked at the computer screen. "You'll see him again soon, Nick. We're not going to let anything happen to Andrew—or even to your ex-wife. I'm calling the office now." She pulled one of the rough-hewn kitchen chairs to the desk. Outside the window, Sharp walked past, glancing toward the house every few seconds.

Sharp's telephone was an old-fashioned desk model, square and boxy with a curly cord. Tolman punched numbers and waited. "Come on, come on," she said under her breath. She looked at Journey while the phone rang. "Think about Mark Twain's nephew, about where we might find those pages." In her ear, the phone connected.

"You have reached Russell Hudson . . . ," the voice mail message began.

"Dammit! Where the hell are you now, Rusty?" Tolman gripped the phone, made as if she were going to throw the receiver, then pulled it back to her ear. After the tone, she said, "Rusty, I'm on a secure landline phone. Journey and I are okay. A little banged up, but all right. Call me back—I can't tell you everything in a voice mail. Here's the number. It's a secure line. . . . Call me, Rusty. Now!"

She hung up. "Jesus, where is that man? Probably at the fucking Hoover Building dealing with the Fucking Bureau of Investigation. The FBI doesn't acknowledge RIO's existence for years, and all of a sudden they want us at the table. Probably so they can blame us for Darlington. Shit!" She rapped on the desk with her knuckles, then rubbed the back of her head. Her hand touched the bandage. "Shit, my head. I need to take some Tylenol." She waved her hand toward Journey. "See if you can find anything about Twain's nephew. Maybe the publishing company had some kind of archives that were passed down. Or maybe some of the family has it."

"Like Evan Lovell's dad."

"We can hope," Tolman said.

She looked at the antique clock that hung above the computer and calculated time zone differences. It would be nearly noon in

D.C. That was good—she knew her father would be at his desk, and his Secret Service phone was secure. She punched in his number, and in a moment, his voice was on the line—the voice that had always pushed her, nudged her, yelled at her, cheered her and, ultimately, comforted her.

"Hi, Dad," she said. "Is your office door closed?"

There was a pause; then Ray Tolman said, "It is. What's up?"

"Two things, Dad. Number one, I hope you've been feeding the cat. Number two, I need your help."

# CHAPTER

# 46

Ray Tolman trusted his daughter.

Meg had turned out surprisingly well, he often thought, despite his wife's long illness, her bizarre death, and his own long absences when he was building a career with the Service.

When Meg was very small, they'd moved every year from one posting to another: from Philadelphia to Portland, Maine to Boston to St. Paul to San Francisco, back to Philadelphia, then on to Washington when he'd been assigned his first protective detail. It had been a hard way for a young girl to live, and being away as much as he was, Ray Tolman did not realize the extent of his wife's bipolar disorder until it was too late.

He'd hospitalized her three times, and each time she came out with new medication, a good therapist, and a commitment to stay on the meds so she could control the disease instead of the other way around. But Janet could never seem to stay on the meds, and when she went off, she would swing from violent, screeching rages to periods where she wouldn't get out of bed for a week at a time.

So Meg was left alone with her mother much of the time. But Ray Tolman always paid for the piano lessons. He'd seen her talent, knew it was something remarkable, but also knew she could never make a living at it. So he'd gently—at least he thought it was gently, but Meg seemed to think he'd hammered her over the head with it—steered her toward law enforcement. She had the analytical mind and the computer savvy that the new generation of cops needed. RIO was a disappointment—he'd actually hoped she might join the Service—but she seemed happy.

And he trusted her. How could he not?

He hung up the phone. His heart didn't pound; he didn't break into a sweat. Ray Tolman had been around far too long and experienced far too much to let anything faze him. He'd protected three presidents personally, and now worked in threat assessment, driving a desk.

Threats against the president of the United States were made on a daily basis, sometimes dozens in a single day. Ninety-five percent of them were nothing at all, pure fantasy. Another 4-plus percent were actually followed up with some investigation, and eventually determined not to be credible. Less than 1 percent were actually serious and became the subject of an ongoing investigation.

Ray Tolman thought he'd just glimpsed a bit of that 1 percent, and it had come from his own daughter. She hadn't elaborated. She hadn't talked about her evidence.

*"Are you okay?"* he had asked her. *"Are you safe? At least tell me that."*

*"For the moment,"* Meg had said, and the words chilled him.

Meg Tolman did not overreact, did not see things that weren't there. Sometimes she could draw conclusions from a small amount of data, and her father knew she had proved to have an uncanny knack for drawing the *right* conclusions.

He did not doubt her. He listened and made notes.

*"Dad, don't trust anyone. It could be someone you think you know well, someone you've served with. But they're going after the president, and they'll have someone inside who can get close to him."*

He asked her only one question: *"In your best judgment, Meg—as a professional now, not as Ray Tolman's daughter—is this a credible threat against the president?"*

*"Absolutely. Dad, there are only two people I trust on this, you and Rusty Hudson, and I can't reach him."*

*"Then I'll get to work on it,"* Ray Tolman told his daughter. *"Take care. Be safe. Keep your eyes open."*

There was no *I love you* at the end of the phone call. They didn't do that. It seemed trite, given the places they had both been. She just gave him the phone number where she was and hung up. The real expression of Ray Tolman's love for his daughter came when he logged on to his computer and pulled up the complete list of personnel on President Harwell's protective detail.

One by one, he started to read the confidential file on every single one of them. Tolman settled in. He turned his little desk radio to an oldies station, keeping the volume low. This was going to take some time.


The Judge was sweeping his floor, of all things, when Washington Four called. The Judge had sought to cleanse his mind of both Dallas Four's failure and his overreaction to it, the fact that a history professor and a government researcher had eluded the Glory Warriors, and that Grant and Lee's signatures—the final piece that would ensure their legitimacy at the head of the government—were still missing.

The Judge ran his hand across the round gold pin and answered the phone in his study.

"We know where they are," Washington Four said.

"Yes?"

"Rural Arkansas, a remote area. The phone number is in the name of a man named Darrell Sharp."

"Arkansas, you say? Then Memphis will be the closest base. I'll have Memphis One take them. Send the location to Memphis Base. We'll get them today. Good work."

The Judge hung up the phone. He was satisfied that the Glory Warriors were back on track to catch Journey and Tolman and get the signatures, and Washington Three was moving into position to do the ultimate job. He opened his desk drawer and read through the first two pages of the document again. Just reading them left him a little breathless. Then he reached farther into the drawer and took out a clear plastic bag that contained more paper. The pages were thick, some smudged, creased by age and handling.

He read the old words again, a different handwriting than that of the pages from Oklahoma and Kentucky. Some of the words were disturbing to him, as they had been to earlier generations, but he possessed a deeper understanding of their meaning. He understood even more than his father had, or his grandfather, perhaps more even than the original Glory Warriors. The fact that he'd sent Washington Three on the final mission proved it. He understood more than any of them.

Washington One rarely drove. In his "official" life, he had a driver at his disposal, but he dared not use the driver when he was on Glory Warriors business. So he drove his Town Car himself, along Columbia Pike in Silver Spring, Maryland. He exited the highway at Industrial Parkway, turned on Tech Road, and drove through the Montgomery Industrial Park to the spot where the road dead-ended.

The low complex of buildings at the end of the road stood behind razor wire fencing. A single, simple sign of black letters on white wood announced MILLER EXPLORATION. It was another of the Glory Warriors' front companies, part of the carefully screened corporate maze.

He passed through three security checkpoints—it was a testament to the operation that even he was required to pass scrutiny—and drove to the main headquarters building. He conferred with the base commander, and together they walked to the converted factories and warehouses where the troops were preparing for the operation to begin.

They were readying their equipment: M4 carbines for the assault, XM107 long-range rifles for the snipers, the H&K MK 23 assault pistols for closer work. Some of the Glory Warriors were simply ready for action—many had waited a long time. Others craved power. Others were bitter, angry that the corruption of the U.S. government had forced the action they were about to take. Some were motivated by history, by Lee and Grant's vision. All were committed.

Washington One and the base commander walked past the last building to the helipads. The concrete clearing was ringed by trees and shielded from the highway and other commercial developments in the area. Half a dozen CH 53-E Sea Stallion choppers with no insignia sat parked on the pads. They were the same type the marines used for troop transportation and assault support.

"How long?" Washington One asked the commander.

"Loaded and in the air within two minutes of your signal, sir."

"Shave that to ninety seconds. Once Harwell is dead, we have to use the immediate advantage of the chaos. The old government can't have the chance to react."

"Yes, sir."

Ten minutes later, Washington One was back on Columbia Pike. He still needed to inspect the other staging areas and call all the regional commanders from Boston to San Diego, Miami to Seattle, then check in with the second wave of the Washington invasion, mobilizing in the Blue Ridge.

*The nation belongs to us,* he thought, *as soon as the president is dead.*

# CHAPTER
# 47

Sharp came and went, rarely speaking but making a great deal of noise. Tolman watched him, watched his haunted eyes as they checked out all corners of a room whenever he walked into it.

When he painted, she watched in silence as he worked with his miniature brushes. When she emerged into the living room after a few minutes, she found Journey standing, pacing in front of the computer. "Tell me," she said.

"Charles L. Webster was married to Twain's sister's daughter," Journey said. "When Twain decided he was going to publish Grant's memoirs, he put Webster in charge of the publishing house. In fact, it was even called Charles L. Webster and Company. Everyone knew who was behind it, but Webster was the front man. Some sources even think it was he and not his uncle who convinced Grant to write the book."

"Is that true?"

Journey shrugged. "Hard to tell. Twain had been friends with Grant for years. It makes sense that he would have had the pull to convince Grant. But Webster ran the publishing company. They published *Huckleberry Finn*, but nothing else was near as successful as Grant's memoir. Then Webster's health started to fail. He'd always had some health problems, but Twain essentially fired him in

1888 when it was apparent that he couldn't keep up with the company any longer. Webster died in 1891. He wasn't even forty."

"So what happened to the papers from the publishing company?"

"It folded a few years later. It wasn't sold to anyone else, it didn't consolidate, it just died. There's no Webster family archive, there's no listing of his letters or papers. I suppose the papers could have gone back to Twain, but if that had happened, surely he would have said so in the Leon letter."

"What about Webster's family?"

Journey tapped his finger three times on the desk. "I confirmed one of his descendants, a J. T. Webster, who lives in Vermont. He would be Charles Webster's great-great-great-grandson."

Tolman rolled her eyes. "Which would make him—let's see, now—Mark Twain's great-great-great-great-nephew."

Journey smiled. "Or something. I was getting ready to call him."

"By all means."

Journey picked up Sharp's heavy phone and called the number he'd found on a genealogy Web site. In a moment, a male voice answered.

"Hello, is this Mr. Webster? J. T. Webster?"

"That's Dr. Webster, and this is he."

Journey nodded. "M.D. or Ph.D.?"

"Ph.D. Who's calling, please?"

"Dr. Webster, this is Dr. Nick Journey. I'm a professor of history at South Central College of Oklahoma."

"What's your research area?"

"The American Civil War. Specifically, the lives of generals from both sides, after the war was over."

"Good enough," Webster said. "I'm a Renaissance man. That's a joke, by the way. I study Tudor and Stuart England, particularly concerning how the different monarchs supported the arts during their reign."

"You're a historian?"

"Ph.D., Yale. Where did you study?"

"University of Virginia."

"UVA. Good for a state school. What does an American Civil War historian need with a Tudor and Stuart scholar?"

"Well, sir," Journey said, "I'm actually not calling about either one of those, directly. I wanted to ask you about your family background."

Webster sighed. "Yes, Sam Clemens was my uncle, many generations back. That's why you called?"

"Yes and no. I'm more interested in Charles Webster, who was in the publishing business with Clemens."

"A great failure," Webster said. "They never duplicated the success they had in publishing the memoirs of Ulysses S. Grant."

"That's why I'm calling. About the Grant papers, I mean. Do you have any of Charles Webster's old papers? Did he leave anything relating to the Grant memoir? I'm working on a major project that is somewhat time-sensitive."

"Young man, every project is time-sensitive." Webster laughed. "I have a few scattered scraps of paper, some things detailing how many books the company sold in a certain quarter, a few notes Charles apparently wrote to himself, that sort of thing. A couple of them are just nonsense. They don't mean anything other than the fact that they belonged to Mark Twain's nephew."

Journey waited a moment. "Dr. Webster, I'm going to ask a huge favor of you. Are those materials scanned? Are they in a computer?"

Webster laughed. "Scanned? Who'd want to scan these things? There's nothing of value here."

Journey drummed his fingers. His eyes fell on Sharp's fax machine next to the computer. "Could you fax copies of them to me? There may be something in them that would help my project."

"I'm telling you, one historian to another, that there's nothing relevant there, just bits and pieces."

"I know, but it might help me to make an important connection." Journey was struggling to keep his voice even, not to sound desperate. Tolman's cell phone rang.

"Bad cell service out here," Sharp said. "Better go outside."

Tolman held up a finger to Journey, then walked out the front door.

"I suppose," Webster was saying. "There are maybe ten pages in all. Give me the fax number."

Journey read the number from the fax machine. I'm not sure how long I'll be at this number, but this should get them to me."

"It'll take me a little while to get them together. I'm retired, but I do have more to do than just play with the Webster family papers."

Journey thanked the man, hung up, and walked outside. A slight rise rolled ahead of the house as the clearing narrowed into the rutted path that led back toward the highway. "It doesn't sound promising, but he's sending what he has."

He stopped short, seeing Tolman's face. She was riveted in place next to Sharp's Jeep, the phone pressed to her ear.

Tolman had seen the caller ID, the phone number preceded by a 703 area code—Virginia, her own home area code. Walking outside, she answered it and heard Kerry Voss's voice. "Meg, I had to call you. I wasn't sure what to do. I left the office sick. But I got your cell number and—"

"Kerry? Kerry, slow down. What's wrong?"

"You asked me to see if those two names you gave me had been receiving military benefits. One of them, Standridge, was a dead end. Basic benefits, nothing out of the ordinary. The other one, Kevin Lane . . ."

Tolman listened without interrupting as Voss told her about the large sums of money paid to Kevin Lane's widow, and the series of pass-through bank accounts. Tolman's stomach started a quiet burn when Voss said *GW One*.

"Meg," Voss said, "I just had to get out of there and think about this, about what to do, who I could trust."

"What, Kerry?"

"The bank account for this GW One. I checked every way I could think of to be sure what I was seeing. There are two names on the account, Meg. The first one is Jackson McMartin. The second one is Russell H. Hudson."

# CHAPTER
# 48

It's a mistake," Tolman said.

"It's not a mistake," Voss said.

"It's a common enough name—"

"Don't you think I thought of that? We traced the computer that originated the first of the money transfers. It was part of the Wi-Fi network at the coffee shop on the corner, Around the Ground. You know the one I'm talking about?"

Tolman squeezed her eyes closed. Hudson bought coffee there almost every morning, and she and other people in the office had lunch with him there from time to time. "I know it," she said.

"And the bank branch is in Silver Spring," Voss said. "I checked the employee directory. Hudson's home address is four blocks from the bank."

Tolman looked up. Journey had come out of the house, Sharp towering in the doorway behind him, a silent sentinel.

"What is this all about?" Voss said. "Meg, tell me what this is about. What's Hudson doing?"

Tolman's mind was trying to shut down. One of the few friends she had . . . Hudson, always allowing her time off to do piano gigs and then asking how they went . . . Hudson, following his losing baseball team . . . Hudson, her confidant . . .

Hudson. Glory Warrior.

She made writing motions with her free hand and gestured at Journey. He disappeared into the house and came out with a pen and paper.

"Kerry," Tolman said. "I can't—"

*I can't believe it. I won't believe it.*

"What's he doing?" Voss said. "Where *are* you, Meg?"

Tolman shook her head. Journey was staring at her with a questioning look on his face.

"I can't—" she said, and the sentence died again.

She thought of the last time she'd talked to Hudson.

*"Talk to no one but me, Meg. . . . Don't trust anyone you don't know well."*

*But I know you well, Rusty,* she thought. *I've known you for five years. You hired me. You brought me into RIO. You listen to me when I need to talk.*

*"You are very, very good at your job, Meg."*

The Glory Warriors would need a person like Rusty Hudson. He was an accountant. He had a law degree. He was low profile, but understood the workings of government like no one Tolman had ever seen. He knew money and budgets and infrastructure. He knew personnel and logistics and details. He was the consummate bureaucrat. He knew everyone, and how to do everything, yet no one knew his name. Through RIO, he had access to incredible amounts of information from several different tentacles of the federal government. He was perfect for the Glory Warriors.

"Meg?" Voss said.

"I'm here." Tolman's voice was very quiet.

"Why?"

"I can't explain it. Not yet. Don't go to the office. Don't go back to work. Call in sick until you hear from me again."

Hudson refused to call in backup until she presented him with written evidence. It hadn't seemed right at the time, though she'd cursed him for being such a bureaucrat, back in Louisville. But now it made sense. The "evidence" he'd wanted was the rest of the Fort Washita document.

Tolman kicked gravel. Dust rose around her like a shroud.

She'd just left him a message. A message with Sharp's number to call back. A number that could be traced to a name and an address.

"Sweet Jesus," she said. "Kerry, what's that other name? The other one on the account."

"Jackson McMartin."

"I know that name," she said. "Why do I know that name?" She repeated it aloud and pointed at Journey—*write that down*. She watched as he wrote the name. "Kerry, I have to go. Stay away from the office."

She hung up, still dazed. Sharp had come into the clearing and stood between the two cars. "Darrell, I'm sorry," she said.

Sharp looked down at her.

"We have to get out of here. This place isn't safe. The Glory Warriors know we're here."

"What?" Journey said. "How—?"

"My boss," Tolman said, and the bitterness crept into her voice. "My fucking boss who lets me take time off work to play piano whenever I want. He's one of them. He's a fucking Glory Warrior."

"How did you—?"

"I was tracking the guys who attacked you at the college. Turns out they were Army Rangers who were supposedly killed in action in Iraq in 2006." She leaned against the Jeep, closing her eyes. "And that explains why Rusty was so hesitant for me to dig around DOD looking for them. Son of a *bitch*! Who knows how long he's been one of them, managing their money, quietly taking care of all the little details so they could do this. God *damn* him!"

She hadn't even realized she was crying until the tears were coursing down her face. She balled both fists and struck the side of the Jeep, her hands hitting hot metal over and over again. Sharp looked alarmed, but didn't move.

Tolman hit the car again. "Goddamn son of a bitch bastard," she muttered through the tears. She struck the car, this time with an open palm. The tears gradually slowed, then stopped, and she said, "I never fucking cry. Never."

"No, you curse," Journey said.

Tolman laughed and wiped her face with the back of her arm. "No shit." The smile faded. "I'm sorry, Darrell. We need to get our things and get out of here. They'll be coming. You can go with us and we can take you—"

"No," Sharp said.

"Darrell, I know you don't like leaving your place, but these are dangerous people."

"So am I," Sharp said.

They tried for the better part of an hour to persuade Sharp to leave, but he insisted he would be ready for whatever came over the horizon. He gave them the keys to his second vehicle, a ten-year-old Dodge Dakota truck—the same kind Rusty Hudson drove, Tolman thought. He also gave each of them a clean, prepaid cell phone and a SIG Sauer 9-millimeter pistol.

"I try to stay ready for anything," he said with a shrug, then looked at Journey. "You know how to shoot?"

"No," Journey said.

"Better learn fast," Sharp said, then looked at Tolman. "I remember how you like the SIG. You were always a pretty good shot."

"I can still hold my own," Tolman said.

"Just get the truck back to me when you can," he said.

"I will," Tolman said. "I bought that car in Kentucky. I guess you can drive it free."

Sharp almost smiled, his mustache moving around a bit. "Where will you go?"

Tolman and Journey looked at each other. "I don't know yet," Tolman said.

Sharp nodded. "I wish you'd played the piano some more."

"So do I."

They parted without touching. Journey thought about a handshake, but settled for a small wave. Sharp nodded in his direction. Tolman got behind the wheel of the Dakota and pulled it from its parking spot behind the house, pointing it toward the road. As they topped the little rise, Journey looked back once. Darrell Sharp was standing in front of his house, still watching them.

Tolman stopped the car at Highway 28, idling as a pickup truck drove past. "Where *do* we go?" Journey asked.

"I'm not sure," Tolman said. "Maybe back toward Little Rock for now. We can regroup in a city. I tell you, I'd rather walk through the worst parts of D.C. at night, unarmed, than spend too much time out here in the woods." She turned left.

They rode in silence for an hour. Radio reception and cell phone signals were spotty in the hills. Journey, in the passenger seat, stared out at the green that surrounded them, his mind playing over all that had happened: a backhoe breaking ground for a new museum at Fort Washita, and the swiftness of all that had come since. The Glory Warriors were well organized, and they had people within the government already working for their cause. Journey glanced at Tolman—the heavy betrayal sat on her face as if painted on, even as she drove the winding road.

Journey turned the thoughts over and over. As soon as the guns and the document had been found at Fort Washita, and plastered all over the media, the Glory Warriors had swung into action, as if . . .

As if they'd been waiting.

But if the pages had really been lost since 1865, why did the Glory Warriors even exist in the modern era?

"You were right," he said aloud.

Tolman jumped, as if she'd forgotten he was there. The truck veered a little into the left-hand lane. It didn't matter—only one car had passed them since they left Gravelly. "What?" she said.

History was about the small details that add up to major events, Journey thought. He preached that to his students constantly: *Look beyond "shots heard 'round the world" and find the shots that were barely heard at all. That's where history really begins, with small things like a casual comment, or one throwaway sentence in the midst of thousands of pages, or the way a person's face looks when something unexpected is suddenly placed in front of them. . . .*

"You were right," he said again. "Those pages—the pages Grant wrote about the Glory Warriors and then asked Mark Twain to leave out of his book. They did wind up in someone's hands."

Then he had it, the thoughts that had fled when he woke up on Darrell Sharp's sofa a few hours ago. He remembered words on a page, a page that didn't seem near as important as others he'd seen recently. And he saw it, unfolding in front of him, just as the Fourche Mountains rose outside the window of the truck.

Tolman alternated her glance between Journey and the road. She raised her hands from the wheel for a moment, asking him the question without words.

"I know where the missing pages from Grant's book are," Journey said. "And here's another thing—Samuel Williams was brilliant, absolutely brilliant. I know where to find the signature page, too."

# CHAPTER
# 49

Ray Tolman took off his glasses and rubbed his eyes. He still couldn't get used to the glow of the computer monitor, and he'd been driving a desk for quite a while now. His eyes felt strained, he had headaches, he had neckaches . . . Hell, his whole body hurt sometimes.

*Can't blame that on a computer,* he mused. *I'm just getting old, dammit.*

Still, he knew that most investigations were conducted like this now, sitting in front of a computer, using mouse and keyboard. His daughter had made a career of finding people and constructing scenarios based on these things.

Ray Tolman smiled, but it faded quickly.

His daughter had told him a group called the Glory Warriors was going to try to assassinate the president, that they were behind the deaths of Jefferson Vandermeer and Nan Darlington and were trying to decapitate the federal government. They were extremists with a military bent.

But it wasn't that simple. They weren't *all* military. They had people submerged in civilian positions as well. They compromised

Justice Darlington's security detail, and had most likely infiltrated the president's as well.

Ray Tolman didn't want to believe it. He had devoted his life to the Secret Service, had served on protective details for three presidents. He'd never seen a traitor in the Service.

But Meg wasn't prone to fantasy. He looked at the screen again, then minimized it and plucked a piece of paper from his desk: the president's itinerary for tomorrow.

He tried to think like an assassin. These Glory Warriors were extreme. Their goal was destabilization. Chaos. Panic. Fear.

Ray Tolman was quiet, listening to the hum of his computer. They would make a public statement. That was what terrorists did, and make no mistake, these were terrorists, American or not. He picked up the itinerary again: Harwell had no public events the rest of today.

There was a National Security Council briefing in the West Wing first thing tomorrow morning, then a Rose Garden ceremony honoring a group of high school kids from Idaho who had collected pennies for five years and raised over a hundred thousand dollars for cancer research, in memory of a classmate who had died of leukemia.

*No.* Not public enough, and the attempt wouldn't take place on the White House grounds. Too difficult, even for someone inside. The logistics would be staggering.

At noon was a thousand-dollar-a-plate fund-raiser for the party's Congressional campaign committee at a downtown D.C. hotel.

*Possible.* He circled the event.

Early afternoon, no scheduled events. Presumably Harwell would be back in the White House.

At three o'clock was a short speech at a new community center in the Anacostia neighborhood of southeast Washington, a project funded partially through a public–private partnership with HUD that the Harwell Administration had enacted in the president's first term.

*Definite possibility.* Even with the area slowly improving, there were still vacant buildings around, lots of areas the advance team would already be working on.

He circled the event twice. No other public events were on the schedule. The president and First Lady were leaving tomorrow evening for a weekend at their home in the Berkshires. If time was critical to this group, and if they wanted chaos and panic, they would go after the president before he left Washington.

That meant tomorrow.

Tolman went back to the members of the security detail. If these Glory Warriors had buried an agent deep in the Service, it would need to be someone who'd been on the detail for a while, building a cover, gaining the trust of both the Service and the president himself.

*Scratch anyone who joined the detail after the president's second term began.*

Normal procedure would be to convene a threat assessment to evaluate the credibility of the information. He had no trouble believing the information, but he wasn't accustomed to operating alone. In the Service, as in most of government, everything was done in teams. People used partners for ideas, to formulate theories, to keep each other in check.

But if there was an unknown traitor somewhere within the detail itself . . .

Ray Tolman ground his teeth, going back to the list, looking at the names of the people who'd been with Harwell since the first term. The list was still too long.

He sat back, thinking. *If I were going to take out the president, Anacostia would be the place to do it. All those vacant houses . . . I would have to check out the place beforehand, find a place to shoot . . . define the access points. If I were a Service insider, I would have to decide what I needed to do to get around my fellow agents. . . .*

So the assassin would want to be on the property before the event. He could volunteer for both today's advance team and tomorrow's detail, and no one would think anything of it.

Ray Tolman checked the duty lists and compared who was on today's advance team with who was on protective duty for the Anacostia speech. There were five names: Anthony Alley, Jay Clare, Ron DeBacker, Timothy Delham, Miranda O'Daniel. He knew all five of them, though only one of them well. Alley was the veteran of the bunch—he and Ray Tolman had served together on the Clinton detail.

*"It could be someone you know well, someone you've served with,"* Meg had said.

O'Daniel was one of only four women on the entire presidential detail. She'd started out in the investigative side of the Service and had later moved into protection. He knew little about her, other than she seemed intelligent and quiet.

Clare, DeBacker, Delham. Names, just names, with faces he saw on occasion.

He couldn't get his mind around it, sitting here at this desk. He needed to see the place. He needed to see the *people.*

One good thing about being a deputy assistant director—Ray Tolman could pretty much pop in on any operation unannounced. He put on his suit jacket, straightened his tie, and grabbed his keys.

When Ray Tolman came home to the District after his second stint in Philadelphia, he'd been told that you simply didn't go into the Anacostia area. Things had changed, and the historic African-American community had gone from stately homes and abundant, if small, minority-owned businesses to drug dealers and random violence that occasionally spilled over and grabbed national headlines. One recent weekend had seen seven homicides in two days.

But President Harwell, as part of the Urban Initiative he pushed through Congress early in his first term, had been promoting partnerships between HUD and the private sector to bring real businesses back to such areas, to foster a sense of community, to reclaim the high ground. It had met with mixed success nationwide, as it had in Anacostia.

Tomorrow's event was in the 1300 block of Valley Place, and the area was downright surreal. One side of the street boasted the new Anacostia Community Center, with its brick and glass, its community kitchen, computer lab, sports complex, meeting rooms, and playground. On the other side were houses, mostly three-story colonials. Many of the ones that were occupied had window-unit air conditioners and sagging porches, though the occasional house had new paint and windows, standing out like roses among weeds. Several were vacant, with plywood nailed over the windows and three-foot-tall grass choking the yards.

Ray Tolman showed his ID to the uniformed officer at the end of the block, parked his Crown Vic, and walked past the barrier. Service agents were talking with residents. Tech teams and dogs were scouring the abandoned houses. Service people and Metro Police were all over the new community center.

Ray Tolman saw John Canton, leader of the advance team, and walked over to him. Canton was a twenty-five-year veteran. Tolman had worked with him for a long time. They'd been to each other's homes. His son and Meg were almost the same age. Canton and his wife, Renee, had come to Janet's funeral.

*"It could be someone you know well."*

"Hey, Ray," Canton said. He was a big man and always looked out of place in a suit, even though he'd been wearing one for all these years.

"Hello, John."

"What brings you down here?"

"Had to get out of the office, see how this is going." He nodded at the community center. "Impressive."

"So I hear," Canton said.

"I'm just going to wander a bit and see what the guys are doing, if you don't mind, John."

"Not at all. Always glad to see a deputy assistant director."

They smiled at each other. A field agent who's been moved inside always seemed a bit out of place, and those still in the field were never sure how to take them. Ray Tolman moved off.

He walked past the makeshift stage that had been erected for the president's speech tomorrow. The presidential seal was already affixed to it. A technician was running cables into the community center. Tolman walked the block, then started back on the other side, where the houses were.

He spotted O'Daniel—she was hard to miss—and then Alley, who waved to him from the porch of a house. He saw DeBacker a few doors down. *Do any of you want to kill the president and suspend the Constitution?*

He stopped at a vacant house, across the street and one door down from the stage. The brickwork of the colonial was crumbling, especially on the second floor. Metal grates covered the two downstairs windows. Of the three windows that marched across the second floor, the two outer ones were covered with plywood. The bottom half of the center one was covered, but it was open on the top. The only third-story window was open. A white sign nailed to the front porch read FOR SALE BY OWNER.

*Good luck*, Ray Tolman thought, and made his way past the sagging fence. He walked a couple more steps and looked up. He couldn't stop looking at the partially uncovered second-story window. A rifle could rest on top of the plywood and have a clear shot across the street.

He heard scratching noises, and a man stepped out onto the porch. Timothy Delham was an agent in his late thirties, a sharp dresser, a bit of a smart-ass, but then, many of the younger guys were.

"Director Tolman," Delham said. "Checking up on us?"

Ray Tolman smiled. "Don't call me director. I'd be getting paid a lot more if I was director."

"True. But you don't *really* want me to call you Deputy Assistant Director Tolman, do you?"

"Good point. Just Ray will do." He nodded upward. "What do you think?"

"This house makes me nervous," Delham said.

"The uncovered windows upstairs."

"Right. And there's a fence in the back that's in such bad shape that anyone could get over it pretty quickly. We'll have uniforms in here tomorrow."

"Good call. It's at a solid angle for a shot."

"That's what I thought."

Delham moved away to check in with Canton, and in another few seconds, the other one of the five agents, Jay Clare, stepped from the house. He was a big, burly guy with reddish hair, getting a little gray, who, like Canton, looked ill at ease in a suit. Clare was in his forties, and never said much.

"Hello, Jay."

"Afternoon. Tim and I were just finishing up in here."

"Don't mind me, I'm just getting some fresh air." Tolman walked into the house as Clare moved away. The wood floors, which he imagined had once been quite stately, were pitted and splintering apart. The walls were down to exposed Sheetrock in places. Tolman took the stairs up to the second landing, where the floors were in even worse condition, and he crouched by the half-covered window, his knees complaining.

He looked down onto the street and across it. From where he was, he could actually see all five of the agents he'd identified as possibles.

*Who are you? Which one?*

After nearly ten minutes, he slowly descended the stairs, holding the rail, which wobbled at every step. Outside he waved to Canton and to Tony Alley, and started toward his car. His stomach was in knots—he wondered if his ulcer was trying to come back.

He had to go back to the office. As the Crown Vic headed away from Valley Place, he wondered which of the people he'd just seen might betray the Service and try to kill the president of the United States.

And if he could stop them.

# CHAPTER
# 50

Darrell Sharp liked living in Yell County because he felt safe. The ancient, rounded hills and the deep forest on all sides sheltered him. No one came looking for him, no one talked to him, and it was always quiet. No one wanted to hurt him here, and he didn't want to hurt anyone else.

Until today.

Sharp also liked living at the end of his own private road because he could see if someone was coming, long before they reached him. This was especially true if that someone was driving a shiny new silver SUV and turning off the highway straight toward his house.

As soon as he saw the cloud of dust on the path, Sharp took his FN Special Police Rifle, the same one FBI snipers now used, and went out the back door. He climbed the ladder that leaned against the rear of the house, walked across his flat roof, and lay prone behind a little lip that curled upward from the top of the house.

He adjusted the telescopic sight, moved his arms around, angled his body. He kept the SUV in sight all the way. The windows were tinted, so he couldn't see how many people were in it, but it didn't really matter. They had penetrated his sheltering hills and trees, and now he would do what he had to do.

The SUV slowed as it pulled into the clearing. It stopped beside his Cherokee, pulling in behind the Toyota that Tolman had driven from Kentucky. The driver's door opened. Sharp adjusted his position a fraction of an inch. A man's head appeared. He had short dark blond hair.

Everything was quiet. Sharp felt nothing but his breathing, his heartbeat. His finger nudged onto the trigger.

The man's head moved out from behind the car door. Sharp took two breaths, letting the second out halfway. He relaxed and slowly squeezed the trigger. The man's head dissolved in a spray of red and gray. He toppled back against the car door and reeled to one side, dropping into the dirt.

Sharp heard voices from the SUV, the sound of the doors clicking, the passenger door opening, but no head appeared. The passenger would be keeping his head down, as he didn't want what happened to his partner to happen to him.

A hand holding a pistol appeared behind the passenger door, in the space where the doorframe separated from the car itself. Sharp calculated distances from hand to head and swung the rifle a little to the left.

The pistol spit in his general direction, but the shot went at least ten feet wide of his position, which told Sharp they hadn't actually seen him yet. The hand holding the pistol wavered. Sharp pulled the trigger. The glass of the passenger door exploded. Some of the shards turned red. The pistol fell, and the hand holding it disappeared.

Sharp listened. With both doors open, he could hear inside the SUV. Another person was in there. He could hear the movements, uncertain, trapped.

Sharp kept staring through the rifle sight, and the other person in the SUV stayed put. That was all right. He was patient.

They stared at each other for five minutes, then another door, the one behind the driver, opened. A pistol came flying out and landed on the ground. Sharp waited.

Two more minutes passed.

More movement from inside the SUV. Sharp steadied the rifle, making minute adjustments, calculating where the third person would emerge. Another gun, this time a rifle, flew out the open door.

"That's it!" said a man's voice from inside the car. "That's all there is! Those are all the weapons we brought!"

Sharp waited.

"I'm coming out!" the man shouted after another minute. "You'll see my hands first. Don't shoot!"

He slid out of the SUV. He was a tall man and younger than Sharp, probably only mid-twenties. He was muscular and would probably be good in hand-to-hand fighting. He edged out, his hands away from his body. He stepped around the body of the driver and into the spot between the SUV and the Toyota.

"I'm unarmed, I swear," the man said. He shuffled a few more feet into the open until he was between the cars and the front door.

"Stop," Sharp said, not raising his voice. The man was almost directly below him.

The young man stopped moving and looked up.

"Turn right," Sharp said. "Around the house. Slow."

He walked around the side of the house. Sharp wasn't worried about him running away. There was nowhere for him to go except deeper into the hills, and Sharp knew he could find anyone in these hills. The FN rifle would drop him in a few steps, no matter which direction he went.

Sharp stood up, walked across the roof, and climbed down the ladder. The man was standing ten feet away from him. He wore fatigue pants and a black shirt with a gold pin clipped to it.

"Inside," Sharp said.

The man walked ahead of him through the open back door, down the hallway, and into the front room. Sharp looked toward his desk. The fax machine was humming, paper sliding out of it.

"Down."

The man lay on the floor. Sharp took the steel cable he kept in his gun cabinet and bound the man hand and foot.

"What are you going to do?" the man asked, out of breath.

Sharp said nothing. He leaned the rifle against the desk and went to the fax machine to see if it was an order for china. He thumbed through the pages until he found what looked like a cover page. Ornate printing read *J. T. Webster, Ph.D.*, with an address in

Burlington, Vermont. The fax was addressed to *Nick Journey, Ph.D.*
Sharp sighed.

The rest of the pages didn't make much sense. There was one that
looked like a receipt for books sold, but it was all in old-fashioned
handwriting. One page looked like a note about a dinner party, with
a reminder that it started at eight o'clock.

A few more pages rolled out of the fax, and Sharp looked at
the man on the floor. "What are you going to do?" the man asked
again.

"Call the sheriff, I guess, and report trespassers."

The man looked at him as if he couldn't believe what he'd heard.

"You ought to leave people alone," Sharp said.

He gathered up the rest of the fax pages. More gibberish, but if
Journey had asked for them, maybe they were important. Sometimes the most important connections in an investigation were the
most obscure.

He glanced at the man on the floor. The sheriff could wait a few
more minutes. What Sharp had told Journey this morning was
true—it was hard to know how you felt after killing someone. Right
now Sharp didn't feel anything.

He put his hand on the phone.


"We have to get back to Oklahoma," Journey said.

"Explain it to me," Tolman said.

"It was too easy," Journey said. "How could the Glory Warriors
have all these people in place, just waiting around, if they didn't already know about the document?"

"Okay, so they knew about it, but they didn't have it."

Journey nodded. "It's a real stretch to think this secret society
devoted to an overthrow of the federal government could go on and
on, recruiting new people, moving money around, building its organization, if it didn't have *something* to go on. There's something to be
said for oral tradition, and I'm sure there's some level of father-to-
son heritage, but I still think they would need to have something
tangible to continue to exist, something they could show to new re-
cruits as part of their sales pitch."

Tolman glanced at him and she saw it in his eyes. "They have the missing pages from Grant's book. They've had them all along."

"I think so. You were right when you said they could have gotten into someone's hands. I don't know *how* they got them, but think about the letter Mark Twain wrote in 1910 to this Leon. The letter wasn't sent. We know it came to Berkeley in 1962. But that's not to say that *someone* didn't read it at some point."

"And someone who read it may have talked to someone else, and somewhere along that chain, the message resonated with a person who read it. How hard would it have been to get the pages from the Webster family? Charles Webster himself died just a few years after the book came out. It was public knowledge that Twain had published the book, and now twenty-five years after the book came out, here's Twain saying that there were these 'lost' pages."

"People would have jumped on that then, the same way they would today," Journey said. "Human nature doesn't change that much over the centuries, does it?"

Tolman nodded into the windshield. "So the pages become their bible, and the treaty between Grant and Lee their holy grail. They dedicate themselves to finding it and being prepared to put their special clause into effect. They tell themselves that when they find the treaty, that makes their power grab legal and that it's just what Lee and Grant intended when Lee surrendered."

Journey spread his hands apart. "So we don't have to find the pages. I think we already know where they are."

Soft pain crossed Tolman's face, but only for a moment. "The other name on the bank account with Rusty. Jackson McMartin."

"He's the leader of the Glory Warriors. He has to be. We have to find him, and we have to get him to come to Oklahoma, to Fort Washita."

"*What?*"

"That's where we can end this. That's where it ended in 1865, and that's where we can end it now."

"You are out of your mind. What makes you think the leader of the Glory Warriors will meet you at Fort Washita?" Tolman said.

"Because he thinks—they *all* think—that I have the signature page. Just like before, I have what they want."

Tolman reached over and flicked on the air conditioner, angling the vent so it hit her in the face. "And you know where the page is."

"I do now."

Tolman drove in silence for another five miles, the hills opening as they approached Little Rock. "Jackson McMartin," she finally said.

"Think it's the same one?"

"Has to be. Reclusive media tycoon, owns at least part of practically everything in the country, stays out of the spotlight. Makes sense, doesn't it?"

Journey nodded. "Heritage News Channel. They even interviewed me the day the guns and the papers were found at Fort Washita. But I doubt we can call up HNC and leave him a voice mail."

"We don't have to find a way to get in touch with McMartin," Tolman said. "Leave that to me."

"Of course. Hudson."

"Yeah." Tolman tapped the steering wheel.

"I'm sorry."

"So am I. Let's say we get them to Oklahoma. Let's say we make them believe the only way they're going to get the signatures is if they meet us face-to-face. They're not just going to let me come along and arrest them."

"No. They've tried to kill me and missed twice and they won't want to miss a third time. They'll have people there. We'll have to be ready for them."

"Don't know how to handle a gun, huh?" Tolman asked.

"Never fired a gun in my life. With any luck, I won't have to now, either."

Tolman shot him a questioning look.

"There is someone I trust," Journey said. "Believe it or not. But first . . . first I want to see my son."

They drove, coming into the outskirts of Little Rock. In a few miles, they merged onto I-40 and turned back to the west. The afternoon rush, such as it was in Little Rock, was just beginning. Tolman pulled into a truck stop—she thought she'd seen more truck stops in the last twenty-four hours than in her entire life—and opened her laptop. She did a quick search for Jackson McMartin.

She didn't even have to use RACER. A simple Google search told her that he came from a family that had made billions in California real estate, he'd gone to college at Stanford and law school at Yale, was a decorated army officer in Vietnam, then worked for the JAG Corps at the Pentagon, where he made one-star general. He served three terms in Congress, was a deputy secretary of defense, then began buying up media properties and pretty much disappeared from public life around fifteen years ago.

They had been back on the road for five minutes when the prepaid cell Sharp had given Tolman rang. "I kept getting your voice mail," Sharp said. "I called until you picked up."

"We were out of range. What's wrong, Darrell?"

"They came, just like you figured they would."

"You're all right?"

"Oh, I'm fine. But this fax came for Journey, from Webster in Vermont."

"Here, hold on," Tolman said. "I'll give him the phone."

She passed the phone to Journey, who said, "Yes?"

"Fax pages," Sharp said. "From this guy Webster."

"And? What do they look like?"

Sharp started reading the pages to him, in the same low, soft Carolina cadence. Bills of sale, book orders, dinner parties, travel plans . . .

"Garbage," Journey said. "There's nothing—"

"Wait," Sharp said.

Journey heard the phone being put down. He thought he heard another voice in the room, but the sound was muffled. He heard a ringing, the sound of a fax kicking in.

"Another page coming in," Sharp said. "No, two pages."

Several seconds passed. Journey heard the muffled sounds again.

"It's from Webster, too. Cover page says, 'Dr. Journey, here's one more, from a family scrapbook my grandmother made. The page talks about "the provisions on the pages preceding," but there are no pages preceding, nothing at all resembling it. It is very vague. Perhaps it is a piece from a manuscript that Charles Webster handled. It seems to be about a post–Civil War political movement, but there is not enough to draw a sound conclusion. Best regards, J. T. Webster.'"

"What?" Journey said, his heart starting to pound. "Darrell, read me the page, the one he's talking about."

Sharp did. When he finished, Journey put his hand over his mouth.

"What?" Tolman said. "Nick, what?"

"Darrell," Journey said into the phone. "Send that fax—please. Just a minute. I have to think of the number. . . . All right, here it is." He told Sharp the number. "Put it to the attention of Dr. Sandra Kelly. On the cover page, tell her it's from me and I'll be calling her, and to hold on to it."

"I'll do it," Sharp said. "Give the phone back to Meg."

Journey passed the phone back across the seat, and Tolman said, "Darrell?"

"You know, Meg, I've talked more in the last eight hours than I have in the last seven years."

Tolman smiled. "I'm glad you're okay, Darrell. Thanks for your help."

But Sharp had already hung up. Tolman looked back at Journey.

"It makes sense now," Journey said. "I haven't been able to understand how two men like Grant and Lee—honorable men who both believed strongly in civilian control over the military—could create something like this and have it out there, just waiting to be found by some nutcases who wanted to call themselves Glory Warriors and run the country. Now I understand, and it changes everything."

# CHAPTER
# 51

Hudson bought coffee from Around the Ground and walked back toward the building that housed RIO. In suite 427, he passed the reception desk, went into his office, and closed the door, finally alone. He placed both hands flat on the desk in front of him and tried to quiet his mind. He steepled his fingers in front of his face, then picked up his coffee as the phone rang.

"Russell Hudson," he said.

"Finally caught you in," Tolman said.

Hudson sat upright. "Meg, where are you? I haven't had time to call you back. I've been dealing with the investigation. Is this a secure line? Can you talk?"

"Oh, I can talk, Rusty."

"What do you mean?"

"Glory Warrior."

"What?"

"You're a fucking Glory Warrior. Don't insult me by denying it."

"Meg, I don't know what you're talking about."

"You prick! All these years, I thought we were friends. Hell, even more than that, I thought you were a professional. As much as

I teased you about being a bureaucrat, I respected you. You fooled me every day for five fucking years."

"Meg, I—"

"I had you over to my apartment. I made you dinner, and I don't even fucking cook! All your interest in my music, asking me what pieces I was working on. I thought you understood me. I let my guard down with you and told you about my mother. And all this time, all these years, you've been planning on overthrowing the U.S. government."

"Meg, what is the matter with you?"

"You're asking me that? You shit, you're asking what's the matter with *me*? After everything you've done, you have the balls to ask me that?" Tolman's voice had been rising, and now she was screaming. "Vandermeer and Darlington, that whole charade of the threat assessment, letting me present it. Oh, that was a good one, that was really inspired. And pretending to call the Pentagon, that was better yet. You knew all along that Lane and Standridge were alive, because you've been paying Lane's wife all this time!"

"Where are you? What do you—?"

"Shut up!" Tolman shouted. "My friend, my mentor, my boss . . . just shut your fucking mouth and listen. You go tell Jackson McMartin—yes, we know who he is—that the two of you are going to meet Journey and me in Oklahoma, at Fort Washita at three o'clock tomorrow afternoon. You like drama, playing your little role all these years? Well, here's a little more drama for you. Journey knows exactly where the signature page is, and you people haven't been able to find a damn thing on your own so far."

"You don't know what you're doing."

"You've screwed RIO and the government and the whole fucking country over for God only knows how long. And you've been screwing *me* over for five years. I know exactly what I'm doing."

Hudson gripped the phone. "You're in no position to talk to me this way."

"You know what? I don't give a shit, not anymore." Her voice took on a bitter, mocking tone. "'Oh Meg, where are you performing this week? Falls Church, how wonderful. How's that new piece coming? Regards to your father, Meg, and by the way, I'm working to suspend the U.S. Constitution and stage a coup. Have a nice day, Meg.'" Tolman lowered her voice. "You make sure McMartin brings the missing pages from Grant's memoir, the ones Grant had Mark Twain take out of the book at the last minute. And call your watchers off Journey's ex-wife and kid. Yeah, I know about that, too. I know about the bank accounts and all the millions of dollars moving all over the place. You covered yourself with all those pass-through accounts and the one in Aruba, but at some point there had to be real names on that money, and that's where I found you. So you go to McMartin and you get moving. If you don't, Journey and the page disappear forever. I'll create new identities for him and his son and they'll vanish. You know I can do it, too. Three o'clock tomorrow, Fort Washita. McMartin probably has a jet, so you can travel in style."

"What do you get out of this?"

Tolman barked a harsh laugh into the phone. "Not a goddamn thing, Rusty." The line went dead.

Hudson sat for a moment, holding the phone before he placed it back in its cradle. His mind raced through the possibilities. He contemplated calling the other Washingtons, but Graves was untouchable at the moment. One was almost always untouchable, and Three was getting into position on Harwell.

He tried to clear his mind again, but all he heard was Meg Tolman's voice.

*No.*

He had worked for twenty-five years, patiently doing his part, becoming Washington Four. In short order, he would become the fifth most powerful man in the country.

He had come too far. They all had.

Hudson looked at his watch. If he left now, he could be in Matewan by midnight. He picked up the phone and called the Judge. "We have both a problem and an opportunity," he said.


Washington Three didn't scare easily. The idea that he was less than twenty-four hours away from assassinating the president of the United States did not bother him. He had trained for it all his adult life. The Glory Warriors recruited him off the campus of Stanford when he was eighteen, followed him through his active duty military years, including a tour in Desert Storm, and facilitated his entry into the Secret Service and his climb through the ranks until he joined the protective detail of newly elected president Harwell seven years ago. Harwell was just another politician, and Washington Three was about to make history.

But driving alone into the Anacostia neighborhood at night came close to scaring him. He passed at least four drug deals in progress and saw one kid who could not have been more than fourteen threatening an even younger boy with a knife. He wondered if one of the boys would be dead by morning.

When he turned onto Valley Place, he showed his Service ID at the end of the block and the D.C. cop on duty passed him through.

"My boss wanted me to check on one more thing," he told the cop, who smiled back at him. They both knew about difficult bosses.

The new community center was well lighted, but no one was around. It didn't officially open until after the dedication ceremony and the president's speech tomorrow. Now, Three thought, the opening would no doubt be postponed further as the nation mourned its fallen leader, just as it mourned the crusty old Speaker of the House and the nation's first female chief justice, the grandmother from Alabama.

He parked three doors down from the house and took his black gym bag from the backseat of the car. He walked to the vacant house with the half-covered window on the second floor, turned in at the gate, and walked right in. The place had no door.

Upstairs, he slipped on a pair of rubber gloves, then opened the bag and reassembled the broken-down sniper rifle in less than two minutes. He inserted a magazine, lay the rifle parallel to the window, and left the house. He had signed off on the house. It was secure. No one would be in it again until tomorrow. And then he would wait.

Washington Three walked back out into the damp night. It had rained in the afternoon and the streets were slick and murky. The tall trees on either side of the community center dripped water onto the pavement. Three scanned the rooftops. The agents up there would be complaining about standing water tomorrow. Some of them would probably ruin their shoes.

He grinned at the absurdity of it, then got back into his car and drove away from Valley Place.

# CHAPTER
# 52

The sun sank ahead of Journey and Tolman after they crossed the Oklahoma line, blazing in shades of blue, orange, purple, and pink. The terrain began to flatten from the Ozark Plateau, ambling toward the Great Plains to the west. They both felt the exhaustion beginning to carry them, to tug at them like an undercurrent.

"I have to see Andrew," Journey said. "This highway takes us straight into Oklahoma City, close to his mother's house. It's another two and a half hours south to Carpenter Center."

"Aren't you concerned—?" Tolman said.

"About his safety. Of course I am. He won't be at the fort with us."

She looked at him but was silent. They were in Oklahoma City by eleven, Journey directing Tolman to take the Classen Boulevard exit. She wound through city streets in Sharp's truck until crossing Dewey Avenue on Northwest Fourteenth in Heritage Hills, which proclaimed itself "the oldest neighborhood in Oklahoma City." Many of the homes were proud Victorians from the earliest years of the twentieth century.

"Here," Journey said, pointing, and the truck coasted to a stop under a huge elm.

A moment later, Amelia had answered the door and was standing, silent as stone, in her bare feet and a long T-shirt.

"Hey," Journey said.

"People were watching my house," Amelia said. "Three men in a van."

"I know, Amelia."

"And who is that Kelly woman who called me? Why couldn't you call yourself?"

"Sandra is a coworker. It wasn't safe for me to call." He looked up and down the quiet street. "The watchers should be gone."

"I think they left this afternoon."

Journey nodded. "How's Andrew?"

"He's fine. Hasn't had any real meltdowns. Very vocal, though. He was being so loud that Paul had to leave."

Journey said nothing. He heard Tolman behind him. "Amelia, this is Meg Tolman. Meg, this is my son's mother, Amelia Boettcher."

"Who's she?" Amelia said.

"I'm with the Research and Investigations Office in Washington, Ms. Boettcher," Tolman said. "Nick has been working with me."

"Working with you?"

"Amelia," Journey said, "are you going to make us stand out here?"

Amelia stood aside.

"Could I just go up and look in on him?" Journey said.

Amelia shrugged. Journey went up the wide staircase with its highly polished banister, the steps covered in expensive fabric, and turned left at the top of the stairs. The first door was slightly ajar, and he could see Andrew's head in the sliver of light from the hall.

He sniffed and caught the smell of urine. The boy had already wet himself in his sleep. But Journey didn't hold his breath, for once. He just watched the boy sleep, a big twelve-year-old kid who had a Winnie-the-Pooh pillow. In sleep, Journey thought, Andrew did not have autism. He was just a child who slept a child's beautiful sleep. Journey caught the trace of a memory from a few days ago, Andrew sitting in the jewelry store in Carpenter Center, squeezing the porcupine ball Marvin Colbert had given him, smiling a real and genuine and happy smile as he felt the little rush of air from the ball on his face. Journey turned away from the bedroom door and went back down the stairs.

At the foot of the steps, he said to Amelia, "We have a lot to do tomorrow. But we're exhausted. I've dozed in cars and had maybe one real hour's sleep in the last twenty-four. Amelia . . ." He put his hands in his pockets. "Could we just stay here for the night? I'll sleep here on your couch, and if you have a guest room, Meg could sleep there."

"Nick, I don't—"

"It's exhaustion. Nothing else. I just need to close my eyes. That's all."

Amelia raised her hands and let them drop to her sides. "We can pack up Andrew's things in the morning. I had to buy him some more Pull-Ups, you know."

Journey nodded. He exchanged a glance with Tolman and watched as Amelia showed her to the guest room.

Unknown to Andrew Journey, the boy slept under the same roof as both his mother and his father for the first time in over three years.

# CHAPTER
# 53

Ray Tolman got up before 5 A.M., showered, and dressed in his suit, minus the jacket. He hadn't slept much. By six fifteen, he was at his desk, staring at the duty rosters again.

*Alley. Clare. DeBacker. Delham. O'Daniel.*

It couldn't be Tony Alley. Ray Tolman knew the man. He was a good man, soft-spoken, easygoing. His background was in accounting. He'd been very good at investigating financial crimes before getting into protective duty. It couldn't be Alley. Tolman had nothing to base it on but instinct. And sometimes, he told himself, all the databases in the world don't mean shit. A good cop is only as good as his instinct.

*Clare. DeBacker. Delham. O'Daniel.*

Would these so-called Glory Warriors really put a woman into this position? On the one hand, the very fact that Miranda O'Daniel was female might lead people to believe she couldn't possibly be one of them, thereby making her the perfect candidate. By the same reasoning, though, there were only a handful of women on presidential protective detail. Therefore she stood out, and this group wouldn't want their sleeper assassin to be one who attracted attention.

*Clare. DeBacker. Delham.*

He went back over their background files. DeBacker had once been a state trooper in Nebraska. Delham and Clare were both from California, though from different ends of the state. Both had been in the army. All three men were in their late thirties to early forties.

Tolman felt the burn in his stomach again. The ulcer. He had developed ulcers only since he'd moved inside. Never had them when he'd been in the field. The disadvantages of being a deputy assistant director . . .

A thought came over him with excruciating slowness. All field agents had regular medical screenings, and were periodically re-evaluated for both physical and mental health. Their medical records were part of their individual personnel files.

If someone were living every single day as a deception, sworn to protect the president but knowing that someday they were going to be asked to kill the man they'd sworn to protect, wouldn't that create a lot of physical stress? Wouldn't maintaining that kind of façade year after year take a toll on a man? He might have medical issues here and there, telltale signs that could be seen—if someone was looking in the right place.

Tolman dug deeper into the personnel files. In half an hour, he knew that Ron DeBacker was the picture of health, and by all accounts had the body of a man twenty years younger. Timothy Delham had complained of dizziness six and a half years ago, not long after coming to the detail. After a battery of tests that took eight months to complete, he was diagnosed with a strange and rare case of visually induced vertigo. He was given medication for it, and he'd had no medical issues since. Jay Clare was constantly fighting high blood pressure, his cholesterol was borderline, and he'd been diagnosed two years ago with severe sleep apnea. He now slept with a breathing mask every night to deal with the apnea.

Clare.

Tolman remembered bumping into him coming out of the abandoned house, the one that had bothered him so much, on Valley Place yesterday afternoon. Had he seemed in a rush to get away from the deputy assistant director?

Ray Tolman hesitated for a long moment. Meg had said the traitor was within the Service. So he couldn't talk to anyone inside, because he couldn't be sure where the traitor was. But she hadn't said anything about the FBI, and Tolman couldn't do this alone. He reached for the phone and called his old friend Pat Moore, who was now a midlevel administrator after years as an FBI field agent. He knew Moore would be awake.

"Pat," he said, "I need your help. I can't trust anyone in the Service, and the president's in danger. Call in sick at the office and meet me. Bring your weapon."

Meg Tolman slept fitfully and woke early. Amelia Boettcher's house was large and comfortably appointed—the guest room sported a queen-size brass bed—but even as exhausted as she was, she didn't rest well. She knew a confrontation was coming in a few hours, the Glory Warriors would be making their move against President Harwell, and she knew she'd have to deal with Hudson's treason.

She got out of the brass bed and showered in the bathroom with its marble surfaces and high-tech showerhead. When she was dressed, she opened the door to her room and turned the corner toward the stairs. As she put her foot on the top step, she heard a sound behind her.

Her nerves still on edge, she froze, her hand instinctively going to her hip. But the SIG Darrell Sharp had given her was back in her room, in her overnight bag. She swiveled her head and saw the boy coming out of the bedroom.

He was a big kid, with brown hair and very large eyes. He was wearing a blue and gold SCCO T-shirt that was too big for him, and loose gray sweatpants. The pants were soaked around his groin area. She caught the strong ammonia smell and had to fight the reflex to gag.

The boy looked just like his mother. His fingers were making unusual motions, the thumb wrapped around the index finger below the knuckle, the index finger almost touching the palm, waggling back and forth. Andrew's eyes found her.

She met those big eyes, and in a very soft voice Tolman said, "Hi."

He looked at her for what seemed like a very long moment; then his eyes flicked away as if he hadn't seen her at all.

Journey appeared at the bottom of the stairs, still in his clothes from last night, and said, "I heard—"

He stopped, looking at both Tolman and Andrew.

"I hope I didn't wake him up," Tolman said.

"He's sensitive to when someone else is moving around," Journey said. "He usually wakes up as soon as someone else in the house gets up." His eyes moved back to his son. "Good morning, Andrew."

The boy looked away and whistled.

"Andrew," Journey said.

Andrew cocked his head away from his father's voice.

"Andrew, good morning."

Tolman looked back and forth, and she was amazed at how level Journey kept his voice, even after the third try. When the boy stuck out his hand in a karate-chop gesture and looked for a brief moment toward the bottom of the stairs, Journey smiled and said, "I sure missed you. Come on, I'll get you changed. I don't know where your mom keeps your things, but I bet we can find them."

He started up the stairs. Tolman stood aside to let him pass.

"Good-looking kid," she said, and didn't know what else to say.

"Thanks," Journey said. "Maybe you could find some coffee downstairs. I don't know where Amelia keeps it."

"I'll find it."

Journey took his son by the hand and steered him back toward his room. "Did you sleep?" he said over his shoulder.

"Not much," Tolman said. "You?"

"I remember sleep as being a good thing. When this is all over—"

"Yeah," Tolman said; then they had disappeared into Andrew's room and the moment was gone.

Half an hour later, Andrew was dressed, and his father had showered and was on the phone with his friend at the Oklahoma Historical Society.

"Bob, it's Nick Journey."

"Nick? Do you know what time it is?"

"It's early, but I was hoping you'd be up."

"I am up, but why on earth are you calling me at six thirty in the morning?"

"You need to close Fort Washita to the public today."

There was a long silence.

"Bob? Did you hear me?"

"Yes, I did. You know I can't just close a state historic site for no apparent reason."

"Bob, get on the phone with your superintendent at Fort Washita and keep it closed today."

"Why?"

"Because someone could get hurt."

Another long silence.

"I know this has to do with the guns and the document, but what aren't you telling me?"

Journey almost laughed. "A lot. Trust me, there's a lot I'm not telling you. We can't have stray people around there today."

"Well, Nick, tourist season is over. We probably wouldn't have big crowds down there today anyway. I can have the on-site people close the front gate, but you know what the layout is there. If someone really wants to get in, they can still get in, and there's access from some of the adjoining private properties."

"I know. In fact, I'm counting on it."


Amelia Boettcher didn't get up until seven thirty, and seemed surprised to see the other three dressed and ready to leave.

"Thanks for keeping him," Journey said to her, and it struck Tolman as a very formal thing to say, the sort of thing one would say to a neighbor or casual friend who'd stayed with a child, but not to the child's other parent.

Amelia nodded, running her fingers through her hair. "Sure. We can just take these days out of next year's June time, okay?"

Journey was silent, working a muscle in his jaw. "Okay."

Amelia knelt by Andrew and touched his arm. "See you later, honey. Don't give your dad too much trouble."

Journey held out Andrew's backpack to the boy and said, "Okay, Andrew, time to go."

Andrew grabbed on to his mother's arm and stepped away from his father.

"No, Andrew," Amelia said, "it's time to go with your dad. Time to go back home. I bet you're ready to go back to school, get back to your schedule, right?"

Andrew angled his body so his mother was between his father and him, never letting go of Amelia's arm.

Journey sighed. "You'll need to walk him out to the car with us, Amelia, or he won't go."

"I'm not dressed."

"We need to go. Andrew, come on, son, your mom will walk out with us." Tolman thought Journey's voice had a weary, seen-it-all-before quality.

They walked to the curb where Tolman had parked the Dakota. "Is there room for him in there?" Amelia said.

"He can ride between us," Tolman said. "It may be a little tight, but he'll fit."

Amelia looked at her as if she'd spoken out of turn, a look that Tolman recognized, a look that only a woman will give another woman when she feels threatened.

Tolman shook her head. "Let's go."

In five minutes, they were away from the curb. In ten, they were back on the highway. Andrew sat between Tolman and his father. He was very quiet, as if he sensed something different about his father.

For the two-and-a-half-hour drive from Oklahoma City to Carpenter Center, Andrew did not whistle or laugh or scream. He made a few small sounds in the back of his throat, and spent most of his time looking from his father to Tolman and back again.

# CHAPTER
# 54

They turned off U.S. 70 and rolled into Carpenter Center at a few minutes past ten in the morning. The carved limestone sign at the city limits read: CARPENTER CENTER, OKLAHOMA, HOME OF LAKE TEXOMA, SOUTH CENTRAL COLLEGE OF OKLAHOMA AND A GREAT QUALITY OF LIFE!

"So this is where you live," Tolman said, behind the wheel.

"This is where I live," Journey said.

She looked at the trees, the abundant greenery, the businesses that served both the college community and the tourism trade. "Nice enough little town, I guess."

"It's not Washington, D.C.," Journey said, "but it's my home."

Andrew grew animated and vocal as he began to recognize familiar sights. Tolman felt him moving in the seat next to her, saw his hands begin to flap, as if he were patting the air. Journey gave her directions and she passed through SCCO's main gate, followed a driveway around, and parked in the lot just off the common. They walked to Cullen Hall and took the elevator to the second floor, Andrew holding on to his father's hand.

Tolman hung back a few steps as Journey was bombarded with colleagues and students, all talking at the same time. Journey deflected as much of the attention as he could, talking on autopi-lot—*I'm fine. It's a long story. I'll explain when I can. Have you seen Dr. Kelly? No, my foot's not broken, only sprained*—and searching for San-dra's red hair in the throng.

He saw her standing a little way back, in the doorway to her of-fice, and he extricated himself from the crowd and made his way to her, still holding Andrew's hand. She was wearing black slacks, a pale burgundy blouse, and the little silver cross around her neck.

"Hi," Journey said.

Sandra smiled. "That's a lousy opening line." She looked down at Andrew and waved her hand. "Hey, Andrew." The boy jabbed a flat hand in her direction, and the smile broadened. "He's okay. I was worried when his mother told me she thought people were watching her house. You got to the message board?"

Journey nodded. "'Radical Redhead.' Thanks."

Sandra's eyes flickered over Journey's shoulder. "You must be the investigator from Washington."

Tolman extended her right hand. "Meg Tolman."

"Sandra Kelly." The two women shook hands.

"Nick speaks highly of you," Tolman said.

The small smile again. "I'm surprised he speaks of me at all."

Journey looked uncomfortable. Andrew squirmed beside him. "Sandra, did you get the fax?"

"It's in my office. I can tell it's related to the Fort Washita page, but there should be something in between. Did *The Poet's Penn* show you what it needed to show you?"

"Yes, and a whole lot more."

"What happened to your foot?"

"I went for an unexpected swim in the Ohio River."

"Ah. I'll just get that fax." She disappeared into the office and came back with the paper. When she handed it to Journey, he caught a bit of her scent—not heavy or perfumed, but clean and fresh and forgiving. "Where are you going now?"

"There's one more thing we have to do today," Journey said, reading the page. *Unbelievable,* he thought. *This sat in J. T. Webster's grandmother's scrapbook for years and years, with no clue as to how it fit in with a much, much larger picture.* Journey looked down at his son, who was scanning the hallway and shuffling his feet. He had let go of his father's hand and was holding Journey by the elbow.

"And I need your help one more time," Journey said. He looked into Sandra's green eyes and saw only openness and concern. He swallowed hard. "Will you take Andrew to school, and then pick him up at three and stay with him for a while, just until I get back?"

The moment was long and excruciating, and Journey saw the doubt in Sandra's eyes; then the eyes softened into recognition of what had just happened.

"Yes," she said. "I can do that for you." Her voice was a little uncertain.

"If it's not—"

"I'll do it. But it would probably be best if I could take him to his own home. He doesn't know my house."

Journey felt in his pocket, then laughed.

"What?" Sandra said. She looked at Tolman. "Why is he laughing?"

"The absurdity of it," Journey said. "House keys and school schedules, in the midst of all this."

"And his keys are at the bottom of the Ohio River," Tolman said.

Sandra smiled. "That must have been quite a swim. I believe, from the sound of this, that you're going to owe me at least two salads at Uncle Charley's. Big ones."

"I believe you're right," Journey said. "And cheesecake for dessert. I left my spare key with Sarah Brandes. She's a student, special ed major, and she sits with Andrew from time to time. She lives on campus, in East Hall."

"I'll look her up in the student directory."

"I'll call the school and let them know you're cleared to pick him up."

"Okay," Sandra said.

"Okay," Journey said.

Journey held his hand, palm out, toward his son, and Andrew hesitated a moment, then laced his fingers into his father's. Then he watched as Sandra took Andrew by the hand and led him toward the stairs. They were out of earshot, but he could see that Sandra was talking to Andrew in a soft voice.

Journey turned to Tolman. "Let's finish this," he said.

"Ray, are you crazy?" Pat Moore asked. "Has being inside gotten to your brain or what?"

They were having coffee in a Starbucks near Moore's house in Arlington. Moore was not a tall man, and Ray Tolman saw that he'd developed a bit of a gut since he'd last seen Moore a couple of years ago. Even though not on duty, Moore wore the FBI uniform of white shirt, dark suit, and red tie.

"No, I'm not crazy. No, I can't give you the source of the information. But I trust the source absolutely. A move is going to be made against the president today, and it's going to come from within the Service."

Moore put down his coffee cup. "Ray, you need to take this up the ladder within your own department. You know better than anyone that there are procedures—"

"Screw the procedures, Pat. The job of the Service is to protect the president, and that's what this all comes down to. I have credible information, and that information points to someone inside."

Moore sat back, rubbing his chin. "Vandermeer, Darlington, and Harwell. I know you're not going to tell me these are all related."

"Pat, I need a man I can trust to cover me."

The two men, career field agents in their late fifties, each now an administrator, looked across the table at each other. "What do you propose?"

"We need to catch this guy at the site so that there's no mistaking who he is and what his intentions are. Since he's inside the Service, he's had access. He could go wherever he wanted and do whatever kind of prep work for what he's planning, and no one would question him."

"Yeah, I understand that," Moore said.

"This guy is very, very smart," Ray Tolman said. "He's been able to stay undercover for a long time." He pulled a folded piece of paper from the pocket of his suit coat. "But he's also arrogant."

Moore nodded toward the paper.

"The duty roster for the president's event in Anacostia this after-noon," Tolman said. "There were a couple of changes late last night."

"But with your position now, you get updates. Damned if there's not some advantage to being on a desk."

"And our boy isn't quite as smart as he thinks he is."

The D.C. traffic was bad as always, and it took over half an hour to get across the bridge to Anacostia. By the time Tolman's Crown Vic turned onto Valley Place, the D.C. police were already out in force, and the Service began filtering in. In a few hours, there would be people on rooftops, people in the trees, people out of sight all around the area.

Tolman's supervisory ID got him past the perimeter, and he parked the Crown Vic just inside the roadblock. He and Moore walked to the house that had concerned him, the forlorn one with the FOR SALE BY OWNER sign tacked to the front porch.

They went in the house, smelling the dampness and the old ciga-rette smoke and fried food and the deadness of a place that hadn't been inhabited for a while. Within sixty seconds, they'd discovered the rifle on the floor beside the open window.

*Yeah, he's a smart son of a bitch*, Tolman thought. *But I'm smarter than he is.*

He looked at the duty roster again, at the event assignments for the day. Things were never what they seemed to be on first glance, he thought.

"Sorry, Pat," Tolman said. "I need you to do closet duty. But I will buy you a case of Glenlivet tomorrow, and I'll buy a steak din-ner for you and Jeannie at the most expensive place you can find."

Moore positioned himself in the closet at the top of the stairs, wedging in behind the door. It was hanging partway off its hinges, but he arranged his body so he was out of sight from the stairs.

Tolman picked up the rifle, withdrew the magazine, and placed the unloaded weapon in the same position on the floor. Then he backed into what had once been a bathroom. The toilet, which was painted a surreal blue, was still in the room, turned on its side. There was no sink, but a cracked mirror still hung over the spot where a sink should have been.

*Come on,* Ray Tolman thought. *Come on and get it.*

He settled in to wait.


Less than two miles from the coffee shop where Ray Tolman and Pat Moore had talked, Washington One sat in his home office and studied the multiple webcam feeds from the different bases. He had told his driver that he would be away from his "real" office all day and that he was not to be disturbed for anything short of a national emergency.

The thought almost made him smile. *National emergency, indeed.*

By the end of the day, the operation would be in progress. In a few hours, the old government's culture of corruption would end and the Glory Warriors would be in control.

They were trained, they were equipped, they were ready. In the Blue Ridge, near Waynesboro, the heavy equipment was preparing to roll. At the bases in Silver Spring, Rockville, Arlington, and Alexandria, the choppers were fueled. The troops were on standby—in a few hours, he would formally activate them, and they would stand ready to deploy into the capital as soon as President James Harwell was dead.

Today was the day.

# CHAPTER
# 55

Tolman and Journey drove to downtown Carpenter Center, to Texoma Plaza with its memorial park in the center of the square and ring of small businesses surrounding it. They parked in front of Colbert's Fine Jewelers, and Journey raced inside. The little silver bell over the doorway tinkled.

Just like the first time he'd been here, the young man with the mixed-blood features was behind the counter. "Help you?" he said.

"Is Marvin here today?"

"Uncle!" the boy yelled, and disappeared into the back of the store.

In a moment, Marvin Colbert came into the showroom. "You're back," he said.

"Yes," Journey said.

"I wondered when you'd come back," Colbert said. "Where's your boy?"

"He's in school."

"He like that little ball I gave him?"

Journey remembered the rush of air on Andrew's face. "He loves it." He leaned on the counter, Tolman standing just behind him. "You know what G.W. is on those pins I asked you about?"

Colbert sat heavily onto a stool. "No, sir, I don't."

"When I sat them in front of you, you got this look on your face like you recognized them. I couldn't quite place it, couldn't remember what was bothering me about that day, and then I figured it out. You know about G.W."

"I know about G.W. I don't know what the letters stand for."

Journey spread his hands apart. "Why didn't you say something that day?"

Colbert's face was stone. "You didn't ask."

Journey felt anger rising; then he realized the old man wasn't being sarcastic. "But what—?"

"I never answer questions that aren't asked," Colbert said. "There's only trouble when you give the answer before the question. Learned that the hard way a few times."

"G.W," Journey said. "It's at Fort Washita, isn't it?"

"Yes."

"But you've never known what the letters mean?"

"No."

"Where is it?"

"In the Chickasaw section, on the west side by the wall."

Journey tried to envision the place. Before the discovery of the guns and the document, he'd been to Fort Washita only twice since moving to Oklahoma. It was a state historic site, but overall it didn't have much relevance to his work. He'd gone once for his own curiosity, and once to take Andrew.

U.S. soldiers who had been posted to Fort Washita, and who had died there—usually from disease or injury, since there was no real fighting near the fort—were buried in the post cemetery, but later reinterred at the Fort Gibson National Cemetery, several hours' drive northeast. Segregated even in death, there was a Confederate cemetery with two hundred unmarked graves at the far west end of the fort. What remained in the post cemetery were a few scattered civilians from the area. Journey closed his eyes.

He snapped them open. "The Colbert family plot. You have a section out there."

"Those are all more recent graves," Colbert said. "You want the old Chickasaw burial ground, outside the Colbert plot."

"But I don't—" He remembered walking over the site the day the guns were discovered. A white picket fence surrounded the cemetery. He'd looked at a few of the old markers, some with splotches of yellow across them. Many children from the nineteenth and early twentieth centuries were buried there. The epitaph on one of them had struck him: A LITTLE FLOWER OF LOVE THAT BLOSSOMED BUT TO DIE.

Outside the white picket fence of the main cemetery was a low rock wall with a small opening that led into it, and a gray granite marker:

CHICKASAW INDIAN BURIAL GROUND—"KNOWN BUT TO GOD."

"But there were no markers," Journey said.

"The old Chickasaw didn't believe in grave markers," Colbert said. "Most of them were buried under their houses. But for the ones who did get buried in a common ground, they weren't marked until way up in the twentieth century."

Journey strained for the memory. It was just a small rectangular section of ground, covered in grass. It was unbroken by . . .

"Right along the wall," he said. "A little stone slab."

Colbert nodded.

"Do you know who he was?" Journey said. His heart was hammering. "Did your family know him?"

"He must have been a white man, since they gave him a marker. But whoever buried him there, they let him lie with the Chickasaw people. Other than that, I don't know. Maybe some of the elders did, but they never told me."

"I know who it is," Journey said.

Colbert nodded, waiting.

"Who owns that part of the land now?" Journey said. "It's within the fort, so—"

"Historical Society."

Journey was nodding. "Yes. Yes, that's it." He looked at Tolman. "It's time for you to use a little of that federal government influence." He looked back to Colbert. "We need to do some digging out there."

Colbert folded his arms.

"People have died because of this," Journey said.

"Because of those pins," Colbert said. It was a statement, not a question.

"Yes. And I think a lot more people could die if we don't do something."

Colbert was silent for another long, long moment. "We'll keep it in the family," he finally said. "One of my great-nephews can help you. I'll give you his number. Just one thing . . ." Journey looked at him. "Leave the Chickasaw alone. Do what you have to do, but don't disturb anything outside that one little corner."

"I won't. His name—the man's name was Samuel Benjamin Williams."

"Then why G.W.?" Colbert said.

"He was the first Glory Warrior," Journey said, and ran out of the jewelry store, Colbert staring after him.

On the sidewalk, Tolman said, "Williams is buried here?"

"Think about it," Journey said. "This is the last place we know for sure he was alive. He was in Appomattox on April ninth, 1865. He rode to Louisville and hid the page in his bank vault. Then he came here to do the same with the front page."

"What if he came here first and then Louisville?"

"That wouldn't make sense," Journey said. "He moved steadily west. Virginia to Kentucky to Indian Territory. In fact, I was thinking today that the route we took from Louisville, down across Arkansas and into Oklahoma, is probably pretty close to what Williams did. This is where the trail ended. We didn't know what happened to him."

"We still don't," Tolman pointed out.

"No, but he died here," Journey said, "and I'm willing to bet it wasn't from old age."

"And one of the Chickasaw buried him. But why—?"

"I think we're going to find out in a few hours." Journey pointed at her. "Call and make sure it's legal for us to dig. Colbert's nephew will do the work for us."

"Dig? Whoa, what . . . you want to dig up Williams's body?"

"We have to."

"Jesus, Journey . . . wait a minute. You think the signature page is buried with Williams? Holy shit, he kept it with him the whole time?"

Journey pointed at Tolman's cell phone. "Start calling."

"What are you going to do?"

He was already on his own phone. In a moment, a voice answered, "Marshall County Sheriff's Office."

"This is Nick Journey," he said. "I'd like to speak to Deputy Parsons."

"Which one?" the voice drawled. "We've got two of them."

"Whichever one is available."

"This is Ricky Parsons," a voice said a few seconds later.

"Deputy Parsons, it's Nick Journey. Do you remember me?"

"Of course I do, Professor. My little brother got killed trying to protect you."

Journey flinched. "In a few hours, you can have the rest of the people responsible for his death."

There was a long pause; then Ricky Parsons said, "I'm listening."

# CHAPTER

# 56

The Judge's jet landed at the Ardmore Airpark at just past noon, piloted by Baltimore Five Bronze. The Judge and Hudson talked little on the flight, other than a terse discussion about what ultimately must be done about Nick Journey and Meg Tolman. Mostly the Judge talked and Hudson was silent.

A white Suburban from Dallas Base waited for them at the small airport, Dallas Three Bronze at the wheel. As the Judge settled into the passenger seat, Hudson bending his huge frame into the second row, the Judge was breathing heavily.

"Sir?" Bronze said. "Are you all right?"

The Judge touched his chest, felt the fluttery beats there. "Air travel doesn't agree with me these days." He gestured at the driver. "You should have the directions. Take us where we need to go."

He sat back against the seat, thinking of the speeches he'd given in his life: orders to troops as a young officer in Vietnam, closing arguments and sentencing statements as a military lawyer and judge, campaign speeches, addresses to shareholders. Nothing could compare to the speech he would give very soon. He went through it in his mind: *My fellow Americans, I join you in mourning the tragedies that have befallen our beloved country in recent times. But out of these tragedies, we will emerge stronger than ever with new directions and a new purpose. . . .*

"*It's in your hands now. Don't fail.*"

"I won't," the Judge said, and he didn't realize he'd spoken aloud.

Bronze drove out of the airport and headed east from Ardmore. Hudson was silent, staring at the Judge from the backseat.


Tolman took three Tylenol for the ache in the back of her head and slid behind the wheel of the Dakota again. She drove as Journey directed, through Carpenter Center to US 70 into Madill, then east on Oklahoma 199. The gently rolling country was mostly cattle pastureland, dotted with the occasional oil well.

Journey looked into the side mirror and saw the Marshall County Sheriff's Department patrol unit behind them, and the unmarked Ford pickup truck following it. The Parsons brothers had made a couple of calls themselves after Journey talked to them.

After they crossed the Washita River, the sheriff's unit passed the Dakota, then slowed and turned left from the highway into a grassy driveway that led to a ranch gate.

Ricky Parsons, the oldest of the brothers, jumped out of his patrol car, opened the gate, and drove through, letting the other two vehicles pull off the road before Scott Parsons, in the Ford truck, closed it behind them. Ricky Parsons got out of his car and walked back to the Dakota.

Journey looked out at him. He was an older version of Pete Parsons, and Journey couldn't look at him without thinking of the young campus cop, body toppling toward him, blood spattering his clothes. They were both—all three, in fact—tall and lean with light brown hair and dark, hungry eyes.

"We'll have to walk in from here," Ricky Parsons said. His eyes moved to Tolman. "Ma'am, you might want to stay with the cars."

"Not on your life," Tolman said. "And don't call me *ma'am*."

"I don't know if I can guarantee your safety."

"I'll guarantee my own safety."

Parsons shrugged, looking in the window. "That foot of yours okay to walk in?" he said to Journey.

"Oh, yes," Journey said. "I can walk. Does your office know where you are?"

"I'm investigating an anonymous tip. Scotty's off-duty, and the other boys happened along while they were going fishing."

Two more men in their late twenties got out of the Ford. Both had handguns. The Parsons brothers each had Mossberg 590 riot shotguns and sidearms.

"Let's go fishing," Journey said, and they began walking east through the pastureland toward Fort Washita.

When the Dallas One team arrived at Fort Washita, they pulled the SUV to the side of the road and gazed across the highway. The old guardhouse that served as an entry to the historic site stood on a rock base, with a raised wooden "crow's nest" enclosure atop it. The enclosure was small, with enough space to admit three adult men, topped by a pointed roof. A sign on the rock front read FORT WASHITA—1842.

A low gate blocked the driveway. On the east side of the entry, a short section of rock wall gave way to wooden fencing, sloping down to wire fence beyond that. Silver—Kevin Lane—saw instantly that security was not a major concern at the old fort. There was enough space on the far side of the guardhouse for a man to slip through.

"On foot," Gold said.

Silver checked the load in the H&K pistol at his side, the same one he'd had the night Gold was killed at South Central College. He wasn't carrying a rifle. He intended to get close enough to Nick Journey to see the man's face when he killed him.

"We're early," Hudson said as the Suburban coasted to a stop. Just in front of them sat another empty SUV with Texas plates.

"We can wait," the Judge said. "We've waited nearly a hundred and fifty years. We can wait another hour or so."

"Sir," Hudson said, "I do not like this. I know Meg Tolman, and she thinks somehow she's going to trap us. It makes no sense for her to dangle the signatures in front of us like this. But she is not a fool, sir. There's something more happening here."

"Of course there is. But the fact is that your subordinate put all this together. You aren't in much of a position to dictate what you do and don't like." He swept a hand at the empty vehicle in front of them. "We're covered here. Professor Journey and young Miss Tolman can pretend they're in control of this situation, but we both know what's going to happen."

"Sir, I think—"

"Do you play chess, Hudson?"

"Sir?"

"Chess. Do you play?"

"No, I don't have time to—"

"When I was a boy, I won the California state scholastic chess championship. My mother was there when I won. My father didn't even know for months. He didn't understand chess, either. I don't think he ever understood that every action—or inaction—has consequences. But I learned that. I suppose both chess and my father taught me that lesson, in different ways."

"With all due respect, sir—"

"The way to control the board, Hudson, is to get a pawn into the other player's territory. Once you do that, the pawn becomes a queen, and of course the queen is the most powerful piece of all and can move anywhere she likes."

The Judge's hand went to his chest again, as if he were smoothing his shirt. He looked toward the fort, thinking of the Glory Warriors who were already inside. He leaned forward and tapped the driver's shoulder. "When we're finished here, take us back to the plane. We'll fly to Dallas and I'll use the HNC studio there to uplink the pages and my speech. By the time Journey and Tolman are finished and I have the signature pages, it will be time."

*My fellow Americans . . .*

At five minutes before three, Tolman and Journey walked into the main body of the historic site from the west, past the ground that had been broken for the new museum, the place where the weapons and the first page of the document had been found. They passed the Confederate cemetery and the restored cabin of General Douglas Hancock Cooper, the man who had ordered his troops to abandon Fort Washita at the outbreak of the Civil War. The Fort Washita visitors' center was just beyond the Cooper cabin, a small gray stone building with a chimney at either end. A CLOSED sign hung on the door. Journey was hobbling a bit on his injured foot, and at times leaned on the much shorter Tolman.

They turned left at the visitors' center, leaving blacktop and turning onto gravel. Ahead, they could see where the road dead-ended at the cemeteries. As they came closer, Journey saw the white picket fence that enclosed the larger cemetery, and the small rock wall surrounding the unmarked graves of the Chickasaw. At the far end of the Chickasaw section was a freshly turned mound of earth. An old wooden-handled shovel leaned against the edge of the rock wall. Marvin Colbert's nephew had already come and gone.

Journey hobbled around the rock wall. The hole was not deep. The coffin was wooden and very crude. At the side of the hole was the slab of stone with the letters *G.W.* carved on it.

"So this is where it ended," Tolman said.

"Someone," Journey said, "and I'm guessing it was one of Marvin Colbert's ancestors, buried Williams here. I don't know what happened to him, and I don't know how he came to know the Indians. But Williams died here. The pages were safe, and the Chickasaw gave him a place among their people and made him a marker, even though they didn't mark their own graves."

"Back in Arkansas, in the car, you said Williams was brilliant. Other than the things we'd already found, what did you mean?"

"He *was* brilliant," said a third voice.

They turned. The frail old man in the gray pants and sport coat, and the huge man wearing a dark suit, were a few yards behind them.

"You've answered a long-standing question, Professor Journey," the Judge said. "The Glory Warriors never knew his real name. To us, he was Edward Hiram."

# CHAPTER

# 57

The old bathroom smelled bad, and Ray Tolman found himself wondering if someone had died in here at some point. In this neighborhood, it was a possibility. If he'd been thirty years younger, the thought might have spooked him a bit.

The media started to arrive on Valley Place. The Service, both uniformed and plainclothes, and the Metro Police were very much in evidence. Technicians began doing sound checks at the podium where President Harwell would speak. Tolman waited and listened and wondered if Pat Moore was cursing him from the closet a few feet away.

The floor creaked below. The footsteps turned toward the stairs and started upward. Tolman flattened himself against the bathroom wall. He held his breath when the burly form of Agent Jay Clare came into view. He saw Clare looking around the landing, then moving toward the window that overlooked Valley Place and the community center.

Clare stopped when he saw the rifle. He knelt beside it, looked up and all around him. He raised his wrist radio.

Ray Tolman stepped out of the bathroom. "Agent Clare, put your arm down."

Clare whipped his head around. "What?"

"You're not going to call anyone on the radio, and you're not going to cause a commotion about that rifle."

"I have to—"

Moore came out of the closet, his own weapon held straight out in front of him.

"What is this?" Clare said.

"Listen to me," Ray Tolman said. "If you care about protecting the president, then you're not going to do anything right this minute. There's not going to be any quick movement in this window, and if anyone looks up here, they're not going to see a lot of hubbub. You're not going to call John Canton on the radio and say, 'Gun.' That rifle is unloaded, and both you and it are going to stay right where you are, as if everything was normal. We're going to keep the president safe, but you have to trust me and not cause a commotion up here."

The presidential motorcade was arriving, the police motorcycles and black Cadillac Escalades and the presidential limousine coming to a stop in front of the community center. Ray Tolman could see the ring of agents around the president, and then there was Harwell's silver hair. He was moving, smiling, waving, giving the requisite thumbs-up signs.

Ray Tolman looked out the window. He could see the men on the roof of the community center, sunglasses on, movements smooth and practiced. He moved his gaze a little to the left of the center and saw what he expected to see.

"Agent Clare, this is Special Agent Moore of the FBI," Tolman said. "Pat, you stay here with Agent Clare. Don't move quickly, don't make a lot of noise. I'm going across the street."

As quietly as he could, Tolman crept down the stairs and toward the back of the house. He walked through the gutted kitchen and out through a screen door into the high grass and weeds. A uniformed officer was on patrol there. The uniform checked his supervisory ID, which Tolman had hung from his shirt pocket, and nodded at him.

An alley ran along the back of the house, and Tolman found more men in it. He walked three doors down, then cut through the backyard of another vacant house. At the edge of the house, before stepping into view of the street, he checked his pistol and made sure the safety was off.


On Washington One's television, HNC tracked the motorcade along Valley Place. Ordinarily, this type of short speech wouldn't have warranted live coverage, but since the assassinations of Vandermeer and Darlington, and given the ongoing investigations, all the media were following the president's every move, hanging on his every word.

*Which works to our advantage,* Washington One thought.

As soon as he saw Harwell step out of the limousine, Washington One pulled his computer's microphone to him and pressed the button. The Web signal was already live, all the bases on standby, just waiting for his word.

"Glory Warriors," he said into the microphone. "You are now active."


The Glory Warriors swung into action in the four Washington-area staging centers. They had their body armor on in less than one minute. They checked their firepower and began to move as one toward their transportation—Humvees and choppers. At the Miller Exploration compound in Silver Spring, and at the other centers, pilots settled into their Sea Stallions and opened the side doors in anticipation of the troops coming aboard.

At points along the Potomac, the fleet of twenty-five-foot response boats, very much like the Coast Guard's Defender Class, powered up their engines. Their .50-caliber M2HB machine guns had been inspected and were fully operational.

They all awaited the single word—*"Go!"*—from Washington One, and the invasion would begin.

# CHAPTER

# 58

"E dward Hiram," Journey said. "He would have appreciated the cleverness of it, Edward being Lee's middle name and Hiram being Grant's real first name."

The Judge smiled and tilted his head toward Hudson. "Mr. Hudson, if you please."

Hudson stared at Tolman. "Meg, you should not have done this," he said. "How can you possibly think you have a way out now?"

"You fucking traitor, you're one to talk," Tolman said. "All of this constitutes conspiracy to commit treason. I won't even mention the murders of Vandermeer and Darlington."

"To the contrary," the Judge said. "We're doing what General Lee and General Grant intended to be done for this country."

Hudson stepped forward. "Give me your bag, Meg."

"Why don't you take it from me, Rusty?"

"Let him have it," Journey said. "Each of us has something the other wants."

The Judge laughed. "You overestimate your position, Professor."

Her eyes blazing, Tolman handed her purse to Hudson. He pulled the SIG Sauer pistol from it. "Were you planning to shoot me?"

"Give it back to me and maybe you'll find out," Tolman said.

"You've created quite a little tableau here," the Judge said. "The Indian burial ground, the open grave. A bit like dressing a stage, isn't it?"

"The pages from Grant's book," Journey said. "You have them. Somewhere along the way, you people got hold of them, even though Twain didn't publish them. You stirred up this whole damn thing, this whole bloody coup, based on those pages. Pages Grant regretted writing and never intended to be read."

The Judge smiled again. "Samuel Langhorne Clemens wrote a letter to a friend in which he mentioned the Glory Warriors and the missing pages to Grant's book. Clemens died before the letter was sent, but shortly thereafter, a man named Alexander Madden came across it. He was a newspaper editor from Connecticut, and an acquaintance of the Clemens family. He was curious about what the letter meant. No doubt he decided it would be worth money to find the 'lost pages' of General Grant's memoir. He found them—we don't know how—but instead of selling them to the highest bidder, he was captivated by what he read, by the ideas. Madden resurrected the Glory Warriors and dedicated his life to finding the treaty, the document that would put the Glory Warriors into power."

"And he recruited others to the cause," Tolman said.

"Yes," the Judge said. "One of them was my grandfather, who became leader after Madden died. It passed to my father, and then to me."

"And then there were people like Layton Detheridge, a jeweler from New York City," Journey said.

"Hiram was a brilliant man," the Judge said. He touched the pin on his collar. "Rather than trust an outsider to create our insignia, he found a way to, shall we say, keep it in the family. He recruited others of like mind. When Madden resurrected the Glory Warriors, he went to New York and found the Detheridge family still in the jewelry business. They've been with us since the beginning. The first Glory Warriors were those in the military who were dissatisfied with the way the civilian politicians ran the country. As time went by, my grandfather expanded the focus. Our family had been very successful in land with the westward expansion after the Civil War, and by the time Madden died and my grandfather took over the

Glory Warriors, we were billionaires. We McMartins had the money and the influence to organize. My grandfather, and then my father, were well connected. My father knew this country's elected leaders were corrupt and immoral and inept, and he knew we would some-day replace them, but he cultivated them. It's quite an irony, isn't it? Becoming connected to those we would replace when Grant and Lee's vision was fulfilled. I, of course, as you know, expanded the universe even further, buying into the media industry. Over time, we realized that it would be to our advantage to have both military and civilian personnel involved, to broaden our influence. I ex-panded my father's vision." The Judge's eyes seemed to lose focus for a moment. "He spent his life waiting. Just waiting."

A breeze kicked up dirt around them. The Judge turned his head, as if hearing something on the wind. When he looked at them again, his eyes were clear. "I took action. Yes, we had to wait to find the documents that gave us our authority. But I wanted to make sure we were ready when this day came."

"So you kept on recruiting, year after year," Journey said, "and searching for the document all the time."

"Yes. We put cells in place in major cities, created teams of mem-bers with different areas of expertise. Bankers, accountants, infor-mation technology specialists, educators, in addition to our military and operational people. We refined our mission, our tactical focus."

"When you wanted someone," Tolman said, "you could create a paper trail to show that they were dead, just wipe them off the face of the earth. Like the ones you sent to attack Nick. But you still paid them, and that money trail had to lead somewhere. Like Kevin Lane—his money went to his wife. That's how we found you. That's how I knew that their deaths in Iraq were faked." She looked at Hudson. "How did they get you into this, Rusty?"

"It doesn't matter," Hudson said. "In any organization, there is a person like me. You should understand that, Meg."

"Oh, yes. You know contracts and budgets and accounts and all those things. You're perfect for this, aren't you?"

Hudson dropped his eyes from Tolman's. He held her pistol loosely in his hand.

"The pages," Journey said. "Show me the pages Grant wrote."

The Judge gestured toward the mound of earth. "Hiram was buried with the signature page. Interesting. He sent us on quite an odyssey, only to have it lead right back here. This seems to be a place of both beginnings and endings, doesn't it?" The old man's hand touched his chest, then reached in his pocket and withdrew the plastic bag with the papers inside.

Journey took the bag, opened it, and pulled out the pages. The plastic bag fell to the ground at his feet. Tolman edged a few steps closer to him. Journey smoothed the paper. On top was the seal of the Glory Warriors. He turned the page and began to read the words of the dying Ulysses S. Grant.

# CHAPTER
# 59

*It is with much deliberation and some hesitation that I approach the subject of the Glory Warriors, but the matter weighs most heavily on my mind and I feel that in the interest of a true unburdening, it should be addressed. I have spent many years considering whether the people should know of this episode, and am by no means certain of the prudence of revealing it even now.*

*It was around 1 November 1864, that the man first approached me. The troops were in winter camps, and I had made my headquarters in the cabin of Dr. Eppes in City Point. It was late at night, with considerable chill in the air, when one of my staff woke me with the news of a man proceeding through the picket lines and requesting an interview with me. I tried to put them off, but the staff insisted the man would not leave without speaking to me.*

*My first impression, of course, was that he was a spy, and I treated the first meeting as such. I ushered him into the cabin and asked the staff to wait outside. I had no fear of my life, as both my sword and pistol were close at hand. When I inquired as to his name, he replied with a smile, "Edward Hiram."*

*I confess, these many years after the fact, that I first believed him* to be mad. *This was not his name, of course, as he had made a clever conjunction of General Lee's and my names, but he would give no other. When I inquired as to his purpose, he said directly, "General, the war is ending. Victory is at hand, is it not?"*

*He hastily informed me that he had served in Mexico with Major McCulloch's company of scouts. I queried him for details, and he was knowledgeable about the engagements at both Monterrey and Buena Vista. He spoke as a man who was there, with some specific authority and understanding of the situations. I did not believe he could have gained such insights from newspapers. I suspended judgment for the moment. As a brother officer from Mexico, I could at least offer him a few moments of my attention. He said that he was now a man of some means and influence, and that he found himself in an attitude of unease concerning the state of the country, both North and South, in the wake of this conflict. He affirmed that while in fact the Union may emerge victorious on the battlefield, that matters may well be acrimonious into the next century if provisions are not made for the postwar government.*

*My own thoughts had lately been oriented this way as well. How would North and South reunite after a conflict of this type? How would we be governed? Would the civil government have the authority and capacity to direct national affairs? There would be many unstable elements in the time to come. There would be those who would do the government ill, in order to foster further instability, to fight another war, perhaps one more dangerous than the military conflict.*

*I entertained all these thoughts as the man stood before me, and he suggested a course of action. When I inquired as to why I should heed any thoughts of his on the matter, as he no longer wore a uniform, he replied, "Because I do not wear the uniform of either side, General, is precisely why you should hear what I have to say."*

*I bade him go then, as I needed rest. But I did not rest that night, nor for many of those nights to come. Through the autumn I thought of "Edward Hiram." I did not know his true name, I did not know where to find him, I did not know from where he came. Yet I could never quite leave off the notions he had articulated.*

*Three days before Christmas, he appeared again during a cold*

rain, and again late at night. When we were alone, he inquired as to
whether I had considered his words. I asked him what he proposed.

"To reclaim the glory of America," he replied.

He envisioned a plan after the war had reached its conclusion,
one that would be enacted if the Washington government was
rendered without a leader in each of the three branches in short order.
Such circumstances would naturally constitute a time of crisis.
Hiram insisted that there would be no need for the plan to be enacted
unless the leaders of all three branches were removed by force. Then
and only then would action be taken.

He proposed a group to be named the Glory Warriors, who
would act in governance of the nation in such time of political crisis
until the crisis abated and the civil government could be restored.
This group would comprise men from both Union and Confederacy,
so as to ensure that it was seen neither as a Northern solution or a
Southern solution, but rather a national solution.

Hiram's proposals gave me much pause, and I considered them
duly. I am a soldier, and as such I am sworn to protect the civil
government of the United States of America. Yet, I confess that I did
not know at that time what lay ahead, and I feared the uncertainty
of the coming years.

When Hiram told me that he would move between General
Lee's camp and my own, and would speak to General Lee just as he
had spoken to me, I was inclined to hear what General Lee might
say on the matter. I knew him to be an honorable man, misguided
though his cause might be. If Hiram could gain access to me, he could
no doubt accomplish the same with General Lee. Of course, General
Lee had been in Mexico as well, in the days when we all wore the
same uniform. I informed Hiram that I would hear what General
Lee might have to say on the subject.

At the same time, and unbeknownst to Hiram, I began to
communicate with Lee as well, without benefit of his intermediary.
We shared a concern for the future, and likewise shared a mistrust of
Hiram. In the end, Lee and I agreed that no matter the outcome of
the fighting in the spring, that a gesture of unity from North and
South that allowed for control of the civil government was in order.

Through my own intelligence network, I discovered a number of *men willing to take on the mantle of the Glory Warriors. Lee did the same. Small numbers of weapons began to be removed from arsenals in the various theaters of the war, and they were routed to the frontier, where little note would be taken. A pair of brothers from Missouri, one who fought in engagements for the Union and one who served the Confederacy, were discharged and sent to the frontier for the purposes of managing the arsenal. They in turn made contact with one of the local natives who would serve to guide Hiram at the appropriate time.*

    *The details of Five Forks, Petersburg, and Appomattox are well known, as is the outcome of the war. Hiram had proceeded to draw up a device by way of explaining the circumstances under which the Glory Warriors would act, and how they would act at such time. He brought the papers to Appomattox on the day I received Lee's surrender.*

    *General Lee and I met Hiram in the McLean home. Lee and I affixed our signatures to the device Hiram had made, with all its implications. Hiram had even created a great seal for the Glory Warriors, which was embossed into the first page of the device. He had additional copies for General Lee and myself. Hiram had clearly expended much thought on the design—Union and Confederate swords crossed at their points, a single star between them to represent unity of purpose, and the most arresting image of all, the American eagle depicted in red, a symbol of the blood that had been shed throughout this land. I saved this seal, have retained it through the intervening years, and have attached it to these pages. It has been a stark remembrance of those final days of the war.*

    *Likewise Hiram had established a relationship with a New York City jeweler by the name of Detheridge, who began to craft a series of gold insignia, by which the Glory Warriors would identify each other, wherever they might be found. I witnessed Hiram wearing one of the insignia for the first time that day at Appomattox.*

    *We sent Hiram on his way west, and as he departed, before the staffs were allowed in to witness the surrender of the Army of Northern Virginia, I said to Lee, "I do not trust him," to which General Lee made the reply, "Nor do I, General. But what choice have we? We have made this bargain with him. We do not know what will occur after today."*

*I informed General Lee of my orders on the matter of "Edward Hiram." General Lee was a pious man, and he took a moment of prayer yet again, then said, "God forgive us."*

*It is an irony, is it not, that in war I ordered many thousands of men into situations of almost certain death—the debacle of Cold Harbor still weighs upon me—and yet I am more greatly burdened by the fact that I ordered one single man—a man not even under my command—to be put to death. For, in the end, I believe that this man "Hiram," though creating an idea that may indeed have had merit in its time, was himself as unstable as what he foresaw for the government.*

*The brothers from Missouri were under orders to detain "Hiram" when he arrived, to receive the device General Lee and I had signed, to secure it with the weaponry, and to remove "Hiram."*

*May God forgive me. As I will meet Him soon, I confess that I face the prospect with some amount of trepidation.*

# CHAPTER

# 60

Journey pictured Ulysses S. Grant, dying of throat cancer and in excruciating pain, wrapped in a blanket in the summer of 1885, twenty years after the events he related, sitting on the back porch of the home in Mount McGregor, New York, scratching out these words.

Only then the general had reconsidered, thinking that perhaps the country might not be well served by knowing about the Glory Warriors, about what he and Robert E. Lee and "Edward Hiram" had done from fear of what would follow the Civil War.

"Fascinating, isn't it?" the Judge remarked. "And quite clear what Grant and Lee intended."

Journey looked up. He'd almost forgotten where he was, and that right here, right now, were modern-day Glory Warriors who had twisted Grant and Lee's vision. He felt in his pocket and touched the page J. T. Webster had faxed. A strong wind gust came up from the south, and he felt it on his face.

"Is it?" Journey said.

"Come now, Professor, you've read the pages. The document the generals signed has the weight of treaty. 'To supersede all others,' as the first page says, and the Lieber Code adds further weight to it. I do know a thing or two about the law."

Journey stared at the old man. "And you've been looking for these pages all these years. A pity Grant didn't help you along by mentioning where on the frontier the guns were being stored . . . where they sent Williams."

"It would have made our lives considerably easier," the Judge said. "But General Grant, of course, was too clever to give away details, even in a memoir written twenty years after the fact. The 'frontier' could have been anywhere from Texas to California. We searched for decades." He swept his hand around. "And this small, obscure little piece of Indian Territory held the answers for all this time. Grant and Lee were remarkably visionary."

Tolman was still looking at the pages Journey held. "The two brothers killed Williams after he got here."

"And the local Indian they'd hired to be his guide buried him here," Journey said. "That has to be what happened. The Chickasaw were peaceful people. They were farmers. When the Civil War broke out, their people were building schools and farms and becoming merchants and teachers. They would have thought it dishonorable that Williams was shot down like that."

"And you have led us here to tell us that the page with Grant and Lee's signatures was buried with him," the Judge said.

"He gave the brothers the document," Journey said, "but he didn't give them all of it. We know that now. He sensed that Grant and Lee didn't trust him—maybe he even knew he was going to be killed when he delivered the document. So he broke it up into three pieces. But the brothers couldn't have known that. They were supposed to 'secure' the document. They took what Williams gave them, and then they killed him, ripped off the G.W. pin to conceal Williams's identity, and to keep it safe, they buried all of it alongside the guns in a copper-coated tin box to protect it against the elements."

Hudson nodded, speaking for the first time since the Judge had handed Journey the pages. "But they didn't realize the document was incomplete."

"Maybe Williams gave it to the Chickasaw guide before he died," Tolman said, "and he buried all of Williams's property with him."

"There's no way to know," Journey said. "There's also no way to know what kind of shape it's in. Just because the first page was buried in an airtight metal box, there's no guarantee about this one."

The Judge's face darkened. "It's time to find out," he said.

Dallas One Silver lay prone behind a two-foot-high cenotaph at the edge of the old post cemetery. The tomb was brick, topped by stone, and a sign before it read CENOTAPH OF GEN. W. M. BELKNAP, DIED 10 NOV 1851. The monument concealed Silver perfectly, and he was able to peek from behind it and take aim at the other side of the Chickasaw burial ground.

He checked positions with his team members: Gold was in the restored South Barracks, closer to the highway, on the second floor, taking the high ground. Bronze was at the guardhouse, covering the fort's main entry.

Silver was under orders not to act until Journey had given the Judge the papers. But now the Judge had just given Journey some papers and watched while Journey and the woman read them.

He edged his finger off the trigger of the H&K assault pistol, still holding his position. He had a clear shot at Nick Journey's head, but he knew he could not shoot. Not yet. When the time came, Kevin Lane would make sure Journey knew he was paying the price for the death of Dallas One Gold—Michael Standridge. Michael's death would not go unpunished. Silver would see justice done when he killed Nick Journey. He couldn't wait.

"Mr. Hudson, the gun," the Judge said, and Hudson handed him the SIG. "I'm an old man, but I still know how to handle a pistol. Mr. Hudson, you and Dr. Journey will lift the coffin out and open it."

Hudson and Journey stepped over the low rock wall to the side of the open grave. The coffin was crude, a few simple, unvarnished slabs of wood nailed together, and the effects of the shallow grave and nearly a century and a half of the elements had rotted the wood almost to the consistency of paper.

Hudson kicked some dirt to one side and bent at the far end, while Journey reached for the end closest to the wall.

"That's right," the Judge said. He gestured for Tolman to walk in front of him, and together they moved to the edge of the wall, standing just outside it.

Journey and Hudson wrapped their hands around the coffin and began to lift. As soon as they touched it, some of the rotting wood at the sides fell away. Hudson jumped, dropping his end, and as it crashed back into the earth, the other side and ends splintered apart.

"Open the top," the Judge said. "Pull the boards off and open it."

Journey stepped to one side and pulled at one of the top pieces of wood. It came off in his hand and he put it aside, then stared down at the skeleton of Samuel Williams.

The bones were gray. Clods of clay adhered to the ribs, the neck, the head. There was no clothing, the fabric having long since decomposed, but Journey saw three buttons on the bottom of the coffin. Brass, he suspected. Brass buttons from the coat of a wealthy banker.

He ran his hands along the sides of the coffin, even touched the arm and leg bones. More of the wood flaked away under his touch. "Oh my God," Journey whispered. His face contorted, he bowed his head and placed it in his hands.

"What?" Tolman said. "Nick, what?"

"The page!" the Judge demanded.

Journey looked up at the Judge. "It's not here. The signature page is gone."

# CHAPTER
# 61

Washington Three alternated his gaze between the podium in front of the Anacostia Community Center and the vacant house across the street. He was in the V of the trunk of a towering oak tree at the edge of the community center. The branches drooped both onto the community center property and the house next door, but there was enough of a break in the leaves for him to have a clear line of sight to the spot where President James Harwell's head would be in a few seconds.

But he needed the diversion that the rifle in the vacant house would bring. He needed panic in the few moments *before* he took his shot. He needed the window of those few seconds when Jay Clare called "Gun!" and all heads turned across the street, before the president was mobbed by DeBacker and Alley and the other agents who were on duty within a few feet of Harwell. The timing had to be precise, and he would be down and running toward Clare and the vacant house along with everyone else, his pistol drawn and ready.

Still, there was no movement from the old house. He saw Clare go inside, but nothing happened. He'd calculated it exactly—he knew how long it would take his fellow agent to climb the stairs, find the rifle by the window, and sound the alarm.

Harwell was ascending the steps to the podium, shaking hands with the community center's executive director, the ward's city councilman, a couple of HUD officials, in all half a dozen or so people who would be on the podium.

Three glanced back to the house. *Nothing.* What the hell had happened to Clare?

Several wild thoughts rolled through him: one of the local drug dealers could have wandered into the house after he put the rifle there last night, and taken it home as a prize. But no, the neighborhood was locked down. No one without the proper ID could get in or out of a three-block radius. Maybe Clare hadn't gone straight upstairs; maybe he was doing a final downstairs sweep, just to be thorough. In which case, all Three had to do was be patient for a few more seconds. . . .

He didn't have a few more seconds. The city councilman was at the microphone, talking to the assembled crowd and media. Three scanned the street, watching the invited crowd, recognizing the Service people sprinkled throughout.

"Damn," Three whispered. He couldn't wait any longer. Without the diversion, his risks had just increased. But the window was closing. He had to take his shot.

President Harwell stepped toward the microphone.


Washington One never took his eyes off the TV screen, watching James Harwell's last moments unfold in Anacostia. The reports from the field had been coming in steadily, by phone, by text, by Web. The invasion force was not overwhelming in numbers, but it was equipped well, and the Glory Warriors had the advantage of the chaos that was about to erupt.

Then the Judge would step into the panic and fear and confusion with his commanding presence on television, on radio, the Web. He would explain what was happening. He would be a voice of reason amongst the clamoring masses. He would have the documents in his hands—the pages signed by two of the most towering figures in American history.

The regional bases would move their forces into the streets of the cities to keep order. The second wave would roll into D.C. from the Blue Ridge Mountains and start taking the representatives of the old government into custody.

Washington One watched Harwell on the TV. The president was about to speak.

"Do it," Washington One whispered.


Ray Tolman emerged into the street three houses down from where he had left Clare, Moore, and the rifle. He stood still for five seconds, watching the tree. He saw the leaves move a little, and a momentary flash of color.

He sighed. His initial theory was wrong—it wasn't Clare, the guy with the high blood pressure and sleep problems, but Delham, the one with the reputation as a smart-ass.

*Always watch out for the smart-ass,* Ray Tolman thought; then he broke into a jog toward the opposite sidewalk.

The president was at the microphone. People were applauding, Harwell was smiling, picking out faces in the crowd and pointing to them with the classic politician's *Good to see you, glad you came!* gesture. The leaves in the tree moved again. Tolman ran faster.


Washington Three glanced once more at the house. He saw no movement. No heads were turned. The block was calm. John Canton would be pleased at how smoothly the event was going.

He was out of time.

He nudged his finger onto the trigger. The pistol was good up to 150 yards, and the tree was a little over half that far from where the president stood. Three knew the exact distance—he'd walked it off yesterday, right in front of all his colleagues.

"Boy, did you fuck up, Delham."

Washington Three jerked at the voice below him.

"You shouldn't have asked for a change in the duty roster at the last minute. You should have left the tree to the uniforms. I know Canton was pleased that an agent of your experience was willing to climb the tree at an event like this, but hey . . . these things get noticed."

The nose of Three's pistol dropped half an inch.

"And your friend Clare? That was a shitty thing to do to him, to try to get me to think he was the Glory Warrior." He bit down hard on the last two words.

Timothy Delham looked down at the face of Ray Tolman, and the automatic pistol aimed at his head.

"I have a better shot than you do," Tolman said. "Want me to take my shot? No? Then you're going to very slowly climb down to the next branch and you're going to give me the weapon, butt first. I may be old, but I don't miss at this range."

"I don't—"

"You're going to come down or I'm going to blow your fucking head off," Ray Tolman said. "You're going to come down and then we're going to talk. We're going to talk about your Glory Warriors and treason and murder. But first things first—get your ass down from there. Now move. Nice and slow."

The failure seared through Washington Three. For a moment, he thought of swinging the pistol around, shooting down through the leaves at Tolman, then going back to the president. But as soon as he shot Tolman, the president would be covered and he would never get to take the shot at Harwell.

He slid his leg down to the next limb. His shot was gone. He would never be able to take it.

"One branch at a time," Ray Tolman said.

Washington Three inched a little farther down. Ray Tolman was speaking again, the gun never wavering. "And the whole gun-in-the-mouth thing is not some noble, honorable act," Tolman said. "I know you're thinking about it. At this point, you have a little possibility of redemption. If you eat your gun right now, all you'll ever be was the guy who was going to sell out his country, but failed and couldn't even do that right. If you talk to me, the world might have a little different take on who and what you are."

Washington Three looked down at him, saw the man's eyes.

"Come on," Ray Tolman said. "Time to go."

Timothy Delham climbed down from the tree and handed Ray Tolman his gun.

"Now," Tolman said. "*Now* we're going to talk."

# CHAPTER
# 62

The Judge extended the gun in front of him, as far as his arms would go. "You're lying," he said.

Journey whipped around to face him as another wind gust stirred the dirt around them. "Look for yourself! Go ahead, Mc-Martin! The damn thing's not there!"

"Hudson," Jackson McMartin said.

Hudson bent his bulk down and repeated Journey's movements, taking care not to touch the bones, averting his eyes from the head, and holding his breath. "There's no paper here," he said.

"Where is it?" McMartin demanded.

"It's not here?" Tolman said. "Jesus Christ, Nick, it's not here?"

"I must have those signatures," McMartin said. "You've hidden them somewhere."

"Where?" Journey shouted into the wind. "Where would I have hidden them?" He pointed toward the grave. "Look at this, Mc-Martin! This is where Williams fell. Those brothers from Missouri killed Williams after he got here. Maybe the guide took the page, maybe one of the brothers took it, maybe Williams was on a steamboat on the Mississippi River before he ever got here and a pickpocket grabbed it from him! What more do you want? *It's gone!*"

Tolman inched a few steps toward the corner of the rock wall. She kept her eyes on Hudson—he was staring into the hole, at the bones of Samuel Williams. Two more steps, three. She saw the handle of the shovel on the ground, protruding from the edge of the wall.

McMartin's face was red. Veins throbbed on his forehead. His white hair whipped in the wind. "The Glory Warriors must have the signatures!"

"Sir," Hudson said, "I do not think—"

"We must have them! As soon as the president is dead, we'll show them to the people. We're ready to move into control of the media, to show the people . . . they are all we need to put the treaty into law, to assure our position. I will make the speech to the people—"

"No," Journey said, his voice lower than a few moments earlier.

The other three looked at him.

"Mr. McMartin, you are a traitor. Nothing more. You've cloaked yourself in this mantle of legality, telling yourself and your followers that if only you had all the parts of the document, your coup would be viewed as legitimate."

"Don't try to bait me, Professor," McMartin said. "All the pages together constitute a legal document, with the power of a treaty. General Order Number One Hundred, the Lieber Code, even lays out the 'hostile country' standard. The Glory Warriors clearly meet the standard. We *must* act."

"You don't understand history," Journey said. His eyes shifted for a moment. Tolman had gained another six inches. Journey lowered his voice. "Grant and Lee never intended for the Glory Warriors to truly be in power in America. The whole idea, as Williams put it forth, was a temporary solution. It was only to get through the very difficult times Grant and Lee thought would come after the war. You read Grant's pages—they were worried about political extremists. And who knows? If John Wilkes Booth's conspiracy had been successful at decapitating the government, instead of beginning and ending with Lincoln, the Glory Warriors may have come into power for a while right then, just days after Appomattox. But the fact is, they didn't, and weren't meant to."

"You're contradicting what you've just read," McMartin said. "Grant was—"

"Yes, Grant and Lee bought what Samuel Williams was selling, at least for a while. I think Williams truly cared about what the country was about to go through. No one knew how Reconstruction would play out. No one could possibly fathom what was going to happen. So Williams's intentions were good, but ultimately, Williams was unstable and Grant knew it. Williams was a man with a lot of money and time on his hands. Brilliant, yes, but there was no way the Glory Warriors were going to be a long-term government."

"You're speculating."

"Am I?" Journey reached into his pocket and pulled out the fax from J. T. Webster.

McMartin's eyes narrowed.

"Here," Journey said, and extended his arm across the wall. "Read it for yourself."

"What is this?" McMartin said.

"In Grant's memoir, the missing pages that were taken from Charles Webster's family sometime after Mark Twain died, the part that has to do with the Glory Warriors stops at the bottom of that page, where Grant writes that he hopes he will be forgiven and he's facing his end 'with much trepidation.'"

"I've read them many times, thank you."

"Sounds like an ending, doesn't it? A man unburdening his soul." Journey shook the paper in the breeze. "But maybe not. This page was somehow separated from the rest of them, and it stayed with Webster's family all this time. It makes no sense at all, unless you already know about the Glory Warriors and the treaty and all of it. Then you can see what Grant and Lee really intended."

McMartin reached for the pages.

*With my own life fading, I take the smallest degree of comfort that when agreeing to the provisions detailed in the pages preceding, we asserted there should be a finite period of time in which the Glory Warriors might act.*

*Our most pressing concern was to be the state of the government in the years directly following the cessation of military hostilities.*

*The Glory Warriors, as explained, could exist as temporary stewards of the government until a certain time had elapsed. After some discussion, we agreed to the period of six years from the date of the surrender at Appomattox. Our common feeling was that this would be sufficient time for the government to have weathered the storms that might well befall it.*

*Of course, there were plentiful difficulties, but never to approach the degree we had feared. The time passed, the Union was indeed reunited, and the Glory Warriors were no more. They were birthed of necessity, of the need to prepare for all possibilities, and it is a happy circumstance that the bleakest of these occurrences never came to pass. The Glory Warriors were allowed to fade into oblivion.*

McMartin shook his head. "No," he whispered.

"You've been telling yourselves for all these years that you had a legal, legitimate right to suspend the Constitution, and you even decided at some point to hurry things along, to bring about the situations Williams and Grant and Lee feared. But Grant knew— –he *knew*—that the country was stronger than that. He knew it wouldn't need such a force for a long period, that they had only to get through the dark days immediately following the war."

"It's a forgery," McMartin said.

"It's *not* a forgery," Journey said. "You've read Grant's pages. The handwriting is the same. It is exactly the same. Ulysses Grant wrote that, and it proves that the Glory Warriors weren't supposed to exist after 1871. Six years . . . six years, that's all! You know what happened in six years? Robert E. Lee was dead and Ulysses S. Grant was president of the United States. There was no need for you then, and there's no need for you now."

McMartin let the nose of the pistol drop. His knees bent. "You won't stop us. Too many have sacrificed too much. We have . . . *I* have—"

Journey said nothing. Tolman took another step. McMartin's hand—the one holding the fax page—went to his chest, crumpling the page. "You—" he said, and his voice was a paperlike rustle. His eyes lost focus again. His lips moved, but no sound came out. Journey thought he formed the words *Don't fail.*

* * *

Silver had watched as Journey handed the Judge the paper, and the Judge read it. He saw the Judge's face change, saw him wobble as if his legs were unsteady. He saw him crumple the paper.

Silver stood, took two steps forward in the direction of the cemeteries, then stopped and planted his legs. He sighted the H&K. At this range, he would not miss.

"Journey!" he shouted.


McMartin jumped at the sound of Silver's voice, his back arching as if he'd been poked with something sharp. But it wasn't the voice of the young Glory Warrior—it was his father.

*Come on, son.*

*Father? But I failed. The Glory Warriors—*

*Are no more. But I'm here now. Time to go, son.*

McMartin's legs were unsteady and a pain was creeping up his left arm. He felt light-headed.

*Son?* Jackson McMartin thought. He swiveled his head toward the voice, then he turned and toppled across the rock wall.


As soon as Tolman saw the motion out of her right eye—the dirt rising around the cenotaph between the two trees, the man she recognized from the SCCO surveillance video as Sergeant Kevin Lane—she lunged forward, grabbing the wooden handle of the shovel. She planted her left foot on the wall, then pushed off with her right foot. As she lunged forward, she brought the shovel around and smashed the metal head of it into Hudson's kneecap.

Hudson expelled air in a grunt, and she thought she heard him say, "Meg." Her momentum propelled her forward and she landed on her butt in the pile of earth, then found herself rolling, falling into the grave, and coming to rest on top of the bones of Samuel Williams.

\* \* \*

Silver watched the heads turn, but didn't see the look of both surprise and pain that crossed the Judge's face. He was focused on Nick Journey, how the man had thwarted the Glory Warriors twice before, and how Michael Standridge's body had looked as the car smashed into it with Journey at the wheel.

Silver squeezed the trigger just as the Judge fell in front of Journey, filling Silver's vision.


McMartin was already falling, hand clutched to his chest, his face gray, when his neck exploded in a spray of blood and bone, covering Journey. McMartin made no sound as his lifeless body tumbled at Journey's feet. For an insane moment, Journey wasn't sure where he was—in the parking lot at SCCO with Pete Parsons falling toward him, or in a Fort Washita burial ground with Jackson McMartin, American media giant and leader of the Glory Warriors, coming to rest in front of him.

"No!" yelled the man with the gun.


The gun roared again, and Journey dived over the rock wall, outside the burial ground. His already-injured foot caught on the wall and sent needles of pain up and down his body.

Another shot exploded into the rock wall.


Tolman didn't know how she got out of the hole.

All she knew was that she felt the bones snapping like dry leaves under her, and that she smelled damp earth and rotten wood. She angled her body around, breaking more of Samuel Williams's ribs, still holding the shovel.

"Meg, now you've gone too far," Hudson said, and she thought she heard his voice catch. He wobbled over her, and she remembered all the times they'd posed for the RIO departmental photo, arms around each other, everyone laughing at them—six feet seven standing next to five feet one.

He stepped toward her and she brought up her arms, swinging the shovel. The point struck Hudson's foot, the one opposite the knee she'd already wounded. She hit him again, ramming the point of the shovel down into his foot.

His hands reached for her neck. Tolman clawed her way backwards out of the hole, dropped the shovel to pull herself out, then grabbed it again, just out of Hudson's reach.

"You miserable son of a bitch," Tolman said, and swung the shovel again, as hard as she could.

*Being short is sometimes an advantage,* she thought as the shovel slammed into Hudson's groin. The big man grunted, and Rusty Hudson fell to his knees.

Dallas One Gold had positioned himself on the second-story veranda of the South Barracks building. A single room at the top of the steps was open to the public, and Gold had found high ceilings, a couple of wooden tables and benches, and a stone fireplace scorched black. Incongruous with the fireplace's appearance was a sign held in place by masking tape: NO FIRES IN THIS FIREPLACE.

Gold patrolled all sides of the veranda and could see most of the property, from Highway 199 to the south, to the ruins of the West Barracks a short distance west of his position. He hadn't been able to see Silver, though, once they were in position and waiting. The cemetery area was at the far north end of the fort, on the other side of the visitors' center.

When he heard shots fired, Gold scrambled down the wooden steps, cradling his rifle, and began to jog across the old parade ground toward the road. Calculating the direction of the gunfire, he ran between the visitors' center and the Cooper cabin, passing the portable toilet that stood between the two structures. As he emerged from the cover of the visitors' center, he heard a door slam and a man in uniform stepped around the corner of the building, holding a riot shotgun. At this range, it was a devastating weapon.

*The building,* he thought. *We didn't recon the interior of the visitors' center.*

"Don't move, asshole," Scott Parsons said. "Drop it or I'll do to you what you people did to my little brother. Just give me an excuse."

*Shit,* Gold thought, and carefully placed his weapon on the ground in front of him.

"Yes, sir, that's right," Parsons said. "On the ground."

Gold lay down and Parsons cuffed him, then jiggled the switch of the police radio that hung on his shirt. "Ricky, I got the one from the barracks."

"The boys and I got the one at the entrance," his brother called back.

Parsons put the heel of his boot in Gold's back. "Welcome to Fort Washita," he said.

# CHAPTER

# 63

In Silver Spring, the commander of the Miller Exploration facility stared at his computer. The feed was live. Washington One's direction to go should already have come down. Something was wrong.

Across the office, his second in command said, "What the hell's going on?"

"What?" said the commander.

"Harwell left the podium." He was watching the TV feed. "Alive and in one piece."

"Oh my God." He pressed the button on his computer mic. "Sir, are you there?"

The commander looked out the back window toward the chopper pad. The men were loaded. The rotors were turning. The force was ready. They only needed the order from Washington One.

"Sir?" he said again into the microphone. "This is Silver Spring calling Washington One. Are you there, sir?"

"Do we stand down?" the second asked. "What do we do? Someone screwed up." He crashed a fist onto the desk, rattling the TV. *"What do we fucking do now?"*

"I don't know," the commander said, and turned back to the microphone. "Washington One, are you there?"

* * *

Washington One sat in his secure command center at the outer edge of the Glory Warriors' Arlington complex and watched Harwell speak, finish to polite applause, and leave the stage. In a moment, the president was back in his limousine and leaving Valley Place.

"What happened?" he whispered; then it became a shout. *"What happened?"*

From behind his closed office door, the voice of one of his assistants: "Are you all right, sir?"

*No, I'm not all right. Washington Three failed, Harwell is still at the head of the government, and I haven't heard from the Judge.* "I'm fine," he called.

The thoughts tumbled around him—he could still order the invasion. The troops were all ready. . . .

But the president still lived. The entire operation was planned around the deaths of all three: Vandermeer, Darlington, Harwell. They were to sweep into Washington to assume control of a government whose leaders had been removed. In the chaos, they would bring order.

The motorcade was calmly making its way down the block. The president was waving. There was no sign of Washington Three.

Washington One picked up the phone. The Judge was somewhere, getting the signature pages—he hadn't said where—and he never carried a cell phone. He tried Washington Two. Brent Graves picked up immediately.

"What happened?" Washington One said.

"No clue. Harwell wasn't to leave the podium. After all this . . ." The man's voice broke. "It's all over. We won't get another chance, and we're about to be exposed. Three will talk; you know he will."

One nodded. "He's always been the weakest link."

"He'll talk. They probably have our names already, our addresses."

"Calm down. The Judge—"

"Is nowhere! It's over. All of this, all these years, and it's over."

One heard a scrabbling sound on the phone. "What are you doing?"

"I'm not letting them come after me. I'm not letting them call me a terrorist or a traitor."

One heard the unmistakable sound of a pistol cocking. "No! Don't be a coward! Remember what we stand for. They can't touch us."

"Maybe they can't touch you, but I'm a nobody. Just a glorified security guard, right? After all this . . ."

Washington Two's voice trailed away. One heard the shot and the body falling.

"Damn you," he said as he put the phone down.

One became slowly aware of the voices from all the staging centers and regional bases, clamoring out of his computer's speakers. *Do we stand down? What has happened? We're ready to attack, sir. Sir? Where are you?* He could hear engines and helicopter rotors in the background. Just one word . . .

Did the Judge have the signatures? He'd said he was personally going to take them from Nick Journey, and then he would address the nation.

But now . . .

He reached for the microphone, held it tightly for a moment, then set it down and turned off the speakers. The room fell into silence.

He could run. He owned property in Belize. His wife's family had a small villa in Italy. He had options. Or, he could take the route Brent Graves had taken. One shot and no pain, no embarrassment, no misunderstanding.

*No.*

*I am an American, an officer, a Glory Warrior. I was doing what is right for my country. I will not run, and I will not die.*

"I will not run," he said aloud.

Then Navy Admiral Carter Smith, vice chair of the U.S. joint chiefs of staff, sat back to wait.

T olman's SIG was still in McMartin's hand, but Journey couldn't get to it. The wall lay between him and McMartin's body, and the man with the gun was closing. He seemed to be ignoring Tolman and Hudson completely. Then Journey realized who he was—it was the second man from SCCO, the partner of the man he'd killed with the car.

He crawled along the back of the wall, listening for the assassin's footsteps. His own foot throbbed. He could never outrun the man, not in this condition—and probably, he mused, not even if his foot was completely healthy. No, he couldn't outrun him—that was not a battle he could win.

He lay still for a moment.

"Journey!" the man shouted again.

*He's not going anywhere, not for a while,* Tolman thought, looking at Hudson. He was on his side, hands shielding his groin. Blood was seeping out of his shoe. She maneuvered around the edge of the grave, watching the Judge's body, her gun still in his fingers.

She shambled around the edge, reached the body, ducked behind it. She reached for the gun.


*It's out of control*, Silver thought. And then he thought: *I'm not Dallas
One Silver anymore. I can be plain old Kevin Lane from Pineville again.
The Judge is dead, the Glory Warriors are compromised.*

All that was left was Kevin Lane, and the knowledge that his
friend, his *brother*, Michael Standridge, had been killed. Lane had
been trained to leave no man behind, and yet he had left Standridge
behind on the SCCO campus. He had failed Michael.

He couldn't see Journey—the professor had disappeared behind
the rock wall. The short woman was moving along the Judge's body.

*The Judge.*

*I killed the Judge.*

Lane squeezed his eyes closed for a moment. The air seemed to
spin around him. A wind gust tugged at his sleeves.

He felt the Glory Warriors pin on his collar. Lane grabbed it and
ripped it from his shirt, taking a good chunk of the fabric with it.

He sighted his pistol. The woman wasn't important. The big
man wasn't important. He was Kevin Lane again, and Kevin Lane
knew what he had to do.


Journey reached the end of the wall, close to the road. He braced
himself against it, and a couple of loose rocks fell to the ground in
front of him.

He could hear Tolman moving, and he wondered what she was
thinking, what direction her mind was going, how she saw the
situation unfolding. Journey adjusted his position and peeked
around the corner of the wall. The man was coming in long strides.
He was in front of the white picket fence that surrounded the main
cemetery.

Journey cocked his head. His hearing, so intensely attuned,
picked up distant steps. They were coming from the direction of the
visitors' center, a walk, a jog, a run. Boots crunched on gravel.

The assassin had stopped. Journey watched him. He saw the little glint of gold in the sun.

G.W.

The pin. The place this had all started, with the discovery of the guns and the document and the pin, just a few hundred yards from where he lay crouched against this rock wall.

The assassin ripped the pin from his shirt, dropped it in the dirt, and started to raise his gun again. Journey's hand brushed one of the rocks that had fallen off the wall.

*I don't hide,* he thought.

He had one chance, and only two or three seconds to gain an advantage. His left hand closed on the rock. He lifted himself up, stood to his full height, and turned.

The assassin looked at him, blinked, and sighted his weapon

Journey reached back and threw the rock as hard as he could. His follow-through was exact, the release point perfect, and the rock struck the assassin on the side of the head.

The man spun halfway around, but didn't lose his grip on the pistol. Then Journey could see Tolman—he had bought her the precious seconds she needed to get the gun from McMartin's hand, and now it was rock-steady in her own hand.

"Drop it!" Tolman screamed. "Drop the weapon!"

Ricky Parsons ran into Journey's field of vision from the left. "Do it!" he shouted at the assassin. "We'll take you apart! Put it down!"

Journey's bad foot gave way and he started to fall. The assassin, blood streaming down the side of his face, raised his gun again.

"Last chance!" Tolman shouted.

The gunman looked at Journey, never wavering, as he fired. Journey felt as though millions of heated spikes had been hammered into his left shoulder. At almost the same instant, he saw the assassin cut down in a hail of gunfire from both Tolman and Parsons.

Journey fell on the shoulder that had just taken the bullet, and the needles jabbed him again, harder. His vision went black; he rolled over onto his stomach, and lay with his cheek against the grass. He could see the legs of the man who'd twice tried to kill him, he could see blood on the ground, and Journey could also see a little glint of gold beside him.

Journey kept blinking, trying to move, but his body didn't want to work. He heard Ricky Parsons on the radio, something about an ambulance, something about an incident report, something about calling the office. Then Meg Tolman was beside him.

"Nick!" She slid down beside him. "Nick!" Her voice faded, as if she'd turned her head. "How long until we get an ambulance here?"

Parsons said something—Journey couldn't tell what—and then Tolman had her hand on his back.

"All right," she said. "All right, he just got you in the shoulder. It's all right, Nick."

Journey tried to nod, his cheek scraping gravel.

"Don't move," Tolman said. She waited a few moments. "Stay with me here, Nick. You're losing some blood, but it's okay. Talk to me . . . come on, talk to me. Hey, was that a curveball you threw with the rock? Damn, that was nice aim. You aim rocks better than most people can aim guns. Come on, don't pass out, man."

Journey felt her hand on his back again. "Five minutes, Nick. Give me five minutes." He felt another set of hands—Parsons?— and then something was being wrapped around his shoulder. Tears welled from the pain.

Tolman was still babbling. "Come on, that'll stop some of the blood loss. Tell me something. . . . Tell me something about Andrew."

"Porcupine ball," Journey said.

"What? Say that again."

"Porcupine ball," Journey said. "Don't you know what a porcupine ball is?"

"No, tell me."

"It's a little plastic ball and it has these spikes on it, like a porcupine, only they're plastic. You squeeze it and air comes out of a little hole. He likes to feel the air on his face."

"Maybe I could get one," Tolman said. "I'll take it places when I play the piano and put it on top of the Steinway."

"You do that."

"Two minutes, Nick." There was a long pause, and Tolman's tone changed. "You're going to be all right. You know, you're pretty damn tough for a professor. Tell me something . . . Nick, can you hear me?"

"Of course I can hear you. You don't have to shout."

"The signature page," Tolman said. "You knew. You knew all along that it wasn't buried here with Williams."

"Yes," Journey said, and he was feeling light-headed.

He heard the siren, the crunch of gravel as the ambulance pulled into the clearing. Then he was being lifted. There were more hands, and it felt like they were all over him.

"I'm going with him," Tolman said. "No arguments."

Then they were in the ambulance, and the paramedics were talking to the hospital in Durant, and Tolman said, "So where is it?"

"What?"

"The signature page. Where is the damn thing?"

Journey closed his eyes. "Go look in the library," he said.

# EPILOGUE

*Thanksgiving weekend*

President Harwell was dead. As the Continental flight touched down at Brownsville International Airport in the southernmost city in Texas, Tolman kept thinking about the president, and all that had happened since Fort Washita.

She and her father were summoned to the Oval Office in late September, after the FBI and ATF had made their arrests. On September 22, raids were conducted in cities from Seattle to Miami. Warehouses full of weapons were seized. Hundreds were arrested.

On September 23, the vice chairman of the joint chiefs of staff, Admiral Carter Smith, was arrested in his office at the Pentagon. As Washington One, he had orchestrated the military component of the conspiracy—faking the deaths of military personnel who had been absorbed into the Glory Warriors, diverting "surplus" equipment and weapons to the Glory Warriors' stockpiles. The official, public line was that Smith had been arrested for misappropriation of DOD funds. Senior Inspector Brent Graves of the U.S. Marshals Service had already been buried by the day of Smith's arrest. Graves's wife reported that her husband had been despondent over the death of Chief Justice Darlington and the lapse in security that resulted in her assassination. Timothy Delham and Rusty Hudson were being held in secret detention facilities somewhere near Washington. Delham had talked and talked and talked, giving the FBI names and locations and a wealth of other information about the machinations to overthrow the United States government. Tolman had not seen Hudson since Fort Washita.

Within two weeks, the Glory Warriors were dismantled, their bank accounts frozen, many of their people locked away. Jackson McMartin's assets were frozen, and the long process of breaking up and selling his media empire had begun.

The American public knew nothing of the fact that James Harwell had come within seconds of being assassinated outside the Anacostia Community Center. The words *Glory Warriors* were never mentioned in any mass media.

So Ray and Meg Tolman sat in the Oval Office, just the two of them with the president of the United States, and listened as Harwell thanked them for what they had done to uncover the conspiracy. He sounded like he was reciting from a briefing paper. After a while, Meg Tolman had tuned it out, thinking of the Rachmaninov piece she'd meant to play for the Vienna Kiwanis luncheon all those weeks ago, but never got to perform. She snapped back to attention when the president said, "I'm ill."

"Sir?" Ray Tolman said after a moment, just to say something.

"I'm ill," Harwell said again.

The three of them looked at each other; then the president dismissed them without another word.

He was dead ten days later. The nation mourned its leader, who had died of a heart attack in his sleep, at age fifty-five. But Tolman was haunted by the words, "I'm ill." What had Harwell really meant? Did he have cancer? Some other physically debilitating disease? Did he have mental health issues, like her mother? And would the president of the United States really have been able to keep such things a secret from those around him? Late at night, Tolman had wondered if the Secret Service found an empty bottle of Ambien or Restoril or some other sleep aid at his bedside. She wondered how the First Lady felt when she woke and found her husband dead in bed beside her. Many questions. No answers.

The vice president was a former senator from North Carolina

named Robert Mendoza. Grandson of Mexican immigrants, he'd proved himself capable during the transition, and had been a gentle, stable hand at the head of government.

"Now we must heal," President Mendoza told the nation on the day Harwell was buried.

Twenty-four hours later, Tolman had sat in the Oval Office again and listened to what the new president had to say. She told him she had to think about it.

*Now we must heal.*

She rented a car, punching her destination into its GPS. Lonely Texas State Highway 4 wandered east out of Brownsville along the flat coastal plain. Mexico looked back at her from across the highway. The road wound north, and then she saw the Gulf of Mexico. Per the directions, she turned left, passing signs for Brazos Island and Boca Chica Beach. Pavement ended and the car passed onto a beach road. It had been a dry season along the Gulf Coast, so the sand was hard packed and smooth. Tolman caught sight of a couple of houses on stilts, but nothing else. Sand, rocks, a little grass farther back from the water.

She parked the car, got out, and walked around a bend. She heard them over the sound of the waves before she saw them: a high-pitched shriek, a loud piercing whistle, a bold laugh. She topped a little rise and saw Nick and Andrew Journey sitting on folding lawn chairs, ten feet away from the Gulf. Journey's arm was still in a sling, and his foot was still wrapped. But his eyes were bright.

Andrew stopped what he was doing with his hands—something involving a straw and a pencil—and looked at her as she walked toward them. He made a sort of hooting sound that she thought sounded vaguely interrogative.

"Hi," she said, raising her voice above the waves.

Journey stood up and they looked at each other. "You look good," he finally said.

"You look like hell," Tolman said, and they both laughed.

"There's so much," Journey said after a long moment. He looked toward the Gulf. "They killed Evan Lovell and they went after your friend Darrell."

"I feel bad for Lovell. The poor guy just tried to help. Darrell's case was self-defense, and the investigation is closed. I guess I feel bad for Darrell, too, but he's . . . maybe 'complicated' is the best word. I suppose that describes my relationship with him, too."

Journey nodded. "So you met the new president."

"Yeah. He asked me to take over RIO."

"Really? Are you going to do it?"

"I told him I'd think about it."

"You should," Journey said. "You'd be good at it."

"We talked about you," Tolman said.

"I guess the subject couldn't be avoided, as the Glory Warriors mess was being untangled."

"The president wants you to work with me."

Andrew whistled as a wave hit the shore. Journey turned abruptly. "Excuse me? I don't think I heard that."

"Don't worry, you can keep your teaching gig and you can stay in Oklahoma. But the president wondered if you might consult with RIO when investigations come up that have a historical aspect."

"You must be kidding."

"You should do it." Tolman smiled. "You'd be good at it."

"You *must* be kidding."

"They'll match whatever you're making at the college."

Journey waited. "You're not kidding."

"Nope. Think about it."

Journey shook his head and they were both silent for a long time. Andrew thrummed out a rhythm with his straw and his pencil, and it seemed to coincide with the impact of the waves on the shore.

"How's Sandra?" Tolman said.

"She's fine. We're friends, and I guess that's a good thing."

"Yes, it is. I hope you two get to talk a lot more."

"Don't get your hopes up. Sandra's a good woman, but it's . . ." He let the sentence die, gazing out at the Gulf.

"Complicated," Tolman said. "I get it." She nodded toward Andrew. "How's this guy?"

Journey squeezed his son's shoulder. "He's the best. He had a few tough days because his routine was off, but he's been fine since then. Good days and bad days, just like anyone."

They walked a few steps. "You're a really, really good dad. You know that, don't you?"

"No, I'm not." Journey smiled. "But I try. Just like your father after your mother died. I try. Andrew deserves that, don't you think?"

"Yeah," Tolman said. "I do. And I also think you should give yourself a break sometimes."

"Aren't you going to ask me?" Journey said after another bit of silence.

"Subject changer. But, since you brought it up, I didn't come all this way to stand on an undeveloped beach, Nick."

"This is where it ended."

Tolman looked around. "What do you mean?"

"The Civil War. It ended here."

Tolman stared at him.

"Did you see the historical marker along the highway outside of Brownsville?" Journey asked.

"No. I don't read historical markers."

"You should. I mean, the last shots of the Civil War were fired not far from this spot."

Tolman folded her arms. "Grant? Lee? Appomattox? Ring any bells?"

"No, the war didn't really end there. Yes, Lee surrendered his army to Grant. But armies were spread all over the place, even this far west. Several battles took place after Appomattox. It took a while for the news to filter down through the country that Lee had surrendered."

"So?"

"So there was this little battle down here on the Texas coast. The Battle of Palmito Ranch."

"Never heard of it."

"Kids are taught in school that the war ended with Lee's surrender at Appomattox. While that may have been the beginning of the end of the war, it was another couple of months before all the Southern armies surrendered."

"Did you drag me down here to give me another damn history lecture?"

"Yes, I did."

They stared at each other; then they both laughed. "What the hell does this have to do with anything?" Tolman finally asked.

"It has everything to do with what we went through in September," Journey said. "There had been a sort of 'gentlemen's agreement' between the Union and Confederate forces early in 1865 that there would be no fighting here along the border. Most of the Union troops had already left, and the Southerners were just a ragtag group, not particularly well organized."

"So someone broke the agreement."

"Both sides knew Lee had surrendered, but they also knew that technically, the war was still going on in the West. But you had the Thirty-fourth Indiana posted here, and one of the black units, the Sixty-second U.S. Colored Infantry. They were commanded by a man named Theodore Barrett, and for some reason, on May twelfth, 1865, more than a month after Appomattox, Barrett ordered his troops to attack the Southern camp nearby. The Union headquarters was right here."

"Here? On this island? What a lousy place to spend the war."

"It was just about as far as you could get away from everything and still be in the Union Army." Andrew ran a few steps ahead, coming close to the surf. Journey kept up with him, limping a little. Tolman watched the two of them together, then had to jog to catch up.

"So why did the Union attack?"

"Who knows?" Journey said. "Barrett wasn't a very distinguished commander, and one school of thought is that he had political ambitions for after the war and wanted to make a name for himself before it was too late. Whatever the reason, he ordered his troops to cross to the mainland and march upriver. I could give you all kinds of details about the troop movements and the time line and all that, but I won't."

"But I'll play along. The Confederates were surprised by this sneak attack, and then what happened?"

"Their commander was a major named John 'Rip' Ford, who was and still is something of a legend in Texas. Soldier, doctor, politician, newspaperman . . . he was quite a character. His group engaged the Union at Palmito Ranch, and it effectively turned into a rout.

When the shooting was just about over, the North was in full retreat, scrambling back across the Rio Grande to the island."

They rounded a curve. The mouth of the Rio Grande lay before them.

"There was still skirmishing going on as they retreated. According to one account, a Federal shell burst right over the head of a young Rebel soldier, and he was so startled, he fired his rifle back toward the soldiers who were retreating. That shot killed a Union private from Indiana. No more shots were fired. That was the last shot of the Civil War."

Tolman looked around at the desolate island, the river, the Gulf, the flat hard-packed sand of the beach road. "Hell of a long way from Virginia."

Journey nodded. "That it is. The Confederates didn't have many supplies, their clothes were worn out. They'd just won a victory in battle, but they stripped the Indiana private of his clothes and all the personal belongings he had with him."

"Why is this important?"

"The Indiana private was named John Jefferson Williams."

"Yeah, so?"

"Meg, listen to me. His name was John Jefferson *Williams*."

"Is that supposed to mean something—?" Tolman's voice died and she stopped walking. "No. There's no way . . ."

"Remember that note we found in Lovell's stuff, the one Samuel Williams wrote when he left in the fall of 1864? It was just one sentence, and it didn't mean anything at the time. We were still trying to figure out what Samuel had done. But he wrote, before disappearing forever, 'I leave all to my younger brother John, who has crossed the river to join the Federals.'"

"Crossed the river," Tolman said. "He crossed from Kentucky to Indiana. So he joined the Indiana troops that eventually wound up here. My God, Nick, you're saying Samuel Williams's brother was the last casualty of the war?"

"That's right. You remember my theory for how Samuel got from Louisville to Fort Washita?"

"He took steamboats as far as Fort Smith, then horseback from there."

"Right. When he changed boats, probably at the mouth of the Arkansas, he could have sent the signature page on another boat going on down the Mississippi. Boats regularly made the run to New Orleans and around the Texas coast to Mexico. We know for a fact that at least some of the troops on Brazos Island found out about Lee's surrender from a newspaper that was left here by a steamboat from New Orleans. All Samuel had to do was pay a messenger to deliver a sealed envelope to his brother, who by then was posted here. He knew it would be safe—nothing was going on down here, after all. His brother didn't know anything about the Glory Warriors. All he had was a sealed envelope that had been sent from his much older brother."

Tolman shook her head. "Sam Williams *was* brilliant. He thought of everything, planned it so carefully. He even figured out that Grant and Lee didn't trust him, and he did everything he could to protect the pages."

"Here's the irony: When Samuel left Louisville back in the fall, that sentence about leaving all to his brother probably *was* just about the bank and his personal belongings. One way or another, he knew he was about to become Edward Hiram and wouldn't be coming back to his old life. But by the next spring, when the war was over and he was putting the Glory Warriors into place, he saw it as a way to keep the signature page away from the other pages. It was a failsafe—he'd created the Glory Warriors, but he didn't want it to be too easy for them to take power. Maybe he thought the power wouldn't be abused that way."

Andrew whistled, then dropped his straw on the sand. Tolman picked it up, brushed it off, and handed it back to him. His eyes flickered across hers before darting away toward the waves.

Tolman looked thoughtful. "So where's the page? The Rebel soldiers stripped John Williams's clothes. If they were that desperate, and they found a sealed letter in the pocket of a dead man, I'm betting they opened it, hoping there was money inside."

"*Someone* opened it, and I think what happened is that they saw the signatures of Robert E. Lee and U. S. Grant with the date of April ninth and Appomattox written on it, and they got scared. Within a few days, everything was back to normal down here on the border, and someone gave the page to an officer, maybe the Union commander at Fort Brown. When the war was officially over, the commander wasn't sure what to do with the page. He knew he couldn't keep it as a souvenir, he knew it had *some* importance, and he was probably nervous holding on to it."

"I know you're not going to tell me he sent it to Washington," Tolman said.

"To the War Department. He washed his hands of it. But of course, the War Department didn't know what it was, either. So I think some clerk in Washington, maybe in a low-level office somewhere—" Tolman smiled at that. "—put it in a drawer and forgot about it for a long time."

They walked a few steps in silence. "At Fort Washita, you knew then the page wasn't buried with Williams," Tolman said. "I understand that we were drawing out the Glory Warriors at that point, but did Williams really have to be dug up? I have to tell you, I keep remembering falling on his bones, and the way they sounded snapping underneath me."

"I'm sorry," Journey said. "I had to convince McMartin."

"Well, you certainly convinced me," Tolman said. "At Washita, you said to look in the library to find the signature page. I thought you were delirious, but I guess you went to the library and put all this together in the last two months."

"Partly," Journey said.

He stopped and looked at her. Andrew pulled on his father's arm, then seeing that Journey wasn't moving, he stopped and scuffed a foot in the sand.

"What do you mean, partly?" Tolman said.

"The page sat around until 1937, when someone finally realized it might be historically significant and sent it to the Library of Congress."

"No," Tolman said.

Journey nodded.

"It was on display in the goddamn Library of Congress all this time," Tolman said.

"Not exactly on display, but it's been there since 1937. There's a note attached to it from the curator at the time, stating that the signatures have been authenticated, and that it is, and I quote, 'likely that a member of either General Grant's or General Lee's staff requested a second copy of their signatures upon Lee's surrender to Grant at Appomattox Court House.'" Journey shrugged. "They think it was someone's souvenir."

"The Library of Congress," Tolman said.

Journey smiled.

"Hidden in plain sight," Tolman said. "The Glory Warriors could have found it at any time."

"If they'd known where to look. It's a bit of an illusion, isn't it? Sometimes things are hiding, even if they're right there for everyone to see."

They looked at each other—a long, long moment of unspoken understanding.

"Maybe that's true," Tolman said. She was thinking of her mother, and President James Harwell. She wondered if Journey was thinking of his parents and brothers, or of his ex-wife and his son and Sandra Kelly. Or maybe he was just thinking about history.

"Then again," Tolman said, "maybe it isn't."

They walked along the beach, close to the shore as the waves rolled in. A wind gust hit them, they felt air on their faces, and a fine, misty spray of water. Andrew Journey held both his hands over his head and waved them back and forth, basking in the November sun and the clear air and the water. He gave a happy, genuine laugh, and then he began to whistle again.

# AUTHOR'S NOTE

We rarely get much measurable snow in Oklahoma, but we do experience our share of sleet and ice storms. In December 2007, the worst ice storm in our history struck and virtually crippled the state. Hundreds of thousands went without power for a week or more. I watched in my own neighborhood as stately, century-old trees buckled under the weight of the ice.

I was fortunate in that the power stayed on in my home, but otherwise my city was shut down for several days and I dared not venture outside. Stranded in the house, I found myself wandering about the Web and landed on an account of Robert E. Lee's surrender to Ulysses S. Grant at Appomattox Court House. General Horace Porter, a member of Grant's staff, had written the narrative and a single sentence caught my attention, words to the effect that the two generals were alone in the Wilmer McLean house for a short time, just the two of them, before their staffs were allowed in to witness the formal surrender.

What did the two men talk about in those few minutes? I wondered. This story was born from that single sentence, that seemingly innocuous line in the midst of one of the most well-documented events in American history.

I feel obligated to point out a few lines between fact and fiction, so here goes: The Glory Warriors are completely fictitious. No such document as the one that forms the basis of this book, was appended to Lee's surrender. However, General Order No. 100, better known as the Lieber Code, is real, as is the fact that it paved the way for many of the modern rules of warfare.

South Central College of Oklahoma and the town of Carpenter Center are my own creations. All other settings are real, although I took a few liberties here and there. *The Poet's Penn* is fictitious, while the relationship between Samuel Clemens (Mark Twain) and U. S. Grant is not. The author and the general were good friends, and Clemens did in fact encourage Grant to write his memoirs and promised to publish them, which he did with great success. The royalties provided an income to Grant's widow for many years after his death.

Private John Jefferson Williams of the Thirty-fourth Indiana was indeed the last man to fall in the Battle of Palmito Ranch, making him the final casualty of the Civil War. The character of Samuel Williams ("Edward Hiram"), however, is wholly fictitious.

The Colberts were prominent leaders of the Chickasaw people for many years. I appropriated the Colbert family name for the character of Jeremiah Colbert ("Onnaroketay"). The Chickasaw burial ground at Fort Washita is as described, with the exception, of course, of the G.W. marker. I remember Fort Washita well from my own boyhood, as I grew up hearing stories and legends surrounding the fort and those buried there. One sad note: in September 2010, while this book was in production, a portion of Fort Washita caught fire, and the restored South Barracks burned to the ground. The descriptions of the fort in the book are as it appeared prior to this tragedy.

I have been asked if it is accurate to ascribe Anglo names to Native people during the Civil War era. Particularly concerning the Chickasaw and the other tribes who were removed to present-day Oklahoma from the Southeast, many of the people used English names as far back as the late eighteenth century, a result of their interaction with, and subsequent intermarriage to, white traders, settlers, and "missionaries." The 1810 rolls of the Chickasaw people, years before removal, show many families with names such as Colbert, Burney, and Smith.

In preparing this book, I read Bruce Catton's classic *A Stillness at Appomattox* and, of course, *Personal Memoirs of U. S. Grant*. Another valuable resource was *The Last Battle of the Civil War* by Jeffrey William Hunt, which covers in broad scope and context the Battle of Palmito Ranch, the desolate spot where the last shots of the war were fired, far away from the legendary battlegrounds of Virginia. To this day, a single historical marker—which has been repeatedly defaced—stands almost hidden along Texas State Highway 4. It is the only outward sign of any kind indicating the location of the final land battle of the war.